Traced and Tracked

Or, Memoirs of a City Detective

James M'Govan

Alpha Editions

This edition published in 2024

ISBN : 9789357968775

Design and Setting By
Alpha Editions
www.alphaedis.com
Email - info@alphaedis.com

As per information held with us this book is in Public Domain.
This book is a reproduction of an important historical work. Alpha Editions uses the best technology to reproduce historical work in the same manner it was first published to preserve its original nature. Any marks or number seen are left intentionally to preserve its true form.

Contents

PREFACE. ....- 1 -
A PEDESTRIAN'S PLOT. ....- 2 -
BILLY'S BITE. ....- 13 -
THE MURDERED TAILOR'S WATCH. (A CURIOSITY IN CIRCUMSTANTIAL EVIDENCE.) ....- 24 -
THE STREET PORTER'S SON. ....- 43 -
A BIT OF TOBACCO PIPE. ....- 56 -
THE BROKEN CAIRNGORM. ....- 67 -
THE ROMANCE OF A REAL CREMONA. ....- 78 -
THE SPIDER AND THE SPIDER-KILLER. ....- 103 -
THE SPOILT PHOTOGRAPH. ....- 114 -
THE STOLEN DOWRY. ....- 125 -
McSWEENY AND THE MAGIC JEWELS. ....- 136 -
BENJIE BLUNT'S CLEVER ALIBI. ....- 147 -
JIM HUTSON'S KNIFE. ....- 158 -
THE HERRING SCALES. ....- 170 -
ONE LESS TO EAT. ....- 180 -
THE CAPTAIN'S CHRONOMETER. ....- 191 -
THE TORN TARTAN SHAWL. ....- 201 -
A LIFT ON THE ROAD. ....- 211 -
THE ORGAN-GRINDER'S MONEY-BAG. ....- 222 -
THE BERWICK BURR. ....- 232 -
THE WRONG UMBRELLA. ....- 244 -
A WHITE SAVAGE. ....- 255 -
THE BROKEN MISSIONARY. ....- 266 -
A MURDERER'S MISTAKE. ....- 277 -

A HOUSE-BREAKER'S WIFE. ....- 289 -
M^cSWEENY AND THE CHIMNEY-SWEEP........................- 300 -
THE FAMILY BIBLE. ....- 311 -
CONSCIENCE MONEY..- 323 -
A WOLF IN SHEEP'S CLOTHING. ....- 334 -

PREFACE.

The gratifying success of my former experiences—25,000 copies having already been sold, and the demand steadily continuing—has induced me to put forth another volume. In doing so, I have again to thank numerous correspondents, as well as the reviewers of the public press, for their warm expressions of appreciation and approval. I have also to notice a graceful compliment from Berlin, in the translation of my works into German, by H. Ernst Duby; and another from Geneva, in the translation of a selection of my sketches into French, by the Countess Agènor de Gasparin.

A severe and unexpected attack of hæmorrhage of the lungs has prevented me revising about a third of the present volume. I trust, therefore, that any trifling slips or errors will be excused on that account.

In conclusion, I would remind readers and reviewers of the words of Handel, when he was complimented by an Irish nobleman on having amused the citizens of Dublin with his *Messiah*. "Amuse dem?" he warmly replied; "I do not vant to amuse dem only; I vant to make dem petter."

JAMES McGOVAN.

EDINBURGH, *October 1884.*

A PEDESTRIAN'S PLOT.

I have alluded to the fact that many criminals affect a particular line of business, and show a certain style in their work which often points unerringly to the doer when all other clues are wanting. A glance over any record of convictions will convey a good idea of how much reliance we are led to place upon this curious fact. One man's list will show a string of pocket-picking cases, or attempts in that line, and it will be rare, indeed, to find in that record a case of robbery with violence, housebreaking, or any crime necessitating great daring or strength. Another shows nothing but deeds of brute strength or bull-dog ferocity, and to find in his record of *prev. con.* a case of delicate pocket-picking would make any one of experience open his eyes wide indeed. The style of the work is even a surer guide than the particular line, as the variety there is unlimited as it is marked. This is all very well; and often I have been complimented on my astuteness in thus making very simple and natural deductions leading to convictions. But the pleasure ceases to be unmixed when the criminal is as cunning as the detective, and works upon that knowledge. To show how a detective may be deceived in working on this—one of his surest modes of tracing a criminal—I give the present case.

Dave Larkins was a Yorkshire thief, who had drifted northwards by some chance and landed in Edinburgh. Street robbery was his line, and, as he was a professional pedestrian, or racing man, he was not caught, I should say, once in twenty cases. The list of his previous convictions in Manchester, Liverpool, Preston, and other places showed with unvarying monotony the same crime and the same style of working. He would go up to some gentleman on the street and make an excuse for addressing him, snatch at his watch, and run for it. More often the victim was a lady with a reticule or purse in her hand, and then no preliminary speaking was indulged in. He made the snatch, and ran like the wind, and the whole was done so quickly that the astounded victim seldom retained the slightest recollection of his appearance.

Yet Dave's appearance was striking enough. He was a wiry man of medium height, with strongly-marked features, red hair, and a stumpy little turned up nose, the round point of which was always red as a cherry with bad whisky, except at those rare intervals when he was "in training" for some foot race which it was to his advantage to win.

Then his dress had notable points. He generally wore a knitted jersey in place of a waistcoat, and he had a grey felt hat covered with grease spots, for which he had such a peculiar affection that he never changed it for a new one. Under these circumstances it may be thought that a conviction would have been easily got against Dave. But Dave was "Yorkshire," as I have indicated, and about as smart and cunning in arranging an *alibi* as any I ever met. No doubt his racing powers helped him in that, but his native cunning did more.

There is a popular impression that a Yorkshire man will hold his own in cunning against all the world, but I have here to record that Dave met his match in a Scotchman who had nothing like Dave's reputation for smartness, and who was so stupid-looking that few could have conceived him capable of the task. This man was known in racing circles—for he was a pedestrian too—as Jake Mackay, but more generally received the nickname of "The Gander."

Why he had been so named I cannot tell—perhaps because some one had discovered that there was nothing of the goose about him. Your stupid-looking man, who is not stupid but supremely sharp-witted, has an infinite advantage over those who carry a needle eye like Dave Larkins, and have cunning printed on every line about their lips and eyes.

The Gander was not a professional thief, though he was often in the company of thieves. He had been in the army, and had a pension, which he eked out by odd jobs, such as bill-posting and acting as "super." in the theatres. He was a thorough rascal at heart, and would have cheated his own grandfather had opportunity served, and had there been a shilling or two to gain by it.

These two men became acquainted at a pedestrian meeting at Glasgow, and when Dave Larkins came to Edinburgh they became rather close companions. The Gander had the advantage of local knowledge, and could get at all the men who backed pedestrians, and then told them to win or lose according to the way the money was staked. A racing tournament was arranged about that time in which both of them were entered for one of the shorter races, in which great speed, rather than endurance, was called for. In that particular race they had the result entirely in their own hands, though, if fairly put to it, Dave Larkins, or "Yorky" as he was named, could easily have come in first. The other men entered having no chance, these two proceeded to arrange matters to their mutual advantage—that is, had they been honest men, the advantage would have been mutual, for they agreed to divide the stakes whatever the result. But in these matters there is always a great deal more at stake than the money prize offered to the winner. The art of betting and counterbetting would task the brain of a mathematician to reduce its subtleties to a form intelligible to the ordinary mind; and the supreme thought of each of the rogues, after closing hands on the above agreement, was how he could best benefit himself at the expense of the other. What the private arrangements of The Gander were does not appear, except that he had arranged to come in first, though the betting was all in favour of Yorky; but just before they entered the dressing tent, a patron of the sports—I will not call him a gentleman—took Yorky aside and said—

"How is this race to go? Have you any money on it to force you to win?"

Yorky, having already arranged to lose, modestly hinted that, for a substantial consideration, he would be willing to come in second.

"Second? whew! then who'd be first?" said the patron, not looking greatly pleased with the proposal. "The Gander would walk off with the stakes. He'd be sure to come in first. Could you not let Birrel get to the front?"

"It might be managed," said Yorky, with a significant wink.

"Then manage it;" and the price of the "management" was thrust into his hand in bank notes, and the matter settled.

Yorky counted the money, and ran up in his mind all that The Gander had on the race, and decided that the old soldier would promptly refuse to lose the race in favour of Birrel. The money was not enough to stand halving, so Yorky decided to keep it all, and also to "pot" a little more by the new turn things had taken. He therefore passed the word to a boon companion to put all his spare money on Birrel, and then took his place among the competitors dressing for the race. The start was made, and, as all had expected, Yorky and The Gander gradually drew together, and then moved out to the front. Birrel at the last round was a very bad third, while the other runners were nowhere, and evidently only remaining on the track in the faint hope of some unforeseen accident taking place to give one of them the chance of a place. They had not long to wait. Yorky, running at his swiftest, and apparently in splendid form, about three yards in front of The Gander, instead of slackening his speed as he had arranged, suddenly reeled and fell to the ground right in front of his companion. The result may be guessed. The Gander was on the obstruction before he knew, and sprawling in a half-stunned condition a yard in front of Yorky's body, while Birrel, amid a yell from the spectators, drew up and shot ahead. The yell roused The Gander, and he feebly scrambled to his feet, and made a desperate effort for the first place, but all in vain, for Birrel touched the tape before him, and he was second in everything but swearing. To the surprise of all, Yorky did not rise to his feet, and remained to all appearance insensible for five minutes after he had been tenderly carried to the dressing tent. Of course there was a protest of the most vigorous description to the referee by The Gander, who not only found that he had laid his money the wrong way, and disappointed numerous friends who had followed his advice, but was not even to have the meagre satisfaction of sharing the first prize. But under the impression that Yorky had simply over-exerted himself, and fainted on the course, the referee, who possibly had money on the result, refused to listen to the appeal, and Birrel got the prize. The Gander denounced Yorky with great vehemence, but was met with the most solemn protestations of innocence. He then put on his clothes and left the tent in a bad temper, but in leaving the grounds was accorded a "reception" which did not tend to soothe his feelings. A dozen or so of his friends, who had received his private "tip" as to the way the race was to go, gathered round the supposed traitor, and, before the police could interfere, had him beaten almost to a jelly. The poor Gander was removed in a cab to the Infirmary to have his wounds dressed, while the elated and successful Yorky went to enjoy himself with his ill-gotten gains.

When the two met again, The Gander appeared to have recovered his temper, and listened to Yorky's explanations of the mishap on the course as pleasantly as if he believed them, which was very far from being the case. Then Yorky so far unbent as to spend some of his money in drinks for The Gander, and was foolish enough to believe that he had cheated the stupid-looking Scotchman very nicely, and that he would hear no more of the matter.

The races had taken place during the New Year holidays, and while the pantomimes were running at the theatres. In one of these The Gander was engaged as a "super.," and it was known to him that the treasurer was in the habit of leaving the theatre for his home, at the foot of Broughton Street, late every night, carrying under his arm or in his hand a tin box resembling a cash-box. This box contained nothing but metal checks, which the treasurer counted at his home. All the money drawn at the doors remained in possession of the manager. Had Yorky not been an unusually cunning man it is probable that The Gander would have manipulated him direct, but as it was, he was forced to confide in another. A loafing acquaintance of Yorky's seemed a suitable tool, and he was engaged and primed accordingly. Bob Slogger had himself an old grudge against Yorky, so, on the whole, perhaps a better choice could not have been made.

The opportunity came when Bob and Yorky were drinking together one afternoon, when the former incidentally remarked that they were doing immense business at the theatre, and making piles of money. Yorky only grunted in reply. It seemed hard that any one but him should be making money, and he did not like the subject.

"I got it out of The Gander that the treasurer can hardly carry the money home some nights," continued Slogger, repeating his lesson. "He lives at the foot of Broughton, and carries it there in a tin box every night about half-past eleven. I could do with that boxful of silver on a Saturday night."

"Ah! Saturday night? is there most in it then?" observed Yorky, suddenly rousing into deep interest.

"Of course there is;" and Slogger at once gave the reasons, and repeated all that The Gander had said regarding the appearance of the treasurer, his hour of going home, and the dark and deserted appearance of the streets at that lonely locality. Yorky snapped at the bait, but did not abandon his usual caution. He said nothing to his informant of his intentions, and much of The Gander's after proceedings had to be founded on mere acute inferences. The spot to be chosen for the attack he guessed at by one of Yorky's questions, and the night most likely to be selected for the attempt was Saturday, for, of course, when the robbery was to be done, it might as well be for a big sum as a little one. He made sure of this last point, however, by trying hard to get Yorky to engage to meet him that night after business, but failed, as Yorky gruffly indicated that he was engaged.

So far all had succeeded to The Gander's satisfaction. It only remained for him to give the finishing stroke. He got a sheet of note-paper, of a kind used in the theatre, and penned the following note to me:—

"If McGovan will watch at the west end of Barony Street between eleven and twelve o'clock on Saturday night, he will see a gent attacked and robbed by a desperate thief who can run like Deerfoot. The gent always carries a tin box, and, as it's supposed to be full of money, it's the box that will be grabbed at. There had better be more than one at the catching, or he's sure to get off."

There was no signature, and at first I was inclined to believe the thing a hoax, or worse—a plot to draw me away from some spot where I was likely to be more useful, but in the end I decided to act on the advice.

I had no idea that the gent described was the worthy treasurer of the theatre, and I suppose The Gander had purposely remained silent on that point lest I should warn the gentleman threatened, and so spoil the little plot.

I was down at Barony Street before eleven o'clock. I took the west end, and planted McSweeny under shelter at the east. It was a dark night, and scarcely any one passed me at my lonely lurking-place. I was so suspicious of a hoax that I was positively surprised when a gentleman appeared at the other end of the street carrying the tin box in his hand, and whistling away as cheerily as if there were no such thing as street robbers in existence. He had scarcely appeared in sight when another man turned the corner walking rapidly in his wake, and looking hastily round to make sure that they were alone in the short street.

The distance between the two rapidly diminished, and then, looking anxiously along behind them, I had the satisfaction of seeing McSweeny's head cautiously appear from his hiding-place at the other end of the street. I had scarcely noted the fact when the footpad was on his victim, making a dash from behind at the treasurer, tripping him up, and at the same moment wrenching the tin box from his grasp.

None but an expert thief could have done the thing so swiftly. The moment the box was in his possession the thief caught sight of me making a dash towards him, and turned and flew towards the end of the street by which he had entered. He flew so fast that his feet seemed scarcely to touch the ground. McSweeny had emerged from his hiding-place at the first outcry, and appeared directly in front of the flying man with his great, strong arms extended for a bear's hug; but the flying man, unable to check his pace, yet unwilling to be taken, merely raised the tin box of tokens and dashed it full in McSweeny's face, flattening my chum's little nose with his face, and laying him on his back on the snowy pavement as neatly as if he had been tugged back by the hair. I paid no attention to McSweeny, but flew on in the wake of the thief; but when I turned the corner of the street into Broughton he had vanished, I knew not in what direction. I turned back, after a run up the brae, and found McSweeny sitting up on the pavement and tenderly feeling the place where his nose had been.

"Oh, you thickhead!" was my only remark, as I passed on to speak to the robbed man.

"Thick, is it?" he dolefully returned. "Faix, it's a great deal thinner than it was a minit ago."

"And you let him off, money and all," I added, in deep disgust.

"Begorra, if you'd felt the weight of the money, like me, you'd wish it far enough away," he returned, busy with his handkerchief; "a steam hammer's nothing to it."

"I am happy to say that there was no money in the box," said the robbed man, who was little the worse of his fall. "Nothing but a number of metal tokens used as checks at the theatre."

"Tokens?" groaned McSweeny, clenching his fists. "I'd like to give him some more."

A few words of explanation followed, which considerably relieved my concern over the loss of the thief; and then the robbed man accompanied us to the Central to report the case, and get a look at the handwriting of the note sent us in warning. He readily recognised the note-paper as of a kind used in the theatre, but could make nothing of the handwriting. However, the fact that the warning had come from some one employed in the theatre was a clue of a kind, and with the promise to give us every help in following it out, he took leave.

Meantime, Yorky had gone with his plunder no farther than a lighted stair at the foot of Broughton Street, which had stood conveniently open when he dashed round the corner of Barony Street. There he quickly wrenched off the lid, plunged his hand into the box to empty big handfuls of silver and gold into his pockets, and found instead only lead. The fact that he was alone draws a veil over the scene which followed. I have no doubt that his words flowed rapidly over his immediate disappointment, and his disgust may be inferred from the fact that he left the box and tokens entire in a corner of the stair. But a deeper rage was to come. Yorky remembered that the first information had come from The Gander, and the fact that we had been in waiting for him, and dummies or tokens substituted for the money the treasurer had been said to carry, seemed to the quick-witted Yorky to point to a plot to trap him. If he could bring that plot home to The Gander he resolved to put a knife in him. I have stated, however, that Nature had favoured The Gander with a look of dense stupidity, and, though Yorky took the first opportunity of seeking his society, and suspiciously sounding him on the subject, he made nothing of it. Bob Slogger he could not get at, for he was already in our hands for a separate offence.

The suspicious manner and queer questions of Yorky alarmed The Gander quite as much as the failure of his plot disappointed him.

"If I don't have him laid by the heels soon he'll shove a knife into me," was his acute thought, which shows how sharp-witted folks can read each other through every fence of face and words.

I took Yorky on the Monday, and we kept him for a day or two on suspicion, but, as the street had been dark and we had but a momentary glimpse of him, he had to be let off for want of evidence. Meantime, The Gander's wits had been at work on a plot which, I must confess, was quite worthy of the object.

When Yorky was set at liberty he was greeted by The Gander, who, with many demonstrations of satisfaction, and to celebrate the occasion, proposed that they should adjourn to Yorky's den in the Canongate and there consume a bottle of brandy at The Gander's expense. No proposal could have been more welcome. Yorky had a weakness for drink at all times, but when some one else paid for that drink it was to him perfect nectar. They had the garret all to themselves, as Yorky's wife, in anticipation of a long sentence on her husband, had fled to her native clime. The drinking began, and from the first Yorky managed to appropriate the lion's share. He was not easily affected by drink, but his ideas were getting a little cloudy by the time the brandy was finished, and readily assented to The Gander's proposal to go for more. Into this second supply The Gander poured a strong dose of laudanum, and, as Yorky swallowed the whole, he was soon insensible. The Gander and he were of about a height and build, but, of course, in appearance and features they were not at all alike. As soon as it was quite certain that Yorky had succumbed, his amiable friend stripped him and tumbled him into bed. He then exchanged his own shabby and paste-spotted clothing for Yorky's trousers, jersey, and pilot jacket. Then, taking from his own pocket a short-haired red wig which he had got from some of the theatricals, he drew it over his scalp, and then with a little rouge did up the point of his nose to resemble the fiery organ of the slumbering thief. Having fastened about his throat the red cotton handkerchief used by Yorky as a scarf, and topped the whole with the greasy and battered grey felt hat, The Gander softly left the den, locking the door after him and taking the key with him. It was between three and four o'clock in the afternoon, but not nearly dark. The Gander got down to Leith Street in his strange disguise, and when near the foot, at that part where Low Calton branches off towards Leith Wynd, he stopped a suitable gentleman and asked the time by the clock. Quite unsuspicious in the broad daylight, the gentleman took out his watch, and in a moment it had changed hands. The grasp had been made at it with such force by The Gander, that the gold Albert attached to the watch was snapped, and half of it left dangling at the owner's button-hole.

The moment the grasp was made, The Gander ran like the wind, and got clear away by Low Calton and the Back Canongate, and never halted till he landed breathless but triumphant at the bedside of the sleeping Yorky. His first business was to resume his own clothing, clean the paint from his nose, and take the wig from his head. Then he took the watch, with the fragment of gold chain still attached, and thrust it as far as his arm could reach in under the mattress on which lay the virtuous form of the sleeping Yorky. This done, he pocketed the red wig, laid Yorky's clothes at the bedside beside his muddy boots, in some confusion, as if they had been taken off somewhat hurriedly, and then left the house, with the pleasing consciousness of having done all he could to help Fate to do the right thing to a great rascal.

While this was being done, the robbed man had made his way to the Central Office to report his loss. He had got a full view of the robber's face and dress—or at least imagined he had—and went over the details with such minuteness and fidelity that I turned to some one and said in surprise—

"Surely it can't be Yorky at his old games already, and he was only let out this morning? It's just his style."

I then went over one or two of Yorky's peculiar features, to all of which the gentleman so eagerly responded in the affirmative that I thought it could do no harm at least to look for Yorky, with a view to bringing him face to face with the victim. I should have found him at once if I had gone to his den, but that was the very last place I thought he would go near when in danger of being taken. I therefore went over all his haunts, but in vain. No one had seen him, and several told me of the flight of his wife, which gave me the idea that Yorky, finding himself "on the rocks," and deserted, had committed the robbery with great audacity, and then left the city for good with the proceeds in the wake of his partner. It was quite late at night when I thought of his garret in the Canongate. I believe it was McSweeny's suggestion that I should go there—at least he always insists that it was, and possibly he is right, for the way in which Yorky had grinned at his damaged face had made my chum certain that the hands which inflicted the injuries were before him, and McSweeny was now eager for revenge.

There was no answer but snores to our knock, so we opened the door and entered.

"How sound the divil sleeps," said McSweeny, with a sceptical grin, as he struck a light. "Sure a fox himself couldn't do it better."

Yorky refused to wake with a word, and even when violently shaken by both of us only half opened his eyes, and uttered some sleepy imprecations. At length, getting impatient, McSweeny lifted a dish containing water and emptied it over Yorky's face, which startled him into a wakefulness and some vigorous protests.

"What do you want now?" he growled at last, when he was able to recognise us.

"I want to know where you were at half-past three o'clock to-day?" was my significant reply. "On with your things and trudge. You've got drunk too soon—you've overdone it. Man, see, there's the slush off your boots all over the floor."

"I haven't been across the door since morning," he solemnly protested, on which McSweeny somewhat savagely remarked that "we believed him every word."

While McSweeny was helping him to put on his clothes, and replying to his protests, I made a search through the room, and finally drew out from under the mattress the stolen watch and fragment of gold chain.

Yorky stared as it was held up before his eyes, and became very sober indeed.

"I never saw that in my life before; somebody must have put it there," he cried, with the most vigorous swearing, all of which we listened to with great merriment and marked derision.

"I thought we should sober you before long," I said to him, as I fastened his wrist to my own. "We'll see what the owner of the watch says to it."

The owner of the watch had a great deal to say, all of which astonished Yorky beyond description. The watch and fragment of chain he identified at a glance, and Yorky as well. He swore most positively that Yorky was the man who attacked him—he had had too good a view of the rascal's features and dress to have a moment's doubt on the matter. Yorky, as he listened to it, was a picture to behold. He scratched his head in the most solemn manner imaginable, and muttered to himself—

"I *was* very tight, but I never yet did anything in drink that I couldn't remember when sober. I can't make it out at all; but I know I'm as innocent as a lamb."

A grin ran round the room as he uttered the words, and, after a word with the superintendent, the "lamb" was led off to the cells. He was next day remitted to the High Court of Justiciary. I strongly advised him to plead guilty, but the wilful man would have his own way, and took the opposite course.

Then the Fiscal pointed out that Yorky had been often convicted of the same crime, and produced a list of these, and demanded the heaviest penalty. The judge promptly responded to the appeal by sentencing Yorky to fourteen years' penal servitude. As he was being removed, a voice among the audience behind exclaimed—

"Ah, Yorky, what a time it'll be before you can make me lose another race!"

The voice came from The Gander. So elated was that worthy over the success of his scheme that he took to boasting of the feat, and giving details to his companions, and thus the story eventually reached my ears. Shortly after, when taking The Gander for helping himself to a bank-note out of a coat pocket in one of the actors' dressing-rooms, I twitted him about depriving the sporting world of such a treasure as Yorky. He denied the whole, but with a twinkle of superlative cunning and delight in his eyes.

"I never before believed it possible to overreach a Yorkshire man," I suggestively remarked.

"A Yorkshire man?" cried The Gander, with great contempt; "if he'd been twenty Yorkshire men rolled into one, I could have done him."

I think he spoke the truth.

BILLY'S BITE.

The boy whose name I have put at the head of this paper was looked upon as a timid simpleton, perfectly under the power of the two men to whom his fate was linked. If Billy had been a dog they could not have looked upon him with more indifference—he was so small, and thin, and insignificant, and above all so quiet and submissive, that they felt that they could have crushed him at any moment with a mere finger's weight.

Rodie McKendrick, the first of his masters, was a big fellow with an arm like a giant, whose standing boast was that it never needed more than one drive of his fist to knock the strongest man down. Rodie was a housebreaker, who filled up his spare time by counterfeit coining and "smashing," or passing, the same. The other, his companion and partner, Joss Brown by name, I can best describe as a comical fiend—that is, he always did the most cruel acts with a grin or a smile, joking away all the while about the wriggles or agony of his victim, as if it was the best fun in the world to him. Joss, I believe, fairly delighted in the sufferings of others, and would have reached the height of happiness had he been appointed chief torturer in an inquisition. He was an insignificant-looking wretch, but an extraordinarily swift runner. These two had settled in Glasgow, for the benefit of that city, and Billy Sloan was their spaniel and slave. There was another spaniel and slave in the person of Kate, Billy's sister, but as she was in bad health she did not count for much. The two children had been left to Rodie by their mother, a Manchester shop-lifter, whom he had brought to Scotland with him, and managed to hurry out of the world shortly after.

They were not his own children, therefore, and that fact encouraged him to deal with them as he pleased. Kate was ten, and Billy nearly nine, and both were small and weakly, so Rodie's treatment of them was not the kindest in the world. Kate's ill health had arisen from that treatment. She had bungled in the passing of some pewter florins made by Rodie and Joss, and not only nearly got captured—which could have been forgiven—but had almost got these two worthies into trouble as well. It was a narrow escape, and Rodie thought best to impress it on her memory by first knocking her down with one tap of his big fist, and then kicking her ribs till she fainted. Billy crouched in a corner, clasping his hands, and looking on pale as death, and with his eyes fixed steadily on Rodie's face. Joss, who was looking on in exuberant delight, noticed the peculiar look, and said—

"Look at the other whelp; he looks as if he could bite, if he'd only teeth in his head."

"Oh, him? Poh!" grunted Rodie in supreme contempt, as he rested from his task; but Joss could not resist the temptation, and reproved Billy's look by sinking his nails into the boy's ear, and then shaking him about till Billy thought that either the ear or the head must come off.

Joss made jokes all the while, and then went back to his supper and his whisky-drinking with fresh zest. Billy crouched in the corner, watching the slow breathing of his senseless sister till he saw that Rodie and Joss were considerably mollified by eating and drinking. Then he crept forward and lifted Kate from the floor, and bore her into a little closet off the room, in which they both slept. Kate moaned a little on being moved, but it took an hour's persistent efforts on Billy's part to bring her back to consciousness, and then he was almost sorry he had restored her, for she suffered dreadful agony where Rodie's iron-toed boots had been at work.

It is possible that some of her ribs were broken,—the dreadful pains and the after-effects all point to that conclusion,—but, though the whole night was spent in sleepless agony by Kate, she was forced to rise next day and attend to her two masters. Kate was the housewife; and though Billy would willingly have undertaken her duties for a time, the comical fiend Joss would not allow it, and insisted, with many jokes, on pulling her out of bed by the ear, with his nails, as usual, and then goading her on to every task which his ingenious brain could suggest as likely to aggravate her trouble.

The children had no idea of resenting this treatment, or of running away, or of anything but their own utter dependence upon these men; and they longed with all the strength of their young minds for the happy moment which should see Rodie and Joss either senseless with drink or out of the house. It happened, however, that the men were alarmed at their narrow escape of the day before, and had decided to keep out of sight for a day or two; so the children had a weary time of agony and secret tears. At night, when clasped in each other's arms in the hole under the slates which was their sleeping place, they sympathised and communed, and mingled their bitter tears; but Kate's dreadful sufferings did not abate much. As weeks passed away she grew shadowy and pale, and a bad cough afflicted her incessantly, so much so that Joss was often compelled to rise out of bed in the night-time and sink his nails into her ears, or stick a long pin into her arm, or wrench a handful of hair out of her head by the roots to induce her to desist, and give him some chance of enjoying his much-needed repose. And the jokes he showered on her and Billy on these occasions would have filled a book. One day both men were providentially out of the house, and Kate, sitting by the fire with her face looking strangely pinched, and her eyes big and shiny, while Billy cooked the dinner by her directions, pressed her hand on her breast, and said to the boy—

"Oh, Billy, is there nothing that would take away this awful pain?"

Billy stopped his stirring at the pot and reflected. His knowledge was exceedingly limited, and his ideas did not come fast at any time; but after a little his face brightened, and he said briefly—

"Yes—I know—medicine."

"Are you sure?"

Billy scratched his head. He wasn't sure, but he thought so.

"Then where could we get some?" was Kate's next query.

They both knew of the chemists' shops, but to go to them required money. At length they remembered of some one in the rookery getting medicine and doctor's advice at the dispensary, and, setting the dinner aside, they decided to slip out of the house, and see what could be done at that blessing to the ailing poor. When they got to the place, and their turn came, Kate went in with great trepidation before a couple of doctors and some students, and explained that she was troubled with a cough and pains in her breast and side. Dozens more were waiting, so there was little time to spare upon each.

"What brought it on?" the doctor asked when he had hastily sounded her lungs. "Caught cold, I suppose?"

Kate blushed and nodded. She did not care to reveal all she had suffered at the hands and feet of Rodie, or she would have told the doctor that far from having caught cold she had caught it very hot indeed. A bottle of medicine was quickly put up and labelled, and Kate was free to depart.

Billy was in high spirits, and danced and pranced all the way home, quite sure that the magic elixir which was to banish all pain from Kate's poor breast was in the bottle she carried. When they got home they found to their great relief that the house was still empty, and after Kate had taken a spoonful of the medicine they hid the bottle away under their bed, lest the comical fiend should jokingly throw it out at the window. The medicine thus applied for and taken in stealth had the effect of soothing the pain somewhat and easing the cough, but it did not stop the decay of Kate's lungs. She got weaker and thinner, till at last even the comical fiend confessed his ingenuity and skill in forcing her out of bed quite exhausted and at fault. Kate spent most of her time in bed in the hole under the slates, while Billy became housewife and nurse combined. Strange thoughts came into her head, and half of the time she was in a hazy dream, through which she saw little but Billy's eager face as he tended, and nursed, and soothed, and consoled, and tried every device for keeping the comical fiend out of the hole. One morning, while Rodie and Joss were still snoring in bed, Kate was more wide awake than she had seemed for a long time, and startled Billy, as she had often done of late, with one of her odd questions—

"Wouldn't it be nice, Billy, if I was to fall asleep, and sleep on and never wake?"

Billy stared at her and tried to realise the thought.

"It wouldn't be nice for me," he said at last, "for I couldn't get speaking to you. You'd be the same as dead."

"Well, what becomes of folks when they're dead?" pursued Kate. "I heard a man say once that there's another world they go to, all bright and beautiful, where there's no pain. I'd like to be there, if there's such a place."

Billy didn't think there was such a place—at least, he had never heard of it, and anyhow he did not wish Kate to die. His heart gave a great pang as he thought for the first time of what it would be to be left in the world—alone—without Kate, and he choked and gulped and would have cried, if it had not been that he did not wish to excite or alarm her.

"But, Billy, I sometimes in my dreams see a hole in the ground, with a light shining through from the other side," persisted Kate. "I see it often, and always want to go into it."

"There ain't no such hole," said Billy, sturdily and determinedly.

"There may be if I die and am put in the ground," said Kate, wearily. "Sometimes I'm so tired that I can hardly wake up again. But, Billy, how would I find the road to the other place if I should fall asleep and not wake again? I've heard it's not easy found, and I think it's only a place for good folks, and we're not that, you know."

"That's true," said Billy, "so you needn't bother your head about going to that place; you're better beside me. You'd never find it; I know you wouldn't."

"That's what I'm afraid of," said Kate, with dreadful earnestness. "I'm afraid I'll be left wandering about in the dark at the other side. I've heard that there's a man with a light shining out of his head walking about ready to take folks' hands and guide them, but he's a kind of an angel, and would never look at me. Isn't it a pity that Rodie kicked so hard? That's what has done it all. And now I'm always sinking. I often catch myself up when I've sunk about half-way through the world, and grip on to your hand just to keep myself here, but if I get much weaker I'll not be able to do that."

Billy clenched his teeth and hands, and said—

"Yes, Rodie did it all. He called me a dog the other day, and maybe I am, for I feel like biting him. Yes, I'll bite him some day, when I'm big enough."

"Could you not help me, Billy?" said Kate, after a long silence. "I'm afraid to go there without knowing something of the road. Couldn't you get some one to tell me how to do when I get through the hole?"

"I tell you there ain't no such hole; and don't you speak about it, for I do-o-o-n't like it," sobbed Billy, almost in anger; "but if there was, I'd be willing glad to go into it to find the road for you," he added, more lovingly, as he noted the distressed look which gathered on her pinched face. "Maybe you need a new kind of medicine. I'll ask them to-day when I'm at the dispensary."

Billy did ask, and in such a way that the doctor's attention was roused, and he whispered a few words to one of the students, who put on his hat and kindly told Billy that he was going home with him. The student was a tall man, and had difficulty in getting into the hole where Kate lay, but when he did, and looked into her pinched face and brilliant eyes, and listened to her quick, gasping breath, he merely gave his head a slight shake, and knelt down by the bedside to take her thin hand tenderly in his own. He had been very merry and chatty with Billy on the way, but now he was grave and solemn, and scarcely spoke a word.

"Will she be better soon?" asked Billy at last, when the silence had almost sickened him.

The student looked down on the white features of the sick girl, and said softly—

"Yes—very soon."

There was another painful silence, and then Kate dropped off into slumber, with her hand resting trustfully in that of the student. Then the gentleman softly disengaged his hand, and motioned Billy out of the hole.

"Where's your father or mother?" he gravely asked, for the room was empty.

"Not got any—mother's dead," said Billy. "Rodie looks after us," and his hands and teeth clenched, as they generally did now when Rodie was in his thoughts, or at his tongue's end.

"Then I should like to see Rodie for a minute," said the student with the same pitying look in his eyes, which Billy could not understand at all. "Could you find him now?"

No, no, Billy could not do that; and did not know when Rodie would be at home, or where he was likely to be found. The student looked round the miserable hovel, and sighed and shook his head, and then left. He had ordered no medicine, he had said nothing about Kate, except that she was to be better very soon, yet Billy felt a vague uneasiness and distrust. The house seemed oppressively quiet, and Kate's slumber unusually deep. What if she should sleep on and never wake?

Billy crept into the hole again, and sat down on the floor beside the bed to listen intently to every breath Kate drew, holding her hand softly the while to make sure that she did not slip away from him as she slept.

"Oh, if Rodie had only kicked me instead!" he thought for the hundredth time. "A boy is more able to stand kicks, and Rodie's so strong—he'd kick anybody right through the world, whether there was a hole or not."

Late in the afternoon Rodie and the comical fiend came in boisterous and gleeful to dinner. They had been unusually successful in passing some bad florins, and had invested some of the proceeds in drink, part of which they had brought home with them to make a night of it, and laughed consumedly over the manner in which they had cheated one of their victims.

Billy served them passively, and then, unable to taste food himself, he crept quietly back to watch Kate. The comical fiend made some splendid jokes, having Billy for their subject, but for once Billy was undisturbed, for he did not hear them. He sat on the floor holding

Kate's hand, and sometimes he put his other arm softly round her neck, lest his hold should not be strong enough to keep her by him.

The men got very noisy and uproarious; Rodie banged the table with tumblers and the bottle, and shouted and stamped his feet, and then the comical fiend, at his own request, favoured the company with several songs.

One smash rather louder than the rest caused Kate to start and open her eyes. She looked up in Billy's face steadily for some moments without moving, and the expression was so strange that in alarm he cried—

"Kate, Kate! don't you know me?"

There was no immediate answer. There was in the slates immediately above them a single pane of glass, which gave light to the closet, and that pane now showed a deep red square of the crimson sky. Kate's eyes wandered to the pane, and became fixed for some moments.

"What's—that?" she whispered at last, with a strange trembling eagerness.

"It's only the winder," answered Billy, a little scared.

"No, it isn't; it's the hole you go through into the other world," said Kate joyfully. "Billy, dear, I can't stay any longer. I'm going through!"

Billy threw both his arms around her slight form, and rained his tears upon her face. At the same moment there was a chorus of gleeful shouts and table-smashing like thunder in the adjoining room. It was the comical fiend applauding his own song. Kate continued to gaze steadily at the crimson pane in the roof with a smile brightening on her face.

"I wish—oh, I wish there had been somebody to tell me what to do at the other side," she said at last in a whisper so low that Billy could scarce catch it. "But maybe somebody will hold out a hand to me. I'll keep feeling about for it. It's growing darker. Am I going through? and is the light only at the door?"

"No, its almost night, and Rodie's lit the candle," said Billy. "Do you hear me, Kate? You're awful dreamy and queer—I'm saying it's almost night."

"Night! night!" feebly and hazily breathed Kate. "Good-night."

Her lips stood still, and her eyes, though fixed on the crimson pane, were strange and big and unearthly. Billy stared at them in awe, and then moved a hand quickly before them to break the steady stare and draw it to himself. There was no response. Her eyes remained fixed on the pane.

"Kate! Kate!" he cried in a scream of alarm.

A slight spasm—almost shaping into a smile—crossed the pinched features; the eyes gazed unwinkingly at the pane—the breath came and went in long-drawn sighs—paused—came again—then paused for ever. Kate had slipped through to another world, where her feeble and groping hand would surely be gently taken by a Guide who Himself knew all suffering and temptation and weakness that can afflict frail humanity, and who will surely be as pitiful to the benighted savages of our land as of any other.

Billy screamed and wept, and threw himself on the still form; and at length even the comical fiend, who had got up on the table to execute a flourishing hornpipe, became annoyed and got down to put a stop to the unseemly disturbance. Rodie, too, who became stupid and sullen with drink just as his partner became lively, roused himself sufficiently to stagger across the room towards the hole, vowing that if he could only trust himself to the support of one foot he would use the other in stopping Billy's howling.

"Kate stares up, and won't move or speak to me," cried Billy in gasps, as soon as he was conscious of the nails of the comical fiend almost meeting in his ear.

"Maybe she's croaked at last," suggested Rodie. "See if she breathes."

Joss hopped in, and soon answered in a gleeful negative.

"It's a good job," said Rodie, "for she'd never have been of any more use."

"Three cheers for her death!" cried the comical fiend, and as there was nobody to laugh at his joke, Rodie being too sullen, Joss laughed the required quantity for a dozen people himself.

Rodie tried to kick Billy, but, finding himself unable to stand on one leg, he contented himself with some horrible threats, and then they went back comfortably to their drinking. Billy cried and cried—softly, so that the men should not hear him—with his arms round the still form, till he fell asleep, and there they lay all night, the living and the dead. Next day Rodie and Joss put all their implements and money out of sight, and sent word to the poorhouse, and a medical inspector came and glanced at the wasted body, and asked a few questions, and signed a paper, which Billy took to the undertaker, who brought a coffin the next day, and placed Kate's form in it, and then asked if they wished it screwed down. Rodie and Joss were too drunk to reply, but Billy, never tired of looking at the wide open eyes, and fancying they were looking at him, said he should like it kept open as long as possible.

The funeral took place the day after, and there was only one mourner to follow the coffin to the grave—Billy himself, in his ragged jacket and bare feet. The only mournings he had to put on were the tears which flowed down his cheeks all the way. Even when the coffin was hid in the ground, and the earth tumbled in, and the turf spread over the top, he could not put off his mournings, or leave the place chatting gaily about business matters, as is the custom at funerals. He still seemed to see Kate's open eyes shining up at him through earth and turf, and he had a firm idea that she could still hear him speak, though herself unable to reply. He loitered long after the gravediggers were gone, and stuck a little twig in the ground so that he should know the spot again, and then, when no one was near to see, he lay down on the grass and whispered to Kate through the openings in the turf. He had but two thoughts to reiterate—the regret that Rodie had not kicked him out of the world instead of Kate, and the wish that he might live to "bite Rodie" for what he had done to Kate. Whenever Billy was in trouble after that he came to the graveyard to whisper his griefs to Kate through the turf. He told her of all his adventures and the tortures of the comical fiend and the kicks of Rodie; and though he got no reply, he felt quite certain that he had Kate's sympathy in every word he uttered. Billy's was not a large mind, or a very acute one, but when an idea did get fairly in, it stuck there firmly. When Kate had been some months in the grave, Rodie and Joss prepared a lot of florins—their most successful effort in base coining—and informed Billy that they were going through to Edinburgh to attend the Musselburgh Races, on business, and that he was to accompany them, and have the honour of carrying their luggage—an old leather valise containing the base florins. Joss and Rodie, for prudential reasons, went by different trains, and Billy, though he accompanied Rodie, had strict orders to sit at the other end of the carriage, and take no more notice of Rodie than of any stranger.

It chanced, however, that by the time the train drew up at the Waverley Station platform, that particular carriage was empty of all but Billy and Rodie, and the base coiner had no sooner glanced along the platform than he uttered an oath and drew in his head with surprising quickness.

"Do you see that ugly brute standing over there, near the cabman with the white hat?" he observed to Billy.

"That ugly brute" was I, the writer of these experiences, on the look out for any of my "bairns" who might be drawn thither by the race meeting, and Billy quickly signified that he did see me.

"Well, keep clear of him, or we're done for. That's McGovan, and he's a perfect bloodhound," and Rodie cursed the bloodhound with great heartiness. "If he gets his teeth on us, we'll feel the bite, I tell ye."

"Ah!" it was all Billy said, and it was uttered with a start, for Rodie's words had suggested a strange idea to him.

"Yes, if he gets us at it it'll mean twenty years to us if it means a day," continued Rodie, still wasting a deal of breath on me. "Now you get out first, and go straight to the place I told ye of, while I jink him and get round by the other."

Billy obeyed, and was soon lost in the crowd, while Rodie—who mistakenly believed that his face was as familiar to me as mine was to him—cut round by another outlet, and escaped to the appointed rendezvous.

Meantime Billy had only gone far enough with the crowd to get behind one of the waiting cabs, whence he watched Rodie leave the station. Then he crept out of his hiding-place, and walked back to the spot where I stood, and touched me lightly on the arm.

"I'm Rodie's boy," he said, while I stared at him in astonishment. "I've come from Glasgow with him, and we're to go 'smashing' at the races to-morrow. Would it be twenty years to him if you caught us at it?"

"What Rodie do you mean?" I asked at length. "Is his other name McKendrick?"

"That's it; and Joss Brown is with him," said Billy with animation. "He says you're a bloodhound, and can bite. Twenty years would be a good bite, wouldn't it?"

"Ah, I see, he has injured you, and you want to pay him back," I said, not admiring Billy much, though his treachery was to bring grist to my mill.

"He kicked Kate, my sister, and she died, and I've told her often since then that I would bite him for it, and now I've got the chance I must keep my word."

I took Billy into one of the waiting-rooms and drew from him his story. Billy told the story much better than I could put it down though I were to spend months on the task. He showed me also the piles of base florins put up in screws ready for use, and offered them to me. But while he had been telling the story I had been studying the position. I had perfect faith in Billy's truthfulness. The tears he shed over the narrative of Kate's death would have convinced the most sceptical. I therefore explained to him that in order to secure Rodie the full strength of a good bite it was necessary that I should take him and Joss in the act, and if possible with the supply of base coin in their possession. To that end I arranged to see the three next day at the race-course, and explained to Billy how he was to act when he got from me the required signal.

I had the idea that Billy was densely stupid—almost idiotic—and that therefore the scheme would be sure to be bungled, but in this I misjudged the boy sadly. If Billy had been the most acute of trained detectives he could not have gone through his part with more coolness or precision. When I had my men ready and dropped my handkerchief, Billy quickly wriggled himself out of a crowd and hastily thrust the valise containing the reserve of base florins into the hands of Rodie, who hid the same under his jacket and looked nervously round. The comical fiend helped him. They had not long to look. We were on them like bloodhounds the next moment. Joss was easily managed, but Rodie fought hard, and struggled, and kicked, and finally threw away the valise of base coin in the direction of Billy, with a shout to him to pick it up and run. Billy looked at him, but never moved.

"You kicked Kate, and she died. It's Billy's Bite," he calmly answered, when Rodie worked himself black in the face, and the comical fiend nearly choked himself with hastily concocted jokes.

The two got due reward in the shape of fifteen and twenty years respectively, but Billy was sent to the Industrial School, and is now an honest working man.

THE MURDERED TAILOR'S WATCH.
(A CURIOSITY IN CIRCUMSTANTIAL EVIDENCE.)

The case of the tailor, Peter Anderson, who was beaten to death near the Royal Terrace, on the Calton Hill, may not yet be quite forgotten by some, but, as the after-results are not so well known, it will bear repeating.

Some working men, hurrying along a little before six in the morning, found Anderson's body in a very steep path on the hill, and in a short time a stretcher was got and it was conveyed to the Head Office. The first thing I noticed when I saw the body was that one of the trousers' pockets was half-turned out, as if with a violent wrench, or a hand too full of money to get easily out again; and from this sprang another discovery—that the waistcoat button-hole in which the link of his albert had evidently been constantly worn was wrenched clean through. There was no watch or chain visible, and the trousers' pockets were empty, so the first deduction was clear—the man had been robbed.

Robbery, indeed, appeared to me, at this stage of the case, to have been the prime cause of the outrage, and an examination of the body confirmed the idea. The neck was not broken, but there were marks of a strangulating arm about the neck, and the injuries about the head were quite sufficient to cause death. These seemed to indicate that two persons had been engaged in the crime, as is common in garroting cases—one to strangle and the other to rob and beat—and made me more hopeful of tracking the doers. On examining the spot at which the body had been found, I found traces of a violent struggle, and also a couple of folded papers, which proved to be unreceipted accounts headed "Peter Anderson, tailor and clothier," with the address of his place of business. These might have given us a clue to his identity had such been needed, but his wife had been at the Office reporting his absence only an hour before his body was brought in, and we had only to turn to her description of his person and clothing to confirm our suspicion.

Anderson, on the fatal night on which he disappeared, had unexpectedly drawn an account of some £10 or £12 from a customer, and in the joy of receiving the money had invited the man to an adjoining public-house to drink "a jorum," and one round followed another until poor Peter Anderson's head was fitter for his pillow than for guiding his feet. On entering the public-house—which was a very busy one, not far from the Calton Hill—Anderson,

I found, had gone up to the bar, and before all the loungers or hangers-on pulled a handful of notes, and silver, and gold from his trousers' pocket, saying to his companion—

"What will you have?"

Afterwards, when they got into talk, they adjourned to a private box at the back; but it was there I thought that the mischief had been done. Anderson had a gold albert across his breast, and might be believed to have a watch at the end of it; but the chain, after all, might have been only plated, and the watch a pinchbeck thing, to a thief not worth taking; but the reckless display of a handful of notes, gold, and silver, if genuine criminals chanced to see it, was a temptation and revelation too powerful to be resisted. The man who carried money in that fashion was likely to have more in his pockets, and a gold watch at least. If he got drunk, or was likely to get drunk, he would be worth waiting and watching for; so, at least, I thought the intending criminals would reason, never dreaming of course of the plan ending in determined resistance and red-handed murder. Your garroter is generally a big coward, and will never risk his skin or his liberty with a sober man if he can get one comfortably muddled with drink.

There was no time to elaborate theories or schemes of capture. A gold watch and chain valued at about £30, and £14 in money, were gone. A rare prize was afloat among the sharks, and I surmised that the circumstance would be difficult to hide. The thief and the honest man are alike in one failing—they find it difficult to conceal success. It prints itself in their faces; in the quantity of drink they consume; in the tread of their feet; the triumphant leer at the baffled or sniffing detective, and in their reckless indulgence in gaudy articles of flash dress. I went down to the Cowgate and Canongate at once, strolling into every likely place, and nipping up quite a host of my "bairns." I thought I had got the right men indeed when I found two known as "The Crab Apple" and "Coskey" flush of money and muddled with drink, but a day's investigation proved that they owed their good fortune to a stupid swell who had got into their clutches over in the New Town. Coskey, indeed, strongly declared that he did not believe the Anderson affair had been managed by a professional criminal at all.

"If it had been done by any of us I'd have heard on it," was his frank remark to me.

I was pretty sure that Coskey spoke the truth, for in his nervous anxiety to escape Calcraft's toilet he had actually confessed to me all the particulars of the New Town robbery by which his own pockets had been filled, and which afterwards led to a seven years' retirement from the scene of his labours.

The hint thus received prepared me for making the worst slip of all I had made in the case. I went to Anderson's widow to get the number of the watch, and some description by which it might be identified. She could not tell me the number or the maker's name; she could only say that it had a white dial and black figures, but declared that she would know it out of a thousand by a deep "clour" or indentation on the back of the case.

"I was there when it got the mark," she said, "and I could never be mistaken if the watch was put before me. A thief might alter the number, but nobody could take out that mark, for we tried it, and the watchmaker could do nothing for it. My man was working hard one day with the watch on, when a customer called to be measured. The waistcoat he wore wasn't a very bonny one, and he whipped it off in a hurry, forgetting about the watch, which was tugged out, and came bang against the handle of one of his irons. The watch was never a bit the worse, but the case had aye the mark on it—just there," and the widow, to illustrate her statement, showed me a spot on the back of my own watch, and then so minutely explained the line of the indentation, its length and its depth, that I felt sure that if it came in my way I should be able to identify it as readily as by a number.

This would have been all very well if her information had there ended, but it didn't.

"You are hunting away among thieves and jail birds for the man that did it," she bitterly remarked, "but I think I could put my hand on him without any detective to help me."

"You suspect some one, then?" I exclaimed, with a new interest.

"Suspect? I wish I was as sure of anything," she answered, with great emphasis. "The brute threatened to do it."

"What brute?"

"Just John Burge, the man who was working to him as journeyman two months ago."

"Indeed. Did they quarrel?"

"A drunken passionate wretch that nobody would have any thing to do wi'," vehemently continued the widow, waxing hotter in her words with every word she had uttered, "but just because they had been apprentices together Peter took pity on him and gave him work. They were aye quarrelling, but one day it got worse than usual, and I thought my man would have killed him. It was quite a simple thing began it—an argument as to which is the first day in summer—but in the end they were near fighting, and after Peter had near choked him, Burge swore that he would have his life for it—that he would watch him night and day, and then knock the 'sowl oot o' him in some dark corner, before he knew where he was.' That was after the master and the laddies had thrown him out at the door and down the stair; and for some days I wouldn't let Peter cross the door. But he only laughed at me after a bit, and said that Burge's 'bark was waur than his bite,' and went about just as usual. And all the time the wicked, ungrateful wretch was watching for a chance to take his life."

"Why did you not tell us of this quarrel at first?" I asked, after a pause.

"Because I thought you detectives were so sharp and clever that you would have Burge in your grips before night, without a word from me; but you're not nearly so clever as you're called."

"But he never actually attacked your husband?" I quietly interposed, knowing that wives are apt to take exceedingly exaggerated views of their husband's wrongs or rights.

"Oh, but he did, though. He came up once, not long after the quarrel, and said he had not got all the money due to him, and tried to murder Peter with the cutting shears."

"Murder him? How could he murder him with shears?" I asked, with marked scepticism.

"Well, I didn't wait to see; but ran in and gripped him by the arms till my man took the shears from him. The creatur' had no more strength than a sparry, though he's as tall as you."

"No more strength than a sparrow?" That incidental revelation staggered me. It seemed to me quite impossible that a weak man could have been the murderer of Anderson, unless, indeed, he had had an accomplice, and that was unlikely with a man seeking mere revenge. For a moment I was inclined to think it possible that Burge might have tracked his victim to the hill and accomplished the revenge, and that afterwards, when he had fled the spot, some of the "ghosts" haunting the hill might have stripped the dead or dying man of his valuables; but several circumstances led me to reject the supposition—wisely, too, as it appeared in the end. Burge, the widow told me, was a tall man, with a white, "potty" face, and a little, red, snub-nose, and always wore a black frock coat and dress hat. I took down the name of the street in which he lived—for I could get no number—and turned in that direction. In about fifteen minutes I had reached, not the street, but the crossing leading to it, when I met full in the face a man answering his description, and having the unmistakable tailor's "nick" in his back.

"That should be Burge," was my mental conclusion, though I had never seen him before. "If he's not, he is at least a tailor, and may know him," and then I stopped him with the words—

"Do you know a tailor called John Burge who lives here-about?"

"That's me," he said, with sudden animation, taking the pipe from his mouth, and evidently expecting a call at his trade, "who wants me?"

"I do."

"Oh," and he looked me all over, evidently wondering how I looked so unlike the trade.

There was a queer pause, and then I said—

"My name's McGovan, and I want you to go with me as far as the Police Office, about that affair on the Calton Hill."

A wonderful change took place in his face the moment I uttered the words—a change which, but for the grave nature of the case, would have been actually comical; his "potty" white cheeks became red, and his red snub-nose as suddenly became white.

"Well, do you know, that's curious!" he at length gasped; "but I was just coming up to the Office now, in case I should be suspected of having a hand in it. I had a quarrel with Anderson, and said some strong things, I've no doubt, in my passion, but of course I never meant them."

I listened in silence; but my mental comment, I remember, was, "A very likely story!"

"I was coming up to say what I can prove—that I was at the other end of the town that night, and home and in my bed by a quarter to eleven," he desperately added, rightly interpreting my silence.

I became more interested at the mention of the exact hour; for I had ascertained beyond doubt that Anderson had not left the public-house and parted with his friend till eleven o'clock struck. He had, in fact, been "warned out," along with a number of bar-loafers, at shutting-up time.

"Did any one see you at home at that hour?" I asked, after cautioning him.

"Yes, the wife and bairns."

"Imphm."

"You think that's not good evidence; but I have more; I was in a public-house with some friends till half-past ten; they can swear to that; and they went nearly all the road home with me," he continued with growing excitement. "Do I look like a murderer? My God! I could swear on a Bible that such a thing was never in my mind. Don't look so horrible and solemn, man, but say you believe me!"

I couldn't say that, for I believed the whole a fabrication got up in a moment of desperation; and little more was spoken on either side till we reached the Head Office, where he repeated the same story to the Fiscal, and was locked up. I fully expected that I should easily tear his story to pieces by taking his so-called witnesses one by one, but I was mistaken. His wife and children, for example, the least reliable of his witnesses in the eyes of the law, became the strongest, for when I called and saw them they were in perfect ignorance both of Burge's arrest and the fact that he expected to be suspected.

They distinctly remembered their father being home "earlier" on that Friday night, and the wife added that it was more than she had expected, for by being in bed so early Burge had been able to rise early on the following morning and finish some work on the Saturday which she had fully expected would be "disappointed." Then the men with whom he had been drinking and playing dominoes up to half-past ten were emphatic in their statements, which tallied almost to a minute with those of Burge. Burge had not been particularly flush of money after that date, but, on the contrary, had pleaded so hard for payment of the work done on the Saturday that the man was glad to compromise matters and get rid of him by part payment in shape of half-a-crown. The evidence, as was afterwards remarked, was not the best—a few drinkers in a public-house, whose ideas of time and place might be readily believed to be hazy, and the interested wife and children of the suspected man; but in the absence of condemning facts it sufficed, and after a brief detention Burge was set at liberty.

About that time, among the batch of suspected persons in our keeping was a man named Daniel O'Doyle. How he came to be suspected I forget, but I believe it was through having a deal of silver and some sovereigns in the pockets of his ragged trousers when he was brought to the Office as a "drunk and disorderly." O'Doyle gave a false name, too, when he came to his senses; but then it was too late, for a badly-written letter from some one in Ireland had been found in his pocket when he was brought in. He was a powerfully-built man, and in his infuriated state it took four men to get him to the Office. He could give no very satisfactory account of how he came by the money in his possession. He had been harvesting, he said, but did not know the name of the place or its geographical position, except that it was east of Edinburgh "a long way," and he was going back to Ireland with his earnings, but chanced to take a drop too much and half-murder a man in Leith Walk, and so got into our hands. On the day after his capture and that of his remand O'Doyle was "in the horrors," and at night during a troubled sleep was heard by a man in the same cell to mutter something about "Starr Road," and having "hidden it safe there." This brief and unintelligible snatch was repeated to me next morning, but, stupid as it now appears to me, I could make nothing of it. I knew that there was no such place as "Starr Road" in Edinburgh, and said so; and as for him having hidden something, that was nothing for a wandering shearer, and might, after all, be only his reaping hook or bundle of lively linen. O'Doyle was accordingly tried for assault, and sentenced to thirty days' imprisonment, at the expiry of which he was set at liberty and at once disappeared. My impression now is that O'Doyle was never seriously suspected of having had a hand in the Calton Hill affair, but that, being in our keeping about the time, he came in for his share of suspicion among dozens more perfectly innocent. If he had had bank-notes about him it might have been different, for I have found that there is a strong feeling against these and in favour of gold among the untutored Irish, which induces them to get rid of them almost as soon as they chance to receive them.

So the months passed away and no discovery was made; we got our due share of abuse from the public; and the affair promised to remain as dark and mysterious as the Slater murder in the Queen's Park. But for the incident I am now coming to, I believe the crime would have been still unsolved.

About two years after, I chanced to be among a crowd at a political hustings in Parliament Square, at which I remember Adam Black came in for a great deal of howling and abuse. I was there, of course, on business, fully expecting to nip up some of my diligent "family" at work among the pockets of the excited voters; but no game could have been further from my thoughts than that which I had the good fortune to bag. I was moving about on the outskirts of the crowd, when a face came within the line of my vision which was familiar yet puzzling. The man had a healthy prosperous look, and nodded smilingly to me, more as a superior than an inferior in position.

"Don't you remember me?—John Burge; I was in the Anderson murder, you mind; the Calton Hill affair;" and then I smiled too and shook the proffered hand.

"How are you getting on now?"

"Oh, first rate—doing well for myself," was the bright and pleased-looking answer. "Yon affair was a lesson to me; turned teetot. when I came out, and have never broke it since. It's the best way."

It seemed so, to look at him. The "potty" look was gone from his face; his cheeks had a healthy colour, and his nose had lost its rosiness. His dress too was better. The glossy, well-ironed dress hat was replaced by one shining as if fresh from the maker, and the threadbare frock coat by one of smooth, firm broadcloth. He was getting stouter, too, and his broad, white waistcoat showed a pretentious expanse of gold chain. He chatted away for some time, evidently a little vain of the change in his circumstances, and at length drew out a handsome gold watch, making, as his excuse for referring to it, the remark—

"Ah, it's getting late; I can't stay any longer."

My eye fell upon the watch, as it had evidently been intended that it should, and almost with the first glance I noticed a deep nick in the edge of the case, at the back. Possibly the man's own words had taken my mind back to the lost watch of the murdered tailor and its description, but certainly the moment I saw the mark on the case I put out my hand with affected carelessness, as he was slipping it back to his pocket, saying—

"That's a nice watch; let's have a look at it."

It was tendered at once, and I found it to have a white china dial and black figures. At last I came back to the nick and scrutinised it closely.

"You've given it a bash there," I remarked, after a pause.

"No, that was done when I got it."

"Bought it lately?"

"Oh, no; a long time ago."

"Who from?"

"From one of the men working under me; I got it a great bargain," he answered with animation. "It's a chronometer, and belonged to an uncle of his, but it was out of order—had lain in the bottom of a sea chest till some of the works were rusty—and so I got it cheap."

"Imphm. There has been some lying in the bargain anyhow," I said, after another look at the watch, "for it is an ordinary English lever, not a chronometer. Is the man with you yet?"

"No; but, good gracious! you don't mean to say that there's anything wrong about the watch? It's not—not a stolen one?"

"I don't know, but there was one exactly like this stolen that time that Anderson was killed."

In one swift flash of alarm, his face, before so rosy, became as white as the waistcoat covering his breast.

Then he slowly examined the watch with a trembling hand, and finally stammered out—

"I remember it, and this is not unlike it. But that's nothing—hundreds of watches are as like as peas."

I differed with him there, and finally got him to go with me to the Office, at which he was detained, while I went in search of Anderson's widow to see what she would say about the watch.

If I had an opinion at all about the case at this stage, it was that the watch taken was not that of the murdered man. I could scarcely otherwise account for Burge's demeanour. He appeared so surprised and innocent, whereas a man thus detected in the act of wearing such a thing, knowing its terrible history, could scarcely have helped betraying his guilt.

My fear, then, as I made my way to the house of Anderson's widow, was that she, woman like, would no sooner see the mark on the case than she would hastily declare it to be the missing watch. To avoid as far as possible a miscarriage of justice, I left the watch at the Office, carefully mixed up with a dozen or two more then in our keeping, one or two of which resembled it in appearance. I found the widow easily enough, and took her to the Office with me, saying simply that we had a number of watches which she might look at, with the possibility of finding that of her husband. The watches were laid out before her in a row, faces upward, and she slowly went over them with her eye, touching none till she came to that taken from Burge. Then she paused, and there was a moment's breathless stillness in the room.

"This ane's awfu' like it," she said, and, lifting the watch, she turned it, and beamed out in delight as she recognised the sharp nick on the back of the case. "Yes, it's it! Look at the mark I told you about."

She pointed out other trifling particulars confirming the identity, but practically the whole depended on exactly what had first drawn my attention to the watch—the nick on the case. Now dozens of watches might have such a mark upon them, and it was necessary to have a much more reliable proof before we could hope for a conviction against Burge on such a charge.

I had thought of this all the way to and from the widow's house. She knew neither the number of the watch nor the maker's name, but with something like hopefulness I found that she knew the name of the watchmaker in Glasgow who had sold it to her husband, and another in Edinburgh who had cleaned it. I went through to Glasgow the same day with the watch in my pocket, found the seller, and by referring to his books discovered the number of the watch sold to Anderson, which, I was electrified to find, was identical with that on the gold lever I carried. The name of the maker and description of the watch also tallied perfectly; and the dealer emphatically announced himself ready to swear to the identity in any court of justice. My next business was to visit the man who had cleaned the watch for Anderson in Edinburgh. I was less hopeful of him, and hence had left him to the last, and therefore was not disappointed to find that he had no record of the number or maker's name. On examining the watch through his working glass, however, he declared that he recognised it perfectly as that which he had cleaned for Anderson by one of the screws, which had half of its head broken off, and thus had caused him more trouble than usual in fitting up the watch after cleaning.

"I would have put a new one in rather than bother with it," he said, "but I had not one beside me that would fit it, and as I was pressed for time, I made the old one do. It was my own doing, too, for I broke the top in taking the watch down."

I was now convinced, almost against my will, that the watch was really that taken from Anderson; my next step was to test Burge's statement as to how it came into his possession. If that broke down, his fate was sealed.

When I again appeared before Burge he was eager to learn what had transpired, and appeared unable to understand why he should still be detained; all which I now set down as accomplished hypocrisy. It seemed to me that he had lied from the first, and I was almost angry with myself for having given so much weight to his innocent looks and apparent surprise.

Cutting short his questions with no very amiable answers, I asked the name and address of the man from whom he alleged he had bought the watch. Then he looked grave, and admitted that the man, whose name was Chisholm, might be difficult to find, as he was a kind of "orra" hand, oftener out of work than not. I received the information in silence, and went on the hunt for Chisholm, whom I had no difficulty whatever in finding at the house of a married daughter with whom he lodged. He was at home when I called,—at his dinner or tea,—and stared at me blankly when I was introduced, being probably acquainted with my face, like many more whom I have never spoken to or noticed.

"I have called about a watch that you sold to Burge the tailor, whom you were working with some six months ago," I said quietly.

The man, who had been drinking tea or coffee out of a basin, put down the dish in evident concern, and stared at me more stupidly than before.

"A watch!—what kin' o' a watch?" he huskily exclaimed. "I haena had a watch for mair nor ten years."

"The watch is a gold lever, but he says you sold it to him as a chronometer which had belonged to your uncle, a seaman."

Chisholm's face was now pale to the very point of his nose, but that did not necessarily imply guilt on his part. I have noticed the look far oftener on the faces of witnesses than prisoners.

"What? an uncle! a seaman!" he cried with great energy, turning an amazed look on his daughter. "I havena an uncle leeving—no ane. The man must be mad," and this statement the daughter promptly supported.

"Do you mean to say—can you swear that you never sold him a watch of any kind—which was rusty in the works through lying in a sea-chest?"

"Certainly, sir—certainly, I can swear that. I never had a watch to sell, and I'll tell him that to his face," volubly answered Chisholm, whose brow now was as thick with perspiration as if he had been doing a hard day's work since I entered. "Onybody that kens me can tell ye I've never had a watch, or worn ane, for ten year and mair. I wad be only owre glad if I had."

I questioned him closely and minutely, but he declared most distinctly and emphatically that the whole story of Burge was an invention. I ought to have been satisfied with this declaration—it was voluble and decided, and earnest as any statement could be—but I was not. The man's manner displeased me. It was too noisy and hurried, and his looks of astonishment and innocence were, if anything, too marked. I left the house in a puzzled state.

"What if I should have to deal with *two* liars?" was my reflection. "How could I pit them against each other?"

Back I trudged to the Office, and saw Burge at once.

"I have seen the man Chisholm, and he declares that he not only did not sell you a watch of any kind, but that he has not had one in his possession for upwards of ten years."

Burge paled to a deathly hue, and I saw the cold sweat break out in beads on his temples.

"I was just afraid of that," he huskily whispered, after a horrible pause. "Chisholm's an awful liar, and will say that now to save his own skin. There must have been something wrong about the way he got it. I was a fool to believe his story. I remember now he made me promise not to say that I had bought the watch from him, or how I got it, in case the other relatives should find out that he had taken it."

"Indeed! Then you have no witness whatever to produce as to the purchase?" I cried, after a long whistle.

"None."

"Did you not speak of it to anybody?"

"Not a soul but yourself that I mind of."

"Well, all I can say is that your case looks a bad one," I said at last, as I turned to leave him. "By the by, though, what about the chain? Did you buy that from him too?"

My reason for asking was, that the chain was a neck one, not an albert, and, of course, had not been identified by the widow of Anderson.

"No, I had the chain; I had taken it in payment of an account; but he wanted me to buy a chain, too, now that I remember."

"What kind of a chain? Did you see it?"

"No; I said I did not need it; but I would look at the watch. He wanted a pound for the chain, and eight for the watch. I got it for £5, 10s., and then he went on the spree for a fortnight."

"A whole fortnight? Surely some one will be able to recall that," I quickly interposed, half inclined to believe that Burge was not at least the greater liar of the two. "His daughter will surely remember it?"

"I don't know about that," groaned Burge, in despairing tones. "That man takes so many sprees that it's difficult to mind ane frae anither."

I resolved to try the daughter, nevertheless, and after getting from Burge, as near as he could remember, the date of the bargain, I left him and began to ponder how I could best get an unvarnished tale from this prospective witness. While I pondered, a new link in this most mysterious case was thrown into my hands.

We had been particularly careful after the arrest of Burge to keep the affair secret, but in spite of the precaution, an account of the arrest, altogether garbled and erroneous, appeared in the next day's papers. From this account it appeared that we were confident of Burge's guilt, and were only troubled because we could not discover his accomplices in the crime, and on that account "were not disposed to be communicative," as the penny-a-liner grandly expressed himself. The immediate result of this stupid paragraph, which seemed to book Burge for the gallows beyond redemption, was a letter from the West, bearing neither name nor address, it is true, but still written with such decision and vigour that I could not but give it some weight in my feeble gropings at the truth. This letter was placed in my hands, though not addressed to me particularly, just as I was wondering how to best question Chisholm's daughter about her father's big spree. The letter was short, and well-written and spelled, and began by saying that Burge, whom we had in custody on suspicion of being concerned in the robbery and murder of Anderson, was perfectly innocent; that the whole of the facts were known to the writer, whose lips were sealed as to who the criminal really was, and who only wrote that he might save an innocent man from a shameful death. The post-mark on the letter was that of a considerable town on the Clyde, or my thoughts would inevitably have reverted to Chisholm as the author or prompter. With the suspicion of this man had come at last an idea that he was in some way mixed up in the crime; yet he did not look either strong enough or courageous enough to be the murderer. Quite uncertain how to act, I left the Office, and wandered down in the direction of Chisholm's home. It was quite dark, I remember, and I was ascending the narrow stair in hope that Chisholm might by that time be out of the house, when a man stumbled down on me in the dark, cursing me sharply for not calling out that I was there. The man was Chisholm, as I knew at once by the tone of the voice, and how I did not let him pass on, and make my inquiries at the daughter, is more than I can tell to this day. I merely allowed him to reach the bottom of the stair, and then turned and followed him. At the bottom I watched his figure slowly descending the close towards the Back Canongate till he reached the bottom, when he paused and peered cautiously forth before venturing out. The stealthy walk and that cunning look forth I believe decided me, coupled with the decided change in the tone in which he cursed me in the dark from the smooth and oily manner in which he had answered my questions during the day. I would follow him, though wherefore or why I did not trouble to ask. About half-way down the South Back Canongate, where the Public Washing House now stands, there was at that time an open drain which ran with a strong current in the direction of the Queen's Park. As it left the green for the Park, this drain emptied itself down an iron-barred opening in the ground, and made a sudden dip downwards of twenty or thirty feet on smooth flag-stones, which carried the water away into the darkness with a tremendous rush and noise. So steep was the gradient at this covered part of the drain, and so smooth the bottom, that miserable cats and dogs, doomed to die, had merely to be put within the grating, when down they shot, and were seen or heard no more.

I followed Chisholm as far as this green, which he entered, and then wondered what his object could be. That it was not quite a lawful one I could guess from the fact that he so often paused and looked about him that I had the greatest difficulty in keeping him in sight without myself being seen. At length he came to the opening in the wall where the open drain ceased and dipped into the iron bars with a roar audible even to me, and then with another furtive look around, and before I had the slightest idea of what he was intending to do, he put his hand in his pocket, drew something forth, and threw it sharply into the roaring, scurrying water. A moment more and my hand was on his arm. He started round with a scared cry, and recognised and named me.

"What's that you threw down the drain?" I sternly demanded, without giving him time to recover, and tightening my grip on his arm.

"Oh, naething, naething, sir—only an auld pipe that's nae mair use," he confusedly stammered.

"A pipe!" I scornfully echoed. "Man, what do you think my head's made of? You didn't come so far to throw away a pipe. Were you afraid that, like some of the cats the laddies put down there, it would escape and come back again?"

He tried to grin, cringingly, but the effect was ghastly in the extreme.

"No, no, Maister McGovan; I was just walking this way ony way, and thought I wad get rid o' my auld pipe."

"More like, it was a gold albert," I sharply said, getting out the handcuffs. "If I had only guessed what you were after I might have been nearer, and prevented the extravagance. You're unlike every one else in the world, throwing away good gold while others are breaking their hearts to get it. Come, now, try your hand in these; and then I'll have to see if the burn will give up your offering."

He was utterly and abjectly silenced, and accepted the bracelets without demur, which led me to believe that my surmise was a hit. The tailor's gold albert, supposing Burge's story to be true, was all that remained unaccounted for, and its possession now was frightfully dangerous. What more natural, then, that Chisholm should take alarm at my visit, and hasten to dispose of it in the most effectual manner within his reach? If he had put it through the melting pot, and I had arrived only in time to see the shapeless nugget tossed out of the crucible, he could not have given me a greater pang; but of course I did not tell him that. I expected never to see it again, and I was right, for the chain has never been seen or heard of since. My thoughts on the way to the Office were not pleasant; afterthoughts with an "if" are always tormenting; and mine was "If I had only seized him before he reached the drain, and had him searched." Then he was so secretive and cunning that I had no hope whatever of him committing himself to a confession. In this I made the error of supposing him entirely guilty. I forgot the case of "Cosky" and "The Crab Apple," who were only too glad to save their necks at the expense of their liberty. Chisholm, though cunning as a fox, was a terrible coward, and as we neared the Office he tremblingly said—

"Will I be long, think ye, o' getting oot again?"

I stared at him in surprise, and then, with some impatience, said—

"About three weeks after the trial probably."

"What? how? will three weeks be the sentence?" he stammered in confusion.

"No; but that is the interval generally allowed between sentence and hanging."

"Good God, man! They canna hang me!" he exclaimed, nearly dropping on the street with terror.

"Wait. If I get that chain out of the drain it will hang you as sure as fate," I grimly replied. I was rather pleased at being able to say it, for I was snappish and out of temper.

"But I never killed the tailor; never saw the man," he exclaimed, evidently fearfully in earnest.

"I've nothing to do with that; it all depends on what the jury think," I shortly answered, and then we got to the Office, and he made a rambling statement about being taken up innocently, and was then locked up.

My immediate task was to have the drain explored, but that was all labour thrown away. The rush of water had been too strong, and the chain was gone, buried in mud and slime, or carried away to sea. I soon had abundant evidence that Chisholm had been on the spree for a fortnight about the time stated by Burge, but my intention of weaving a complete web round him was stayed by a message from himself, asking to see me that he might tell all he knew of the watch and chain. He did not know that I had failed to get the chain, or he might have risked absolute silence.

"Ye ken, I'm a bit of a fancier of birds," he said, in beginning his story.

"Including watches and chains," I interposed.

"I was oot very early ae Sunday morning, for however late I'm up on a Saturday, I can never sleep on Sunday morning," he continued, with a dutiful grin at my remark. "I gaed doon by the Abbey Hill to the Easter Road, and when I was hauf way to Leith I saw a yellow finch flee oot at a dyke where its nest was, and begin flichering along on the grund to draw me away frae the place. Cunnin' brutes them birds, but I was fly for it, and instead o' following it, and believing it couldna flee, I stoppit and begoud to look for the nest in the dyke. But before I got forrit I had kind o' lost the exact place. I searched aboot, wi' the bird watchin' me geyan feared-like a wee bit off, and at last I found a hole half filled up wi' a loose stane. Oot cam' the stane, and in gaed my haund; but instead o' a nest I fund a gold watch and chain; and that's the God's truth, though I should dee this meenit."

"Did you mention the finding to any one?"

"No me; I didna even tell my daughter, for I kent if it was fund oot I might get thirty days for keeping it up. I had an idea that the watch had been stolen and planted there, or I might have gaen to a pawnshop wi' it. It was kind o' damaged wi' lying in the dyke, so at last I made up a story and sellt it to Maister Burge."

"You are good at making up stories, I think?" I reflectively observed.

"I'm thinkin' there's a pair of us, Maister McGovan," he readily returned, with a pawky dab at my ribs.

But for his coolness and evident relief at getting the thing off his mind, I should have set down the whole as another fabrication. But when a man begins to smile and joke, it may be taken for granted that he does not think himself in immediate danger of being hanged. His story, however, might have availed him but little had I not chanced to turn up my notes on the case at its earlier stages, and found there the hitherto meaningless words muttered by Daniel O'Doyle. "Starr Road" muttered in sleep might be but a contraction of Easter Road, or be those actual words imperfectly overheard. Then there were the words about something being "hidden safely there," and the whole tallied so closely that I was at last sure that I was on the right track. These additional gleanings made me revert to my anonymous correspondent in the west. It was scarcely likely that I should be able to trace him; but he spoke in his note of the guilty one being a person or persons outside of himself—known to him. This lessened my interest in him personally, but made me think that if I visited the town I might get hold of O'Doyle himself, which would be quite as good, if not better. I accordingly went to the place, in which there is a public prison, and as a first step called on the police superintendent. An examination of the books at length sent me in the direction of the prison, in which a man answering the description, and having O'Doyle for one of his names, had been confined on a nine months' sentence for robbery. I was now in high spirits, and quite sure that in the prisoner I should recognise the O'Doyle I wanted; but on reaching the place I found that a more imperative and inexorable officer had been there before me in shape of death. Immediately on getting the answer I made the inquiry, "Did he make any statement or confession before he died?" This was not easily answered, and before it could be, with satisfaction, a number of the officials had to be questioned, and then I found that O'Doyle had been attended, as is usual, in his last moments by a Catholic priest.

This gentleman was still in the town, though not stationed in the Prison, and knowing something of the vows of a priest, I despaired at once of extracting anything from him, but became possessed of a desire to have a look at his handwriting. Accordingly I sent him a polite note requesting him to send me word when he would be at liberty to see me for a few minutes' conversation. I fully expected to get a written note in reply, however short, but instead I got a message delivered by the servant girl, to the effect that her master was at home, and would see me now. I grinned and bore it, though it is not pleasant to feel eclipsed in cunning by anyone. I went with the girl, and found the priest, a pale, hard-worked looking man, leaning back in his chair exhausted and silent, and certainly looking as if he at least did not eat the bread of idleness. I felt rather small as I introduced myself and ran over the case that had brought me there, he listening to the whole with closed eyes, and a face as immovable as that of a statue. When I had finished there was an awkward pause. I had not exactly asked anything, but it was implied in my sudden pull up, but for a full minute there was no response.

At last he opened his eyes—and very keen, penetrating eyes they were—and, fixing me sternly with his gaze, he said—

"Did you ever come in contact with a Catholic priest before Mr McGovan?"

"Frequently."

"Did you ever know one to break his vows and reveal the secrets of heaven?"

"Never."

"Do you think one of them would do it if you asked him?"

"I think not."

"Do you think he would do it if you threatened him with prison?"

"Scarcely."

"Or with death—say if you had power to tear him limb from limb, or torture every drop of blood from his body?"

"I don't know—I shouldn't like to try."

"Then what do you come to me for?" he sharply continued, with a slight tinge of red in his pale cheeks. "Am I, think you, more unworthy than any other that has yet lived?"

"No, I should hope not," I stammered; "and I did not come expecting you to reveal what was told you in confession——"

"What then—you wish to know if I wrote that letter maybe?"

"Yes."

"And you'll be satisfied that I speak the truth when I answer?"

"Yes."

"And you'll ask no more?"

"I'll ask no more."

"Then I didn't. Bridget, show the gentleman out."

I was so staggered and nonplussed that I was in the street before I had time to ponder his reply. I was convinced then, as I am now, that the priest spoke the literal truth; how then had the letter been written? Certainly not by O'Doyle himself. Was it possible that a third person could have got at the information?

Back I went to the jail, and by rigid questioning discovered that at the time of O'Doyle's death there was one other person, a delicate man of some education, in the hospital, who complained of pains in the head, and of having grown stone deaf since his incarceration. This man had been set at liberty shortly after, and made no secret of having malingered so successfully as to get all the luxuries of the hospital instead of the hard labour of the other prisoners. There was then an excited and prolonged conversation between this man and the priest I had visited; and as they were of the same faith I have little doubt but the father had bound him down in some way to keep secret what he had chanced to overhear of O'Doyle's confession. This at least was my theory, and a peculiar flash of the priest's eyes when I afterwards hinted at the discovery convinced me that I was not far off the truth.

Chisholm, for his bird-nesting experiment, got thirty days' imprisonment, and Burge, after about a month's detention, was discharged.

THE STREET PORTER'S SON.

The old street porter appeared at the Central Office one winter morning, but refused to reveal his business to any one but me. I had been delayed a little beyond my usual time by other work, but Corny Stephens patiently sat there the whole time. He appeared to know me, too, for the moment I entered the "reception-room" he rose and deferentially touched his forelock. He was an old man, very thin and bloodless, with poverty shining out of every bit of his meagre clothing and decayed boots. He wore at his lapel the polished badge of a licensed street porter, and over his shoulder had slung a hank of frayed rope, apparently as aged and weak as himself. It is not unlikely that I had seen him often before, but my interest is not so strong in honest folks, and, as he belonged to that healthy majority, I did not remember noticing him particularly. He was blue with cold, but the hand touching his forelock trembled violently, not so much with cold as strong excitement.

"It's your help I want, sir," he said, when I had tried to dispel the awe and dread with which he seemed to regard me, "and mebbe I can give you some news that'll be of use to you; only I'm afeared I might get mixed up in it myself. I've been honest for sixty years now, and it would be mighty hard to be mistook for a thafe and a villain now."

These words put me upon my guard, and while he was speaking them I was reading his face closely. Listening to the specious stories of rogues makes one suspicious of everything. He did not suffer under the ordeal, but I still made no sign, merely asking him to go on.

"Do you know a man called Micky Hill?" he abruptly resumed.

I started a little, for Micky had been in my thoughts more than once lately. I knew him, of course—a convict and ticket-of-leave man, who had already endured two long terms, and who knew me just as well as I did him, and never passed me without an impudent grin, as much as to say, "Your mighty smart arn't you—why don't you get hold of me?" Micky had small eyes set deep in his head, and every twinkle of them was full of cunning. I believe those eyes of his irritated me more than the man himself. I hated them from the depths of my soul.

"Yes," I quietly answered, "what of him?"

"Well, it's him I'd like to see with your bracelets on," answered Corny with fearful energy, "to see booked for ten years, as he will be, I've no doubt, if you can prove a good case agin him."

"You've quarrelled with him, then?" I remarked, with some surprise at the association of an honest man with a thief.

"Not me," cried the old porter, with warmth. "Ye don't think I'd speak to the likes of him? But he's brought me bitter sorrow, and it's only fair he should suffer for it. I think I can do that, and do you a good turn at the same time, sur, and him never be a bit the wiser. There was a grocer's broke into down at Greenside last week, was'nt there? and a lot of brandy and things took?"

"Ah! did he do that?" I cried, for it was in connection with that very case that Micky's name had cropped up in my mind, coupled with the fear, I confess, that I should never bring the crime home to him. Micky did a deal in shebeening, and who more likely to find a use for strong spirits which cost him nothing? but experience told me that he would never be the dolt to keep the plunder where any connection between it and himself could be traced.

"Will no harm come on me or mine if I tell ye all I know?" tremblingly inquired Corny.

"Had you anything to do with the affair yourself?" I sharply demanded.

"No, by me immortal sowl, no!" cried the old man, "I'd sooner drop dead with starvation than rob any one of a hap'orth. But my son Pat—he's a labourer, sur, and been out for two months with the frost—he has been too much in Micky's company—mebbe you've seen him—and it's him I'm afeard for. He got fourteen days just for being in Micky's company, yet he won't keep away from the villain. My belief is, Micky has throw'd a charm over him, and Pat's being led off his feet without the power to help himself. Oh, sur, it's an awful thought to me and to his sister, that would give the very heart out of her own breast to keep him straight."

There could be little doubt of his sincerity now, for his whole heart was in his eyes, and he had broken down pitifully as he spoke. I now dimly understood the case, for it was not the first by many dozens which had come in my way.

"Tell me all you know, and I will do what I can for you, though I can promise nothing," I said, thinking that the son might be involved more than the father was aware.

"I'm content with that, sur," he gratefully responded, "for I hear there's thaves that think your word surer than the bank. But it's not much I do know. There's an empty place in the court down there where Micky lives. It used to be a coal-house, but nobody uses it now, and the roof's nigh dropping to pieces. Well, I believe if you go to that place and get the door open, and dig up the dross, you'll find a good deal of what was tuck out of the grocer's. I think Micky did the job, but anyhow he has a key that opens that place, and nobody but him ever gets a finger near the stuff."

"How did you find out all that?" I promptly demanded. "Did your son tell you?"

"Him tell me? Do you think Pat 'ud betray any one, even a black-hearted villain like Micky Hill? No, he's too honourable, though Micky, I'll swear, wouldn't have any such scruples. Must I tell you how I found it out?"

"You'd better, if only to save your own character, and take all suspicion away from yourself."

"Well, then, his sister Annie heard him speak it all in his sleep."

I whistled aloud, and the glance I turned on the trembling old man was one more of pity than pleasure. Before the son could have been so full of the knowledge as to be oppressed by it in his dreams, he must have been very deeply involved—probably one of the actual perpetrators—and in that case how could I possibly save him? At the moment I heartily wished that the old man had never come near me. If only he and Micky were in the job, and I nipped up the elder rogue, I knew for certain that he would at once suspect treachery, denounce Pat, and put proof in our hands as well. And then another difficulty immediately occurred to me—even if we searched the cellar and found there the stolen goods, how would that bring conviction on Micky? He had not the shed rented, but had cunningly taken possession unknown to any one, and probably entered it only by night when no one was likely to see him. Altogether the case seemed a knotty problem, and I had to send away Corny with less encouragement and hope than he had looked for. If the old porter had known what awaited him outside, his trembling and fears would have been increased rather than diminished, for in an entry in the close was snugly ensconced the very man he had been denouncing.

Micky did not allow himself to be seen, but followed the old man down to the Cowgate, and there allowed him to be some distance along before he made up to him and addressed him.

"Fine morning, Corny," he said, with a wicked leer, which struck the old man with a nameless dread.

"Is it, then?" he hotly retorted; "then you'll see to keep away from me."

"Where have you been so early?" asked Micky, smiling and looking more wicked than ever.

"Where you'll———" The Irish blood of the old man was up, and the two words were out before he knew. He checked himself, however, and walked off without a word more.

But the worst was now known to Micky. He now *knew* that he had in some way, incomprehensible to himself, been betrayed. His suspicions could fall on none but his partner, the porter's son, and on him he resolved should fall the full brunt of the punishment. He abused himself roundly for taking such a greenhorn into his confidence, but, on the whole, thought that he had so managed matters as to keep his own skin safe. The porter's son being out of work, was not difficult to find; but Micky was rather surprised to find that his most ingenious hints and questionings did not for a moment disconcert or disturb Pat Stephens. He began to think the labourer more cunning than himself, when in reality the other was a perfect child in comparison. The apparent innocence of Pat only added to Micky's rage and hatred, and, taking the labourer home with him, he told him vaguely of some one having seen him going to his hide, and pressed upon Pat the key of the cellar, with the request that as soon as it was dark he would go to the shed and bring out certain bottles which Micky was in need of for the concoction of the peculiar "fire water" which he doled out as whisky. Quite unsuspicious, Pat took the key and carried it about with him all day; and late that night, when all was quiet in the court, he went to the shed, unlocked the door, and was busy digging up the stuff when we entered and offered to help him. He dropped the spade at once, and then dropped himself right into the grave of coal dross he had made, where he sat helplessly staring at us, speechless with astonishment and terror. We had been watching the place since nightfall from a safe hide close by, and were as much astonished at our capture as the cowering culprit himself.

I had made sure that none but Micky himself would have the run of that cellar, and was intensely chagrined to find in our clutches only a rather stupid-looking fellow, who had not even the daring to attempt resistance or make a dash for liberty.

"What's your name?" I demanded, while the others rapidly unearthed the contents of the hide.

"Patrick Stephens," he nervously answered.

"Good gracious! you don't mean to say that you are the porter's son?" I exclaimed, more vexed than I cared to show.

He nodded, but then perhaps conscious that he had said too much, he took refuge in silence. Behold the stupidity of the man; just when speaking would have benefited him he closed his mouth. I asked him what he was doing there; if he had been sent by any one, and how he accounted for some of the bottles bearing the address of a Greenside grocer; but to all these questions he remained perversely dumb. He had not the slightest suspicion that Micky had betrayed him, still less that he owed his capture to his own tongue and his anxious father. His idea was that he had been suspected by us, watched and followed to the place, and thus captured in the ordinary course of events. Finding him so stubborn, I sent him to the Office in charge of the others, leaving a man to guard the plunder till it could be taken away in a barrow, while I went up to Micky's house and considerably surprised him by telling him to get up and come with me—for the cunning rascal had, for the sake of appearances, got into bed, where he stared at me, the very picture of virtuous innocence.

He showed every one of his yellow teeth in that devil's grin of his when I sharply repeated the command, and then I inwardly guessed that I should have some trouble in getting him convicted. My hope, however, was strong in the porter's son, who, I was convinced, was by far the more innocent of the two, so I snapped the bracelets on Micky with apparent zest, and he was locked up till morning, when I again visited Pat, and found him as obdurate as before. I had still one resource—the old porter, and to him I went as soon as I could get away.

His distress—and that of his daughter, who appeared to keep house for them—was overwhelming, and, not unnaturally, the heaviest of their reproaches fell upon me.

"You tuck him away after promising that you would do your best to save him and ketch the other villain!" cried the old man, with bitter tears. "Saints above us! and I've been the means of sending me own heart's blood to prison. Och! och! the curse of Heaven be on me for that, and may the tongue that betrayed him wither in me head!"

"I may save him yet, if you can only get him to speak—if you can get him to denounce Micky. Could you not prove an *alibi* for the night of the robbery?"

The old man paused in his lamentations to think for a moment, and then honestly confessed that the night of the robbery and that which followed were two on which he was certain his son was not at home. I had therefore no doubt but Pat had actually been engaged in the robbery, which had been executed in a clumsy and haphazard fashion, quite in keeping with the two men in custody. I got the porter to see his son in prison, but the effort was made in vain, for Pat would not open his mouth. Tears, prayers, and entreaties were showered upon him in vain, and the only thing which moved him was his old father lifting his hands to invoke the curse of heaven upon his ungrateful head.

"Don't, father, dear!—don't," he piteously cried, grasping through the bars at the feeble arms of his father as they were about to be upraised; "don't say the black words, for sure I've an oath on me sowl, and I can't break it!"

"Well, well, poor lad!" and the father struggled no more. "May the Almighty give ye strinth to throw id off;" and so they parted, and the misguided victim went unflinchingly to his trial. There was not the smallest tittle of evidence to connect Micky with the crime, and after a short detention he was liberated. Pat was tried shortly after at the High Court, and sentenced to eighteen months' imprisonment.

"Oh, Patrick dear! it's somebody else should be in your shoes this day," came like a "keen" from among the audience as he was led out; and the cry seemed to unman him a little, for it came from his sister.

Some time after, when the circumstances had faded a little in my memory, I was over in the jail seeing a prisoner who worked near Pat. I noticed the porter's son, whose head was now closely cropped, and his appearance considerably changed by the prison dress, and, half recognising him, I said dubiously—

"Well, what are you in for?"

"It's yourself should know that, sur," he said, with a sad smile. "I'm Patrick Stephens. Could I have a word with you, sur?"

"Yes, if you look sharp about it," was my answer, for my time had nearly expired.

I expected that he had thought better of the case which had landed him there, and was ready to denounce Micky, but in that I was mistaken. He had not a word to say on that point; his sole concern was for his father and sister.

"When Micky was in on suspicion he found out that it wasn' me, but my father or my sister, that betrayed the hiding-place," he said to me in a hurried whisper. "He's sorry now that I was took, but he's mad agin them, and has sworn to be even with them. You've no idea what a divil he is when he takes it into his head. Now, sur, if you'd only take the hint and watch him and them, for though they are as honest as the babe unborn, he'll get them into a scrape as sure as he's sworn it."

"Ah, it's easy getting into scrapes," I significantly rejoined, glancing at his oakum heap and his prison garb; "the difficulty is to get out of them."

"Sure, I know what ye mane, sur," he returned, with a slight flush of shame, "but since I've been in here I've got a mighty load off me sowl, and, if I'm spared to get out, please the Lord, I'll never take it on again."

I thought of a certain road being paved with good intentions, but said nothing. There was one chance in a thousand that Pat's might hold good. Even if the thought only comforted him in his seclusion, a blessing was gained.

I questioned him further on the matter he had placed before me, and learned that the information had reached him through a newly-incarcerated prisoner. I could not but admire through the whole revelation the quick intelligence of Micky in piecing together facts which to anyone else would have indicated nothing. From the mere excited exclamation of old Corny, and that of the sister in the Court-room, he had gathered that it had been intended to trap him and save the porter's son. He knew that as well as if I had revealed to him the whole particulars of my interview with Corny. I began to envy Micky his quickness. But though he was just the man to thirst for revenge, I did not think that he would interfere with the old street porter, and it is probable I said so to Pat at the time, and his warning would speedily have been forgotten but for the curious events which followed.

A month or two after my interview with Pat his father was accosted while on his stance by a well-dressed man having the appearance of a commercial traveller, and asked to carry a rather heavy portmanteau to a certain address. The job was executed with alacrity, and liberally paid for. A few days later the same man hired Corny, after dark, to carry a box to another part of the town, paid him with the same liberality, and told him he might need him again soon.

The occasion came only two days later. The man, who was well dressed, and always carried an ivory handled umbrella in his hand and a cigar in his mouth, stopped the old porter on the street, and in an off-hand way asked him if he could carry some crystal and china from a house at the south side to an address at the opposite end of the city. Of course the porter was eager and willing.

"The only awkward thing is that I won't be there till nearly nine o'clock," said the man; "would that be too late for you?"

"Sorra a bit, sur," was the ready response. "Any hour will suit me, more by token there's no wan likely to be needing me so late."

Punctually at the hour named, Corny appeared at the place—a common stair in Clerk Street. As he was ascending the stair in search of the name furnished by his employer, that gentleman appeared descending the stair, and carrying in his arms a good-sized square parcel.

"I was beginning to think you had forgotten me," he pleasantly observed to the old porter, "and was afraid I should have to send the things over in a cab, at the risk of getting half of them broken."

Corny apologised for the trouble he had given, adjusted the bundle to his own shoulders, and prepared to go.

"You will get half-a-crown, which I left for you when you deliver them," said the man graciously, "and there is little danger of you breaking anything, as they are all carefully packed in soft goods."

Corny was pleased with the explanation, for the weight of the bundle did not suggest china or crystal to him, and in taking and adjusting it to his ropes, he had heard not a single clink or rattle from within. He went his way with the load, while his employer reascended the stair and was gone. Corny was not a robust man by any means, so it was past ten o'clock before he reached his destination. Then he found that there had been some mistake in the address, for he could not find any one who expected such a consignment, or answered to the name he sought. After trailing about for half an hour, Corny was reluctantly compelled to turn southward once more, with the intention of returning the load to its owner. But there a fresh difficulty awaited him. He found the stair easily, but in the whole land could discover no one answering to the name given him by his employer. Corny got a good deal of abuse, indeed, for rousing some of the tenants out of bed, and as he was now thoroughly knocked up with his weary trailing, he resolved to let the matter rest till morning, and turned his face homeward.

Now, at that moment, by a curious train of circumstances, I was sitting in Corny's house patiently waiting for him. That very afternoon I had been passing down one of the closes, when my eye caught a bright-coloured and new shoulder shawl decorating a woman moving in the same direction.

"Hullo, Bess," I said, stopping short, "let me have a look at your shawl."

She stopped with wonderful willingness, saying—

"Ah, you think it's one of the lot taken from that shawl shop on the Bridge, but you're wrong. I bought it this morning in another place, and there's the receipt," and she produced one of those little flimsies which drapers give with their goods, showing that three shillings had been paid for the shawl that very day. "Would you like to know who did that job?" she added with suspicious loquacity.

"Yes—had you a hand in it?"

I was only chaffing her. I never expected to get a single grain of truth out of her, for she was bad to the very heart's core.

"Me! No; but I heard about it, that's all."

"You're an awful liar, Bess; but go on," I calmly answered.

"Well, I believe an old porter called Corny Stephens had the big hand in it," she boldly continued.

"I don't believe it," was my answer.

"Well, please yourself; I only heard it; but if you went to his house late to-night you might find something, that's all," and away she went, singing unmusically.

I knew very little of the old porter, but, had I put my impressions of him against my knowledge of Bess, her statements would at once have kicked the beam. Still I could not deny that the taint of Pat's conviction and sentence extended in a certain sense to his relatives, and my duty was to act on any hint, however meagre, so that I decided to visit Corny the same night, at an hour when he was likely to be at home and in bed. I got there at ten o'clock, and was frankly received by his daughter, who told me he had a late job, and would not be in for an hour or so. She was preparing his supper, so I decided to accept her offer and sit down by the fire till he came.

In the ordinary course of events Corny should have appeared, bearing his undelivered load, about eleven o'clock, and this had probably been calculated upon, but I waited till midnight, and much to the concern of Annie his daughter, no Corny appeared. How that happened was simple enough, though not in the programme.

Corny was slowly trailing through Argyle Square with his load, on his way home, when he chanced to be met by McSweeny. My chum was in a good humour, for he had been spending a night jovially at a friend's, where a widow had made a dead set at him; and McSweeny's joy arose from the fact that at the last moment he had ingeniously saddled the widow on to an unsuspicious friend, while my chum took his way home in happy freedom alone. But though elated and exultant, at peace with all the world, and trying his best to merrily whistle "The Poor Married Man," McSweeny's duty was not so far from his mind as to allow him to pass Corny and the big bundle at such an hour.

"Stop, you!" he imperatively commanded. "What's that you're carrying on your back? and where are you going with it?"

"It's some chany and crystal I got to carry over to the New Town, and I couldn't find the place, so I'm taking it home," said Corny.

McSweeny suspiciously poked his fingers into the bundle, but could feel nothing like china or crystal.

"It's uncommon soft," he said, with a grunt. "Who gave it to you to carry?"

"The gintleman."

"The gintleman, ye blockhead; hasn't he got a name?" said McSweeny wrathfully.

"He has; it's written on that paper; but I couldn't find him when I took the load back."

"I daresay not," said McSweeny, dryly. "Well, you'll need to come up to the Office wid me, till we see what's in the bundle."

"I'm an honest man," said Corny indignantly. "Do you take me for a thafe?"

"Well, you don't look like one of my bairns," said McSweeny, in imitation of me; "but you'll have to trot all the same. Mebbe you don't know that I'm McSweeny, the detective, that all the books has been writ about?"

"I know the other one," said Corny simply. "McGovan'll spake a good word for me."

"You'll not need that if your bundle's all right," was the lofty reply, and to the Office they went.

The bundle unfortunately was not all right. It contained a deal of rubbish of no use to any one, but it also contained a number of bright-coloured shawls of a certain pattern, which were already down in our list as having been taken from a shop on the Bridge.

Corny seemed thunderstruck at the grave looks of every one about him, and wildly went over the details I have put down, but without impressing his hearers much. The story seemed such a poor one and so common. There is not a "smasher" taken with the counterfeits in his possession but volubly declares that he got the parcel from some one on the street, either to hold or to take to some address. Corny seemed to realise his position only when he was handed over to the man to be taken down to the cells. Then he dropped on his knees before the lieutenant, and, clasping his hands, besought them to spare him the disgrace.

"I'm not a thafe, sur, and though I'm sixty years of age I never was in a cell in my life. Send to the praist and ax him what he knows of poor owld Corny Stephens."

The tears of the quivering old man, and his desperate energy might have had some effect, but just then one of the officers present, touching his cap to the lieutenant, said briefly—

"His son got eighteen months lately for shopbreaking."

That settled the matter. It was the old doom reversed—the sins of the children coming back on the father.

Before Corny was locked up he besought them to send word to his daughter, so that his absence might be accounted for, and it was from the messenger thus sent that I learned these facts, and that further waiting was useless. I was considerably staggered by the news, and had now so much suspicion of Corny that I took the precaution of searching his house thoroughly before I left. That was the first impression. Next morning, after I had seen Corny, I began to think differently, though still puzzled. It was well on in the forenoon, and after Corny had been remitted to a higher Court, that I remembered about the warning of his son Pat. Curiously enough, the thing which brought it to my mind was the presence of Micky Hill among the audience of the Police Court, coupled with the fact that he left as soon as Corny had been removed.

"A plant! a plant, I believe!" was my mental exclamation, but I was too busy for some hours to give the matter further attention. Then I began my work. I found that Bess had followed me from the Office down the close in which I had addressed her about the shawl, and it now recurred to me that she and Micky were old acquaintances, and very likely to work into each other's hands. Then she had volunteered the information about Corny, without my asking for it, and I knew her so well that I had not for a moment believed it until Corny was taken with the goods in his possession. I did not know very well how to act, but there was no time for delay, and I began by pouncing upon Bess. She was so frightened that she let out a word or two more than she intended, and in a short time I was at Micky's house inquiring for him.

Micky was drunk—speechlessly drunk—to which state he had reduced himself, I think, in joy over the success of his scheme; but the capture of the shebeener was a trifle to the one which accompanied it.

In the same room with Micky, and not much more sober, was a swell-mobsman, who had been lodging there for some time. He had come down for the purpose of attending the races, and was a smart man altogether. He did not get to the races that year, for the old street porter easily identified him out of a dozen men as the man who employed him to carry the bundle to the New Town. His ivory-headed umbrella and his cigar case were also identified as promptly—a clear proof that a rogue should not indulge in easily recognisable finery.

Before the day of the trial we had also discovered a person living in the stair in Clerk Street who had seen the smart man loitering in the stair with the bundle and handing it over to Corny, and that, with a stolen shawl found on the back of Micky's wife, served to successfully rivet the fetters on both.

The actual perpetrator of the robbery had really been the swell-mobsman, Micky having had no hand in it but the resetting of some of the things; but some of the evidence appeared to implicate him, and he was found guilty, and sentenced to the same term as his companion in the dock—seven years' penal. Corny, of course, had been released as soon as we got Bess to make a clean breast of it, and he appeared as a witness at the trial, and got some handsome commendations from the presiding judge. His case attracted some attention, and a gentleman willing to help the old porter came to me for advice in the matter, to make sure that the case was a deserving one. The result was that Corny's lot was made more easy; and when his son was released, they were all helped out of the country by the same generous hand, Pat proving one of the exceptions to the rule, "Once a thief, always a thief."

A BIT OF TOBACCO PIPE.

Criminals vary in character and degree of guilt as much as the leaves of the forest do in form and colour, but there is always a large number whom no one of experience ever expects to reform. They are the descendants of generations of thieves; they have known nothing else from babyhood, and will know nothing else till they are shovelled into the earth. It would be far cheaper to the country to keep them in perpetual imprisonment, but so many objections can be raised to such a scheme that I question if it will ever become law.

To this class belonged Peter Boggin, otherwise known as "Shorty." He had received this name not so much on account of his height, which was medium, as on account of his temper, which was of the shortest. I question, indeed, if Shorty would ever have been in prison at all but for his temper.

Shorty's boon companion and working pal was a quiet, lumpish-looking fellow named Phineas O'Connor. Phineas, when his tongue was loosened by drink, was wont to assert that he was descended from the Irish Kings, and therefore had been derisively dubbed "The Fin." He was a still man, rather sullen, and not lacking in deadly ingenuity, as will appear before I have done.

Among the many schemes proposed or tried by Shorty and The Fin was one for entering a big house in the New Town, occupied by a fashionable family much given to receiving company. The Fin had noted this circumstance, and had also ascertained beyond a doubt that the family were really, and not apparently, wealthy. By following the line of houses with his eye to one of the common streets of Stockbridge, close by, The Fin then decided that to enter the upper part of the major's house would not be difficult. The place was marked and watched for some time before the opportunity occurred, as no intimation of his intention regarding parties was ever sent by the major to either Shorty or The Fin.

One evening, when the season was at its height, and the nights conveniently long and dark, the two, when taking their customary stroll for inspection, found the house lighted from top to bottom, and the longed-for party in full swing. The usual dinner hour they knew was six o'clock, and, as that hour was approaching, Shorty set out for a tour of inspection in the next street, while The Fin patiently waited for the dinner gong to sound.

The first warning had been given by the gong when Shorty returned and reported the road clear, and the two took their way to the next street, where they ascended a common stair, and by standing on the railing at the top managed to reach the hatch leading to the roof, by Shorty climbing up on The Fin's shoulders and then pulling his helper up as soon as he had forced the hatch and reached the low den between that and the slates. There was another hatch yet to force—that which led out on to the slates—and to reach that the two had to crawl along in a stooping position, carefully feeling with their feet for the cross beams lest they should suddenly plunge through the lath and plaster into the room below. In crawling along thus they felt and passed the water cistern which supplied the whole tenement beneath them, which stood as close in under the slope of the roof as its height would admit of. Getting open the upper hatch proved no difficult task, and then they tossed up who should get out and make his way along the housetops to the major's house.

The lot fell to Shorty, and he got out and patiently worked his way along the slates and over ranges of chimney cans to the more aristocratic street hard by. When he reached the attic windows of the major's house he looked at his watch and decided that the whole household and all the guests must then be busy downstairs, the dinner in full swing, and the servants too excited and flurried to think of coming near the bedrooms or upper flats. One of the attics, presumably occupied by the servants, had its window open, and Shorty had merely to raise the sash a little higher to pass within and have the free range of the whole of the house but the area and first flat.

An experienced man, Shorty did not hurry with the task. He went over the trunks of the servants first, but found nothing worth lifting but a small gold brooch and a silver ring. The ring was not worth two shillings, and Shorty was at one moment inclined to toss it back into the box, but he changed his mind and took it with him. He should have left it. Leaving the servants' room, with many an inward imprecation on them for keeping bank books instead of money in their boxes, Shorty softly ranged through all the other rooms and bedrooms within his reach, and soon had quite a respectable pile of plunder gathered into his capacious coloured cotton handkerchief. He took nothing but articles of jewellery and the contents of two ladies' purses, which he found in one of the bedrooms; and among the articles there chanced to be a very heavy gold chain—either a bailie's or a provost's chain of office. Although the haul was a fair one, Shorty was dissatisfied, for he had expected to get something out of the plate chest in the tablemaid's room. He found the room and the chest in it conveniently open, but inconveniently empty. All the plate was on the dinner table, or downstairs ready to be placed there, and Shorty, forgetting that he owed his ease and success to the dinner and guests, was ungrateful enough to curse both. Even thieves are never content.

In leaving by the attic window Shorty was careful to close the window after him, a circumstance which afterwards led to some confusion on our part, as the servants, finding it thus closed, declared most positively—probably to screen themselves from blame—that the window had not only been closed, but firmly fastened on the inside. This statement led us to think that, during the confusion of the party, the thief might have entered by the front door and made his escape in the same manner. There was some hunting and examination in the direction of the roof, and the hatch in the adjoining street was found to have been forced, but at the time that led to nothing. Had we even guessed at the curious incident which had followed Shorty's exit on to the roof our action would have been very different. It is these unlooked-for events which continually trip up the most astute. We suffered by the slip, but we did not suffer alone.

When Shorty got out on the slates, carrying his handkerchief of valuables, he found something more deserving of cursing than the dinner—namely, a clear sky and a tolerably bright moon. Speaking rapidly and energetically under his breath, he crawled along, keeping on the safest side of the roof till he could do so no longer, having to go forward to make his way over a range of chimney cans. As chance would have it, at the same time he glanced anxiously down on the steep street running down towards that spot, and saw the policeman of the beat looking, as he fancied, in his direction. Not only did the officer look, but he made some motion with his hand, and crossed the road as if to come nearer.

"Spotted!" cried Shorty, with an oath; and the rest of the journey across the roofs to the hatch where The Fin awaited him was performed in "the best time on record." As a matter of fact the policeman had neither seen Shorty nor made a motion in his direction, but Shorty hurriedly explained the position to his chum, and after a brief council of war they rid themselves of the plunder, dropped through the inner hatch, and escaped downstairs, by the backdoor, across some greens. They took separate routes, certain that they were being hotly pursued, and got into hiding at once.

A few hours later the robbery was discovered and reported at the Office. As in few cases of the kind, we were able to take down a pretty full and accurate list of the articles stolen, including, of course, the silver ring of the servant and the heavy gold chain already noticed.

With this list, and the knowledge that so many of the articles were easily identifiable, I had little doubt but we should soon lay hands on either the thief or part of the plunder. I was mistaken. None of my "bairns" showed an overflow of money; not the slightest sign of "a great success" appeared anywhere; and none of those had up on suspicion had heard of the deed. Some of them strongly asserted that the whole thing was a sham, and really done by an amateur—one of the servants or some of her followers. One of the boldest to assert this was Shorty himself, whom I had invited to accompany me to the Office, and who had followed me with an alacrity which caused my hopes to sink at once to zero. As for The Fin, he was not a man of words, and only scowled, and told us to hurry with our investigations, as he did not care for the Lock-up, and wanted back to his den. We did not hurry particularly, knowing that both were safer and more harmless under lock and key than at liberty, but events hurried for us in a manner anticipated neither by them nor us. While the two worthies were still in our keeping, I chanced one day to call upon an honest jeweller who dealt in the precious metals, and was shown by him a piece of a heavy gold chain which he had that day bought from a lad whose name and address was in his book. The piece was about eighteen inches long, and at one end showed a clean cut, as if it had been either clipped through with strong shears or cut with a chisel, half of the severed link being still attached to the chain. It was fine 22 carat gold, and so uncommon-looking that the jeweller had questioned the seller closely as to how it came into his possession.

"He said that it had belonged to his mother, and they had had it for years locked away, but, seeing that it was of no use, they thought of having it made into a brooch," continued the jeweller. "He was just a working lad,—not at all like a thief,—so I believed him, and paid him for it according to weight and quality."

"Why did he not have it made into a brooch?" I sceptically inquired.

"Because there was not enough of it to make one such as he desired, and none of those I offered him in exchange pleased him."

"I daresay not," I dryly returned, and then I decided to take the piece of chain over to the major's, and at the same time hunt up the lad who had sold the old gold. The result of my visit to the major's was that the piece of chain was strongly believed by that gentleman to be part of that taken from his house, and the hunt for the lad who had sold it proved only that the young rascal had given a false name and address.

So much was gained, however, for we were a step nearer the criminal, as we imagined. We had a full description of his age and appearance, and there was a strong probability that, being a novice, he would not stop short at his first attempt to dispose of the plunder. A very stringent order was issued to all the jewellers likely to be visited, but as it turned out, the order was not needed, for, not many days later, the lad again appeared with another piece of gold chain to sell.

"We've found the other piece at the bottom of a drawer," he said, "and we thought you might give more for it, as it might be joined on to the first piece and sold as a chain, instead of being melted down as old gold."

Scarcely able to believe his eyes, the jeweller asked him to sit down while he went into the back shop to assay the gold. He did not set about the task with great alacrity, but contented himself with sending an apprentice out by a side door with a message to the Central Office, while he stood and watched the lad through the glass door. The message was handed to me, and I went to the shop at my smartest.

As I entered I saw the lad seated in the front shop in the overalls of a working joiner. At the same moment the jeweller came from the back shop with the piece of chain in his hand.

"A piece of old gold which this lad wants me to buy," he observed, and then, while the lad started and glanced at me, I, with apparent carelessness, and without looking in his direction, took from my pocket my little staff of authority, as if to polish up with my sleeve the silver crown. The lad's eyes became fixed on that in a kind of fascination, and when I took the bit of chain and glanced full in his face, I was not astonished to find him deadly pale, and almost tottering on his legs.

"Where did you get it?" I demanded, and then, after a feeble grip at the counter, he sat down, looking ghastly indeed.

"At home; it's my mother's," he stammered; then he seemed to think better of it, for he hastily added, "No—I found it."

"Imphim; where the Hielantman found the tongs—at the fireside, eh?" I returned, after cautioning him. "Did you find any other things in the same place?"

"No." It was a lie. I saw that, but then it was meant more as a dogged refusal than a denial. A reaction had come to his terror; he had pondered the position for a moment, and decided to take shelter in silence.

"Where do you live?"

"I'd rather not say," was the tardy answer.

"Very well; work at anything?"

"Yes; I'm a joiner." He appeared to regret the admission, for he bit his lip the moment he had said it.

"Apprentice or journeyman?"

"Apprentice. I'll be out with my time next year."

"Maybe you will," I significantly answered; "meantime you'd better come with me and see what the Fiscal has to say to it."

He objected most strongly to have his wrist fastened to mine, but the jeweller happened just then to address me by name, and my prisoner collapsed and submitted to the degradation. We had no great distance to go, but the road seemed long enough to him, for, though anything but an honest-looking fellow, I guessed rightly that it was his first experience of the handcuffs. At the Office he took refuge in silence, or tried to screen himself with absolute falsehood. He gave a false name; would give no address; denied that he had a mother living; would not say for whom he worked; and altogether emitted as stupid a declaration as any one could well have done. I believe he meant well—he meant to screen himself from further trouble; to save his friends from disgrace along with him; and to keep the knowledge of the scrape into which he had fallen from his employer and acquaintances generally; but then every liar has exactly the same excuse.

It was simply a little more work for me, and as the task was gradually accomplished, the facts revealed seemed to point to his guilt with no uncertain finger.

The discovery of his identity was made simply enough by his mother coming to the Office next morning to report her son missing. He had been absent all night, and had not returned to his work on the previous afternoon, and she was greatly distressed and concerned for his safety. It was the mention of the trade he followed, and the name and address of his employer, which first gave me the idea that we had the missing son; and when she was shown our prisoner he did not appear at all grateful for the boon, but swore at her in a manner in which no mother should be addressed, and which would have put many a professional criminal to the blush.

The mother appeared stunned and stupefied by the discovery that she had helped to rivet fetters on him, and that he was likely to be tried for housebreaking with an alternative charge of theft. How the charge came to assume this form is the most striking and curious feature of the case. As soon as I got the two addresses I went first to the home of the prisoner, Alfred Scott, and searched in vain for the rest of the plunder; then I went to his employer's workshop, and unearthed the treasure-trove from a most ingenious hiding-place under a pile of wood which took us ten minutes to remove. Everything was there but the gold chain and the servant's silver ring, and the whole were still wrapped up in Shorty's spotted cotton handkerchief, which unfortunately did not bear either name or address. But this discovery was not the most important made at that place. From Scott's master we learned that our prisoner, along with a journeyman, had been employed making some alterations or repairs in the major's house about six months before the robbery. The natural inference then was that he upon that occasion had provided himself with casts of some of the keys, and so prepared to commit the robbery—hence the framing of the charge on the serious lines I have indicated.

As soon as these facts were made plain, and when the major had identified Scott as one of the joiners who had worked in his house, I went to Shorty's cell and said that we had got the thief, and that in all probability he and The Fin would be soon at liberty.

Shorty received the news not with the satisfaction I had expected, but with a stony stare which seemed to me absolutely idiotic. He made no remark of any kind, and showed neither gratitude nor resentment. It turned out, however, that he and The Fin did not get off so easily, but were convicted and sent for thirty days to prison for "loitering with intent."

Meanwhile Scott persisted in his fatal and blundering silence, and his case came on for trial. He pleaded "not guilty," and the case went to proof, when the evidence, which, link by link, appeared to demonstrate his guilt beyond the shadow of a doubt, took him completely by surprise. There was the selling of the chain; his contradictions and prevarications; the finding of the plunder, and the fact that he had worked on the premises—all damning.

The summing up of the evidence had been completed, and the jury were about to find him guilty without leaving the box, when Scott excitedly asked to be allowed to make a statement in his defence.

"I am innocent of either theft or housebreaking—such crimes never entered my head," he tremulously declared. "If I've done wrong at all it was only in not giving up the articles when I found them. I was sent to a land in H—— Street to repair the fastenings on the hatches leading to the roof, which had been broken by the sweeps or some one. The landlord had been ordered by the police to have them repaired, and I was sent to do it. There were two hatches—one at the head of the stair, and one in the roof; and in the loft between was a cistern. It is a big one, and stands at the side of the loft. I had to get a candle to see my way across the beams, and when I was coming back, after putting on a new hasp, I saw something like the corner of a cotton handkerchief in the space behind the cistern. It just caught my eyes as I was passing, and I went round and pulled it out, and found in it all the things I am accused of stealing. I had no idea they were stolen, or how long they might have been hidden there, and I thought I might keep them."

This statement produced no impression either upon the Bench or the jury, or, if it did, the impression was damaging to the accused. In the first place, there was an air of romance about his story—it looked like another ingenious lie—and did not account for the plunder being left there, or give any clue to the real thieves. Then, even supposing the strange statement to be true, it still left Scott self-convicted of a serious crime—appropriating to his own use what he perfectly well knew did not belong to him. Without hesitation the jury found him guilty, and he was sentenced to six months' imprisonment, it being his first offence.

And he was innocent! what a shame! some one exclaims. Well, I don't know. He was not innocent in intention. He was actually a thief, though not the actual first thief, and he suffered a just punishment.

And now to return to Shorty and The Fin. It does not appear that these amiable gentlemen met Scott in prison, or, if they did, that they exchanged confidences on the case which interested them so deeply, and in their seclusion the newspapers were not regularly placed upon their breakfast table, even had they been blessed with the ability to read them. It was agreed that Shorty should go over to the hide and get the plunder, while The Fin went to a safe reset to arrange about its disposal. This programme worked perfectly in all but one trifling item—the finding of the plunder. Shorty did himself up with soot to resemble a chimney-sweep, and with a ladder and the proper key of the hatch got up to his hide behind the cistern, only to groan and curse over the fact that the cotton handkerchief and its contents were gone. The truth flashed on him at once—some one had found the plunder. Shorty was as much enraged as if he had been robbed. While he stood there cursing, something bright caught his eye between the beams behind the cistern, and, stooping down, he picked up the servant's silver ring—the sole remnant of the valuable plunder, which had in some way fallen out of the cotton handkerchief. Shorty was so furious that he was near pitching it as far as he could throw, but again that fateful second thought came to restrain him, and he put it into his pocket and returned to The Fin, to whom he related the facts, with the exception of the finding of the ring. The Fin, as I have noticed, was a silent man. He heard the whole with open eyes and shut mouth, and Shorty was himself too much enraged to notice that The Fin was displeased and suspicious. Some men would have stormed, and taunted, and uttered their suspicions, and even fought over it, but that was not The Fin's style. He uttered no reflection, but when Shorty left him, The Fin took the precaution of following him.

Being newly out of prison, Shorty's funds were low, and he went to the reset who had just been visited by The Fin, and managed to extract two shillings out of him in exchange for the servant's silver ring. Every article of the plunder was by that time known to The Fin, having been frequently described by Shorty, and more particularly this ring, which Shorty had been so near leaving behind.

Scarcely had Shorty got into a public-house and exchanged one of the shillings for some brandy, when The Fin was up at the reset's house demanding to know what Shorty had sold, and how many pounds sterling he had got for it. The reset, rather staggered, at last declared that Shorty had sold only the silver ring, and showed the trinket in confirmation.

The Fin did not believe a word of it, but he was a still man, and said nothing. Before three hours were gone he was with me, and had given me such information regarding another feat of Shorty's that at last I drew a long breath of satisfaction, for I was sure of a conviction and a good long sentence.

As soon as I had taken Shorty—not without a fight—The Fin regretted his hastiness. He saw that if Shorty got a long sentence, he, The Fin, would perhaps never get near him for vengeance, whereas, had he allowed him to remain at liberty, a quick shove down some stair or toss out at some window when Shorty was drunk would have settled the whole business. The Fin's regret did not last long, for before many hours he was in the cells too, Shorty having in turn revealed some awkward facts which seemed likely to put The Fin as long out of harm's way as himself. These expectations were fully verified shortly after, when they both received sentence of seven years' penal, and were duly removed to the penitentiary.

And now I come to the bit of tobacco pipe, which will prove how a mean and insignificant trifle often comes into the world to accomplish a great work, and confer a blessing on all mankind. Every one who knows anything of prison life can understand how a bit of an old tobacco pipe is valued by convicts shut off from tobacco for years. The smallest crumb of it, having the faintest taste of nicotine, is treasured and passed from prisoner to prisoner, to be sucked and finally broken up and chewed to its inmost recesses. It is worth twenty times its weight in gold to them. When The Fin had spent a year in prison in almost absolute silence, he got into hospital for some trifling complaint, and so ingratiated himself with the doctor that he was once or twice allowed into the laboratory. There by some means he had managed to secrete a minute quantity of a deadly poison, which he inserted into the hole in a piece of old tobacco pipe shank. This bit of tobacco pipe he concealed till he was again among the working convicts. He and Shorty were tacit foes, but this difficulty The Fin got over in a manner worthy of the cause. Once, when the warder was approaching, and a search possible, he managed, in sight of Shorty, to conceal the bit of tobacco pipe in a place easily accessible to his old pal, and then, when the danger was past, forgot to go back for it until Shorty had had a chance of appropriating the treasure. Not many minutes later Shorty took a fit and dropped dead among the convicts.

Every one was horrified and astonished, till one of the warders noticed a smell of tobacco about the mouth of the dead convict, and fished out of his clenched teeth the bit of tobacco pipe. It was then supposed that part of the pipe shank had been bitten off by Shorty and drawn back into the windpipe so as to cause his death; and he duly occupied his six feet of prison soil.

And was The Fin convicted and hanged? Not a bit of it. He lived out his sentence and was released, and went about long enough to boast of his deed, though I am bound to confess that few believed him, and the general opinion was that Shorty died of the bit of tobacco pipe without the poison. However, The Fin claimed all the credit, and insisted that he was not to blame for the result, seeing that he did not administer the poison, and that Shorty, in appropriating what he knew was not his own, committed a grave offence against convict society, and could not complain if he suffered for the crime.

The Fin should have been a lawyer, and with education might have risen to be one, had he not been soon after choked by an overdose of shebeen whisky.

THE BROKEN CAIRNGORM.

I had to take Jess Murray for her share in a very bold robbery, in which a commercial traveller, peaceably walking home to his hotel, had been waylaid and stripped of pocket-book, purse, and watch, the haul altogether amounting to upwards of £100 in value, the greater part of which was not his own. The gentleman could give no description of the men, but remembered that they had been assisted at a critical moment by a woman, who, so far as he could judge, was tall and handsome, and not very old. It was the style of the robbery as much as that brief and imperfect description which directed my attention to Jess Murray. She was a bold wench, strong as a lion, and so thoroughly bad that I took the trouble of hating her—an exceptional case indeed, as in general one gets to look upon her kind with as much indifference as a drover does upon a herd of horned knowte, under his care one day and gone the next.

I believed Jess to be one of the few who have not one redeeming quality or trait, and was eager for the chance which should put her out of harm's way for a good long term of years.

I had really no evidence, but an instinctive feeling, connecting Jess with the robbery; but when on my way to her place I chanced to pass one of her acquaintances on the street. I let him pass, and then a thought struck me, and I turned back and stopped him. A scared look at once came into his face, so I asked him to come with me—back to the Office. He came reluctantly, and the cause I speedily understood when he tried to throw away behind his back a £20 bank note taken from the pocket-book of the commercial traveller. The number and description of this note was already in my possession, and I picked up the paper money with the most lively satisfaction, when the fellow immediately began to protest that he had only been sent to change the note, and was willing to tell all about the robbery if things were made right for himself.

The result of this chance capture was that we had abundant evidence against Jess and another, and I went for her with the greatest of pleasure. She was in the "kitchen" of the place among a crowd of her kind when I entered, and it needed only a motion of my finger and a nod of my head to chase the merriment from her face, and bring her slowly across the floor to my side. It is not usual for me to be communicative, but on the present occasion I was elated, and said in reply to her sullen inquiry—

"It's that affair of the commercial traveller. It's all blown, and you are in for five years at least. Jim White is in the office already, and the £20 bank note with him."

Jess seemed struck in a heap with the news. She flashed deadly pale and sank feebly into a chair, with her bold, bright eyes becoming shiny with tears.

"Where's Dickie?" she faintly articulated to some of the silent onlookers, and, fearing treachery, I snatched out a double brass whistle which can be heard a whole street off, and swiftly raised it to my lips.

"Stop! you needn't," Jess quickly interposed, understanding the motion. "Dickie's only my laddie. Oh, what will become of him when I'm away?"

Dickie was said to be playing down on the street, so I told her we might see him as we left. Jess began to cry bitterly—Jess! whom I believed to have not one genuine tear in her! and thus we descended the stairs together. In the street a ragged and unkempt boy of seven or eight was brought to her side, and she clutched him to her breast, kissing his smudged face with a passionate fervour which gave me quite a fresh insight into her character. The boy resembled her in features, and would have passed for good-looking had he only been washed and dressed up a little.

"What's to 'come o' my bairn?—oh, what's to 'come o' my bairn?" wailed Jess, and the boy began to howl in concert, and I saw that it would be useless to try to separate them just then.

"Oh, he'll be looked after as he has often been before," I carelessly answered. "He'll go to the Poorhouse. He'll be safer there than under your care—and cleaner."

The remark did not appear to console Jess in the least. Dickie was her only child, and the whole strength of her nature seemed concentrated in her love of that boy. I was astonished, and speculated on the matter all the way to the office, quietly wondering what "line of business" that same gutter child was destined to torment me and others by adopting, when he should be a few years older.

I had made a pretty shrewd guess at Jess's sentence, for the list of previous convictions was so strong against her that she was awarded exactly the number of years I had named. I was convinced by that time that she did not grieve over the punishment at all, but over her separation from her child, and I remember thinking—"We are poor judges of one another. What a strong hold could be taken of that woman through that child, if one only knew how to use the power."

Dickie was allowed to see his mother once before she was sent to the Penitentiary, and then he went back to the Poorhouse. He was a good deal cleaner by that time, and had on different clothing, but there was one plaything, or fetish, with which he had resolutely refused to part, and that still hung from his neck. It was a broken cairngorm stone, with a hole drilled at one end, through which a bit of twine had been drawn, that he might suspend the trinket from his neck. I had noticed the stone when I took him to the office with his mother, but merely glanced at it, thinking that it was but an imitation moulded in yellow glass. I was mistaken, for it was part of a real stone, and had probably been set in some stolen brooch which had been broken up for the metal.

It was of no great value, but it pleased Dickie, and kept him from wearying during his long confinement in the Poorhouse, which to him was as irksome as being shut up in a prison. He was a lively, spirited boy, and had never been checked or curbed, so it may be imagined he got into as many scrapes as the average boy of his age.

However, in spite of his mischief and wild pranks, Dickie had a soft spot in his heart, and could be tamed by a gentle word or appeal when lashing had been tried in vain. When he had been about eighteen months in the Poorhouse, a poor knife-grinder was admitted for a day or two, who told Dickie such grand romances of his free life on the road that the boy took an insatiable longing for freedom. Squinting Jerry was the man's name, but though he had an evil look, he was really an honest fellow.

Jerry had been driven to the Poorhouse for a night's shelter, and while there had been laid up for a day or two with a bad leg which troubled him at times, but as soon as he was able to move he hastened to quit the oppressive confinement. Before he had done so, Dickie, by a series of pathetic appeals, had extracted from him a consent to receiving him as an apprentice.

Jerry was really not reluctant to having an assistant, whom he needed sorely at times, but he was afraid that the arrangement might get him into trouble with the parochial authorities, should he be followed and Dickie taken back. Then there were Dickie's antecedents to be considered—he was the son of a convict, and might have the "bad blood" in him, as Jerry expressed it. The old knife-grinder therefore agreed to the proposal with reluctance, as we often do with what turns out a great blessing. Dickie had no difficulty in fulfilling his part of the agreement, for he had already run away twice, and each time gone back of his own accord.

He therefore got out of the Poorhouse easily, and joined Jerry a mile or two out of the city. He took with him his only treasure, the broken cairngorm, which some one had declared to him was a diamond, and worth a great deal of money. This opinion was not shared by Jerry, who failed to find a purchaser for the stone, and finally relegated it to a little box in the grinding machine, which they trundled before them wherever they went. Perhaps the parochial authorities were glad to get rid of Dickie, for he was not followed or taken back. The new life suited him—it was free and untrammelled; it had constant variety, and there was a certain spice of romance about it, which made sleeping in the open air, or getting drenched with rain, or lost and benighted, as they often were, mere trifles, to be forgotten with the first blaze of sunshine. Compared with his life in the Poorhouse Dickie found it heavenly, and very soon a new and altogether unexpected result began to arise from his changed condition.

When Dickie had taken to the road it was sheer impatience of restraint that sent him thither, and he had many ideas of right and wrong which are tolerated only among my "bairns." Now Jerry was an ignorant man, who did not know one letter from another, but there was one lesson he had learned—that a life of crime is the worst paying trade in the world. Halting by roadside hamlets, resting under shady hedges, or wandering along green lanes, Jerry laid down his ideas to Dickie in a homely fashion, which would have thrown a teacher of grammar into hysterics, but which nevertheless carried conviction to the heart of the boy. Not that Dickie had ever meant to wrong Jerry, but he had only taken to this life as a make-shift till his mother should be released from prison.

When questioned as to his intentions for the future, and especially after rejoining his mother, he coolly said that he supposed he should take to her trade. It was this callous idea that Jerry set himself to undermine, and admirably the old man succeeded, thus affixing a brighter gem to his brow for all eternity than if he had gone as a missionary to the heathen and converted a whole troop of savages. Dickie first listened in respectful patience to the new doctrines of honesty and hard work, then began to imbibe them and manfully adopt them himself, and finally became as firm and resolute in their dissemination as Jerry himself. Out of this sprang a strange act. Dickie had once written to his mother describing his new life, and promising to rejoin her on her liberation; he now wrote a final letter, asserting his intention of separating himself for ever from her and her influence, and declaring his intention of growing up "on the square." Jess was nearly insane over the news—not that she cared whether he grew up honest or a thief—but that he should think of separating his life entirely from her own. Three months elapsed before she was able to reply to his letter, and by that time Dickie was hundreds of miles away, leaving no address, and the letter was returned to the Penitentiary, marked *"Not Found."* Jerry was an Irishman, and though he always earned less money in his own country than in Scotland or England, he inclined more to wander at that side of the Channel, where, if the people could give nothing else, they were always ready with a kindly greeting or a sympathetic answer, and, of course, Dickie accompanied him, and gradually acquired such a strong smack of the Irish brogue that he would have passed for one of themselves.

When the queer partnership had first been formed, Dickie did little but go round the houses at which they paused and ask for knives or scissors to grind, but gradually, as he grew stronger and mastered the intricacies of the grinding as taught by old Jerry, the position of the partners became inverted, Dickie taking the heavy part of the work and Jerry the light. A strong affection had sprung up between them, and Dickie never thought he could do too much for the feeble old man, whose bad leg at times held them in a poor locality till they were literally starved out of it. During these detentions, Dickie, not at all dismayed, sturdily faced the road alone, sometimes making a round of thirty miles in a day, and faithfully returning with the grinding machine and his earnings at night. In this way he had "eaten the district bare," as he said, while Jerry's leg showed no sign of mending or allowing him to move.

"Ye'll have to take another county, Dickie, darlint," he said, after they had discussed the matter, and found some action imperative. "I'm not afeard of ye running away an' forgetting your poor owld grandfather. I've teached ye better nor that, more by token they can never expect to prosper that wrongs the helpless or the suffering."

"May I drop dead the minute such a thought enters my head!" said Dickie with energy. "Rest where you are, Jerry dear—and get well and take all the comfort ye can, for sure ye've been a blessed friend to me, and made a man of me when I'd have turned out nothing but a jail bird and a vagabone."

The "man," as he termed himself, was then just twelve years of age, but his sentiments, as the reader will admit, were worthy of twice that number of years.

Thus it was that Dickie came to face the world as an independent traveller. He moved over a great part of Ireland in this way, always sending the net gains regularly to old Jerry, and, on the whole, doing nearly as well as before the separation. He almost invariably met with kindness and sympathy, but once he was attacked and robbed of three days' earnings. But in taking the money the wretches took also Dickie's carefully cherished talisman, the broken cairngorm, and by that they were identified and convicted, while the trinket was returned to Dickie, who cherished it and guarded it, with greater faith than ever in its power. He would not have parted with that senseless bit of stone for a twenty-pound note, for it was the only link which connected the present with the past, and he never looked at it, as he was wont to declare, without remembering what he might have been but for old Jerry.

"Faith, I believe if I were to lose that stone my good luck would go with it," he repeatedly asserted, from which it will be seen that there was mixed up with Dickie's well-doing a spice of superstition, which, however, is not a bad thing, when it keeps in the straight path feet inclined to wander.

On one of the rare occasions when Dickie was able to get back as far as Belfast to see Jerry, he found the old grinder unusually weak and worn. Hitherto Jerry had doctored his leg himself, but now it had assumed such a strange appearance that he was glad to have Dickie by his side to advise him. It had begun to grow black, and, what was more strange, the pain had all gone out of it. Dickie had been doing pretty well on his travels, so he promptly decided that they should call in a doctor.

When that gentleman came he looked at the leg, and then at the emaciated face of the old man, and then said compassionately—

"Why did you send for me?"

"To mend me leg, plase God," said Jerry.

The doctor quietly covered up the limb and shook his head.

"Ye've more need of a praist, good man," he said, shortly, but not unkindly. "No doctor alive will ever make you well."

Dickie felt his heart suddenly grow cold and empty within him; then a revulsion came and he burst into tears. Jerry alone was calm, and even radiant.

"I've been expecting the message," he quietly returned. "Plase the Lord, I'm ready to die. Dickie, avourneen, don't sob the heart out ov ye like that. Sure, it's rejoicing ye ought to be that I'm getting rid of all my troubles and pains at wanst; and, blessed be God, it's aisy dyin' when love smooths the pillow. Ye've been a true son to me, and my own heart's blood couldn't have been affectionater. Pay the gintleman for his trouble, Dickie, aroon, and then run for a praist, for I feel the blackness creeping up on me, and when it covers my heart I'll be in heaven. The Lord is always good; He's kept me alive till you got back, Dickie, to take my hand an' help me over the dark stile."

The doctor would accept of no fee, and Dickie ran off and got a priest, who came and went, leaving Jerry happy and peaceful, with one arm round Dickie's neck and the other clasping his hand. He had a great deal to tell his young partner, but the most important of all was a strong injunction that he should continue honest and industrious.

"There's some money in the owld snuff-box under my head," he continued. "I've tuck care of it for ye, for ye've earned the most of it, and deserved it all. You'll get all that, and give me a dacent funeral, and keep the rest. It'll maybe start ye in a better way of doing some day, but if the other way isn't the straight way, ye'd better pitch the money into the salt say and go on as ye are."

The next morning the blackness crept up on Jerry's tender heart, and Dickie, still clasping the old man's hand and wetting it with his tears, helped him over the dark stile, and stood alone in the world.

The courage had nearly gone out of Dickie under this blow, but youth is buoyant, hopeful, and active. After laying the head of Jerry in the grave, and paying every one, Dickie found that he had nearly £20 left, all in gold sovereigns, for Jerry had imbibed the national distrust of bank notes. Dickie left the money in safe keeping, and started once more with his grinding machine. It was only when going over his old rounds that he discovered how much Jerry had been beloved and respected—truly another testimony that "honour and shame from no condition rise." Every one had a good word for his memory, and many a tear was shed as Dickie described his peaceful and courageous end. After another year of this wandering in Ireland, Dickie crossed to Liverpool, and spent a year in England, at the end of which time he sold his grinding machine, and became a hawker of cheap jewellery.

He was now a smart-tongued lad of fifteen, nicely dressed, with a good stock, all bought with Jerry's careful savings, and found the new line much more congenial, and quite as profitable as the old. Much of the Irish accent dropped from his tongue, and at length it would have puzzled even an expert to decide his nationality by his speech. As he increased in experience and accumulated capital, he was enabled to deal in a finer class of jewellery, which he carried about in a mahogany box having several lifting trays and compartments, and having on the side a stout leather handle, and on the top a brass plate bearing the words—

"RICHARD MURRAY,
Licensed Hawker."

Till he was seventeen he never thought of coming near Scotland, and had long since forgotten his mother's features, and given up any idea of seeking her out, or joining his fortunes with her own; but some one then fired his mind with a glowing account of what could be done in his line in some of the towns, and Dickie crossed the Border and worked his way to Glasgow, in which city he succeeded well. Saturday afternoon and night were his best times for business, as then the working folks were all free and plentiful of money.

After one of these successful days he had wandered into a big, flashy public-house, close to one of the theatres, for a last effort before going home to his humble lodging. The place was crowded, bar and boxes, for the theatre had just disgorged its contents, and it was near closing time. Dickie sold some of his wares, and then found himself in one of the boxes offering a silver brooch, set with imitation diamonds, to a company of three there seated—two men and a big muscular woman, with some traces of beauty still about her face.

The woman fancied the brooch, and appeared resolved on buying it, but among them they could not muster the price of the trinket, and as Dickie would not abate to their price, the brooch was reluctantly handed back and shut up in his box. The moment he had gone a significant look ran round the three.

"It would be easily done, and he's quite a boy," said Jess Murray eagerly. "He won't give it for a fair price; if you've any spirit at all, you'll take the boxful."

One of the men, Bob Lynch by name, was indifferent whether they adopted the suggestion or not, and rose carelessly to follow the lad;

the other, known as "Jockey" Savage, thought that the boy, as Jess called him, was not such a stripling, and might give them more trouble than they bargained for. They all agreed, however, that it was worth while following him, and, if a suitable spot were found, making the attempt. They left the public house and separated, one man going on either side of the street, and Jess following some distance behind, to assist in any emergency. Dickie's lodging was in a narrow close off the Gallowgate, and they had to follow him thus far before any opportunity occurred for attacking him, as, though he did no business on the way, he kept persistently to the main thoroughfare, thronged with passengers. The moment he entered the close the men exchanged signals and dived in after him. Dickie had scarcely walked twenty yards when a garrotting arm was thrown round his neck, and a snatch made at the box in his hand. But Dickie had not knocked about the world so long without learning something. He held on to the leather strap of his box with all his strength, and at the same time delivered a backward kick at Jockey Savage's shin bone, which made him slacken his grip, and squirm and howl with agony. As the intended victim made a great outcry at the same moment Bob Lynch made a desperate effort to bring out a leaden-headed life-preserver, but then Dickie, divining what the motion meant, grasped at the villain's arm with his disengaged hand while he tried to pin the other to Lynch's side with his teeth. Just then there was a swift rush to the spot, and Jess Murray, snatching the "neddy" from Lynch's pocket, brought it down with a crashing swing on the fair brow of the lad. Dickie dropped like a log, and Jess caught the box as it fell from his hand, tossing the neddy back to its owner, and saying—

"You bunglers would take all night to it. Now bolt! I'll take care of the swag."

They vanished from the spot like magic, and by different routes gained a den further east, known to them all, and peculiarly handy in their present condition, as it was kept by a man who would reset anything—the Great Eastern, even, if anyone chose to steal it. Jess was the last to arrive, with the box hidden under her shawl, and she tossed it down on the table with much pride and satisfaction.

"You hit him twice, Jess," observed Lynch, who was a bit of a coward, and was now very pale and concerned. "I hope to goodness you haven't croaked him."

"His own fault if I have," coolly answered Jess. "Turn out the box and see what we've got, and then into the fire with it before the spots come."

The order was speedily obeyed. The stock was of greater value than they had anticipated, but in addition, in the bottom compartment of the box, they found five or six pounds in money, and a bank-book representing a good deal more.

"What a pity! what a pity!" cried Jockey reflectively; "banks are a nuisance—if the money had only been here instead of the book!"

"What's that in the tissue paper?" said Jess eagerly—"a pile of sovereigns, very like. Turn them out—the greedy beggar was as rich as a Jew."

Jockey obeyed, and gave a whistle of disappointment. All that the tissue paper contained was a broken cairngorm stone, with a bit of dirty twine drawn through a hole at one end.

"There's your pile of gold," he said, tossing Dickie's talisman over to Jess. "I hope you like it."

Jess lifted the trinket and stared at it with her face slowly becoming ghastly, and her heart freezing within her.

"I've seen that before!" she slowly whispered, as the men stared at her in awe-stricken wonder and silence. "It was his when he was taken from me. Perhaps it is a mistake—perhaps I have not killed my own bairn. Read! read! you that can read—read what is on that brass plate on the lid of the box."

Jockey glanced at the plate, and sprang to his feet in horror.

"God alive! it's there," was all he could articulate.

"What? what? tell me what?" moaned Jess, beginning to clutch at her breast with her hands, and to writhe about like one grown mad.

"RICHARD　　　　　　　　　　　　　　　　　MURRAY, Licensed Hawker."

was the awe-stricken response, and only the half of it was heard. Shriek upon shriek went pealing through that rookery. Nothing could check her outcry; she screamed at every one; tore at them like a tiger; denounced them with every gasp and mad exclamation, and finally drew to the spot the police by struggling to throw her two accomplices out at the window. They were all marched off to the Central—with the reset as a make-weight, and Jess was there put in a padded cell and watched the long night through, or she would never have seen the light of another day. The first thing that helped to soothe her was the news that Dickie was not killed, and though there was concussion of the brain, he was likely to recover. When he did recover he was allowed to visit her in prison, and put his arms through the bars and clasp her close and hear her say that she was done for ever with a life of crime.

Jess and her companions were tried shortly after, when she, on account of the peculiar circumstances of the case, and the tearful appeal to the jury by the chief witness—Dickie—got the mild sentence of two years' imprisonment. Jockey and Lynch got ten each, as by a fiction of the law Jess was supposed to have acted under their influence.

When Jess was released, Dickie waited for her, and they vanished together.

THE ROMANCE OF A REAL CREMONA.

A grand ball was being given one night in November at the mansion of the Earl of ———, a great castellated place a good bit within a hundred miles of this city. The dancing room was a perfect picture—the floor polished mahogany in mosaic work, the walls panelled in white flowered satin, with gold slips at the edges, and the whole lighted by hundreds of wax candles inserted in brackets and chandeliers of cut crystal, glittering with pendants, while flashing in the head-dresses and on the necks and bosoms of the fair guests were enough diamonds and other precious stones to have bought up the Regalia twice over.

It was in this scene of brightness and grandeur, and strictly exclusive gaiety, that the curious robbery which was to cause me so much trouble and concern took place.

In an assemblage of this kind, one would expect a thief, if he managed to get into the place at all, to turn his attention to the guests and their jewels; but such was not the case, and it was there that the first puzzling element came into the affair.

At one end of the room, partly in a large recess formed by one of the bow windows, and partly in a portion of the room screened off by a rope covered with red cloth, was a raised kind of a dais for the orchestra. This corner was at the end nearest the door, and clustered within the rope, with stands and music complete, was an orchestra of local musicians, under the leadership, for that night only, of a more distinguished player from England. This gentleman, whom I may name Mr Cleffton, had been engaged at some high-class concerts in Edinburgh, and was about to return to England when he was asked as a great favour and at a high fee to play at this distinguished gathering. To play at a dancing party was rather out of this gentleman's line—to accept a high fee was not, so he went—much to his grief as he soon found.

About midnight, when the room was beginning to become uncomfortably warm, the guests filed out grandly to a supper room close by, and shortly after the musicians were similarly entertained in a smaller room, to which they were led through a long range of carpeted lobbies by the butler himself. Most of the players left their instruments on the seat they had occupied or on the music stand or floor—Mr Cleffton alone took the trouble to return his to its case. He was about to shut and lock this for additional security when he chanced to notice that all the others were waiting on him, and said hurriedly to the butler—

"I suppose the violins will be perfectly safe here? No one will meddle them while we're out?"

The butler smiled lightly at his concern, and said emphatically—

"Not a soul will go near them."

So the fiddle case was left open and unlocked, and its owner went away with his companions to regale himself upon cold fowl and tongue and champagne, or whatever wine he fancied most.

Now, when I say that Mr Cleffton fairly worshipped his own instrument, I am, I believe, giving only an ordinary case—all fiddlers, I understand, do that, and the more wretched the instrument the more devout is their homage. Whether this particular fiddle merited the slavish devotion I cannot say. It was very ugly, and rather dirty-looking; but its owner, besides never tiring of admiring it from every possible point of view, had given £40 for it, and afterwards spent a good many more, as I shall presently show, in trying to establish at law that the fiddle he had bought belonged to him; so I suppose it must have had good qualities of some kind.

When, therefore, the orchestra had finished supper and strolled back under the guidance of one of the servants to the ball-room, Mr Cleffton's first look was towards his fiddle—or rather towards the case in which he had so tenderly deposited it before leaving the room. Then he started, and blinked sharply to make sure that the champagne had not affected his vision. The case was there, as was also a beautifully quilted bag of wadding and green silk in which he was wont to tenderly wrap the fiddle when done playing, and before inserting it in the case; the fiddle bow, too, was there, but the Cremona was gone.

"Hullo! what's this!" exclaimed Mr Cleffton, in his quick, sharp way, and trying to smile in spite of his concern and pitiable pallor. "Which of you has been meddling with my fiddle."

Nobody had been touching it, as they all hastened to assure him, reminding him at the same time how he had been the last to leave the room; and then, with concerned looks and widely opened eyes, they looked everywhere about the recess for the missing fiddle, narrowly inspecting every one of the instruments left; but it was all in vain—the fiddle had vanished.

"My beautiful *Strad!* my beautiful *Strad!* worth £400!" was all Mr Cleffton could moan out, as, wringing his hands, tearing at the few hairs left in his head, and almost shedding real tears of grief, he trotted feverishly and excitedly round the ball-room, peering into every corner in search of his treasure.

"Perhaps some of the servants may have taken it out to have a scrape while we were at supper," suggested another player, keeping his own instrument tight under his arm so that there might be no danger of a second tragedy. All the other fiddlers echoed the suggestion, and, carrying their instruments under their arms, followed the distracted leader through the lobbies in search of the butler, or any of the servants likely to throw light on the strange disappearance.

The butler was soon found, and brought out from the supper room proper to hear the story of the Cremona; and in amazement and incredulity he followed the players to the ball-room, where, however, he could only stare and count over the instruments left, with the invariable result of finding them one short. Then the servants were questioned closely and searchingly, but not one of them had thought of looking at the fiddles, far less of taking one out of the room to try it, and the end of the investigation found them exactly where they had begun—that is, staring blankly at each other and saying, "Well, that is strange—how on earth could it have gone?"

By and by odd couples of the guests began to drift into the ball-room, and at length Lady ——— herself, the amiable hostess, appeared, and was informed in a whisper by the butler of the unexpected difficulty.

"One of the violins taken out of the room? oh, impossible," she incredulously echoed, with a coolness which must have stabbed Mr Cleffton like a sword of ice. "You will find it lying about somewhere when the dancing is over. Could you not play on one of the other violins, Mr Cleffton, and look for your own afterwards?"

Mr Cleffton looked at the honourable lady in pitying and profound contempt for her ignorance, and deep reproach for what to him seemed an indifference absolutely brutal. What! sit down and calmly play on another instrument while his own—to him the best in the world—might be speeding in the hands of the exultant robber to the other end of the world.

This was more than fiddler humanity could endure. High fees and even the countenance of earls were not to be despised, but they were as nothing compared with the loss of his darling instrument, and in a torrent of excited language, such as the lady was seldom favoured with hearing, the bereaved musician told her so. Not another note would he play till he got his own fiddle.

A horrible pause followed, but in the end a compromise was effected, by which all but Mr Cleffton continued to play, while he followed the butler from the room to prosecute his inquiries in the regions below.

A tardily stammered-out word from one of the servants had given them a slight clue to the strange disappearance. During the interval occupied by supper, some of the strange servants being entertained below—that is, the coachmen and footmen of those who had come a distance, and merely put up the horses to wait till the party was over—had proposed that they should take a peep at the glories of the empty ball-room, and, this being readily agreed to, they slipped quietly upstairs under the guidance of one of the servants, and gratified their curiosity.

"But they had been only a moment in the room," the quaking servant added, "and hardly inside the door."

The butler made no reply, but to Mr Cleffton he hopefully remarked—

"I suspect some of the coachmen will have your fiddle down in the kitchen," and to the kitchen they went to find there more than one coachman, but no fiddle, or trace of one. Every one there seated swore that they had not as much as noticed the fiddle, and then they voluntarily underwent a process of searching. Greatcoats were produced and inspected, pockets turned out, and every means tried without success. Then some suggested that they should see if all in waiting were there; they counted off at once, and found that, by comparing the number with that of the plates set for supper in the servants' hall, they were exactly one short. Who was the missing one! No one could tell, till one jolly-faced coachman said—

"Where's the surly chap that sat next to me, and never took off his driving coat all the time?"

"Ay, where was he?" every one echoed, and soon to this was added the question, for the first time asked, "Who was he?"

There was no answer to either question. Nobody had noticed the man particularly, though to the jolly-faced coachman he had gruffly said that his name was "Smith, or Jones, or something," and that he had been "driving some of the folks up stairs."

Every one in this case, down to the servants of the house themselves, had imagined that every body else knew all about the strange man, and so had paid little attention to him and his odd manner.

Smith had done little but smoke and stare, though he had shown great alacrity in going up to see the ball-room; some, indeed, insisted that it had been he who proposed the treat. More, he had gone up with his heavy driving coat on, and some of the servants had a faint recollection of him loitering near the music stands while the rest of the servants walked round the room looking at the decorations.

"That's the man that has stolen my violin," cried Mr Cleffton at this stage of the inquiry. "He would have a big pocket inside his coat,—probably made for the occasion,—and has slipped my Cremona into it when no one was looking or thinking of him. Who does he serve with?"

"Who, indeed?" All echoed the question; but when guest after guest had been enumerated or appealed to by the butler, there came the still more surprising discovery that Smith served no one—came with no one—and was known to no one—had gained admittance, indeed, entirely by the dress he wore, his own cool audacity, and the general flurry in which every one was plunged by the party being held up stairs.

"Get out your horses, and let the villain be pursued," cried Mr Cleffton, more and more distracted, "the whole robbery has been systematically planned and carried out; but the wretch can't be far off, and we may overtake him yet. I will give ten pounds to any of you who help to put it into my hands again."

The incentive was little needed, for a good deal of Cleffton's excitement had communicated itself to those about him. In a few minutes several vehicles were horsed and ready in the stable yard behind, and on one of these Mr Cleffton took his place beside the driver and with a grand lashing of whips and excited whooping they were off down the avenue, at the foot of which they separated to take the different roads running from the spot. Mr Cleffton, from some idea of his own, had chosen that leading to Edinburgh; but, though the night was clear, and the moon and stars out in the sky, not a trace of the fugitive did they come upon between the mansion and the city. Several tramps they did overtake and rouse up and search without ceremony, but as none of these answered the description of the surly Mr Smith, they were allowed to resume their tramping or snoring, while the agonised fiddler entered the city. Of course his first visit was to the Central Police Office, where he made known his loss to the lieutenant on night duty, and then excitedly demanded to see a detective. It was explained to him that detectives require sleep as well as ordinary mortals, and are not usually kept at the office during the night waiting for such exceptional cases, but this produced little impression upon the musician.

"Everything depends on this matter being seen to with promptitude," he said. "Give me the man's address, and I'll go to him myself."

They ought to have given him McSweeny's address, considering the hour and the work I had done the day before, but they didn't; they gave him mine; and out to Charles Street he came at half-past four in the morning, and roused me out of bed, sleepy, stupid, and dazed with having got only three hours rest instead of eight, and, without waiting to see if I understood him, at once began to bemoan his loss.

"My lovely Cremona! my beautiful *Strad!* spirited away—stolen from under my very eyes! Good heavens, what am I to do? What is to become of me if you don't trace out the thief?"

"Strad! Strad! Who is she?" I vacantly asked, thinking from the man's tears that he must mean some young and beautiful maiden, violently abducted from her home and friends.

"The best fiddle in the world—at least, the best that I ever tried, and I've tried a few," he moaned, wringing his hands. "I'd rather have had a leg broken, or lost my head, than that Cremona."

I stared at him, only half understanding the speech, and inclined to think that he had lost his head.

"You don't mean to say that it's a—a fiddle you've come to make all this fuss about?" I at last found voice to say.

"A beauty—and the tone of it, three fiddles in one, and as sweet and soft as a flute," he cried, not noticing my rising anger.

"Good heavens, man!" I shouted at last, "you don't mean to tell me that you've come here and roused me out of bed at four in the morning about a miserable fiddle that you've lost? I thought it was something serious."

"And do you not call that serious?" he returned, after favouring me with a pitying look which was meant to kill me, but did not. "It is serious for me. I'll never sleep till I get it."

"I'm sorry for you, but you might at least have let me sleep—till morning."

"Worth £400—refused £200 for it the other day," he continued, quite undisturbed.

"£400!" I echoed. "Is it possible you gave that sum for a fiddle?"

"No, not quite so much, but that's its value," he slowly admitted.

"How much did it cost you?"

"£40," he rather reluctantly answered.

"There's a slight difference between 40 and 400," I ventured to remark.

"A mere nothing," he said, with the greatest gravity stumbling on a joke; "that's common in fiddle buying. You don't always give for an instrument exactly what it's worth."

"Then its value is just the price which you choose to put on it?"

"That's about it;" and then he hastily changed the subject by narrating all the circumstances of the strange robbery much as I have put them down, only taking much longer to go through.

When he had finished I quietly returned to the point at which he had broken off, pretty sure that he had a reason for avoiding it.

"If the fiddle is worth £400, and you got it at a tenth of that price, you must have got a great bargain?" I observed.

"I am coming to that," he answered, with a groan. "A great bargain? Yes, I thought so too at the time, but I've never had peace since I bought it. It has a history, and as that, I am sure, has something to do with the robbery, you may as well hear it now."

"Then there is more to listen to?" I ruefully returned, with something like an echo of his groan, and a wistful thought of the cosy blankets I had left. "Will it take long to tell?"

"Not very long—it must not, for I must have you and some of your comrades out to watch the departure of the Newcastle trains."

I groaned in reality then, and resignedly began to dress.

"Well, go on—I'm listening," I said, with a very bad grace, which, however, he was too grief-stricken to notice.

"Well, I was swindled in buying the violin—regularly diddled," he said, with some exasperation.

"*You* were swindled? I thought it was the other way?" I said, stopping in surprise.

"So did I, but I was mistaken," he answered, with a writhe. "This was how it happened. I was playing at Newcastle last year, when a man named John Mackintosh, who said he had a real Cremona violin, or one that was said to be real, called upon me, and said he wanted my opinion of it. I had nothing to do during the day, so I went to his shop,—a little den down near the New Quay, in which he sold ginger beer, sweets, and newspapers,—and saw at a glance that it was a splendid instrument. It was of no use to him, for he is only a wretched scraper, who would be as happy with a twelve-and-sixpenny German fiddle, so I determined if possible to get him to sell it. He asked what I thought of it, and I said indifferently that it might be a real Cremona and it might not, but it was worth about £10."

"That would be a lie, of course?" I quietly observed.

"Well, in a sense, yes," he stammered, flushing a little. "You know I was speaking professionally."

"Oh, indeed? Professionals always lie, then?"

"No, no—you mistake. I mean that professionals can never afford to give so much as ordinary buyers with lots of money. But the man was deeper than I had expected—he's a Scotchman, you know, and they're always cursed long-headed. He said, 'Ah, but I wadna gie that fiddle for twice £10.' I laughed at him, but at length I said I would buy it from him, and give him the £20. Blast him, then I found he wouldn't sell it at all!"

"And you came away without it?"

"I tried him every way—pointed out how much more useful the money would be than the fiddle to him, but he only said dryly that 'he would think aboot it,' and thus I left him. The next time I was in Newcastle I called upon him again, and saw the violin, but this time Mackintosh was not in the shop, but an uncle of his, who said he could not sell the fiddle without the owner's consent, but hinted that if I made a reasonable offer for it he had no doubt I might make a bargain the next time I came. Well, I did call on my next visit, and saw the uncle, who said that Mackintosh had decided to sell it if I would make the price £40, and I snapped at the offer at once. I asked when I could see Mackintosh, but the uncle only said, 'You can get the fiddle frae me as weel as frae him—if ye hae the money wi' ye?' I had the money, and counted it out at once, while he wrote out a receipt, put a stamp on it, and signed it 'John Mackintosh.' Then I got the fiddle, and thought as I bore it off that I was happy for life."

"But you weren't?"

"I wasn't. I had not been home many days when I got a note, vilely written and spelled, from Mackintosh, demanding back his fiddle, and saying hotly that his uncle, the drunken beast, had no right to *lend* the fiddle to me, or even let it out of the shop. I replied sharply that I had bought it, paid £40 for it, and held the receipt; to which he replied that his uncle had left him, and gone no one knew where, but the fiddle was never his uncle's, nor had he power to sell it, and that Mackintosh himself had never fingered a penny of the price, and did not mean to, but insisted on getting back his Cremona. Here was a nice swindle; yet what could I do? I offered him other £20 to let me keep it, but he laughed at the offer, and then brought an action-at-law against me for the return of the fiddle."

"And what was the result?"

"The result as yet is only that I've had to pay away nearly £20 in lawyer's fees; but, as I stick to the fiddle, and would burn it sooner than give it up to him, I suspect that in desperation he has planned this robbery, and now is making his escape to Newcastle with the fiddle in his possession."

"Oho! and that's the end of it," I exclaimed, now seeing the awkwardness of the case he was putting into my hands. "Was it this man Mackintosh who offered you £200 for the fiddle the other day?"

"No, no! That was another person altogether. But what has that got to do with the case in hand?"

"Nothing, perhaps, but we'll see. Who was he?"

"Oh, a curious, half-daft customer, who has a craze for buying fiddles. He lives a mile or two out from this city, but heard me play on mine at one of the concerts, and invited me out to try his and compare them with mine."

"Did he seem very anxious to buy yours?"

"Oh, fairly daft about it—offered me my pick of his selection of fiddles and £200 down for it, but I only laughed at him. He doesn't play at all, so of what earthly use would it be to him? He has been in an asylum, I understand, at one time, and I could believe it, for none but a daft man would give the prices he has given for the fiddles he has. One wretched thing, with no more tone in it than a child's sixpenny toy, cost him £180. He's been beautifully swindled."

"Swindling seems to be rather a prominent feature in fiddle-buying," was my comment; but while I made it I was thinking of something else.

It is a pity that he told me of the Newcastle affair, for from the first I had caught the idea that the offerer of the £200 would be found to have some connection with the theft. The bringing in of another clue completely upset my first instincts, and made me give them less prominence than I should otherwise have done. The description of the surly, sham coachman, too, did not tally in any particular with that of either Mackintosh or his uncle, though, as Cleffton remarked, that did not go for much, as they might have employed another to do the job for them.

There was little time for either thinking or further inquiries, for on consulting the railway time tables I found that trains started by both lines for Newcastle at a few minutes past seven, and as I could not divide myself into two, I would have to rouse McSweeny—rather a joyful task—and prime him with details and descriptions, and set him on to watch one station, while I and Mr Cleffton took the other.

As the early train from the Waverley Station did not run farther than Berwick without a break, I thought the Caledonian more likely to be tried, and decided to take that one, while McSweeny took the Waverley. There was no boat for Newcastle from Leith till next day, so we were pretty safe in trying only the railway stations.

We got down to the Pleasance, roused McSweeny without compunction, and then hurried off to our different posts of observation. I took up my stand close to the booking-office, with Cleffton watching close by, and there we stood till every passenger had been served with tickets, and the train moved out of the station. Not one carried a fiddle, or suspicious bundle, or had any appearance of having one concealed about them, and not one answered the descriptions either of Mackintosh, his uncle, or the sham coachman. Cleffton was manifestly disappointed, and eager to know what I thought.

"Wait till we hear what McSweeny has to say," was my reply, and we drove along to the other station to find that my chum had actually made a capture, and lugged him off to the Office, fiddle and all. Cleffton was in high spirits, but swore horribly when he found that the prisoner was only a harmless blind fiddler, with an instrument having more patches and splices than his coat, and worth only half-a-crown. Then I gave my opinion freely—

"I'm afraid we're on the wrong scent."

Cleffton, however, had formed his own theory, and insisted on all the trains for Newcastle being watched that day; and this was done, but without success. Even then he would have held out, but in the course of the day I sent a telegram to a skilful man on the Newcastle staff, asking him to find out if Mackintosh had been out of town, and at night I had an answer giving a decided negative. Not only was he at home, and serving his customers as usual, but he had even spoken confidently of recovering his valuable Cremona, in a month or two at the most, by the ordinary processes of law.

"Recover it, the cheating scoundrel!" cried Cleffton, when I read him the message, "after me paying him forty pounds for it!"

"Not him—you did not pay him," I quietly corrected.

"A regularly planned swindle!—all made up between them," he hoarsely iterated.

"I have little doubt it was," I thoughtfully replied; "but did it never strike you as curious that a man in his position should possess such a valuable instrument. Did he never tell you how it came into his possession? It is just possible that it was not really his to sell."

"Do you think so?" eagerly cried the excited victim. "By heavens, I would give a ten pound note this minute if you could fasten a crime of any kind on him. That would be revenge! He always declared to me that he bought it in a disjointed state from a broker in Edinburgh here for £3. Perhaps it was stolen."

I said nothing, for either way Cleffton would lose his fiddle, and probably the money he had paid for it. I had no doubt that the false sale had been planned and arranged by Mackintosh; and was quite sure that the man who could do so would not stick at trifles, but it did not therefore follow that he had stolen the fiddle. I gave the whole matter a night's thought, and in the morning wished heartily that the fiddle had been burned to ashes a year before I was born, for I seemed to get deeper into troubles and difficulties the more I studied and investigated.

I now put Cleffton and his theories aside, and began to work the case in my own way. After getting from him the address of the gentleman who had offered him £200 for the Cremona, I made my way out to the mansion which had been the scene of the robbery. I then worked my way in towards the city, and, after two days' hard work, at length discovered two persons who had seen a man answering the description of the sham coachman at an early hour on the morning of the robbery. One had seen him on the road, another had seen him in the city; but neither seemed to have any suspicion that under the big coachman's coat there was concealed a bulky thing like a fiddle.

From some of the servants I had learned that the man was red-haired and big boned—that he had a slight cast in the eye, and that he undoubtedly knew something about horses and driving. I therefore decided that if I should have the good fortune to discover him I would find him to be some dodging groom or stableman of doubtful reputation rather than one of my own family of recognised "bairns."

My next step was naturally a visit to the eccentric connoisseur, whom I shall call Mr Turner. It happened, however, that before I had advanced to this stage Mr Cleffton had to leave the city for England to fulfil several important engagements, and I was for a little rather puzzled as to how I should be able to identify his violin, if I were lucky enough to get my eyes on it. Fiddles, of course, are all alike to me, and unless by some marked difference in the colour I could not tell one from another. Mr Cleffton tried to prime me a little by speaking of certain marks and printed tickets which I would find about the fiddle, but when he admitted that some of the fiddles already in Mr Turner's possession had these very tickets and marks I was more helpless than ever. At last a happy thought struck him just as he was leaving town, and he dropped me a note directing me to an old Edinburgh musician who had been playing second fiddle with him on the night of the ball. This gentleman had seen and closely examined the Cremona more than once, and, having a perfect knowledge of all the peculiarities of such valuable instruments, would know the missing one, I was assured, among dozens. To this gentleman, therefore, I went, and we arranged that he should take me out to Mr Turner's as a friend wishing to see the rare collection of old violins. We then set out for the nearest cab-stand, as the place was three miles out of town, and on the way I chanced to say—

"But are you perfectly sure that you would know this fiddle so as to be able to swear to it? It would be very awkward for us all if we made a false accusation."

"I'll know it when I see it," was the confident reply, "and I'll tell you why. I have a strong suspicion that I've seen the fiddle before—ay, and played on it, too. If it's not the £50 Cremona that my old chum, M——, of the Theatre Royal, lost about ten years ago, it must be its twin brother."

"Lost? How could a fiddle be lost?" I faintly returned, as with a sinking heart I anticipated fresh complications.

"Well, or stolen—it was never rightly known how it happened," promptly returned my companion. "I was there at the time myself, and I'll tell you all about it as we go out."

I groaned, and resigned myself to listen.

We got to the cab-stand, and were soon rattling out from Edinburgh, and when out on the smooth country road my new assistant very eagerly threw off the following information:—

"We were playing at a ball out by Penicuick—six or seven of us altogether—and as it was a jolly affair at a gentleman's seat, we were driven out and in in an open trap. My chum, M——, of the Theatre Royal,—he's dead now, as you know,—was leader, and had his best fiddle with him—a splendid *Stradivarius* Cremona, which cost him £50. I had a great liking for the instrument, and used often to try it, and have got the loan of it often when I had a solo to play. We were through with our business about three in the morning, and I remember perfectly that it was a clear, cold night, with plenty of moonlight. We had had some refreshments during the night, but every one of us knew perfectly well what he was about. M—— was the last to step into the vehicle that was to bring us in, and he came out with his fiddle and case in his hand, and said, 'Mind yer feet or I pit in my fiddle—better that you sud be crampit for room than that my fiddle sud come to ony herm.' We made room—the fiddle case was shoved in on the floor of the vehicle among others there lying, the door at the back was shut, and we drove off, singing, laughing, and joking, and as jovial and happy as kings. There was a toll-bar some distance in, and I remember some of us getting out to knock up the toll-keeper and get him to open the gate; and it is possible that the door of the trap may not have been shut immediately on the journey being resumed, but, at all events, the door was found open when we came to the next toll, which was near Edinburgh. When we got to the Theatre Royal—the most central place for us all—we got out, and M——, who was joking and laughing till we had all got out our instruments, began groping about under the seats, and then said, 'Some o' ye hae taen my fiddle.' We counted over, and searched everywhere, but the Cremona and case were gone."

"Lost on the road, I suppose?"

"Yes, or stolen—it was never found out which. The loss was not thought serious at first, for there was a brass plate on the case bearing the owner's name, and it was expected that the fiddle would be picked up by some of the early carters coming in to the market, and that a mere advertisement and small reward would ensure its restoration. But though the advertising was tried, and every inquiry was made, the fiddle has never been heard of since."

"And did you not tell Cleffton all this when you saw the fiddle in his possession?"

"No; I was not sure that it *was* the fiddle. But I thought of it, and was very near saying it."

I made no further comments on the new information. I was not anxious that he should prove correct in his surmise, but hoped that the case would be narrowed rather than broadened. With this end in view I thought proper to prime my companion well as to the questions he was to ask the gentleman we were on our way to see, leaving to myself rather the task of watching and analysing.

Mr Turner had a craze for buying fiddles which he never did, and never could, play upon, and I mentally placed him in the same position as a bibliomaniac, who would sell his soul to get hold of some old musty volume not worth reading, simply because it happened to be the only copy in existence. Such a man, I had no hesitation in deciding, would steal as readily as a man drunk with opium. My only difficulty was how to make sure that the fiddle had been stolen at his instigation, and, if that were made clear, how to get at the stolen article.

The cab stopped at a little hamlet about three miles from the city, and I was shown into the drawing-room of Mr Turner's house, in which we were speedily joined by a dirty-looking man, very shabbily and raggedly attired, and evidently straight from digging in the garden, whom I had difficulty in believing to be the wealthy gentleman I had come to see.

The face was rather repulsive, on the whole, until my companion spoke of his rare fiddles, when it became animated and bright with the ruling passion of his life. Then he turned to a cabinet in the room, and unlocked it as solemnly as if it had been an iron safe full of diamonds and gold, and brought out several old fiddles, very much cracked and mended, and every one, if possible, uglier than another, and which were placed successively in my hands, with a triumphant look, which evidently meant, "Admire that, or be for ever condemned as ignorant and stupid."

I examined them closely as I had been instructed by Mr Cleffton, and even brightened a little when I found one which had the printed ticket inside of which he had spoken, but on referring the matter to my companion, he only smiled and said—

"Oh, that's a *Strad.*, too, but it's only a copy, and a very poor one. The other was a *real* Cremona. By the by, Mr Turner," he abruptly added aloud, in response to a signal from me, and while I pretended to bend over the fiddle in my hand in wrapt devotion and admiration, "Do you remember that *Stradivarius* which Cleffton refused to sell you?"

"Yes; what of it?" The words were somewhat hastily thrown out, and I fancied I noticed a kind of nervous flutter in his voice as he spoke.

"It has been stolen."

"Stolen? Impossible!"

These were his words, and natural enough under the circumstances, but it is impossible to convey in print the whole effect of the exclamation. There is more in the manner in which words are spoken than in the words themselves. The appearance of surprise and incredulity was—or appeared to me to be—manifestly forced; the eyes of the man had an absent and uneasy expression, as if, while he was mechanically pronouncing the words, he was saying to himself—"Is there any danger? Can any one have hinted to him that I might have been the thief?"

"It is not only possible, but a fact," pursued my companion.

"And how was it done?" asked Mr Turner, with more coolness.

The fiddler briefly ran over the incidents of the theft, but when he came to explain that all the suspicion rested on the sham coachman, Mr Turner dissented warmly. "They'll find that that has been a cock and bull story of the servants to screen themselves," he said decidedly. "The whole thing is absurd; and my opinion is that the fiddle is safely hidden somewhere about the house in which it was missed."

"The police don't seem to think so," I quietly observed.

"The police!" he scornfully echoed, "a parcel of blockheads—they'll never lay hands on it, I'll swear. When anything is stolen, of course, they have to make a show of activity, but it's all humbug. They never recover the stolen thing."

"I think you're mistaken," said I, with some truth, as the reader probably is aware.

"They'll never see it," he hotly and positively persisted. "I'll stake twenty pounds on it."

"Perhaps you'll lose," I laughingly returned. "Now, Mr ———, you bear witness that Mr Turner has promised to pay £20 to the—say the Royal Infirmary—if the police get back Mr Cleffton's fiddle."

Mr Turner appeared to think this a very good joke, and laughingly repeated his offer. We had by this time looked over every fiddle in his possession, as he averred, and as I had no search warrant, and no grounds for trying to get one, we had to take leave without any further discovery. But while we were being shown to the door by the shabby and ragged proprietor, I busied myself with inquiries as to the number of servants he employed. The house was a big one, and there was at least half an acre of garden ground attached to it, and I was in hope that he might keep a man, or hire one to help him to keep it in order. In this I was disappointed. He kept but two servants, and never hired a man for his garden, unless when actually forced to it by bad health. He kept neither horse nor machine, and always walked in to Edinburgh when business called him thither, so my sniffing after a horsey manservant went for nothing. I knew, however, that Mr Turner had been perfectly aware of Cleffton's engagement to play at the Earl of ———'s, and was loath to believe that I was on the wrong scent.

I therefore bade the eccentric man rather an absent-minded good-bye, and had moodily settled myself in the cab for a good think, when a sudden thought came to me as we were leaving the hamlet behind. A little further down the road from the house we had visited was a wayside cottage with a few jars of sweets and biscuits and a couple of tobacco pipes stuck prominently in one of the windows, thus intimating that the place was meant for a shop. If any gossip—any news or information was to be collected regarding any one in the place, it was surely to be got in such a house as this, and my hand was on the check string in a moment.

When I got inside the cottage, a clean, tidy woman came bustling through from the back room, wiping her hands on her apron as she came. I was a little at a loss how to begin till I noticed some bottles of lemonade in a case behind the little counter, and asked to be served with two.

Chairs were handed us, and we decanted the lemonade in comfort, talking about the weather and roads as we did so, and then I indifferently turned the conversation to the strange customers that the good woman would be in the habit of noticing on the road.

"I suppose you never notice any men coming to see Mr Turner up the way there—a coarse, red-haired man, for instance, in a big coachman's coat, and having a slight cast in his eyes?"

"Mr Turner's no ane to hae mony folk coming aboot his hoose—he's owre greedy for that," was the answer, "but I think I did see a man like that a day or twa syne—no gaun to Mr Turner's, but coming the other road. He cam' in here and bocht a half-ounce o' tobacco and a pipe."

"Going in towards Edinburgh, you mean?"

"No that either, for he asked the nearest road to the railway station."

"He couldn't be going to Edinburgh, then, for the station is two miles farther on, and he would have been nearly as quick to have walked. Have you any idea if he had been at Mr Turner's?"

"No me; I never clapped een on the man afore."

"Was he carrying anything?—a fiddle case, for instance?"

"No, no—naething but a deal box, tied roond wi' a string. It wasna sae big as a fiddle case. He laid it doon on the counter while he filled his pipe. I think there was a ticket on it—put on wi' iron tacks—and a name on the ticket."

"What name?"

"I never lookit. Maybe it wasna a name. I never like to be impident, and didna look very close."

I questioned her closely on the man's appearance, and found that it tallied very closely with that of the sham coachman. Yet I was anything but hopeful of the result. The description might have suited fifty innocent men who might pass her little shop in the course of a forenoon. Still I resolved to follow the clue a little further, and directed the cabman to turn his horse off at the first bye-road, and make for a railway station two miles further on. It was quite a small place, a branch from the main line, and to my satisfaction I found the booking clerk who had been on duty on the day named by the woman. This lad recollected the red-haired man perfectly, but when I said, "Where did he book for?" he looked at me with a puzzled expression, then thought a moment, and said—

"*Did* he book for any place?"

It was now my turn to look puzzled.

"I don't know—I suppose he did when he walked two miles to get to the station," I said at last. "Why else would he come here?"

"He brought a parcel," said the lad, turning to one of his ledgers and flapping over the leaves. "He booked *it*, I know, but I don't think he took out a ticket or waited for the train."

"What kind of a parcel?"

"A light box. I think he said it was to be kept dry, as there were artificial flowers and ribbons in it. Ah, here is the entry—it is not paid you see—he said we'd take greater care of it if it wasn't prepaid—'Sent by James Paterson, to Robert Marshall, Linlithgow. To lie at station till called for.'"

"Was the box big enough to have held a fiddle?"

"About that size, sir. I don't think it would have held the fiddlestick too. The fiddlestick is longer, and would take more room."

"Was the box called for at the other end, do you know?" I asked, beginning to be more hopeful.

"I don't know about that—it was sent away, and that's all we have to do with it. These parcels are generally expected, and don't lie long unclaimed."

"You've got a telegraph handy—would you just send a message through, particularly asking if that box has been called for?" and I calmly sat down and motioned the clerk to his place at the instrument; and in a short time had the welcome news that the "box was there still, and had not been asked for."

I looked at my watch and then consulted a time-table, and found that if I drove smartly into Edinburgh I could easily get a fast train to Linlithgow, without waiting for the slow connection with this out-of-the-way branch line. Afraid of looking foolish if I found myself mistaken, I dropped my companion at Edinburgh and took train for Linlithgow alone. The moment I got out, and the bustle of the train's arrival and departure was over, I got the booking-clerk to turn out his parcel press, and easily found the box I was in search of. It was but roughly put together, and appeared to have been made out of the undressed spars of an old orange box; but by shaking it sharply I soon ascertained that it contained something harder than either flowers or ribbons. After a consultation, I was allowed to use a chisel to the lid, and easily prised it up sufficiently to pull out the paper and straw with which it was padded, and found snugly reposing underneath, a fiddle which in every respect answered the description of that stolen from Mr Cleffton.

I had little doubt that I had fairly recovered the stolen property, but I was just as anxious to get hold of the thief. It appeared to me that the sending of the fiddle by rail to this quiet station was merely the adoption of a safe hiding-place till the hue and cry of the robbery were over, and that as soon as the actual instigator felt safe he would appear to claim the box. I could not afford to wait so long; so I got permission to fasten up the box and leave it, while I returned to Edinburgh bearing the fiddle.

My first visit was to the gentleman who had introduced me to Mr Turner, and he identified the fiddle at a glance as Cleffton's; but he did more. Getting out a fiddle bow, he ran his fingers over the strings in a testing way, and at last said decidedly—

"I could stake my life on it that that's M———'s £50 Cremona that was stolen as I told you. Suppose we go along to his house and see?"

"I thought you said he was dead?"

"So he is; but his widow is alive, and may know the fiddle. We will not prompt her in any way, but just show it her and see if she has any suspicion of the truth."

I was so pleased at the identification of the fiddle as that stolen from Cleffton—which was all I had been employed to find—that I offered no objection, and we walked through a street or two to a semi-genteel place, where I was introduced to the widow of the musician, and found her a shrewd and superior woman—one picked out of a hundred, I should say, for quick intelligence.

My companion opened the conversation by asking to see one of her late husband's instruments to compare it with that we had with us, and in the course of the testing he managed that our fiddle should find its way into the widow's hands. In a moment or two I saw her start and look at it more closely, then take it nearer the light and examine it closely at the scroll work close to the screwing pegs, and then she turned to my companion perfectly amazed, and said—

"Do you know what I've discovered?"

"What?"

"This is my fiddle—the one that was stolen from M―――the £50 Cremona lost on the Penicuick road."

"Impossible!—that one was bought in Newcastle."

"That's nothing. I don't care though it had been bought in Australia—it's his fiddle. Look here"—and she pointed to some scratching on the varnish in among the scroll carving—"what do you call that?"

We both looked very closely, and I said at last—

"It's like the letter M scratched with a pin."

"It is just that, and was scratched with a pin in this very room. He did it one night before me, saying, 'If ever any one runs away with my fiddle I'll know it by that whether they change the ticket or not.' You need not take the fiddle away with you, for I claim it as mine."

Here was a poser, but I was not to be so easily deprived of what was mine only on trust. I quietly took the instrument into my hands, saying—

"At present, Mrs M―――, the fiddle is in the hands of the police, and as soon as you make good your claim to it I have no doubt it will be surrendered to you, but it seems to me that you will require to advance better evidence than that of a mere scratched letter."

"I for one can swear to the instrument," observed my companion.

"And half a dozen more, when they see it," added the widow warmly. "I will raise an action for its recovery to-morrow."

"Tuts! do not be so hasty—save your money in the meantime," I advised. "I may get the evidence for you quite easily, if I can get the thief to confess. But that will necessitate a journey to Newcastle, so it can hardly be done in a day."

I said this pretty confident that the swindling Mackintosh who had sold the fiddle to Cleffton would turn out to be the original thief, and took away the instrument and made preparations to secure him. I had before this made an arrangement whereby any one calling for the box at Linlithgow station should be detained and arrested; and the whole case now presented the curious spectacle of two robberies, two claimants, and two thieves. A telegram to England, according to arrangement, brought Mr Cleffton down in joy and ecstacy to claim his beloved fiddle, but only to be all but heart-broken with the intelligence that it was believed to be stolen property, and could not be given up till all claims had been fully investigated. The day after,

I managed to run down to Newcastle. I easily found the little shop of Mackintosh, and considerably startled him by saying—

"My name is McGovan, and I have come from Edinburgh about that affair of the Cremona. I want you to come with me."

The name appeared to be known to him, for he became ashy white before I had done speaking, and then with chattering teeth managed to say—

"I can't leave my business; but I'm willing to lose the money. I'll pay Cleffton back the £40 out of my own pocket, if he gives me back the fiddle."

"Out of your own pocket?" I growled. "Man, don't try that on me. The whole thing was a regular plant. But, as it happens, it's not that part of the business that has brought me here. It's the way you got the fiddle—it was stolen."

"Stolen? Then it wasn't by me," he cried, with fearful earnestness. "I can swear that with my hand on the Bible. I bought it from a broker in the Cowgate, in Edinburgh."

"That's a common story—you'll have a receipt, I suppose?" I answered, with a grin.

"I have, and I'll show it you," and much to my surprise he very quickly produced a badly written and spelled receipt for £3, bearing a stamp, and signed "Patrick Finnigan."

"Now, be cautious what you say," I returned, after a long look at the paper. "I happen to know Finnigan, and know him to be an honest man. You declare that you bought the fiddle from him—the fiddle which Cleffton bought from you for £40?"

"I declare that solemnly."

"Then how did he get it?"

"I don't know; but it runs in my head that he said he bought it at a country auction sale. It was in two pieces when I got it—the neck was away from the body."

All this seemed probable enough, but I thought proper to take Mackintosh with me to the Newcastle Central, and have him locked up, while I returned to investigate his statements. Taking the fiddle and receipt with me, I called on Finnigan and asked him to try and recall the circumstances of the sale. That he managed to do when prompted by several statements of Mackintosh to me—particularly one as to the fiddle being in a broken state, and having hung in the back shop in a green bag, when Mackintosh asked to see it. Questioned then as to how it came into his possession, he said—

"I was out in the country at an auction sale—it was at a farm about six miles from here—and there were two or three fiddles put up. This was the last, and as it was broke—though the auctioneer declared that it only needed a little glue and new strings to make it play beautiful—nobody would bid for it, and I got it for five shillings. I always meant to sort it up, but was afraid I mightn't do it right. One day the man who bought it came in and looked at a fiddle I had in the window, and then asked if I had any more. I showed him that, and saw him look pleased and eager like, so when he asked the price of it I thought I'd drop on him, and said £5. He prigged me down to £3 and then took it away, saying he didn't think it dear."

"You can't remember the name of the farm, I suppose?" I wearily remarked, beginning to despair of getting to the bottom of the strange complication.

"I don't know the name of the farm, but I think the name of the farmer who had died, and who had owned the fiddle, was Gow, or something like that. I could take you to the place though, and maybe that would do as well."

I thought the proposal a good one, and got a cab the same afternoon, and drove out towards Penicuick, then by some cross roads, through which the cabman was unerringly directed by Finnigan, we reached the farm in question. Here I was not surprised to learn that nothing was known of the Gows who had formerly occupied the farm. Gow himself was dead, and his surviving relations gone, none knew whither; but, in the course of my inquiries, I came across an old man—a ploughman or farm worker, who had served with Gow for many years, and to him I turned as a kind of forlorn hope, though, as it happened, I could not have hit upon a better if I had hunted for years.

"It's about an old fiddle that was sold at the roup when the old man died," I explained, in rather a loud key, for the old man was a little deaf. "It was broken at the time, and was sold for five shillings."

"I mind o'd perfectly," said the old man. "It was the fiddle that we fund on the road gaun to market. The maister was on ae cairt and me on the tither; and it was quite dark at the time, but there was a heavy rime on the grund, and the fiddle was in a black case, and I noticed it as we drave by, and stoppit my cairt to pick it up. The maister stoppit his too, and then when he had lookit at the fiddle, and tried hoo the strings soonded, he said, 'Them 'at finds keeps, Sandy. I'll gi'e ye five shillings to yoursel', an we'll say naething aboot this to naebody.' So we shoved it in alow the strae, and there it lay till we got back frae Em'bro'. The maister played on it, and likit it better nor his ain; but on the Saturday after he cam' to my hoose late at nicht, wi' the case and fiddle in his hand, and said, kind o' excited like, 'Sandy, in case onybody should ask after this fiddle I think we'd better pit it ooten sicht for a wee. Get your shuill, and dig a hole ony place where it's no likely to be disturbed.'"

"And you did it?"

"Deed did I. I dug a hole, and the fiddle and case lay there for mair nor a year. But it was never claimed, and we got it oot, and he played on it for a while, but the damp ground had spoiled it in some way, and he never likit it sae weel as at first. Then it gaed in twa ae day in his hands, and was put awa in a bag till the day o' the sale."

"And what became of the case?" I asked, with great eagerness.

"Ou, the maister used it for a long time to haud ane o' his ain fiddles, and it went wi' it at the sale to Thompson o' the Mains."

"Was there not a brass plate on it bearing a name?"

"A brass plate? I raither think there was a brass plate on it when we fund it, but I never saw it after. Maybe the maister had ta'en it aff."

"Not unlikely," I dryly observed. "Did you never hear of the fiddle being advertised for?"

"No me; I didna fash muckle wi' papers at that time."

"You must have known that you were as good as stealing the fiddle?—that it must have had an owner?" I sternly pursued.

"I said that at the time, and advised the maister to adverteese it in the papers, but he only laughed, and said he would tak' a' the risk."

"Can this Mr Thompson who bought the case be found now?"

"Naething easier, sir," the man readily returned. "The farm's no a mile off."

I began to see the end of my task now, and, with the old ploughman to lead the way, at once drove to the Mains and was introduced to Mr Thompson. The fiddle case was at once produced, and then I smiled as I discovered on the top of the lid a square indentation and two rivet holes, which had evidently at one time contained a brass name-plate. With little difficulty I got the fiddle case away with me, and drove back to Edinburgh, where it was identified by the widow at a glance as that of her husband's lost instrument.

I now had the whole case traced out to its core, and lying clear as a written history before me, but as there was only one fiddle to give away among the claimants, it will be seen that the task before us was not only difficult, but almost certain to bring upon us the dissatisfaction of some of the so-called owners.

While I had been investigating, Mackintosh, thoroughly frightened, had sent a draft for £40 to Cleffton, asking him to return the fiddle at his leisure and say no more about it; but when he was set at liberty he had the doubtful satisfaction of finding that he had lost both the money and the fiddle. I waited patiently to see if the box at Linlithgow would be called for, but evidently the senders had become alarmed, for they never turned up. I then tried to ascertain from Mr Turner's servants if a man like the sham coachman had been seen about that gentleman's house, but they were too wary for me, and denied it point blank. I then turned to Mr Turner himself, and, hinting in no measured terms that he was the prime mover in the robbery, *commanded* him to pay over to the Infirmary the sum of £20, which the grasping villain very reluctantly but abjectly consented to do.

There now remained but the two rival owners to deal with, and I am certain the case would have gone to the Court of Session but for a thought which struck me when Cleffton was one day arguing his view of the case to me.

"You gave £40 for the fiddle, and thought it well worth the money," I said. "How much do you really think the fiddle is worth?—I mean privately, between ourselves."

"It would be cheap at £400," he said with a sigh. "I should never have sold it for that."

"Then I'll tell you what to do," was my prompt rejoinder. "The widow to whom the fiddle undoubtedly belongs never speaks of it as worth more than £50, she has no use for the fiddle herself, and would doubtless be glad of the money. Go to her and offer her £50 for it, and that, according to your own confession, will be £350 below its value."

"Hang it! I never thought of that! I'll try it," he exclaimed, "though I'm afraid even fifty pounds will not buy it, and I don't know how on earth I'm to raise more."

"Perhaps you'll get it for less," I hopefully suggested, but I was mistaken. The value of the fiddle had risen in the widow's estimation, but in a day or two Cleffton came back with a carefully-worded receipt, penned by his own lawyer, and empowering us to hand him the Cremona, which he had bought from the widow for £65. When the fiddle was placed in his hands he fairly hugged it, and kissed it as fervently as I have seen mothers embrace their lost children. I smiled pityingly at the spectacle, but perhaps he would have done the same had he seen the mothers getting back their idols. We are good at pitying each other.

THE SPIDER AND THE SPIDER-KILLER.

In some of the isles of the Pacific, I have been told, it is not uncommon for a spider, while in the act of seizing and sucking the heart's blood of a tender and juicy fly, to be himself pounced upon by a larger insect peculiar to the clime, having as keen a zest for raw spider as the spider has for fresh fly. Nature repeats itself in all its grades and conditions. Human spiders abound among my "bairns," but then fortunately the spider-devourer occasionally crops up in the same class.

In passing through one of the fashionable crescents down in the New Town, one day about noon, on some business which admitted of little delay, I was a little surprised to see one of the most cunning rogues within my ken ascend the steps of a big main-door house, and ring the bell as coolly as if the residence had been his own. Peter Hart was an exceedingly cautious rascal who could never be caught napping, or booked for anything like the sentence he deserved, from the fact that he never personally conducted any operation which he could conveniently transfer to a "cat's paw."

That was the man whom I saw ascend the steps of that fine residence. What was the villain after there? My business was urgent, but the effrontery of the knave pointed so clearly to some carefully-planned crime that I instinctively slackened my pace to watch if he should enter the house. Unfortunately I had been almost upon him before aware of his identity, and these quiet crescents are almost deserted by day, so there was no opportunity for concealment before his quick eyes, ever on the alert, had turned round and taken in the position at a glance. Peter's impression probably was, that I had been following him all the way from his house in James' Square. He might have known me better. Had the meeting been anything but a purely accidental one, I should never have allowed him to get a glimpse of me, more especially at that critical moment.

I fully expected Peter to cave in at the first glimpse of me, and slink off from the house at his smartest; but, to my surprise, he only bestowed upon me a patronising wink and a confident grin, and stood still to await the answering of his ring. His coolness did not seem to me that of sheer impudence or audacity. It seemed to be boastful and exultant—as much as if he had said, "Ah, Jamie, what a lot of trouble you have had for nothing. Here I am safe from you; just try me and see."

There was something irritating in the challenge, although it was given only by a look, and, in spite of my anxiety to get away, I determined to wait a little, and possibly do the very thing he defied me to attempt. I therefore only passed on slowly, far enough to hear the door opened, then I turned, never expecting to see him admitted. The cunning rascal was watching me all the time, and possibly guessing my thoughts, for when I looked round he was being admitted by the smart servant maid, and in the act of disappearing favoured me with another exulting grin and wink, which said as plainly as words could have done, "Sold for once, Jamie."

I did not believe it, and determined to let all other business stand that I might see the end of this adventure. With this object I loitered about, never within sight of the windows of the house, yet always having my eyes on the front door till Peter reappeared. There was no name on the door of the house he had entered, but by questioning a servant who passed I learned that the occupant or owner was an independent gentleman named Matthew Bannister, who had taken some degrees at college, and was a kind of *savant* in his way, having published some works on chemistry. The gentleman was well known to me by reputation, and the moment his name was mentioned I decided that Peter Hart's visit to the house could have no connection with him. Mr Bannister had a young and beautiful wife, who had bestowed not only herself and her love upon the somewhat elderly gentleman, but a fortune as well; but she came of a high family, and I as emphatically decided that Peter's visit could have no connection with her. There then remained only the servants, and, knowing Peter's reputation and his modes of working, I quickly decided that he was in collusion with some of them, and working out some scheme entirely unknown to their employers.

Peter did not remain long in the house—possibly ten minutes at the most; and when he did appear I thought best to be out of sight. To my surprise he had no bundle or trace of one about him: nor did his person appear more bulky than when he had entered. He looked carefully around in every direction—for me, of course—and, apparently slightly relieved at seeing no one, started off in the direction he had come. He made his way by Broughton Street to Greenside, where he entered a favourite public-house. Not two minutes later the pot-boy came out with something like a bank note in his hand, and, knowing the boy well, I stopped to make inquiries for Peter.

"Where are you running to now?" I carelessly asked, not wishing to be too sudden in my questions.

"To get change for a £5 note," he smartly answered, with a peculiar wink, at the same time opening the crisp note for my inspection. "We've lots of change, but it's aye safer to try a big note outside."

I examined the note carefully, and found it to be perfectly genuine.

"You might have risked it with that one," I said at last, handing it back. "Who offered it?"

"Ah, that's just it," said the quick-witted boy; "even a good note isn't quite safe from him; it was Peter Hart. You'll know *him* I daresay?"

"Oh, indeed!" I cried with a start, and a thrill of satisfaction. "He offered this to be changed, did he? Then you needn't bother going any further with it. I particularly want to see Peter."

The pot-boy was quite accustomed to such events, and did not seem surprised. We entered the shop together, and the boy conducted me to the box in which sat Peter. I had in my hand the £5 note. Peter had in his a glass of brandy, which he was in the act of raising with manifest gusto to his lips. He was transfixed in the act, more by anger, it seemed to me, than fear.

"This is yours, isn't it?" I said pleasantly, whereupon he scowled most malignantly. My "bairns" take pleasantry very badly from me.

"Yes, it's mine," he said with an oath at me, which, being quite undeserved, need not be put down. "What do you want with it? It's good enough, isn't it?"

"I believe so. Where did you get it?"

"What's that to you?" was the bullying reply.

I folded up the note and put it into my pocket, and then produced my handcuffs.

"Everything in the world," I replied. "You must either answer that to me or put on these before answering it to the Fiscal."

Slightly disconcerted, but still defiant, he thought for a moment, and then said—

"Well, I got it from a gentleman—a friend of mine I was a-calling on this morning."

"His name?"

"Mr Bannister," he sullenly responded, after another pause.

"I believe you!" I returned with marked scepticism. "You had better say no more, for you'll have to go with me."

Peter lost his temper, and said he would see me very much altered first, but he didn't. He was foolish enough to resist, so I got another man, and after much kicking and struggling on Peter's part we landed him at the Central Office. This resistance on Peter's part seemed so utterly unlike him—his usual conduct being cheerful and polite to an irritating degree—that I rashly considered that for once I had caught him napping, and that by the merest accident.

At the office I stated all the facts, how I had seen Peter entering the house of Mr Bannister, and watched him leaving it, and knowing his character and antecedents had followed him and arrested him passing a £5 note, for the possession of which he could not properly account. Peter, on being searched, was found to have in his possession other £5, in one pound notes, thus clearly proving that the changing of the large note had been a matter of choice or policy, not necessity. To the Fiscal, however, he boldly declared that he had got all the money in way of business from his very good friend Mr Bannister, and he was put in the cells till I should go over to that gentleman to make inquiries. What the "business" was for which he had been paid ten pounds he refused to state, and I concluded that that business existed only in Peter's imagination.

When I reached the house and was shown in, the impression I had formed was strengthened. Everything in the place seemed so stately and grand that I could not conceive how the possessor could be beholden to such a crime-stained wretch as Peter Hart. Mr Bannister at length appeared, and accompanied by his amiable young wife. I studied their faces closely as they entered, and it struck me that that of the husband was careworn, fearful, and anxiously watchful in expression; that of the young wife looked tenderly solicitous, and somewhat saddened and subdued.

"I have called about rather an awkward business," I at length said, not knowing very well how to begin. "My name is James McGovan, and I am connected with the detective staff——"

I would have proceeded to say that I had watched and arrested Peter as already described, but I was at that juncture interrupted in a manner altogether unexpected. The gentleman who had an appearance at once refined and dignified, started back at the mention of my name, with his face as suddenly changed to a deadly and anguished expression as if he had been at the moment stabbed to the heart. He seemed ready to drop to the floor in his pitiable agony, and his wife saw the change even before my eye had taken it in.

"O Matthew! dearest!" she cried, starting forward, with her own face flashing almost as white as his own. "What is wrong? What is to happen to you?"

I scarcely caught his answer, it was so huskily spoken, but it seemed to me something like—

"The very worst that could happen to me."

Then the young wife gave a low moan, and fell slowly forward in his arms. She had fainted, and her very helplessness, I believe, was all that kept him in his senses.

Mr Bannister rang for a servant, and had his wife removed, and then with a blanched face turned to me and said—

"Now, sir, I am ready to attend to you. Will you state your business with me?"

"A man named Peter Hart entered your house this morning, and shortly after left, having in his possession £10 in bank notes, which he declared had been given him by you. Is that actually the case?"

I had expected Mr Bannister's face to lighten up and express astonishment as I proceeded, but instead it became darker and more troubled.

"Why do you ask?" he at length answered in a helpless tone.

"Because we know him to be a daring criminal, and suspect that the money was obtained by robbery, and possibly without your knowledge."

"Is that all that brought you here?" he demanded, with a look of intense relief. "Did he make no other statement of any kind?"

"None except that we could refer the matter to you for confirmation of his statement, and for that purpose I have called."

"Oh, if that is all," he readily answered, looking now positively radiant, "I can readily relieve your anxiety. I did pay him the money, freely and willingly, for work done."

"For work done!" I echoed, a good deal staggered, and thoroughly puzzled. "Have you any objection to say what kind of work it was?"

"I have. It is not necessary to go into details," he coldly returned.

"You are aware, then, of the character of the man you have employed?" I continued, with undisguised disappointment.

"I believe him to be a scoundrel," he faintly and somewhat wearily answered. "I know nothing of his private character, and care less."

"Then we are to conclude that we have made a mistake in arresting him, and that we have no just cause for detaining him?" I pursued, trying in vain to read in his face the real secret.

"Exactly. You have made a mistake, but it was a natural one on your part, seeing, as you say, that the man is a professional criminal," he dejectedly responded. "By the way," he added, with more animation, "I wonder that a man like you does not lay such a rascal by the heels. Is he too clever for even you?"

"That remains to be seen," I dryly returned. "He will not be at liberty a moment longer than I can help."

"I am glad to hear you say that," said the gentleman, shaking me warmly by the hand. "When you do get him, and ensure his conviction, come to me and I will put a £5 note in your hand as an honorarium."

"Honour among thieves!" was my contemptuous thought. "There is some bond of villainy between the two, and now this man wishes to get rid of his leech. I wonder if I could not take them both?"

I left the house, after bidding Mr Bannister a not over-gracious farewell, and Peter Hart was promptly set at liberty, with much crowing and exultation on his part. The next day or two I spent chiefly in trying to guess at the nature of the hold which Peter exercised over the gentleman. That he was the spider and Mr Bannister the fly, I felt certain after making some inquiries regarding the character of the latter. Mr Bannister was spoken of by all as the soul of honour and goodness. I was more than disappointed at losing Peter—I was angry; for in leaving he did not scruple to say some nasty things regarding my capacity, and to hint in a lordly fashion that any other attempt to interfere with him would be followed by a letter "from his lawyer." I replied, in the irritation of the moment, that I should probably interfere with him before long in such a way that his lawyer would be powerless to help him or injure us. I ought not to have spoken so rashly, but then I felt savage, and, as good luck would have it, the very boldness of the threat added to my reputation when the spider-devourer had adjusted things nicely to my hands. Thus many of us live—continually tottering between a great success and a great failure. To the spider-devourer I now come, though, of course, I did not at first recognise him in that character.

Not many days after Peter's release I was accosted at the head of Leith Walk by a sharp-witted fellow, pretty well known to me, named Dick McQueen. Dick was not a thief, but one who lived chiefly by billiards and cards. He had been ostler, waiter, boots, groom, cabdriver, and I know not all what by turns, and was about as keen a blade as it is possible to become by continually rubbing edges with others as sharp. He was always poor, and I think was partly supported by relatives at a distance.

"I believe you said you'd take Peter Hart before long," he said to me, after some of that preliminary talk which conjurers and men of the world use to throw one off his guard.

"Did I?" was my careless reply.

"You'll never do it single-handed," he darkly continued, "but if you could make it worth my while I'm ready to give you the straight tip, which will book him for twenty years."

"What do you mean?"

"Twenty years to him is surely worth as many pounds to me?" he suggestively returned.

"Perhaps, but I'm not in a position to offer anything; indeed, I'd much rather do the work myself."

"You can't, for Peter's got a gent at his back who'll stand any amount of bleeding, and he doesn't need to put out a hand now. Now, if you could only help me to find out who that gent is, I believe he'd stand a poney to get rid of Peter."

I watched Dick's face keenly for some moments in silence.

"You don't know who the gent is, then?" I said at last, suspiciously.

"No; I've tried hard to find out, and I've watched Peter all over the town to no purpose. He's too blessed fly for me."

"Have you any idea what hold Peter has upon the gent?" I asked, after a pause to think.

Dick bestowed upon me one of the most superlatively cunning winks that humanity could create.

"I've an idea," he curtly answered.

"Well, what is its nature?"

"Look here, McGovan, you're a detective, and pretty fly, but you don't come it over me so easy," he retorted sharply, but without any anger. "I'll swop secrets with you, there! Nothing could be fairer, could it? You find out the gent's name and address and gi' me them, and then I'll tell you what hold Peter has on him."

"Is it anything in connection with that hold which is to book Peter for twenty years," I quietly continued.

"Oh, no; that's a different affair altogether—a job Peter did years ago down in Sunderland. I was there at the time, and know all about it, and I'm the only one who has the real tip in his hands."

"Why are you so anxious to get rid of Peter?" I presently inquired. "Have you quarrelled?"

"No, not exactly, but Peter cheated me out of half-a-crown months ago, and I've never forgotten it, nor never will."

Half-a-crown! fancy a man being threatened with twenty years' entombment—probably the whole term of his life—through cheating a companion out of a miserable half-crown! If Peter had only known that a spider-devourer was on his track, would he not have hastened to place a whole heap of half-crowns at his enemy's disposal, and have abjectly craved his pardon as well?

I took the proposal of Dick to *avizandum*; and shortly decided to let him have the desired information. I had first paid a visit to Mr Bannister, and found him not only willing but eager to pay twenty pounds to any one who would give such information as would lead to Peter's incarceration, conditionally, of course, that his name did not appear in the case. I made no conditions, but allowed Dick to settle his own terms. Before I gave him Mr Bannister's name and address, I insisted on being told what hold Peter had on that gentleman, when Dick readily answered—

"Do you know Bell Diamond—she who's said to be Peter's sister, though her name's different? Well, I don't know all the outs and ins of it, but Bell is said to be that gent's real and lawful wife."

"Never!"

"A fact, I believe. Peter's got all the papers somewhere to prove it. They were married quite young—twenty years ago, at least—when Bell wasn't such a harridan as she looks now."

The moment this information was tendered I regretted my compact. What though I sent Dick to Mr Bannister, and the money were cheerfully paid, if the arrest and imprisonment of the gentleman himself on a charge of bigamy followed? The very execution of my duty would then look, in the eyes of those most interested, an act of the deepest treachery. There was no going back, however, and I could only hope that Dick had been misled or mistaken. The same afternoon Dick appeared at the office, and gave minute details of a daring forgery case in which Peter Hart had been engaged years before. The facts were so striking that we were for a time doubtful of their reality, and telegraphed south for information. The answer put at rest every doubt. Two men had been tried and convicted in connection with the affair, but they were mere tools, and the principal had escaped. That man was said to be Peter Hart, changed only in name; and an officer able to identify the real culprit was on his way to Edinburgh when the reply had been despatched.

So far Dick's information seemed valuable and accurate, and with the greatest alacrity and delight I went for Peter Hart, whom I found sitting at his ease in his inn—the same public-house in which the former arrest had taken place.

He returned my salutation rather sternly and haughtily, and resumed his game with the air of a man who was certain to be the last to be "wanted" by me.

"I'm waiting on *you*, Peter," I at length pointedly remarked.

"Oh, you are, are you?" he snappishly and defiantly answered, jumping up with the greatest readiness. "Perhaps you'll take me to the office and lock me up as you did before, and risk me bringing an action of damages against you and the rest of 'em? Perhaps you'll be kind enough to call in a policeman to hit me over the head and arms like as he did the last time, eh?" and after this scathing and satirical outburst he paused for breath, to pose grandly before his friends, thinking doubtless that he had quite cowed and overawed me.

"There is a man at the door," I quietly answered, bringing out my bracelets, "but he won't need to hit you over the head unless you act as foolishly as you did the last time. You're not afraid of these!"

"Afraid of them? Not me. I want them on—I want them on badly. See, I'll put them on myself. Now take me away, and abuse me, and lock me up, and then take the consequences!"

Delighted to find that his facetious mood made him so pliant, I obeyed him in every particular, and Peter's exultant smile only faded when the first two or three questions had been put to him at the office. The moment "Sunderland" was mentioned his jaw fell, and he fixed upon me a look of hatred most flattering and pleasing to me. On searching the lining of Peter's coat we came upon a flat packet of papers. There were some six or seven letters, and a properly authenticated certificate of marriage, all proving that Isabella Diamond had been courted and married some twenty years before by Matthew Bannister. Peter's rage had been working up during the search, and he now shouted out that he knew who had set that "bloodhound," as he was pleased to name myself, on his track, and after a burst of the most awful language, he wound up by accusing Mr Bannister of having two wives living, and commanding us to go and arrest the gentleman as smartly as we had arrested the rogue.

When the papers had been discovered I fully expected to have that disagreeable task to perform. The whole case seemed clear and the proof positive to my mind, for I had seen the working of the hidden springs from the first. But the law has certain forms of its own; and I was sent first to Bell Diamond herself, who was the proper person to make the charge. To my surprise, though she gave vent to rage and vituperation over the capture of Peter, she most positively refused to charge Mr Bannister with bigamy; nay in the very face of the discovered papers she swore most positively that she had never been married in her life, and had never spoken to Mr Bannister. My firm conviction, upon hearing this extraordinary denial, was that Bell had a spark of generosity in her breast, low as she had fallen, and wished to save the man who had once loved her from the ignominy of a prison; but in that I was very far mistaken. Bell was actuated by a very different motive—a desire to get well out of an awkward plight and a very threatening complication. The secret was partly laid bare by referring to Mr Bannister, but it was not wholly made clear till long after.

Mr Bannister had really married a girl named Isabella Diamond, who drifted away from him and was lost sight of. That lost wife, after sinking lower and lower, died in a lodging-house in Glasgow, in which Peter Hart and his sister at that time lived. Nelly Hart was in trouble and likely to be taken, and the name of the dead woman was boldly given in as Helen Hart, while the living owner took the name of Bell Diamond, as well as the papers left by her, and vanished in the direction of Edinburgh. There they remained for some time, till, by merest accident, they discovered that Mr Bannister was newly married, and conceived the plan of frightening him into paying black mail, under the idea that his lost wife was still alive.

Where there is real love there is always perfect trust, and Mr Bannister had confided the whole story of his life to the devoted girl who had laid her all at his feet; and it was that knowledge and the idea that she was to be torn from him for ever which had caused her terrible agitation and swoon on the occasion of my first visit to the house.

Peter Hart duly received his sentence of twenty years, and Dick McQueen, the spider-killer, as I may name him, was avenged of his half-crown.

THE SPOILT PHOTOGRAPH.

The photographer had put up a rickety erection in shape of a tent close to the grand stand at Musselburgh race-course. He was a travelling portrait-taker, and his "saloon" was a portable one, consisting of four sticks for the corners and a bit of thin cotton to sling round them. There was no roof, partly from poverty and partly to let in more light. It was the first day of the races, and masses of people had been coming into the place by every train and available conveyance.

The photographer's name was Peter Turnbull—a tall, lanky fellow, like an overgrown boy who had never got his appetite satisfied. He was clad in the shabbiest of clothes, but talked with the stately dignity of an emperor or a decayed actor. In spite of the gay crowds pressing past outside, business did not come very fast to Turnbull, so, after waiting patiently inside like a spider for flies, he issued from his den and tried to force a little trade with his persuasive tongue.

In front of his tent he had slung up a case of the best photographs he could pick up for money, which were likely to pass for his own, and occasionally some of those bent on pleasure paused to look at the specimens, when Turnbull at once tackled them to give him an order. Women he invariably asked to have their "beautiful" faces taken; men, who are not accustomed to be called beautiful, or to think themselves so, he manipulated in a different fashion. He appealed to them as to whether they hadn't a mother who would like a portrait of them always beside her, or a sweetheart who would value it above a mountain of diamonds. Turnbull's appearance was against him—he looked hungry down to the very toes of his boots—and most of those he addressed were as suspicious of his eloquence as of that of a book canvasser.

At length, however, he did get a man to listen to him—a sailor, evidently, with a jovial, happy look about his face, and plenty of money in his pocket.

"You'll be just off your ship, I suppose, you're looking so fresh and smart," said Turnbull at a venture. "Your sweetheart will be pleased to see you, but she'd be more pleased if you brought her a good portrait to leave with her."

The sailor laughed heartily.

"Sweetheart?" he echoed between his convulsions of merriment. "Why, I'm a married man."

"So much the better," returned the photographer, not to be daunted. "She'll want your portrait exactly as you stand—not as you were before this voyage, or when you were courting her. Folks' faces change so soon."

"Maybe they do, but their hearts remain the same," returned the sailor cheerily.

"Well, not always—they change, too, sometimes," said Turnbull, with the air of one who had bitterly experienced the truth of his words; "but with your portrait always beside her, her heart couldn't change. Just step in—I won't keep you a moment, and you can take it with you. You'll have it, and she'll have it, long after the races are forgotten."

The sailor easily yielded, and followed him into the tent, and then Turnbull, having now a professional interest in the man, took notice of his dress and appearance particularly for the first time. The man was low in stature, thick set, and evidently a powerful fellow. He wore an ordinary sailor's suit of dark blue, but had for a neckerchief a red cotton handkerchief loosely rolled together, and so carelessly tied that the ends hung down over his breast.

In order to get all the sailor's face into the portrait, Turnbull with some difficulty persuaded him to remove his cap, and then drew from him an admission that his objection arose from the fact that there was a flesh mark on one side of his forehead which he did not wish to appear in the portrait. The difficulty was got over—as it was with Hannibal—by taking a side-view, and the first attempt came out all right, so far as the portrait was concerned. But the sailor wished to appear as if he had just removed his cap, and with that in his hand, so the first was put aside as spoilt, and another taken, which, though not so successful, pleased the owner better, as in that the cap appeared in his hand. The portrait was finished and framed, and so free and good-natured was the owner that he insisted on paying for the spoilt one, which, however, he refused to take with him. While Turnbull had been putting a frame on the portrait, the sailor took out a long piece of tobacco and a pocket knife and cut himself a liberal quid, at the same time offering a piece to the photographer, which was accepted. The knife with which the tobacco was cut was a strong one, with a long, straight blade and a sharp point.

The whole transaction over, they bade each other good-day, and the sailor disappeared among the crowds of spectators and betting men on the course with the avowed intention of enjoying himself, and scattering some money before he went home.

Six or seven hours later a man was found lying in one of the narrow back lanes of the town, so inert, and smelling so strongly of drink, that more than one person had passed him under the impression that he was drunk, and without putting out a hand to help. At length the ghastly hue of his face attracted attention, and it was found that he was lying in a pool of blood, which had flowed from two deep wounds in his breast and side, and thence oosed out at the back of his clothes on the ground below.

Some of the crowd who gathered about him as he was being carried to a house close by identified him as a baker named Colin McCulloch, belonging to a town some miles off, but who was well known in a wide district from the fact that he went about with a bread van. He was not quite dead when found, but an examination of his wounds soon indicated that life was ebbing away.

One of these was as deep as the doctor's finger could reach, and appeared to have been inflicted with the narrow, straight blade of a long, sharp-pointed knife.

I had been on the race-course for the greater part of the day looking for a man who did not turn up, and heard of the occurrence only when I called at the station before leaving for town. It had been decided that McCulloch was not fit to be removed, and I went to see him, but found him far beyond speech or explanation. By visiting the spot on which he had been found I discovered a girl who gave me the first clue.

She had been passing along the lane, and had been "feared" as she expressed it, to pass McCulloch, who was tottering along in the same direction, very drunk and demonstrative, though all alone. Every one was away at the races, and the narrow lane seemed quite deserted, but there appeared in front a sailor, who had no sooner sighted McCulloch than he began quarrelling with him and threatening him. Thankful of the opportunity, the girl slipped past during the quarrel, having just time to notice that the sailor was a short, thick-set fellow, and that he wore a red cotton handkerchief for a necktie. When she was at a safe distance she chanced to look back, and saw the sailor give McCulloch "a drive in the breast," and so knock him down. She did not wait to see anything more, but hurried home, thinking that it was only an ordinary drunken quarrel.

Questioned by me, she could not say whether the sailor had used a knife. Her idea was that he had only given the man a drive with his hand to knock him down or get him out of the way. The sailor spoke in a low tone; McCulloch was noisy and defiant. She saw no knife in the sailor's hand, and was sure he was a stranger. She did not think she would know him again, as she did not look at his face, but she knew every one about the town, and was positive that the sailor did not belong to the place. It was the sailor who stopped McCulloch, whom he seemed to know; and she thought he was quite sober, though pale and angry-looking. "Look me in the face and say it's not true," were the only words she could remember hearing, and they were spoken in a fierce tone by the sailor, just as she was getting beyond earshot.

Having thus a little to work upon, I tried all the exits of the town for some trace of him, without success. He had not gone away by rail or coach, and no one had seen him leave on foot, so far as I could discover; but that was to be expected in the state of the town. Dozens of sailors with red neckties might have come and gone and never been noticed in such a stir. In the town itself I was more successful. To my surprise I found that a man answering the description had visited nearly every public-house in the place. He had never spoken or called for drink; he had merely looked through the houses in a pallid, excited manner, and gone his way.

"He seemed to be looking for some one," a publican said to me, "but he was gone before I could ask him."

I spent a good deal of time in the place, though not sure that if I got that man I should be getting the murderer, and returned to Edinburgh with the last train. I went back again next morning, and found McCulloch still alive, and sensible enough to be able to give an assent or dissent when asked a question. But about the murderous attack upon himself he could not or would not give a sign. He would only stare, or shut his eyes, or turn away. The doctor thought he did not understand me—that the patient's head was not yet quite clear; I thought quite the reverse. The same curious circumstance occurred when it was suggested that his deposition should be taken. McCulloch had no deposition to make, or would not make one. He seemed quite prepared to die and give no sign.

Not an hour later I was favoured with a visit from Turnbull, the travelling photographer. He had been lodging in the town, and of course had heard of the strange crime. He had heard also of my unsuccessful hunt for the sailor, and would probably have gone up to Edinburgh to see me had he not been loth to lose another day at the race-course, his stance being taken for three days.

I could not conceive what the lank, hungry-looking being could want with me, or why there should be about his lean jaws such a smirk of intense satisfaction, as he gave his name and occupation.

"A murder has been committed—or what is as good as a murder, for the man, I believe, is at his last gasp," he exultingly began. "There will be a hanging match—that is, if you can trace and capture the murderer. Now, Mr McGovan, you're said to be clever, but you haven't got him yet, and never will unless you get my help."

"Your help?" I echoed in amazement; "why, who are you, and how can you help me?"

"My name you know, and I am not unknown to fame, I am an actor as well as a photographic artist. I have trod the boards with some success, and you know that that in itself is a kind of training in acuteness eminently fitting one for detective work."

I could not see it, and said so. I thought him an escaped lunatic.

"Mark me, Mr McGovan," he continued, quite unabashed, "I have in my possession the only means whereby you can trace and arrest the murderer. Now just tell me what it is worth, and we may come to a bargain."

"What it is worth?" I said, with a grin. "I don't know that it is worth anything till I try it."

"A hundred pounds? Surely they'll offer that as a reward for such information as shall lead to the capture of the murderer?"

"I don't know that they'll offer a hundred pence," was my reply. "Tell me what you know, and if it is of any use I will see that you are suitably rewarded."

"Ah, that won't suit me," he answered with great decision. "I will leave you to think over my offer; you know where to find me when you have made up your mind."

He was moving off, after making a low and stagey bow, but I got between him and the door, and brought out a pair of handcuffs.

"I know where to find you now, which is far more convenient," I quietly remarked. "You have admitted that you know something of the murder—I shall detain you on suspicion."

"What! arrest me? an innocent man; lock me up in prison!" he exclaimed, in genuine terror. "You cannot—dare not! I know nothing of the murder; I merely think I can put you in the way of tracing the man who did it."

"Do so, then, if you would prove your innocence," I said, rather amused at his terror and dismay. "Were you an accomplice?"

"An accomplice! how can you ask such a question?" he tremblingly answered. "You are taking a mean advantage of me, for I feel sure that my secret is worth a hundred pounds at least. But I will trust to your honour, and put it all before you. People will give *you* all the credit. Everyone will say 'McGovan is the man that can do it; we might have known he wouldn't escape when McGovan was after him.' Nobody will think of me, or hear of me, who have given you the clue. It's the way of the world; one man toils, and ploughs, and sows, and another man reaps the harvest."

"Ah, nothing pleases me so much as envy, flavoured with a little spitefulness," I quietly returned. "It is the most flattering unction you can lay to a man's soul."

"I am not envious," he dolefully replied, "but it is hard to supply another with brains."

"Especially when he has none of his own," I laughingly retorted. "Well, come along; bring on your brains—I'm waiting for them."

"I really believe you are laughing at me in your sleeve," he observed, with a half pathetic look. "It is brave to crush the poor worm under your heel when you know he can't retaliate."

"You're a long worm—six feet at least," I solemnly answered; "a long-winded one, too, unfortunately. I must leave you in the cells for an hour or two——"

"Oh, no! I will speak; I will tell you it all in half a minute," he wildly answered. "The murderer is said to have been a sailor—a short, thick-set fellow, wearing a red neckerchief. I photographed such a man in the forenoon, and I have the first portrait, which didn't please him, though it is like as life."

"Ah! let me see it. Have you it with you?" I cried, with sudden interest and great eagerness.

"Now you change your tune," he reproachfully answered. "I have it with me, or I should not have given in so easily. I was afraid you might have me searched, and, finding the photo, think me an acquaintance or accomplice of the man," and, with a little more wearisome talk, he produced the portrait, and slowly put before me the incidents already recorded.

When he had done I was not greatly elated. The thread which connected his early customer with the man supposed to have attacked McCulloch was of the slenderest. Then I was disappointed that Turnbull's story looked so real. I had fondly hoped he would stumble and prevaricate enough to allow us to lock him up on suspicion—in other words, that we should find him to be an accomplice, anxious to save himself at the expense of a companion in crime. I took the photograph, but plainly told him that I feared it would be of little use to me.

"Ah, you wish to undervalue it in order to get out of paying me a good round sum when the man is caught," he answered, with a knowing wink. "I haven't knocked about so much without being able to see through that dodge," and away he went, as elated and consequential as if he had really laid the man by the heels.

When I was alone I had a long study over the notes I had taken during the interview. The sailor photographed had stated that his ship only got in the day before, and that he was on his way home, and merely visiting the race-course in passing. He had not said where he lived or at what port he had come in, but the general impression left on Turnbull's mind was that the port was not far off. Leith or Granton seemed to me the likeliest places, and I turned to the shipping lists to have a look at the names of new arrivals. At Leith only one vessel had come in on that day, The Shannon; and at Granton, though there were several arrivals, none of them were from long voyages. The sailor had hinted that he had not been home for eighteen months, and that to my mind implied a long voyage, or long voyages.

To Leith accordingly I went, and found The Shannon, her cargo already discharged, and only a few of the men on board. Some had been paid off and some were off for a few days on leave. The man whom I questioned—for the captain had gone home too—seemed to me sullen and suspicious. He did not know if one of the men had gone eastwards to see his wife; if any of them lived in that quarter he had never heard of it, and so on. I was dissatisfied with the answers and the man's manner, and had he resembled in the slightest degree the portrait in my pocket I should have arrested him on the spot. I thought I would bring out the photograph as a test. Holding it up before him, I said sharply—

"Do you know that man?"

"No, I don't." The answer came out almost before he had time to look at the features. It was too prompt. It was a lie. The falsehood told me more than the truth would have done. It not only convinced me that I was at least on the track of the photographed sailor, but roused in my mind for the first time a strong suspicion that he was the knifer of McCulloch. I went from the ship to the shipping agents. I found the clerk who had handed their pay to all the men; and on producing the photograph saw that he recognised it instantly.

"Yes, that was one of them," he said, "but he was paid off, and has gone home."

I asked the man's name, and, on referring to the books, he gave it as Tom Fisher. With some difficulty he got me the man's address—which was in a town some miles east—and his trouble arose from the fact that no money had been sent to Fisher's wife for nearly a year.

The sailors' wives often drew one half the men's pay, but she had not applied for it during that time, and was supposed to have changed her address.

"I didn't say anything of it to Fisher," said the clerk in conclusion, "and he seemed quite elated at having so much money to draw. It's a kittle thing interfering between a man and his wife, and it might have alarmed him needlessly. If there's anything wrong he's best to find it out himself."

I left the shipping office, and took the first train for the town in which Fisher had his home. If he was to be found anywhere, I thought it would be there—and especially so if he turned out to be innocent. It is a quiet country place in which everyone knows his neighbours, and I had no difficulty in finding the house. But it was occupied by an old woman, who said she had been in it for nearly a year. I asked for Mrs Fisher, the sailor's wife.

"Oh, she was a bad lot," was the blunt rejoinder. "She sellt a' her things, bit by bit, and gaed awa' in the end withoot paying her rent and other debts."

"Where did she go to, do you know?"

"Oh, dear kens. She was a drunken hussy, and thought hersel' bonny. Some say that she went awa' wi' a baker-man they ca' McCulloch, and was aboot Leith for a while, but maybe it's no true. He used to hae a great wark wi' her."

"And her husband—has he never been here?"

"Never since I cam'; but I heard that McCulloch was stabbed at the races by a sailor and I wadna wonder if that sailor turned oot to be Fisher himsel'."

I thought the old woman the most acute I had met for a while; we always do when we find a person's thoughts and opinions tallying with our own. I left the house and pursued my inquiries elsewhere. I found no one who had seen Fisher near the town, or in it; but at length there was mentioned to me the name of a man who had been at the races, and had there seen Fisher and spoken to him. This man I found out, but he was not nearly so communicative to me as he had been to others. He admitted that he had seen Fisher and spoken to him, but couldn't remember what they had talked of. He knew McCulloch also, and had seen him at the races, too, but in a drunken condition, and not fit for conversation. Questioned more closely, he admitted that Fisher was an old friend of his, and that the last thing in the world he would wish for would be to do Fisher any injury by what he should say. He had heard of the stabbing of McCulloch, and did not wonder at it, the man was so quarrelsome, but he had no idea who had done it. Fisher might have done it, or anybody else— he knew nothing about it, as he was out of the place two hours at least before the attack was made.

I could read the man as plainly as if he had spoken all he knew. There was the same reticence which the sailor had shown on board The Shannon, and it probably arose from the same cause—a desire to screen and save a friend. I got back to Leith, and found with some relief that no vessel of importance had left during the two days; I then tried Granton with the same result. "Glasgow" then rose promptly in my mind, and I drove to both the Edinburgh railway stations to make inquiries. At neither had any person resembling the photograph been seen, but a telegram to one of the stations a mile or two from the city elicited the news that a man in sailor's dress had taken a third class ticket thence to Glasgow. He had driven out to that station in a cab, and the cab had come from the direction of Edinburgh. I telegraphed to Glasgow, and followed my message by the first train. When I got to that city I found my work nearly all done for me. Fisher had been traced to an American liner, in which he had shipped under the name of George Fullerton.

Strange fatality! George Fullerton was the name of the man who had seen him at the races, and so clumsily tried to screen him from me. The vessel in which he had shipped was gone—it had sailed the night before—but there was a chance of it stopping at Liverpool. I telegraphed thither and took the night mail, in case the vessel should touch, but the weather had proved too stormy, and she held on her course. Being so far on the way, and now perfectly sure of my man, I did not dream of turning back, but took passage for New York in a fast liner, which would easily have outstripped that in which the fugitive had got the start, but for one or two unforeseen accidents on the way, which added three days to the length of the passage. When we landed, the vessel in which "George Fullerton" had sailed was in the harbour, and my man gone. He was described to me by one of the sailors as depressed and sullen, but singularly free with his money. He had been taken on at the last moment in place of a man who had failed to appear, and so, instead of working his passage, had received full pay. On landing he had treated several of his mates liberally, and had seemed bent on nothing but getting rid of his money.

"I believe I could find him for you," said the man at last, and I readily accepted the offer.

We made our way to a tavern near the harbour much frequented by seamen, and there, sitting alone with some drink before him, I found the counter-part of the spoilt photograph. I should have easily recognised him in a crowd, but with a foolhardiness almost incredible, he wore the fatal red neckerchief, which proved to be of silk, not cotton.

I said nothing to my conductor beyond ordering for him a drink at the bar, and then went up and took a seat opposite the red necktie.

"You're a Scotchman, I think?" I said to him at last.

"So are you," he said, a little startled.

"Yes. Long since you left the old country?"

"Long enough," he growled, "and it'll be longer or I go back."

"Nonsense, man," I said, without a smile. "I'm going back by the first ship. Suppose you go back with me?"

"Never!"

The word was accompanied by a deep oath, but I was busy with my hand in my pocket, which came out as he made a gulp at the drink before him, and brought up the barrel of a pistol levelled straight at his eyes.

"Hands up! Tom Fisher," I shouted as he staggered back, and the bystanders came crowding round. "I believe that's the custom of this country, or the right thing to say when two are likely to play at one game. I've come all the way from Edinburgh to arrest you for stabbing Colin McCulloch. My name is McGovan, and I've the warrant in my pocket."

He gave in in the most sheepish and stupefied manner imaginable, and some one was obliging enough to snap my handcuffs on his wrists. I took him away in a *coupé*, and had him locked up till I should get the necessary papers filled up for his conveyance across the Atlantic.

On the passage home we got quite friendly, and he told me the whole story of the attack. He had met George Fullerton, and been told by him of his wife's faithlessness and flight, coupled with McCulloch's name. He was quite frenzied, and went off at once to look for McCulloch, whom Fullerton had seen not long before in the town. He met him at last by chance, and stabbed him twice, meaning to kill him.

When he came to be tried, which was two months later, on account of the state of his victim, he pleaded "Not guilty" by advice, and McCulloch was called as a witness, when, to the astonishment of all, McCulloch declared most positively that he could not remember who stabbed him, but that he had a strong impression that the assailant was *not* the man at the bar.

None looked more astonished than the prisoner, but a moment later he recovered himself and rose to his feet.

"He's telling a lie! I did stab him. I'm guilty, and I'm not sorry. He led away my wife, and she's now on the streets. Ask him if it's not true? That's all I've to say."

McCulloch, when questioned, made some shuffling answers, and was finally ordered out of the box. Then Fisher, in consideration of the peculiar circumstances of the case, and his having been already two months in prison, was sentenced to a month's imprisonment.

I saw him after his release. He was searching for his wife, and had come to me to get my assistance, but we only found her grave.

THE STOLEN DOWRY.

In a public-house in the Saltmarket of Glasgow there had been a leak in a barrel of spirits which stood in a dark corner inside the counter. The whisky was pure and unreduced as it came from the distillery. Before being retailed it would have been mixed with water in certain proportions, according, to the price labelled on the fancy-painted casks ranged along the wall, to which it would have been partly transferred on the day after its arrival. As it happened, however, that particular barrel was not to be sold. An old spigot had got loose during the night, and the pot-boy who opened the shop waded into what he thought was water instead of the thick coating of sawdust generally covering the floor. The shop was dark, and the boy got a stump of candle and lighted it, to have a search into the cause. The smell might have enlightened him. Behind the counter the floor was covered with escaping whisky. The boy crouched down and poked the candle-stump in under the barrel, and at the same moment was burnt by some of the melted grease. His fingers were of most importance to him, and he dropped the candle with a howl. If the whisky had been gunpowder, it could scarcely have put him out of the shop more quickly. There was a blaze and a roar, and then an explosion, and the boy had scarcely reached the opposite side of the street, with more burns than the candle had inflicted, when the whole shop was in flames.

The land of houses above the shop was a high one, and crowded in every flat with families of the poorest. Before these unhappy inmates were well aware of the calamity the flames and smoke had burst through the ceiling of the shop, and into the stair, thus cutting off the only means of escape. Then followed a scene exactly like that which happened in our own Canongate, when a maker of fireworks had his shop blown up about his ears. The terrified inmates gathered at the windows shrieking for help—those in the lower flats being gradually forced upwards by flame and smoke. In a few seconds beds and mattresses began to fly out at the windows of the adjoining houses, and these were held up by the eager and excited crowd below to break the fall of those leaping from the high windows. Some were killed on the spot, many were injured, but a great number were successfully caught, scarcely the worse of the fall. At one of the top windows two women stood in desperation and despair. Though living in the same land, and possibly on the same flat, they were strangers to each other till that moment. One had a child of five clinging to her, white and speechless with terror, and this woman was a poor, hard-working seamstress, a year or two widowed, and having nothing but her needle to depend on for support. The other was Bet Cooper, as bold and irrepressible a thief as ever infested Glasgow.

"We'll have to jump—it's the only chance," said Bet, addressing the terrified dressmaker. Bet was scared and awed herself, but her terror had not the effect, as in the person beside her, of rendering her limbs perfectly powerless.

The poor dressmaker shook her head, and feebly moaned out something about the child clinging to her.

"If my wee Mary was only safe I wadna care for mysel'," she hysterically exclaimed at last.

"Then throw her down—they'll catch her safe enough," said Bet with energy.

"I couldna dae't—ye couldna dae't yoursel' if she was your ain bairn," sobbed the poor mother.

"Then I'll do it for you, if you like?" volunteered Bet.

"Oh, no, no!" screamed the mother, and the child echoed the terrified cry, which was faintly caught and responded to by the anxious crowd watching them and urging them from below.

"Then I'll take her in my arms and jump with her?" said Bet generously. "If I am killed, she'll fall soft on top of me and be saved."

The perfect antipodes of each other in character and training, these two women were for the moment drawn together by the warm humanity which makes the whole world kin. The weaker spirit, the half-fainting dressmaker, clung to the bold thief, and mingled her tears with those of Bet as trustfully as if she had been the purest in the land. It is doubtful if she would have consented even then, but a great cloud of smoke and flames sweeping and roaring in their direction hastened the decision. The child screamed and shrank towards the outstretched arms of Bet, and the mother let her go with an effort.

"You'll take care of her?" she tremulously said, as she kissed the child's white face over and over again.

"I'll take care of her," said Bet, shortly. "Now stand back a bit, and let me jump."

She grasped the clinging child high over her shoulder and sprang into the air, while a sympathising roar from the crowd below greeted the action. Four men were holding aloft one of the beds, and Bet sank into the yielding mass almost as softly as if she had descended only her own height. The child was breathless and a little shaken, but quite sensible. Bet sprang to her feet and waved the rescued child in triumph in the air towards the mother far above, though the ringing cheer rising around must have carried to her the glad tidings even before Bet's cry rang out.

"She's safe! Now jump! jump for your life!" was Bet's eager exclamation. But the mother still clung to the window in powerless terror, and finally motioned to those below that she would try to escape by the roof. Her gesture was not understood at the moment, or a dozen voices would have been raised to warn her that that means had already been tried in vain. The building by that time was filled with smoke, and the unhappy mother had never got farther than the passage leading to the stair landing. Her body was found there, scarcely scorched, with the features calm and placid as in a gentle slumber. Little Mary, the rescued child, when shown the still form, cried out joyfully, "Mother's only sleeping." So she was, but it was that blissful rest which knows no troubled dreams, the last and longest that is sent to weary humanity.

Bet took the child with her for that night. She had no lack of acquaintances to give her shelter, but Mary appeared to be without a friend in the world. Bet was not easily moved, but somehow that last speech of the poor mother, and her appealing gaze as she uttered it, had got imprinted in her memory—"You'll take care of her?" Bet fancied she heard the words still, and determined to keep the child under her own eye till its nearest relatives should be sought out and found. Bet was then comparatively young—still under thirty, but she had never had a child of her own, and it was a queer sensation to her to be treading the streets with that little innocent one's hand so trustfully reposing in her own.

The talk of the child was also different from anything Bet had ever listened to; it actually seemed for the time that Bet was the child, and Mary the woman. With a gentleness quite new to her, Bet tried to explain to Mary that there was a possibility of her mother sleeping on and never waking, an idea which Mary utterly derided, though in the end she said contentedly—

"If mother doesn't wake, you'll be my mother instead?"

"No, no; that would never do," said Bet hurriedly, and with some agitation. "I'm not good enough, and it wouldn't be allowed."

"I think you're *very* good," said Mary, with the air of a judge. "You saved me from the fire. Oh, what a jump it was! Won't you let me sleep with you to-night, and cuddle close in your arms, if mother isn't back?"

Bet wasn't sure, and she mumbled out something to that effect, which Mary chose to take for consent to the arrangement.

They made their way, thus talking and considering, to the house of an acquaintance of Bet—a thief, of course, like herself, and almost as well known. Bet was careful to keep the child apart from her friends, that their strange talk might not reach or contaminate its ears, and early in the evening undressed Mary with her own hands to put her into the bed under the slates which had been appropriated to her use. She tucked the child in very tenderly, and got a hearty kiss for her pains, and was then about to leave the little closet, when Mary called her back with the words—

"But I haven't said my blesses."

"Jerusalem! and what is that?" said Bet, for a moment puzzled.

"Oh, you just sit there, and put your hands together like mine, while I say them like a little angel," said Mary, and to teach her new pupil she illustrated the matter by getting out of the bed-clothes and kneeling beside Bet, clasping her hands and beginning to repeat her prayers. Bet's attitude—expressive more of astonishment than anything—not quite pleasing her, Mary had to stop and place her new friend's hands in the same position as her own; and, that being adjusted, she proceeded—

"God bless mother; bless Bet, my new mother; bless everybody—for amen. Good-night. This night I lay me down to sleep; I give my soul to Christ to keep. If I should die and never wake, I pray the Lord my soul to take. For amen. Good-night. Our Father which art in heaven, hallowed be Thy name. Kingdom come. Thy will be done—earth as 'tis heaven. Give us this day our daily bread. Forgive us our debts, as we forgive those trespass against us. And lead us not into temptation. But deliver us from evil. For amen. Good-night."

Bet was hushed and subdued, and the second kiss which she imprinted on the child's lips was very near being a tearful one. Possibly the simple utterances of the little one had awakened in her breast some memories of her own childhood, long dormant; or perhaps the pure radiance of the child's innocence was showing her the darkness of her own heart and life. At any rate Bet left the little closet very bad company for her friends, and was more than once twitted by them upon her solemnity. Bet had begun to think; but as yet the only tangible idea that came to her out of that whirl was expressed in the words—

"I wish the bairn's friends would not turn up. I think I should like to keep her myself."

Next day inquiry proved that Bet's "bairn" was literally without friends. Her mother had been in receipt of parochial aid on account of the child and her own poverty, and the parochial authorities could prove beyond question that she had been friendless and alone. Under these circumstances the glad wish welled up naturally to Bet's lips—she would take it; she would be a mother to the orphan, and seek help from no parochial board. Alas! Bet forgot in the warmth of her newborn love that all her past life was against her. What kind of guardian for a tender and innocent child was a woman who had spent most of her life in open defiance of the law, when not actually in prison?

The truth only dawned upon Bet when those who had the power evaded her request by saying that they would consider the matter, make inquiries, and let her know. Meantime the child was allowed to remain with Bet, and, as she slowly sauntered home, the thought rose in her mind—

"They'll take her from me; they'll never allow me to keep her. I'm too bad; too well known. They'll ask the police about me, and take her away to-morrow. And they're right. I'm not fit to bring her up—not unless I make a change."

That was the thought which pulled Bet up, and made her pace the streets for hour after hour before returning to her charge. Change!—was it possible for her to change sufficiently to bring up a child to a good and useful life? Bet was afraid that it was not. But then her very boldness and seeming callousness covered a strong will and a passionate nature, which, once roused to love, loved with headstrong impetuosity.

The more imminent the separation from the child seemed, the more Bet longed to keep her, and the result of her long thinking on the plainstones of Glasgow was that she went home to nestle down beside Mary, saying to herself, "I'll try! I'll try, for her sake!"

Her case, however, was desperate, so Bet was awake very early in the morning, and had Mary up and dressed and out into the cool morning air before the bells and steam whistles had begun to call the factory folks and ironworkers from their homes. Bet's intention was to make her way to Edinburgh, but as she was fearful of her destination being suspected, and herself pursued, she took a very different route when leaving the city. She had not a penny in her pocket, and, as a matter of fact, had to beg her way, by a long and circuitous route, to the capital. We were duly informed of her disappearance, and, though there was no special charge against her, we should doubtless very soon have had her in our hands had Bet resumed her own line of business. But this did not happen. Bet, while begging at a farm outside the city, had been told to go and work, and replied that she was willing to do so there and then. This resulted in her being employed on the place for nearly a month. At the end of that time she had a little money to draw, and entered the city to have a struggle for honesty and a new life.

I am afraid that Bet's resolve would have all gone to the wall through the taint of crime and the power of hunger had she not chanced to meet an old prison companion who had been struggling in the same way for some months. This woman not only gave temporary shelter to the wanderers, but introduced Bet to a lady who, with some of her friends, had formed a kind of private prisoners' aid society. Mrs Colbrun—as I shall name her, knowing her aversion to publicity—heard Bet's story, which, probably for the first time in Bet's life, was a truthful one in every detail, and, with many a warning that the new life would be full of hardship and temptation, agreed to give her a start by recommending her among her friends as help in rough house-work. Thus Bet was secured from absolute want, and, as she was a strong-bodied woman and eager to do her best, it was not long before she had a regular round of houses employing her at stated intervals at washing and cleaning, besides occasional jobs from outsiders. During the first few years of this life Bet had many a hard struggle and sore temptation; but then the innocent prattle and loving caresses of Mary made all smooth and endurable. Bet, I should have observed, was by no means a good-looking woman. She had an evil look which was very much against her in her new line. People often employed her with reluctance on that account, and got rid of her as soon as possible, so with all her willingness she was always very poor. Her life was a lonely one, and I have no doubt she often asked herself with bitterness whether the change from her former reckless course was altogether a good one. As Mary grew in years and cleverness, however, and became more of a companion to her protector, her gentle influence gradually asserted itself, and chased many of these clouds from Bet's half-savage mind. When she was just twelve Mary insisted upon being taken from school and set to work, and through Mrs Colbrun was apprenticed to dressmaking in a big establishment in Princes Street. Mary did not grow up a great beauty, but she had a quiet, engaging manner, and an artlessness and simplicity which made her a favourite. She remained in that establishment for six or seven years, by the end of which time the relative positions of Bet and her had changed, for Bet's health had become uncertain, and Mary's wage formed almost their sole support. Mary had forgotten many of the incidents of her youth, but singularly enough, the scene at the fire was imprinted on her memory as vividly as the day after it had occurred. She often spoke of it, and speculated on how different both their lives might have been but for that great calamity. She never really understood Bet's shudder at the thought, for Mary did not know that her second mother had been a thief, and saved from a life of crime by her own innocent prattle. We are all children alike in that respect, and never know a tithe of the good we have done.

At this time came the grand turning-point in Mary's life, for the son of one of the partners of the firm, who acted as cashier, fell in love with the quiet, lady-like Mary Cooper, passing over beauties in dozens to do so, and, after a long course of opposition from his parents, which as usual only strengthened his passion, succeeded in so adjusting matters that Mary consented to become his wife. When the matter was settled Bet looked as if she did not know whether to cry or rejoice, and, I believe, did a little at both.

"How am I ever to fit you to go among such grand folks," she said in manifest distress.

"You have been fitting me all my life," said Mary, with a bright look and a soft embrace, which she had generally found effectual in banishing all objections.

"That's all very well," answered Bet, only half mollified; "but where is your outfit to come from? You must have dresses, and no end of things. Ten or twenty pounds would not be too much. Only think! if you went among them in your poor rags, wouldn't they sneer at you all your life after?"

"I don't know; I never thought of that," was Mary's simple rejoinder, "but so long as Herbert does not sneer at me I shall never care for any one else. He will shield me from all trouble."

"Ay, you're like every one else in love, you see nothing but sunshine before you," dryly returned Bet, "but it's possible that even he would turn round and sneer at your former poverty if I allowed him to provide your outfit, as he offered to do. 'Nothing of the kind,' I said, quite sharp; 'Mary will provide all that herself.' But though I said that to look independent, I can't for the life of me tell where the money's to come from. I have not one pound to rub on another."

"Don't distress yourself about that, mother dear," said Mary, with another nestling kiss; "for if he cannot love me for ever without a paltry dress or two, his love isn't worthy the name. And if his devotion is to change to sneers, all the outfits in the world would not prevent it. So just let the matter rest. I'll take all the risk. He knows we are poor in everything but a good name, so where is the shame?"

Mary thought she had effectually settled the difficulty; but Bet continued to harp on the same theme. It was an awkward position certainly. There was Mary living in a house of one room and a closet, in a not very choice locality, and her affianced in one of the biggest villas in the Grange. The inequality of their positions cropped out painfully whenever he chanced to visit the humble home, and Bet was in such a feverish state of distress over her poverty that she would have made any sacrifice for a little temporary grandeur. As the time drew near when Mary was to leave her for another's care, Bet's uneasiness increased. She had rashly pledged herself to provide Mary's outfit, and was now further from that than ever. It is difficult to analyse her feelings so as to account for all her actions; but I suppose her mind had got into such a morbid state that she was scarcely responsible for her own actions.

At this critical juncture Bet's old friend and adviser, Mrs Colbrun, sent for her and Mary to congratulate them on the approaching event, and make some small present to the bride. What the present was I have no recollection, but it was something which led Mrs Colbrun and Mary to leave the room for a few minutes.

Bet had often been left with the free range of the whole house before with no evil result. In the room in which she was now left there stood a writing table, one drawer of which was open, showing quite a pile of bank notes and other money.

Bet fought valiantly with the temptation till Mrs Colbrun was actually crossing the lobby to re-enter the room, when the old thieving nature struggled uppermost, and Bet, with one swift movement of her hand, had possessed herself of a bunch of the notes, and concealed them with magical celerity about her person.

The remainder of her stay in the house was torture to Bet, not only on account of the fear of discovery, but because she had a conscience, and could not disguise even to herself the dastardly act she had committed in robbing a benefactor.

They got away at last, but Bet was nearly an hour at home before she ventured to bring out the notes, which she did with a shaking hand, telling Mary they were for her marriage outfit, which she had better go and purchase forthwith.

Perhaps it was the tone in which the strange request was made, or the guilty look which accompanied the offer of the money, or possibly sheer astonishment at Bet possessing such a sum, that roused Mary's suspicions; but she had scarcely taken the notes and counted them when a chill thought fell on her heart.

"Where did you get so much money, mother dear?" she tremulously asked. "Did Mrs Colbrun give it you?"

"No, no! ask no questions, but away you go and spend it to the best advantage," hurriedly responded Bet, in a strange voice.

Mary stared at her for a minute, then began to tremble violently, and finally sat down with the notes in her hand, and burst into tears. Thoroughly alarmed, Bet sprang up and tried to soothe the young girl, but the first words which Mary could articulate stabbed her through.

"Mother, dear," she cried, clasping the guilty woman in her arms, and trying in vain to get a clear look into the shrinking eyes, "tell me true and plain. There was a drawer in Mrs Colbrun's room with a pile of bank notes in it. I saw them. You didn't—oh, mother! forgive me for the horrible thought!—but say you didn't take them—steal them—from Mrs Colbrun."

"I didn't" was shaped on Bet's lips, but the words stuck in her throat, and the guilty look on her face, and her abashed attitude as she shrank before the accusing eyes gave the lie to the husky response.

"Oh, mother, how could you?—you have ruined us!" was all Mary could utter, but after an agonised pause she sprang up with startling energy, and said—

"I must take them back! I shall never allow her to be robbed!"

"And send me to prison for ten or twenty years?" cried Bet in reproach. "No; rather throw them into the fire. That will hide all."

"I shall not! Mother, you are mad—you are not in your senses to propose such a thing. It would be robbery just the same, whether we use the notes or not, if we do not restore them. I shall take them back, but try to give them in a way that will not criminate you. Yes, whatever happens, you must be safe."

Mary hurried on her things and left the house, amid the feeble protests of Bet. She had not been out of the place many minutes when I knocked at the door and entered. Mrs Colbrun had missed the notes immediately on the departure of Bet and Mary, and, shocked and indignant, had brought word to the Central. It needed but a word or two regarding Bet's past life to convince me that she was the thief, and I took the address and went there direct. Bet, however, was bold as brass, and denied all knowledge of the notes, and officiously assisted me to search the house for them. I left her at last baffled, but not convinced, and made my way to Mrs Colbrun's for consultation and advice. It was nearly dark when I reached the place, which was at the outskirts of the city, and on a very dark and badly-lighted road. As I approached the place I fancied that I saw a skulking figure cross the road and move round towards the back of the house. It was Mary, who had loitered about vainly trying to think of some mode of restoring the notes which should not re-act upon her benefactor, Bet. At length she had conceived the project of getting round to the back, raising the window of Mrs Colbrun's room, and tossing the notes into some corner. Quite ignorant of these facts, I followed the figure; saw the dark window stealthily approached, and then was witness to an attempt to force up the window, which chanced to be fastened on the inside. When this had continued for a short time I slipped rapidly up behind, and laid a hand on the woman's shoulder. She uttered a scream of terror, and instantly dropped the bunch of notes, which I as quickly picked up. I took her round to the front door, and introduced her to Mrs Colbrun, who besought me, as I have seldom been pleaded with, to let poor Mary go, "and say no more about it."

That was quite beyond my power, and Mary—who had not a word to say in her defence, and even faintly admitted the identity of the stolen notes—was taken away and locked up.

No sooner did Bet hear of the capture than she appeared in a frenzied state at the office, tearing her hair and altogether conducting herself like a maniac, and loudly declared that she and not Mary was the thief. I had known so many cases in which a mother sacrificed all, even her reputation, to save her offspring from prison, that I felt certain this was but another instance of the kind, and we paid little attention to Bet's story.

The same day Mary's affianced appeared at the office, and was allowed to see the prisoner, when he besought her in the most piteous accents to declare the truth and save her name, but to all this Mary would say nothing. At the trial she was informed that her sentence would be lighter if she pled guilty, and "Guilty" she pled accordingly.

Her sentence was one month's imprisonment, but the moment it was pronounced she turned to her affianced, who had been seated behind her, and whispered with a face positively radiant—

"Now, I may speak, Herbert. Yes, I am innocent."

Strenuous efforts were immediately made to quash the conviction and have Mary released, but the law gives forth no uncertain sound on the point, and Mary served the full month like an ordinary malefactor.

When the position was explained to me by her lover, I said to him—

"Stick by her. She is a noble girl. Marry her when she comes out; for, when she could sacrifice so much from love of her mother, what would she not sacrifice for her husband!"

He thought the advice good enough to act on, and I believe has never regretted his choice.

McSWEENY AND THE MAGIC JEWELS.

A kick from a brute having iron toe-plates on his boots had placed me on the sick, or rather the lame, list, and so the scientific gentleman, with his strange story of robbery, was referred to McSweeny. The gentleman, who was well known as an author and student, and whom I may here name Mr Hew Stafford, insisted that none but the very cleverest and most acute detective on the staff could properly follow and understand the almost supernatural events connected with the robbery of the jewels, and as my chum's opinion has always been that he answers to that description, and every one else was busy, he was allowed to take the case in hand.

"I'm Detective McSweeny, at your service, sur," he said, bowing stiffly, as the old gentleman blinked at him through his spectacles. "I daresay you'll have read my experiences? They are published in books, and that's how some call me the great McSweeny."

"No, I have not had that pleasure," politely responded Mr Stafford. "I never heard the name before."

"Ah, I know how that is," returned McSweeny, with alacrity. "It's because a kind of assistant of mine puts his name to the books. Ye see, sur, I'm troubled wid a kind of stiffness in me right hand, and writin's bothersome to me, so I let him do it. His name's McGovan, and he gets all the praise and all the money for the books, which I wouldn't mind at all, at all, if he didn't try to make me look as small as possible. If ye believe him, I can't do a dacent job without him. For a story-teller, I'll back him agin all the world."

"Yes, I think I have heard his name, but I never look at that kind of literature," wearily answered Mr Stafford.

"An', good for you, sur; for the lies that's in it—especially about me—no wan knows better than meself; but it's no use me saying anything, for paiple believe every word he writes. He drives his own carriage, while I've to walk on futt. Never moind! I've the pull on him in cleverness. Give me your difficult job, and see if I don't run down the thafe better than a dozen McGovans rolled into wan."

"I understand—you mean that he is but a lame detective?"

"He is that," said McSweeny, with a twinkle in his eye, as he thought of the kick which had laid me up. "If there's a lame detective annywhere in the world this minit, it's him."

"Then I am delighted to have met you instead," exclaimed the innocent Mr Stafford, "for of all the mysteries that ever were brought here to unravel, none could be more incomprehensible than the robbery which has brought me here. You can understand how valuables might go where there are hands to take them,—servants or professional thieves,—but for jewels to vanish before one's eyes in a locked room, with windows fastened, and not a living creature near, seems as nearly impossible as anything I can imagine, yet that is exactly the case which I have brought to you."

"Nothing at all—nothing at all to us," said McSweeny, with the most unbounded confidence in himself. "Just go over the whole story, and I'll soon put it all to rights."

"Well, I am, as you probably know, a bachelor, and live out at Newington in a self-contained house of my own. My servants are a housekeeper, a kitchen-maid, and good-for-nothing page—a boy of thirteen, who eats his own weight of food every day, and torments the life out of me generally. I must tell you at once, however, that it is quite impossible that any of these three servants can be the thief."

McSweeny smiled knowingly to himself, but made no remark. He had already decided that the good-for-nothing page-boy was the thief.

"You will understand how it is impossible that the servants could be involved, when you learn the circumstances," pursued Mr Stafford. "A young relative of mine is getting married, and, as I am not exactly a poor man, I decided upon giving her a handsome present. I said nothing about my intention to anyone, but went to the bank and drew £200."

"£200," said McSweeny, gravely noting down the facts, with a severe official frown on his brow, in imitation of some peculiarity of my own.

"With that money in my pocket I went over to Princes Street, and bought, in a first-class jeweller's, a necklace, brooch, and ear-rings. They were set with diamonds and pearls, and, I believe, full value for the money I paid for them, which was only a pound or two less than I had drawn from the bank. They were very pretty trinkets, and, though no admirer of such things generally, I could not help looking more than once at these. I mention these facts just to let you understand that they were *bona-fide* jewels, paid for at the highest price, and bought from a man above suspicion, and no trick affairs made up in some magic way to deceive the eyes or fingers, and then vanish into gas or air before one's eyes. After I had paid for the jewels they were put into a small casket covered with morocco and lined with velvet, and this casket, wrapped in paper, was placed in my own hands, and carried by me to my own home. I still said nothing of my purchase to anyone. The page-boy was in the hall as I entered, but the casket was at that moment in my coat pocket, and he could not possibly have guessed that I carried anything uncommon. I left my hat, and umbrella, and boots in the hall, and went straight up to my study. This room is always closed with a check-lock, and no one can enter it during my absence. There is no furniture in the room which could screen any person from sight. When you enter the room you see at a glance all that is in it—my book-case, my writing-table, and a sofa and four chairs. There is a fire and fire-place, of course, but no one could conceal himself there, as the grate is a small register one, and the fire was blazing up when the magical disappearance took place. I always light the fire and trim it myself, and the page never gets further than the outside of the door when he fills and brings up the coal scuttle. The floor is covered with one piece of wax-cloth, so there are no crevices or holes into which any small trinket could drop or roll. You are following me clearly, I hope?"

"Yes, sur—as clear as day," answered McSweeny, with rather less confidence in his tones.

"Well, on entering the room, I knocked up the fire, put on fresh coals, and then seated myself before my writing-table, directly in front of the fire. I took out the casket of jewels and placed it on the table before me. The door, you will remember, was shut, and cannot be opened from the outside except by me, who carry the only key. I could see all the room, and both door and window, and am certain no human being but myself was in that room. I thought I should like to have another look at the trinkets, and opened the casket and laid them out, one by one, on the writing-table before me. I felt them—touched them—turned them over, and in every possible manner was convinced that they were exactly as I had received them from the maker. Now listen. After I had admired them for some little time, I replaced them in the case, which was fitted with grooves to hold them. I did not close the case, but began to reflect on the possible weal or woe which might await the young girl who was to receive them. While thus reflecting, my eyes left the table for a few minutes, and rested on the window and the distant green hills and clear sky. I was in what is called a brown study for perhaps five minutes. When

I awoke from that reverie, and brought my eyes back to the table, the jewels were gone!"

"Gone?" echoed McSweeny, incredulously.

"Yes, gone—casket, and necklace, and brooch, and ear-rings had vanished bodily, leaving not a trace of their existence before me on the mahogany table."

"You'd drapped them on the flure, mebbe?" suggested McSweeny, whose hair was beginning to rise on end.

"Not at all, though, like you, I thought at first that that was possible," calmly continued Mr Stafford. "I looked at my feet, over the table, under the table, and into every drawer and cranny about the table. I did not find them. I tried the door; it was firmly closed. The window the same. I felt every pocket. All in vain. The jewels and the case were gone."

"Ay, but how? There must have been some greedy fingers to take them," said McSweeny, who seemed to instinctively guess the suggestion that was coming.

"Perhaps not," said the old gentleman, as calmly; "a spirit hath not flesh or bones. Did you never hear of evil spirits?"

McSweeny almost jumped to his feet, and fumbled apprehensively with his red scalp.

"Faith have I," he answered, with a shudder, thinking probably of the "Spirit Rappers" described in "Strange Clues." "If it's a good healthy ghost of the owld-fashioned kind your going to mintion, it's all right, but your table-rapping ones I'll have nothing to do with."

"I don't profess to say what kind of spirit took them," solemnly replied Mr Stafford, "but it must have been a covetous spirit. I've told you all I know of the affair. The jewels are gone, and that's exactly how they vanished. I could not ask the servants about them, for they never saw them, and were not near me at the time. I don't feel inclined to lose them, yet I am certain that no human hand took them."

"Rats, mebbe?" hopefully suggested McSweeny.

"No; there is not a hole in the room."

"A jackdaw then—it might have come down the chimney."

"Impossible. I must have heard it, and seen it. No; the jewels disappeared right under my nose, without a sound. I leave you to solve the mystery and recover the property."

McSweeny had asked for a difficult case, and now that he had got one he was bound to express himself highly elated at the apparently unsolvable mystery. He volubly promised the robbed gentleman not only that he would speedily lay the thief by the heels, but that, spirit or no spirit, he would recover the property as well. His inward resolve, of course, was that if he found himself making no progress with the case, he would shove the finishing of it on me, while, if by some rare stroke of good luck he did succeed, the greater renown would attach to his efforts on account of his emphatic declarations. Full of these assurances, he accompanied Mr Stafford out to that gentleman's house at the South Side, and was taken up to the room in which the jewels had so magically disappeared. He got Mr Stafford to sit down in the exact spot and attitude he had occupied when the robbery took place. When this had been done, and every part of the room examined, McSweeny was more puzzled than ever. His reason told him most emphatically that the valuables could not have gone without hands, and yet he could not suggest even to himself how fingers could have got at them. There was not a crevice in the room—the house was a modern one, and therefore could not have any invisible stairs, doors, or passages in the walls; and even if these had existed, he could not conceive it possible for anyone to enter the room and remove the jewels before the owner's eyes, and he sitting there wide awake, looking straight before him. However, he had promised great things, and by his confident looks, and winks, and nods hinted at greater, so all he could now do was to take refuge in a little boldness. In entering the house he had got his eye on the page-boy, who was in the act of stuffing something out of sight into one of his pockets. As McSweeny reached the boy's side a whiff of the page's breath ascended to his nostrils, and seemed to point to the cause of the hurried act of concealment.

"Tobacco, the young spalpeen!" was McSweeny's mental exclamation. "The boy that can smoke is fit for anything. Just wait a minit, my jewel, and I'll frighten the very sowl out of ye."

Having inspected Mr Stafford's study, and made nothing of the work, McSweeny had no difficulty in working himself up into a fit of rage against the page.

"Just ring the bell, plase, for that boy in the tight jacket and buttons," he said to Mr Stafford when they had returned to the sitting-room.

The bell was rung, and the page appeared, when McSweeny grandly requested to be left alone with the quaking boy. Mr Stafford accordingly withdrew, when McSweeny elaborately took from his pocket first a note-book and pencil, and then a pair of handcuffs, which he clanked noisily down on the table before the boy's eyes.

"Now, you boy—your name?" he sternly began.

"William Lister, sir," said the page, visibly alarmed.

"Well, William, I'm the great detective McSweeny, and I've come here on a great case. You know what I can do to you, I suppose?"

"Ye—ye—yes, sir," stammered the page, nearly crying, and shaking on his legs.

"Now look me in the face, sur," and McSweeny grabbed the boy suddenly by the arm, and forced him down on his knees—no very difficult task—while he chained him with his fierce eyes. "Now, sur! you've been robbing your master!"

"No—no—no—sir!" cried the boy, clasping his hands in an agony of terror, and beginning to howl.

"You tuck them; I can see it in your eye," sternly returned McSweeny. "Now, where have ye hid them? Out with it, or off to jail ye go!"

More abject howling and protesting, and then the boy blubbered out—

"It was for my mother I took them."

"Your mother, ye villin. She's fond o' them things, I s'pose?" derisively returned McSweeny.

"Ye—ye—yes, sir."

"And she's got them now, eh!"

"Yes—oo! hoo! hoo!"

"And where does she live?"

"Bu—bu—bu—ccleuch Street, sir."

"Then we'll go there now," sternly observed McSweeny, highly elated with the success of his bold measures; "and luck here now, if ye try to escape I'll shoot you—shoot you! with a double-barrelled poker."

The terror-stricken culprit rose and got his cap; and they were moving out of the lobby when Mr Stafford appeared.

"It's all right, sur," whispered McSweeny, with a significant wink; "you'll have them here for identification in an hour."

"But how was it done?" cried the gentleman in amazement.

"Done? What trick is there that's too difficult or dirty for an idle vagabone of a boy?" responded McSweeny with a wise look. "I knew what a scamp he was the minit I smelt tobacco on him," and McSweeny got out his own pipe ready for lighting when he should be outside the door.

The boy, all the way to his home, was tremulously asking what would be done to him, but his captor smoked away in dignified silence, more terrible to the prisoner than the most voluble of threats. At length the great oracle spoke, and gave the boy to understand that the nature and duration of his punishment would depend very much upon himself—if he agreed to tell how the robbery had been accomplished, and all other particulars, his punishment would probably be extremely light. This gracious concession gave great comfort to the boy, who instantly promised to keep back nothing. They had then arrived at the house in Buccleuch Street.

It was a poor hovel of a room, both damp and dark, being on the ground floor. A woman who opened the door was promptly introduced to McSweeny as the boy's mother. The boy whispered to her for a moment, and then led McSweeny to the fireplace. A small fire burned in the grate, and on that fire was a pot of broth. The boy lifted down the pot on to the hearth, and, handing an old ladle to McSweeny, told him to "take them out."

"What a hiding-place!" was McSweeny's inward comment. "The young scoundrel's as clever as if he had been wan of my bairns all his life. To think of him making broth of jewels!—begorra, he deserves a prize for fine cookery."

As he made these comments McSweeny began to rake up the contents of the pot, but found no trace of the magic jewels.

"What do ye mane, ye young spalpeen?" he cried at last, in terrible tones, to the boy and his quaking mother. "Didn't you say they were here, in the pot?"

"Yes—that's them," said the boy, stopping his whimpering to point to a heap of beef bones, with some shreds of meat still adhering to them, which McSweeny had removed one by one from the pot.

"What?" The thought was too humiliating—too horrifying; and McSweeny could find voice for only the one word.

"That's them," repeated the boy, touching the steaming bones, "and I'd never have taken them, only the servant said they were no use."

"It's jewels I'm after!" shouted McSweeny in a great rage. "Jewels! £200 worth of jewels!"

"Jewels? I never saw them," cried the boy, drying up his tears with marvellous alacrity. "You said bones, I thought—at least it was the only thing I ever took, and thought you meant them."

All this was dreadful to McSweeny, and yet it was so simply and naturally spoken, that he could not for a moment doubt the truthfulness of either. With a great show of bluster and official activity he searched the whole of the little hovel, but, of course, found no trace of jewellery of any kind; indeed, the page-boy protested loudly that he had never seen his master with jewellery in his possession, and so could not possibly have stolen it.

The return to Mr Stafford's house was not quite such a triumphal procession as McSweeny had expected, and when there he had nothing but utter failure to recount. He went over the whole house, and questioned the other servants, with a like result. He was not a step nearer the solution than when he began. There remained then but one slender hope—that the thief might attempt to dispose of the jewels, so McSweeny finished his work by taking a minute description of these valuables, and having them inserted in our printed lists sent round to all dealers and pawnbrokers. A tour round the most of these produced no better result. No one had offered such articles either for sale or pledge. At the end of a week, when I was beginning to "hirple" about again, we were in one of these dealers' places, when I suggested that the description of the jewels was rather vague for the pawnbrokers, and that we might go along to the jeweller who had sold them to Mr Stafford, and have it made fuller and more complete. A reference to the scribbles which McSweeny called notes revealed the fact that no such name was recorded. I sent McSweeny out to the South Side to have the omission rectified, not being able to walk as far myself, and on his return learned that Mr Stafford had had some difficulty in remembering the name himself. However, on McSweeny naming two or three of the principal ones in Princes Street, he at length spotted one as the right one. In the evening I chanced to be in Princes Street, and went into the shop to get the description. To my surprise, the jeweller and all his assistants declared that no such purchase had been made in the shop. Back I sent McSweeny to Mr Stafford, when that gentleman at once smiled out knowingly, and said—

"I think I understand that statement of the jeweller. It is all a plot between him and my servants—he is to swear that he never sold them, and they are to declare that they never took them. The jeweller will thus get them back, and they will divide the spoil."

McSweeny scratched his red pow, looked up at the ceiling, and then down at the carpet, and finally confessed that he did not exactly catch the drift of the gentleman's reasoning.

"I will explain—I will confide in you as a friend," said Mr Stafford, waxing warm. "I am a lonely man, without wife or children to look after my interests and protect me from designing persons. The consequence is that I am continually being persecuted, robbed, and cheated. One of my acquaintances, whom I never injured by thought or deed, carried this torture to such an extent that I was forced to leave the city."

"Could you not have got the protection of the police?" suggested McSweeny.

"Useless. How could I prove the persecution? I fled to London; the wretch followed me there; I took the first train from the place; it landed me at one of their pleasure gardens—the grounds of the Crystal Palace, I think. I enjoyed myself there; when all at once my fiend—my tormentor—as I must call him—appeared before me. I ran from the spot; a balloon was just starting; I leaped in, cut the rope, and shot up into the air, laughing in triumph at the chagrin of my persecutor."

"That was a neat escape," observed McSweeny; "but how did ye get down again?"

"The most awful part of the adventure was to come," pursued Mr Stafford. "When I had got up a certain distance I got freezing cold, and thought to warm myself with a smoke. In striking a light some of the gas escaping from the balloon must have touched and exploded, for the next moment the whole thing was in shreds and flames, and I was flying towards earth with the speed of a cannon ball."

"And ye was kilt? Smashed to atoms?" exclaimed McSweeny in earnest horror, with his hands raised, and his eyes almost starting from their sockets.

"No; fortunately I fell into the water, and, being an excellent swimmer, I managed to save myself. I returned to Edinburgh, but my tormentor was soon upon my track again, and even yet he continues his persecutions upon every occasion when there is no chance of being seen. Possibly he is at the bottom of this mysterious robbery."

McSweeny asked the name of this persecutor, and after a good deal of demur on the part of Mr Stafford, the name was given, when it proved to be that of an eminent professor, as renowned for his learning as for his goodness. McSweeny was a good deal staggered, but took leave, saying he would make inquiry into the matter, and see that Mr Stafford was annoyed no longer.

When he came to me with his report I laughed outright, and said—

"Why, the man's mad! I wonder you did not see it in him before."

"What man? The Professor?" inquired McSweeny, with great simplicity.

"No, this Mr Stafford."

McSweeny would not believe it, and I suggested that we should ascertain if he had really drawn £200 from the bank on the day of the alleged purchase of the jewels. I did not believe that he had, but was surprised at the bank to find that he had really drawn that sum. We then went over every jeweller's in Princes Street, but could not discover one who had sold to any one on that day the jewels described as stolen so magically. After thinking over these discoveries for a little, I formed in my mind a theory, which proved pretty sound in the end, and which I proceeded to test, by going out to Mr Stafford's house in company with McSweeny, and having a talk with that gentleman upon general topics. When done, I felt slightly disappointed. I could find no trace of insanity about the man, but then I ought to have remembered that my profession is not to detect lunacy, but thieves. Still, acting on my theory, I requested permission, and Mr Stafford's assistance, to search the whole house. This was given with the greatest alacrity. We went over every room and closet, but Mr Stafford's study, without discovering anything. Then we came to that room, and I promptly asked for his keys. The request appeared to stagger him, but was granted, and I turned out all the drawers in his writing-table. At the bottom of one of them was an envelope or thick packet, which I took up, but which he as hastily tried to take from me, saying—

"That's only some bank notes—some money of mine."

Very impolitely, as it may seem, I retained the envelope, turned out the contents, and found, on counting the notes, that they amounted to £200 exactly. I then handed them to the owner without a comment, and searched no more. With a shrewd suspicion of what I might expect, I went to the Professor whom Mr Stafford had named as his persecutor, and from him learned Mr Stafford had, on a former occasion, been unfortunate enough to injure his brain by over-study, and was by the Professor's advice removed to an asylum for the insane. That gentleman, who evinced the liveliest friendship for Mr Stafford, agreed to see his friend at once, and report on his mental condition. The result was, that Mr Stafford was proved to be not exactly insane, but in a condition of mental derangement which threatened to become more pronounced, and it was decided that he had better have an experienced attendant from one of the asylums. This was arranged quietly, and with very little demur on the part of the patient, but his condition became more grave, and eventually he had to be removed to an asylum, in which, with one brief interval, he has remained ever since. His mind, however, has taken firm hold of the story of the magic jewels, and the development which that incident has now assumed is that I, the writer of these sketches, was the robber of the jewels, and that, in fear of detection, I smuggled the money I had received for them into his drawer. He also asserts that I declared him insane only to protect myself from the consequences of the crime, and that if I could be removed from power his liberation would at once follow. Poor, suffering humanity! who shall minister to a mind diseased?

BENJIE BLUNT'S CLEVER ALIBI.

How Benjie Blunt came to get his name I never could discover—possibly it was prompted by the law of contrariety, because Benjie was so sharp. His real name had not the remotest resemblance to this, but as he refused to answer to that, he was always put down in the prison books as Benjamin Blunt.

Benjie's vanity was much greater than his acquisitiveness. He liked to boast of the feats he had done, hence the cases in which he was mixed up generally showed a superlative degree of ingenuity and cunning, however small the stake. I do not find, however, that Benjie's cleverness produced any marked diminution in the number of his convictions—indeed, it was the grave length of that list which prompted him to make such elaborate preparations in the following case.

Close to the Meadows, and before that quarter was so much built upon, there was a cottage occupied by an old army surgeon, whom I may name Dr Temple, and his servant, Peggy Reid. This gentleman was a bachelor, and somewhat eccentric, and, as he had spent the most of his life in India, he was supposed to be very rich. Dr Temple was as exact and punctual in his habits and engagements as if he had been still in the army. Everything went on like clock-work in his snug little home, and if a servant did not please him in that respect, he discharged her on the spot. One of his habits was to spend every Thursday evening at a friend's house, leaving his own house at seven o'clock, and returning at half-past ten. His house was full of Indian curiosities and nicknacks, but most of them were of a kind which could not have been readily turned into money. The cottage had a little garden in front, railed in, and had also a space at one end, in which stood a coal cellar, a wash-house, and an empty dog kennel.

A working joiner happened to be passing this cottage about nine o'clock on a Thursday night, and, glancing up towards the front door, was surprised not so much at seeing it standing half-open as at noticing something like a human foot and the skirt of a dress lying motionless on the lobby floor. There was a light in the lobby, and the inner glass door was also ajar. The man stopped and stared, wondering whether it was not some servant busy scrubbing the floor, and lying on her side to reach some corner scarcely accessible. But the foot did not move, and as the place was lonely and dark, the man suspected something was wrong, looked round for a policeman in vain, and then pushed open the gate and advanced towards the strange object. He found Dr Temple's servant, Peggy Reid, lying on the lobby floor behind the outer door quite insensible. At first the man thought she had been knocked down, and so stunned, but seeing no traces of a blow, and finding that she breathed calmly and regularly, he came to the conclusion that she was drunk, and vainly tried to arouse her by shaking her and propping her up on a lobby chair. As she gave but faint signs of awaking, he then tried to call the assistance of the household by ringing the bell, and, getting no response, concluded that the house was empty, and went in search of a policeman. At the Middle Walk he was fortunate enough to catch the glare of a policeman's lantern, and soon had the man informed of the strange discovery. They went back together to the cottage, and found the servant girl still sitting in the lobby, and looking stupid and confused.

"A man rang the bell and said the doctor sent him for his stick," she feebly explained in reply to the policeman's questions. "Then he shoved himself in and held something to my mouth, and everything grew dark."

"Chloroform," said the policeman shortly. "The house has been robbed, I'll swear. Let's look through it and see."

With some assistance Peggy was able to get on her feet and lead them through the house. A great deal of damage had been done; ornaments and curiosities smashed and tossed down in sheer wantonness or anger, but not much of value taken. Some silver ornaments and jewellery, and an old-fashioned gold watch, were all that the servant could say positively were gone; but it turned out afterwards that a considerable sum of money in gold and bank notes had been taken besides these valuables. An Indian casket of carved wood, ornamented with ivory, was also missed on the day following. It was not worth sixpence to any one but the owner, and why it had been taken was a mystery to all.

While this discovery was being made, or possibly a short time before, a curious arrest was being made in the High Street, which, as everyone knows, is about seven minutes' walk from the Meadows. Benjie Blunt had made his appearance in the High Street, not far from the Central Station, uproariously drunk and apparently reckless of all consequences. He staggered about, shouting out sundry sounds which were supposed to represent a song, he insulted everyone within his reach, and, finally, in making a mad grasp at some of the tormenting gamins clustered about him, he fell forward on his face, and was so overcome that he could not get up again. A crowd cannot gather in the High Street at any time without almost instantly attracting our attention. The man on the beat was soon at Benjie's side, and on telling him to get up was rewarded with a kick on the shin bone. Another man had to be summoned, and between them, with the greatest difficulty, they managed to carry the limp and drooping figure of Benjie into the station, by which time that worthy was quite incapable of speech, and was locked in a cell to sober at leisure. Benjie passed the night in a profound slumber, and was next morning placed at the bar of the Police Court, and fined in five shillings, or seven days. When had a professional thief five shillings to spare? or the inclination to part with the sum, unless he had urgent and profitable work awaiting him outside?

Benjie declared himself bankrupt, and made a pathetic appeal to the Sheriff to be let off "just this once," and was then hustled out and taken to the cells, no more depressed than if he had been starting for a week's holidays. Indeed, from the manner in which he thrust his tongue into his cheek, and bestowed on me an impudent wink as he was led off, it struck me that Benjie was highly delighted with himself or his oratorical display. I failed to see any cleverness in it; I was to think differently later on.

I had been out at Dr Temple's cottage not an hour after the discovery; and as I found the servant perfectly recovered, and with not a scratch to show as the result of the attack, I rashly concluded that she herself was the thief, with or without an accomplice. My idea was that the lying in the lobby with the door open and apparently insensible was a mere feint to throw suspicion off herself while her companion escaped with the booty. My only wonder was that she had not been found bound and gagged as well, and it was that omission which made me wonder if she had done the whole thing single handed. With this thought uppermost I searched the whole cottage and garden very carefully, expecting to find the plunder there buried or hidden. The dog kennel already noticed stood on feet, and was about four inches off the ground, and it seems strange to me now that I did not have it moved or looked below. However, the oversight—which I actually made—mattered little, for at that time the plunder was not there. I merely mention the fact to show what a narrow escape the girl made, for had the stolen things been got there she would certainly have been arrested; and that they were not there found was not through any planning or skill of the thief. That which complicated the case to all concerned proved a blessing to the servant girl.

Peggy Reid, when questioned by me, asserted her belief that she would know the man again who had held the handkerchief over her mouth and nostrils, and stated that she had noticed a man resembling him hanging about the place, and passing and repassing some days before. I had no faith in her ability to do so, for at that time I strongly suspected herself, but I made a raid among "my bairns," and picked up two fellows, who were shown to her without success.

She was positive that neither of them was the man, and they were liberated. If Benjie Blunt had been at liberty I might have thought of him, but at that time he was demurely picking oakum in Calton Jail to wile away the tedium of his sentence of seven days. He had been carried into the Central Office, dead drunk, an hour before the robbery was reported, and what could be more satisfactory to us? Candidly, the thought of Benjie in connection with the singular and daring robbery never once rose in my mind.

Failing with the two first arrests, I kept my eyes open for the spending of the money which had been the chief part of the plunder. A flutter of interest quivers through the whole thieving community the moment a big haul is taken by any of their number. It will not hide; you see it in their faces, in their manner, in their gorging and drinking, and in a certain indescribable furtive uneasiness and excitement which they show when visited and questioned.

The only one whom I found to be unusually flush of money was a man named Pat Corkling, better known as "Pauley." Pauley was more a beggar and tramp than a thief, and had got his nickname by evading hard labour during a sentence for vagrancy by pretending that he had a "pauley," or paralysed, right hand. Pauley, then, was spending money freely, and yet always too drunk to go out begging. I therefore removed him to the Central, and had him searched.

We found more money on him than he could account for, but none of it could be identified, and Peggy Reid, on being shown Pauley, declared most positively that he was not the man.

Pauley was therefore released, and went away triumphant, with the money in his pocket, to resume his drinking and gorging.

At this stage of the affair there occurred a most singular and unaccountable event. Benjie Blunt was set at liberty, having duly served his term of seven days, and that very night the policeman Bain, on the beat past Dr Temple's cottage, was suddenly attacked in a ferocious manner by a man who ran off the moment the assault was made. Since the discovery of the robbery Bain had been ordered, with Dr Temple's permission, to enter the garden by the gate during the night, and make the circuit of the cottage to see that all was secure. He had done so on that occasion, and was scarcely out of the garden when a powerful hand drove the hat over his eyes, while a powerful foot administered a vicious kick to the small of his back. While he was dropping to the ground in agony a voice growled out something to the effect that he was to "take that you thief!" Bain managed to spring his rattle; but when he scrambled to his feet again he found himself alone, the nimble assailant having flown like the wind. No arrest was made, though Bain had to get a substitute for the rest of the night, and go home to bed.

Next day, as if to add to the complications, a note was handed into the Office addressed to me, with twopence of deficient postage to pay, and which ran thus—

"A blake Sheep. yul finde the rober of mr temples is thee Peg on the bete. serche him an his howse an yul see. giv him 10 yers the vilin."

The most of this precious epistle was written in a species of half-text, which did not seem altogether unfamiliar to me. So impressed was I with the idea that I went over to the prison and had a look at the copy-books of most of those in the school or who had been in it lately. I did not come on any resembling it, and it was not till Benjie Blunt came up to me on the street a few days later that the possible connection between him and the curious writing flashed upon my mind.

"Now, I remember—Benjie used to write a hand something like that," was my thought when he addressed me, and I fully expected that Benjie's first words to me would have a reference to the policeman Bain, a most sterling and tried man, in whom we had implicit confidence.

Benjie took a long time to work round to the subject uppermost on his mind, but at length he said—

"I know you're always on the look-out for hints, and you're so kind and attentive when I'm in you're hands that I couldn't help coming to you with what I've found out."

I grinned unfeelingly into his solemnly puckered-up face.

"O Benjie, try that on somebody else," I rejoined, with a look which must have convinced him that I was wide awake to his clumsy flattery. "Out with what you've to say; I'll find out your motive afterwards, if it's of any importance."

"What's it worth to put the thief in your hands?" he asked with cunning look, which could not possibly be described on paper.

"It's worth about as much as the thief or yourself—nothing," I calmly answered.

Ah, well, he was sorry for that, but he was still anxious to help us—virtuous Benjie!—and would not mind doing a good action for once.

"You know Pat Corkling? Pauley, they call him," he continued.

"Why! is he the man?" I cried in surprise. "I had a letter accusing Bain, the policeman on the beat, of the crime, and I strongly suspect, Benjie, that that letter came from *you*."

Oh, no, it was quite a mistake. Benjie protested strongly—a trifle too strongly—that he had never written such a letter in his life; and I immediately concluded that he had written that letter, but was puzzled to think why he should now come to me accusing Pauley.

"How do you know that Pauley did the job?" I asked, when Benjie had done protesting.

"I didn't say he did, and I'm not going to say it. I'm not to appear as a witness in the case at all, mind—that must be the agreement, or I tell nothing."

"All right; I agree to that; go ahead with your story—I daresay it's a lie from beginning to end, so it doesn't matter much."

Benjie smiled delightedly at the compliment, and proceeded—

"When I got out of quod and heerd of the thing—which had been done when I was in—I had a idee that the peg was the man that did it, just like the man, whoever he was, that wrote to you," demurely observed Benjie. "Pegs is an awful bad lot—except you, of course—oh, honour bright, except you," he added, catching himself up barely in time. "But then I found out that Pauley had been flush of money for near a week, and I took to watching him. I didn't get much out of him, for he's fly, I tell you."

"That's a great compliment from you, Benjie—what a pity he can't hear it," I remarked.

"But there was some Indian ornaments took, wasn't there?" Benjie added, suddenly coming to the point, and looking innocently anxious for enlightenment.

"Yes."

"Well, I saw Bell Corkling with one of them—at least I think it would be one of them—a silver thing, made like a butterfly—and I heerd that others saw her with more, which she had put away in a safe place. O Jamie! ye had Pauley up on suspicion—why didn't you keep him while you had him?"

"That's a mistake which may be easily rectified, if we can find any of the things in their possession."

"Trust you for that, Jamie," said Benjie, in servile admiration, at the same time giving me a poke in the ribs for which I did not thank him. "And, mind, be awful suspicious of him if he tries to prove a *nalibi*, as they call it," he added, with careful concern. "He's an awful liar, and could get others to swear anything."

"Ah! he's not alone in the world in that respect, Benjie," I significantly rejoined, "and has no chance to be till the hangman gets you."

Benjie gracefully acknowledged the compliment, and, after some more advice and instruction, left me.

I knew, from the moment that Bell Corkling was named, that I should have some trouble in getting evidence against them. They had no fixed abode, and generally lodged at a place where dozens besides themselves might as reasonably be suspected of the crime. This beggars' howf was in the Grassmarket, and its occupants had such a reputation for stealing from one another that I scarcely expected Bell or Pauley to be so foolish as leave their plunder about that place. My opinion to this day is that Benjie *did not* see the Indian trinket in Bell's possession, but merely inferred their guilt from circumstances which I shall notice further on. Therefore the task which Benjie conferred on me was much more difficult than I imagined. I had Bell watched for a day by a smart little ragamuffin whom I engaged for the purpose, and then I broke in on them at what I thought was the most favourable moment—about ten o'clock at night. The "kitchen" was full, but Pauley and Bell were in more select and favoured society— the room of the lodging-house keeper, who was helping them to dispose of some bad whisky. Bell looked angry and excited when I appeared and my men closed the door; Pauley looked concerned, and hurriedly said something across the table to Bell in an undertone, when she made a swift motion as if to wipe her mouth with her hand. All that took place while the fat lodging-house keeper was rising, and, in tones of innocent wonder, asking what I sought at such a time.

I had not an answer ready, for I was thinking of Bell's peculiar action, and watching her closely the while; but at length I said pleasantly to Bell—

"I want to know how old you are, Bell."

"Then I won't tell you," she fiercely answered.

"I didn't ask you. I mean to find out for myself. You're such a horse of a woman—I want to see if I can tell by looking at your teeth. Come away, now, like a good soul, open your mouth."

Pauley turned pale, and Bell closed her lips more rigidly.

"Sha'nt," she defiantly answered, in a mumble through her teeth.

"Ah, ladies are always shy on that point; I must take you to the Office, and get a crowbar to prize open your jaws," and I got out my handcuffs to fit one on her, when she suddenly made a desperate gulp, and then turned crimson in the face, and began to wave her arms and kick her legs at a fine rate, gasping, and choking, and sputtering, but failing to get the impediment either up or down her capacious throat. She opened her mouth now without being asked, and the chasm thus displayed was enough to frighten the bravest, but she was so evidently in pain, and urgent in her motions, that I made an attempt to relieve her.

Others tried in turn, but at length we had to send for a doctor, who, with a peculiar instrument—like a long bent pair of forceps—managed to bring out of her throat an Indian gold coin. As soon as I had examined the coin, and made some pleasant remarks thereon, which were very badly received by Bell, I asked for the remainder of the plunder, and not getting it, searched the place thoroughly, when I at last found a small paper parcel tied with a piece of twine, and fastened up inside the chimney with a table fork. In this parcel was most of the plunder, including the old-fashioned watch, which seemed not a bit the worse of its smoking. The landlady was loud in her denunciations of my prisoners, and they were good enough to confirm her protests, by declaring that she knew nothing of the hide. Still all three had to trudge, though the landlady afterwards got off with an admonition. It was the table fork which saved her, for it was proved that she had missed the fork days before, and kicked up a terrible row, accusing one of the lodgers of having stolen that useful article.

The arrest, and the manner in which it had been accomplished, seemed to impress Pauley with a more exalted opinion of my powers. He did not know that it was by a mere chance that I entered at the moment when Bell had the Indian coin in her possession, and seemed to think there was something uncanny about me. That was his first impression. A day or two's reflection made him veer a little. He had never told the particulars of the robbery to a living being—even Bell had not been so trusted. How then could I have known that he must be the man? That was Pauley's puzzle, and it led his thoughts insensibly in the direction of Benjie Blunt. He sent for me at last, and asked me point blank if he had been informed on by that worthy. I was a little staggered by the question, and Pauley took me up at once.

"I see it was him that set you on to me and Bell—and there's nobody else could," he bitterly continued. "Well, I can be even with him, for I'm not the real man after all. If you'll undertake to get me off, I'll put you up to the whole plant."

I could make no such pledge, but Pauley's anger was roused, and he had resolved that Benjie should suffer, so he made unconditionally the following statement:—

"That night when the robbery was done I met Benjie in a public-house in the Pleasance. He pretended to be very drunk, but he wasn't, and I knew it, and wondered what he was after, as I smelt chloroform, and knew he was the only one who could have it about him. He got quarrelsome and broke a glass, and was put out of the place. I didn't stay long after, as I was curious about him. He went along a street or two pretty drunk like, and then got as sober as a judge, and went out very smart to the cottage at the Meadows. The whole job didn't last five minutes, and I watched it all a bit off. When he came out again he had a narrow box in his hands, and he went to the dog kennel and pushed the box in below it, and then bolted. I went for the box, and got it, and bolted too, for I was frightened, seeing the servant's foot in the lobby, and thinking maybe he had given her too strong a dose. I burned the box whenever I got under cover, and hid everything but the money. I heard that Benjie was locked up for being drunk and abusive the same night. He was no more drunk than I am now, but I s'pose he thought he'd be safer in there than out."

This story was too wonderful for me to credit at a moment's notice, but I thought there could be no harm in getting hold of Benjie. I had pledged my word to him that he was not to appear in the case as a witness; his appearing as a prisoner was quite outside of the bond.

I went to look for Benjie soon after my interview with Pauley, and chanced to meet him coming up a close in the High Street, when he graciously smiled out, and seized hold of my hand to shake it warmly, while he thanked me most heartily for so neatly securing Pauley and Bell. He seemed to look upon the capture as a personal favour done to himself. He was shortly to change his opinion.

"I'll go up the close with you," I quietly remarked, turning and accompanying him as far as the High Street. "There are some points in that affair I'm not quite sure of, and I want you to go with me as far as the Office."

"All right, but I am not to appear as a witness," he warningly observed.

"No, no, not as a witness," I assuringly returned, "and, lest anyone should suspect you of peaching, suppose I put one of these on you and take you along on suspicion?"

He looked at me suspiciously, but recovered and grinned out as I snapped the steel on his wrist—

"It's a good joke," he said delightedly.

"I don't mean it for a joke at all," I said, becoming serious. "Really and truly I am arresting you on suspicion."

His whole countenance changed, his jaw fell, and for a moment he stopped walking, and looked as wicked as any human being could look.

"You can't prove anything against me," he at length answered, moving along with me in apparent confidence. "I can prove a *nalibi*, as it's called. I was in Fernie's public-house in the Pleasance all the afternoon, and was put out there drunk, and lugged into the Office long before the robbery came off. I was drunk, but I knew what I was about, and I know I was never near the Meadows."

"Done!" I cried. "Oh, you fool! Why did you say so much? You've convicted yourself by speaking of an *alibi*. It was the only link awanting in the chain of evidence, for I could not conceive why you should pretend to be drunk and then get back to the High Street and have yourself locked up as drunk and incapable. Thank you, Benjie, for your help in this matter. It was all a clever *alibi* you were arranging?"

Benjie emitted one oath, and then became silent, conscious, doubtless, of the soundness of my remarks. An hour or two after he had been locked up, I had Peggy Reid brought to see him, when she unhesitatingly identified him as the man who had held the handkerchief to her mouth on the night of the robbery. This drove the last prop out from under Benjie, and he plaintively asked if Pauley was to be accepted as evidence. Being informed that that was a likely contingency, he thereupon stated that he would prefer to plead guilty, in order that Pauley might suffer along with him. His benevolent intention was humoured, and the three went to the Penitentiary together, Benjie getting the lion's share in the number of years.

JIM HUTSON'S KNIFE.

Jim's mother touched me on the arm as I ushered him into the Police Court for the first time. I remember it all as well as if it had happened yesterday. She had been loitering about the lobby, tearful and oppressed, but was roused as by an electric shock when "James Hutson!" was shouted out, and echoed through the corridor. She gripped my arm as I was hurrying him in at the door, and the whole arm attached to those rigid fingers shook as with an ague. The tearful eyes brimmed over freely, and the parted lips moved, but for a moment no sound came forth.

"Jim was aye a guid laddie," she at length chokingly articulated. "He's been led away; he was never meant for a thief. Save him! make it licht for him, and he'll never come back here. Oh, Maister McGovan, he's the only ane left me—the only ane oot o' six."

I did not hear any more, for I was in a hurry, and the roll that morning rather long, but the appealing face, the tears, and hurriedly breathed outpourings of that poor mother's heart, followed me right into the court-room. Frantic and voluble appeals under such circumstances are common, but this one was quiet, sudden, and overpowering. I looked at the prisoner for the first time with special interest. He was a young lad of sixteen or so, rather strongly built, and manly-looking, but, of course, hanging his head in shame as they generally do the first time. The case was a very simple one. Jim was an apprentice plumber in a big workshop; quantities of brass-fittings, copper wire, and tin had been missed, and at last I was set to watch the workers. I followed several innocent ones for a time, but at length came to Jim. I should have overlooked him, for he had rather an innocent face, but for a certain bulkiness about his body. Jim did not go straight home, but took a certain broker's on the way. He went through to the back shop, and I surprised him there in the act of unloading. The broker, of course, protested perfect innocence, but I took them both. The broker got off by some means, and Jim now stood there alone. The charge was theft, and confined to the articles taken with him, though that did not cover a hundredth part of his pilferings. Was he guilty?

"Yes sir, guilty," was Jim's hurried answer, with his head lower on his breast.

"Hae mercy on him!" rang out from the benches behind in the unmistakable tones of Jim's mother, as the magistrate paused in doubt, possibly feeling to send such a fine lad to prison. "Let him off this time, and he'll never come back again."

I was motioned to the side of the magistrate to give my opinion in an undertone. I did try to make it light for the lad. I said I thought he had been prompted to the acts by some one who was uncaught, that his home training had been against such a course, and that he had never been in court before. But I could not refute the statements of his employers, that their losses had extended over more than a year, and been serious indeed. A few moments thought, and the magistrate spoke out without comment of any kind—"Thirty days."

There was an impassioned outcry in a woman's voice, but I did not turn in that direction, as I did not want to see anything. I hurried out the prisoner by the side door a moment or two later, and was again clutched by the mother.

"He'll come oot waur than he gangs in," she exclaimed in despairing accents, and with bitter reproach.

"Exactly, there's little doubt of that," I answered with assumed coolness.

"Is that a just punishment?" she pursued, almost choked with tears, as she clung to the arm of her son, who now seemed to shrink from her in shame, and to long for the seclusion of the cells.

"It's the Nemesis of crime—the chief part of the punishment," I returned; "they should think of that before they begin."

We had to part them by force, and she called me a monster and a brute, which I don't think I am, though I did feel a little like one at that moment.

Whether Jim had any prompter to his first crime, other than poverty or the desire for tobacco and other luxuries, I never knew. If he had, the man was probably one of the working plumbers, and possibly took warning by Jim's detection and pilfered no more. At the end of the thirty days his mother was over at the jail door to receive him with open arms and take him home with her. He promised there, at the jail gate, that he would have done with crime for ever. I heard him speak the words, and I believe he sincerely meant to keep the pledge. But there were two things which neither he nor his mother calculated upon. The first was that the taint of crime was now upon him. Who would employ a lad who had been convicted and imprisoned for theft? The second was still more serious, though at the time it probably seemed trifling indeed. In prison, Jim had met his fate in the shape of a young fellow of about his own age, named Joe Knevitt. Joe was the very antipodes of Jim in nature and disposition, yet a very strong friendship appears to have sprung up between them. Joe was sly, cold, cautious, and thoroughly unscrupulous with friend or foe; Jim was daring, hot-headed, impulsive, and passionate. Joe was a professional thief by birth and training; Jim was the reverse. Joe was as cunning a rascal of his age as ever came through my hands, and could never be limed for any but the most trifling sentences, and probably did not reveal his real character to his new acquaintance. When Jim was set at liberty Joe had a week or two to remain in jail, so they might have been separated for ever but for the taint of crime.

Jim was really not much worse through being in prison, but things were very much worse for him. He tried to get work, and was everywhere asked for his character. Sometimes he took courage and confessed the truth, but when he did he was invariably dismissed at once without further parley and with marked distrust. Then his mother scraped together enough money to send him to Glasgow, in the hope that he would succeed better where he was not known. Jim used every penny of the money, and tramped back the forty miles in a half-famishing state. Of course his mother cheered and consoled him, and slaved for him at her wash-tub without a murmur; but a young lad must fill up his time in some way. He could not sit all day looking at his fingers, and he needed a little money if only to keep him in tobacco. He met Joe Knevitt one day, and from that hour his troubles seemed at an end; his silence and sullen despair vanished, he was always cheerful and kind to his mother, and never wanted money. But how the money was earned and how his time was spent he never could clearly explain. He was not much in the house, and was never absent for a night at a time, but his mother was deep in her work and knew nothing, whatever she may have feared. I daresay she had many a sorrowful hour, and pleaded and remonstrated with him unceasingly, for the singular feature of Jim's case was that his new life did not harden him against his mother. If he was becoming dissipated and brutalised, no trace of that was ever expended upon her. With her he was always subdued and silent or full of promises for the future. There were thus two influences at work—one dragging him downwards and the other tugging him back. Joe Knevitt's proved the stronger, for when this had gone on for some time Jim was again in my hands. This time it was for an attempt—the very daring of which almost took my breath away. I suppose the planning had been done by Joe Knevitt, but the execution—the lion's share of the work—fell to Jim.

The place chosen was a clothier's at the South Side—a shilling-a-week clubman—whose business premises were the third flat of a land of houses, the fourth of which was the top. There was not the slightest chance of getting in unseen by the door, as one part of the flat was let to a person who was seldom out of the house. The remainder was locked up when not occupied by the clothier and his band of tailors, and most of the windows looked to the back. It happened that the house was a corner one, and after much study and reconnoitering the intending thieves decided upon a mode of entering which I would not have risked for all the webs of cloth that ever were woven. A quiet and very dark Sunday night was chosen for the attempt. The two got up on the roof of the corner house joining that occupied by the clothier, and Jim, who had under his coat a long length of rope wound round his body with which to lower the webs of cloth to his pal, crept down to the edge of the slates, and loosened with his practised hand the zinc roan or rain gutter running along the edge of the slates. This precarious bridge he sloped over the angle to the window of the clothier's store-room, a distance of only about twelve feet, but with a slope on it that would have made anyone shudder had they been forced to walk that plank against their will. Joe steadied the top end of the frail bridge, and Jim went sliding down and across with his life in his hands. He was *seen* doing it, and the accidental spectator afterwards assured me that his own hair nearly stood on end as he saw it done. The passage was accomplished swiftly, and in safety, but Jim's difficulties were only begun. He stood on the window-sill, three storeys from the ground, but tug as he could the window-sash refused to move. Fancying that it might have been fastened inside he removed one pane of glass in a fashion of his own, inserted his arm, and found to his dismay that the window was not bolted in any way, but only paint-fast. To attempt to move it he knew would be folly, and yet he could not go back to the opposite roof. There was only one way out of the fix—to strip off his jacket and the rope he had brought and try to wriggle through that open pane. He removed as many of the points of broken glass as he could with the aid of his jacket, but in doing so let go the end of his rope, which dropped into the green behind, and left him there isolated and helpless. He cursed over the loss, doubtless, but quickly began the wriggling business, and in a few minutes had struggled through—his shirt sleeves and waistcoat, and even his skin, considerably torn and damaged in transit. When he was in, and the whole coast clear, he thought little of the trouble and danger. He passed to the next room, found the window of that more manageable, and coolly proceeded to select his plunder. He did not hurry himself, for he had not the slightest suspicion of having been seen, every window near him being dark. Having made his selection, he was in the act of tearing up a web of cloth into strips to replace his lost rope, and lower the plunder by, when he was startled by a sudden, shrill whistle, at the far-off end of the green below. He knew the whistle, and what it meant—danger! but could not conceive why the shrill sound should have been thrown out at such a time. Joe was surely growing childishly timid. Jim went to the window, ready opened, and peered out. Not a soul was in sight. Reassured, he went back to his rope-making, but had made no progress worth recording, when a loud knock at the outer door of the house brought him to his feet, with his heart beating fast with dismay. Only till he heard the door opened and a rough voice say something about "thieves in the house," did he delay. He did not even think of a rope of cloth strips. The hands of the police were already on the door of the room. He sprang at the window, remembering as he did so the exact position of the roan pipe running down outside the house into the drains below. The pipe was of cast-iron, and fastened to the wall with strong stancheons. Jim grasped it from his perch on the window-sill, and ran down it hand under hand as if it had been a rope. It was a feat he would never have attempted in cold blood. He reached the green just as the policemen thrust out their heads at the window above and sprang their rattles. Then he dived for the nearest doorway, but was there met by a man who had helped to give the alarm, and who collared him and gave him a hard struggle for liberty. Jim was younger and lighter than his captor, but he was desperate, and he came off victor, and, leaving the man almost breathless on the ground, he was off into hiding as fast as fear and his supple limbs could carry him. The struggle, however, had taken place near a bright stair-light, and the vanquished man had a full and clear view of Jim's features, and was able to give me, an hour or two later, such a description that I had little doubt of being able to trace the scared thief. Only *one* had really been seen at the job, and I was not surprised, on making inquiries for Joe Knevitt, to hear that he was "away in Glasgow, and had been there for a week." The same could not be said of Jim Hutson, for I found him in his mother's house demurely kneeling by the hearthstone, and helping his mother by chopping sticks. He denied having been out the night before, and his mother with tears supported his statement—doubtless believing it true—for he might have waited till she slept before he went out. But I had to take him, and, of course, he was identified—picked out of a dozen men without a moment's hesitation—and locked up. His mother was at the Police Court next day (in tears, of course), and with her old appeal on her lips—

"Jim was aye a gude laddie; he may be guilty, but he's been led away."

I could not listen to her this time, and kept out of her reach. How could I say a word in favour of him now, when I knew him to keep company constantly with the worst of my "bairns?" Jim was remitted to the High Court, where he got a year's imprisonment. I nipped up Joe for another affair some time after, so in misfortune they were not divided.

I have not yet noticed Jim Hutson's knife. It was at this capture that I saw it first, when I emptied his pockets at the Central Office. It was a murderous looking weapon with two blades. The big blade was at least six inches long, but was not fitted with a spring back, or Jim would have looked upon it for the last time, as it is illegal to carry such a knife. Perhaps it would have been well for Jim if such a confiscation had taken place. The knife was of a peculiar make, probably foreign, and had a hole drilled through the buck-horn handle, as for a cord, and most likely had been stolen from some sailor. Across the buck-horn handle Jim had made two deep notches with a file, with a cross cut between, forming the letter H.

This knife, after some joking comments by me, was put away with Jim's tobacco pipe and other treasures, to be returned to him when his term expired. But before that time came Jim had done something which quickened curiously the interest I already felt in his career. One of the warders had in some way excited the rancour of three prisoners, and they laid their heads together and recklessly resolved to "pitch into him." By a most ingenious plot they managed to get him alone, and then ferociously attacked him with hammers. Jim, however, had taken a liking to the man, and, happening to be near, he at once, with that bull-dog bravery which had always distinguished him, took the part of the warder. He fought two of them single handed, though a good deal pounded and hurt in the struggle, and was seized with them, by mistake, and hurried off to the dark cell. As soon as matters had been explained by the rescued warder, Jim was brought forth and handsomely complimented by the governor, and from that day till the expiry of his sentence treated with marked lenience and favour. I was over in the jail shortly after this affair, and, chancing to see Jim among the workers, I took him aside for a word. "Jim," I said, putting my hand on his shoulder and speaking with great earnestness, "you're in the wrong line entirely. You are just the stuff a good soldier is made of. Get into that as soon as you are let out. It'll be a new life—an honest one—and advancement is sure for you. It's a sheer waste of material to have you herding here with these louts. Rise above them. These cowards are fit for nothing else, but you, you can be a man if you choose."

While I spoke I saw his eyes—which were fixed somewhat shame-strickenly upon the ground—gradually light up. A new possibility had dawned upon him.

"I think you're right, sir," he said at last, very gratefully; then he added with great firmness—"I'll enlist whenever I get out."

He meant to do it, and would have done it, but for his mother. What fatality prompted her to veto the whole plan?—to abjure him with tears and clinging love, which were resistless, to remain at home and not trouble himself about the future while he had her to slave for him? She shuddered at the idea of her boy—her youngest, and the last of them all, going into a battle, and recklessly tearing through showers of bullets and walls of steel, as she knew he would do. But, could she have looked into the future, as I can now look back on the past, she would have seen there something more to be dreaded. So Jim continued to loaf about and live upon his wits, and when Joe Knevitt joined him, the old practices came as a natural result. I saw Jim once or twice and tried to reason with him, but his answer was always the same—

"Mother won't let me list."

"Then I'll have you again soon," I gravely remarked.

"I can't help it," was his cool reply, and I suppose he thought the event far off. With the confirmed thief it is always some one else who is to be taken, never himself. Jim had really not over-rated his cleverness. He had grown more cautious by experience, and might have eluded me but for his rock a-head—Joe Knevitt. I believe there was a woman in this rupture—one of those flashy shop girls who sell cigars and tobacco and flirt with everybody, and whom Joe wanted entirely to himself; but the ostensible reason was a difference about their respective shares in the plunder from a certain robbery down at Greenside which puzzled us not a little. There is a certain style in every thief's work. In any kind of job where Jim's old plumber experience helped him, he was perfectly at home, and had this affair shown any trace of that, I should have gone for him at once. But there was no trace of violence or tearing down of wood-work, or wrenching or unscrewing. It was a shop, and the door was found locked as usual when the owner entered it next morning and found the most valuable part of his stock gone, and about twenty pounds in silver as well, which he had thought too heavy to take home the night before. I searched the whole shop *carefully*, and found no trace of the thieves or clue to their identity; and candidly may now confess that I suspected the *owner* was the thief, that for some purpose he had robbed himself. I was mistaken, of course, for the door had been opened and locked again with skeleton keys made by Knevitt.

Meanwhile Joe and Jim were quarrelling, and Joe proceeded to settle the dispute in a fashion of his own. On the second morning after the robbery, the shop boy in sweeping out the place found a big clasp knife, which he had not noticed before, in a dark corner behind the counter. The knife was shown to his master, and finally brought up to the office to me. The moment it was placed in my hands I exclaimed—"What! did you find that in the shop? How did I miss it when I was there? It's Jim Hutson's knife. I'll soon have the thieves now, and possibly the plunder too."

Down I went to Jim's home in College Wynd. He was not in.

"He's got wark," his mother explained.

"So I think," was my dry rejoinder. I looked over the house, and finally under the bed found a parcel tied up in brown paper.

"He brocht it in last nicht," his mother simply remarked. "He's keeping it to obleege a freend."

I opened the parcel, and found it contained part of the stolen goods. I was explaining this to the mother when Jim appeared in working garb for his breakfast. He changed colour at once, and sat down, or rather dropped down, into a seat by the fire.

"It's all up, Jim," I said with some pity. "I told you I'd have you soon."

He stared at me, not in resentment, but with a strange, thoughtful look in his eyes. "Have I been sold?" he at last inquired, rather quietly. "Did he—I mean—did anyone betray me?"

"No," I promptly answered, believing what I said. "Have you your knife about you?"

He dived his hand into his pocket, and then appeared to reflect.

"You needn't look there for it," I remarked. "I'll find it for you when we get up to the office."

"I had it yesterday—I'm sure I had it yesterday," he said, after a horrible pause.

"I don't think so," I gently observed in correction. "You dropped it the night before."

"What! do you mean to say you found it *there?*" he cried, his whole face becoming white with fury.

"It was found," I oracularly returned; and then, taking my advice, he relapsed into silence, and quietly accompanied me.

Of course the mother had to go too, but she was speedily released, as it was quite evident, from her artless admission to me, that she knew nothing of the robbery, and her character was above suspicion.

Jim did not deny his knife. He only said occasionally under his breath—"He has done it! Wait; I'll give it him back!"

His suspicion, which was probably sound, was that Joe had picked his pocket of the knife, and then made some errand into the shop, and so managed to drop the tell-tale article where it was likely to be found.

From these muttered imprecations I guessed that Joe was his partner in the crime, and went for him as soon as Jim was locked up. An ordinary thief would have betrayed his pal at once after such dastardly treatment, but, as I have indicated, there was about Jim a kind of manliness which scorned such a mean revenge. He remained absolutely silent regarding Joe's complicity, and, as that rascal was cunning enough to take care of himself, we had no evidence against him, and he was released.

In order to have his sentence shortened Jim pleaded guilty, and got off with eighteen months' imprisonment.

"When your term is up, Jim, go for a soldier," I whispered to him as he was led down stairs.

"Maybe I will—it depends," he grimly answered with set teeth, and so he disappeared for a year and a half's moody reflection.

When the time came for his release he was fearfully excited for a little over the fact that his beloved knife could not be found among his treasures.

"My knife! my knife! I must have my knife!" he feverishly exclaimed, and he absolutely refused to stir out of the prison till he got it. When it was found and placed in his hands he appeared exuberantly happy, and as impatient for liberty as he had before been reluctant to leave.

At the gate, his mother, as usual, was there to receive him, but she found him a good deal changed. He was moody and strange, except when questioning her regarding Joe Knevitt. The little she knew of his old pal was eagerly devoured, but beyond that he had little to say. At home his first task was to get out his knife and grind its edge to a razor-like keenness. His mother noticed the fact, and fancied that he appeared specially careful with the point, but the only answer she got was—

"Ah, it's been lying a long time unused, mother. Eighteen months is a long time—in prison;" and Jim's teeth became set, and his two hands shook as he tested the keenness of the point of the knife with his thumb. His mother saw that she had touched a sore spot, and remained silent. As soon as Jim's task was over he set out to look for Joe. He wanted him particularly, and was quite joyful when he learned that Joe was still about the city, and not in prison. But search as he could he did not find Joe, and at length learned that that cautious customer had left for Glasgow on the very day of Jim's release. No matter, Jim thought distance a trifle, and followed as soon as he could scrape enough money together. He took his knife with him. On the second day he did see Joe for a moment or two—met him full in the face in an entry off the Gallowgate; but the moment their eyes met, and Jim's hand went into his pocket, Knevitt ran like a hound, and managed to distance Jim completely and escape. Next day Knevitt left for Perth, after saying that he was off to Edinburgh; but Jim met a man who had seen Joe take a ticket for Perth, and he followed. At Perth he traced Knevitt without difficulty to a house known to them both. But the hunted man had seen him approach, and by slipping on a woman's skirt and shawl and bonnet boldly passed him on the stair, and escaped. Jim fathomed the trick a few minutes later, and cursed his own stupidity in allowing the unnaturally tall female figure to pass him; but by that time Knevitt was on his way to Dundee. The next train took Jim there also. After a day's hunting he met his man in Couttie's Wynd.

"By G—d! your hour has come!" he cried, darting his hand into his breast pocket; but again Knevitt put on that fearful speed and ran for life. Not far from the place is a ferry across to Fife. The pier at which the boat starts is guarded by a gate which is closed when the boat is about to move. Knevitt managed to get within that gate just as it was being closed, and scrambled into the boat nearly dead with terror, while Jim was thundering and shouting in vain outside the gate in hope of admission. Knevitt had thus a whole hour's start, and, besides, had more money in his pocket. Jim, when he reached the other side, was uncertain whether the hunted man had decided to walk or ride; and his own funds being low, he resolved to walk. He had no doubt as to the next goal.

"Edinburgh! he'll be sure to land in Edinburgh!" he muttered to himself, and thus he confidently tramped through Fife, reserving the little money he had to pay the ferry at Burntisland. It was the dead of winter, and bitterly cold, and when Jim arrived at his mother's house he was nearly dead beat. He had got over with a goods boat, and reached home early in the morning. He lay down and slept all day—a fevered, unrestful sleep, full of dreams and mutterings, and suppressed threats and deadly words, which filled his mother with terror. At night he awoke, and moodily consumed the meal placed before him, and then limped to the door.

"Where are you for now?" asked his mother with a palpitating heart.

"Just going out to look about me," was the answer, and then he was gone. His mother thought she would look about her too, and threw a shawl over her head and followed. During the two hours' wandering which followed, she never lost sight of him. At last she discovered that he was following a man—Joe Knevitt—who appeared quite unconscious of the fact. Knevitt made for a tumble-down rookery in a close a little below the Bridges. It was his home, and had the advantage of being accessible from two sides—by the two flights of wooden steps on one side, and by a back window on a level with a higher close beyond. The garret on the top flat was all Joe's, and he clearly indicated to his foe that no one else was within by unlocking the door as he went in. Jim had his shoes off in a twinkling, and then crept up the first flight of steps and patiently waited in the dark, with his knife ready unclasped in his hand. The poor mother understood it all now, and, having before heard the place described, she slipped round to the next close, clambered upon an outhouse, and astonished Knevitt by tapping lightly at the window and madly motioning him to come out and fly for his life. Knevitt needed no explanation; her face was enough, and he was out at the window and gone before she had well got over her excitement and terror. She waited there for a full quarter of an hour to give him time to escape; and then resolved to go in, open the door, and go down and tell Jim that his plot was discovered and his intended victim far beyond his reach. The door was opened, and Jim, watching below with the knife in his hand, dimly saw a female figure descend where only a man had entered.

"That trick won't deceive me!" he cried, as he dashed up the steps and drew back his right arm. "You've tried it once too often, Joe!"

One plunge of the sharp steel with all the strength of his powerful arm, one low groan as the poor victim sank back on the steps, and it was done, and Jim flying for life and liberty. His mother was not dead when she was found, but it was quite evident that she was mortally wounded. When her state was known, and preparations made to take her deposition, she persisted that she had been stabbed by Joe Knevitt. The knife found by her side was Jim Hutson's, but his mother, innocently or knowingly—I cannot tell which—said—

"Jim was aye a gude laddie, and though he was led away he wadna lift his hand against his mother. Joe Knevitt did it, the ungrateful scoondrel, after me daeing him a gude turn. *But dinna tell Jim* or he'll kill him, and twa deaths winna mak' ae life."

We easily picked up Knevitt, but he denied the whole with such manifest horror, and gave such explanations, that we set out to hunt for Jim, and I was the one destined to unearth him; and also, I regret to say, to inform him of the fearful crime he had committed. That scene I can never describe. He dropped on his knees, rolled and writhed on the floor, tearing his hair in a frenzy of agony, moaning out but the two words—"My mother! My mother! My mother!" Of course he confessed the whole crime in every detail; but his mother was never told of the hand that gave her the death-blow. She lingered for some months, and, the doctors said, did not actually die of the wound, but of some trouble of the heart, brought on by the excitement and pain. Jim was tried and convicted of manslaughter only, and was sentenced to two years' imprisonment. The sentence may seem light, but *that* was not his punishment. He carried that within him. Joe Knevitt's bones now lie in the prison yard, but Jim's dust is in a foreign land, where he died on a battlefield in a way that made men call him a hero. They did not know the secret of his daring.

THE HERRING SCALES.

The hawker of the herrings was not of the class usually seen in the streets of Edinburgh, where they seldom own more than the wheelbarrow containing the fish. He was a man of some substance, having a donkey to draw his cart, and a number of pigs, and a big garden, in which he worked during his spare hours. The place in which he lived is a town some miles from Edinburgh, and the time when the quarrel began the month of July. The quarrellers were a baker named Dan Coglin, and the herring hawker aforesaid, Jamie Burfoot by name. The baker was also a man of some means, being in business for himself, and he would have prospered had it not been for his uncontrollable temper. Coglin had in his time threatened to murder every friend and acquaintance in the place, and doubtless in the heat of his passion really meant to do so, but fresh objects for his resentment constantly arose to divert him from his purpose. He was one of those unhappy beings who meet with mighty wrongs, and slights, and insults every day of their lives, and feel called upon to set the world right in that respect, no matter at how great a risk to themselves.

The quarrel took place at the bakehouse door, and was witnessed from a stairhead above by a tailor named Thomas Elder, who had already had more than one disagreement with the hot-headed baker.

Burfoot had stopped his donkey cart at the bakehouse door, and offered some of his herrings for sale. They were fresh herrings, but that was just the point on which the dispute began. Coglin said they were stale, and added that Burfoot had cheated him often in the same way before, adding some lively reflections on his character, from which it appeared that the herring hawker ought to have been hanged many years before.

Now, as often happens quite providentially in such cases, only one of the men was violent. Burfoot was a quiet, canny customer, who only laughed at the most outrageous of the baker's remarks. His character was in no danger from the insane ravings of such a man, and the herrings were there to speak for themselves. He lifted one of the finest, and handed it to the baker, saying simply—

"If that isn't fresh out of the sea this morning I'll give you the whole load for nothing."

This was said laughingly. Coglin took the herring, affected to sniff at it, and then, with an expression of disgust, threw it back. Burfoot's mouth was open, and the pitched herring dived into the cavity as neatly as if it had really been, what the hawker asserted, "living." Burfoot sputtered and choked, while the tailor above, though wishing the quarrel to go the other way, could not restrain a burst of laughter at the comical appearance the hawker cut. There is a limit even to the endurance of a peaceable man. Burfoot no sooner was free of the unexpected mouthful than he wildly grabbed a handful of herrings from the cart, and battered them, as fast as he could fire them, in the direction of the baker's head. Coglin retreated and closed the bakehouse door, and after some storming and threatening Burfoot picked up the missiles he had used, tossed them back into the cart, and drove on, shouting "Fine fresh herrings!" Four or five of them, which had been dashed in at the open door at the retreating baker, that worthy gathered up and complacently put into a dish in the oven for his dinner. He was in a good temper, for he thought he had got decidedly the best of the quarrel. He was to change his mind next morning. Coglin's business was a small one, and, except at specially busy times, he did all his baking himself. He was therefore the first and only one on the spot next morning. The hour was an early one, but it was quite light, and he noticed at once that something was wrong. The principal window to the bakehouse had been raised, and the lower sash left wide open. The circumstance excited his curiosity and surprise, but did not at first greatly concern him. There was little of value in the bakehouse for thieves to take, and he thought the raising of the sash might be only the trick of some mischievous boy. He unlocked the door and got inside, looked around the place, and then groaned and cursed to his heart's content. The batch for his early baking had been carefully "set" the night before, that is, the dough had been carefully mixed in a wooden trough, covered over with a board and some empty sacks, and left to "rise." It had not risen as he had expected, for the coverings had been removed; his bakehouse "bauchles" had been stuck into the soft mass, with all the shapes and biscuit markers, and a dirty can of sugar and water, with its paint-brush, with which he anointed cookies when they came hot from the oven, added on the top. That was not all. A bag half-full of flour, which generally stood in a corner, had been dragged forward and turned out on the floor, while into the white heap had been poured his whole supply of barm.

When he had quite exhausted his stock of language, Coglin rose, and, closing the window and door, made his way to the chief constable's house, where he roused that worthy man out of bed, and insisted upon him dressing and coming to see the wreck.

The constable came and examined all, and then very naturally asked who had been quarrelling with the baker. With a man of Coglin's disposition it would have been safer to ask whom he had not been quarrelling with. Coglin went over the names of some of his foes, but, having had the best of the slight affair with the herring hawker, he never thought of naming Burfoot.

The constable made no great progress with the case, and I suspect did not exert himself much, as there was general rejoicing over the baker's calamity, which was thought to be well deserved. Finding this to be the case, Coglin insisted on having a detective brought from Edinburgh. The case was important, he declared—nothing but a conspiracy conceived and executed by half of the town's folks, including a magistrate and several leading town councillors, and he would have the law to them though he should have to call in the aid of the Home Secretary himself. Accordingly I went down to look at the place, and was greatly amused by Coglin's wild statements of his troubles and daily martyrdom. In looking over the bakehouse, I chanced to notice on the board which had been used to cover the "batch," or "sponge," a number of herring scales—almost enough to convey the idea of a hand-print.

I said nothing of the circumstance till I had examined the window sash, and found two similar hand-prints of herring scales there also.

"Are you in the habit of handling herring often?" I asked, to which he gave a prompt response in the affirmative.

"Oh, yes; there's often as many as two dozen dishes of them here in the morning to be fired in the oven."

"And you take toll of a herring out of each?" I laughingly observed.

"No, no, I never touch them," he hastily returned; and then I showed him the herring scales on the board and the window sash. He looked grave enough for some moments, and then burst out into a ferocious "Aha!"

It was all he said for a few moments, but it clearly indicated that the herring scales had suggested a great idea to him. What the idea was I soon knew, for he proceeded to describe the encounter with Burfoot, and ended by boldly affirming that the herring man and no other was the author of the outrage. The inference seemed a very fair one, and after getting a description of the quarrel, I decided to see after the herring man. The result of my investigations in that direction was absolute failure, so far as bringing home the guilt to Burfoot was concerned. I not only got clear proof that Burfoot on the night and morning of the outrage had been out of the town altogether, but that he had been confined to bed and too ill to move out of the house. Nothing could be clearer than the evidence on this point; and when I had finished I was convinced that, whether Burfoot had planned the outrage or no, he at least could not have been the actual perpetrator.

Nothing more seemed to come of the herring scales, and I reported the result to Coglin, who received it with a burst of abuse.

"And you call yourself a detective?" he scornfully shouted, and his private opinions which followed are not worth recording.

"I believe that is what I am called, and what I earn my bread by," I quietly returned.

"Well, I'll tell you what you are!" he shouted, working himself nearly black in the face; and he then proceeded to declare that I had been bought over by his enemies, and that he would now trust, not to the police or the law for redress, but to himself. He looked so like a maniac in his rage and fury, that I did not trouble to reply, but left him and got back to Edinburgh, where other work soon drove the recollection of the baker's petty affair out of my head.

Coglin's detective work did not begin where mine left off. He had quite settled in his own mind who was the guilty one, and his only difficulty was to decide on what punishment should be meted out to the herring hawker. Many plans suggested themselves, but they mostly had the objectionable feature of bringing the self-appointed judge and executioner within reach of the law. At length a chance remark of Burfoot—who, all unconscious of impending evil, was still on friendly terms with the baker—prompted him to a scheme as ingenious as it was diabolical. A son and heir had been born to Burfoot, and he gleefully told the baker that he should soon hold a party of rejoicing over the event, when the christening could conveniently take place. He did not invite Coglin to form one of the party, but that oversight did not distress the baker.

"I wish I could poison the whole of them," was his inward comment as he turned to his bakehouse, and out of that remark sprang the great scheme.

Coglin of course knew something of the baking of fancy bread, and the same evening, as soon as his ordinary work was over, he set to and made a fine christening cake. He was careful to cover up the windows and every chink in the door before beginning. In making up the cake he hesitated long between some arsenic which he had got for the rats in the bakehouse and another powerful drug as a seasoning; but, having made his choice and hurried up the cake, he waited and watched the firing of it as eagerly and attentively as if a Princess Royal had been intended as the joyful recipient. The cake did not rise well, probably owing to the queer spicing it had got, but Coglin chucklingly decided that the sugaring would cover that. He snowed it over with a preparation of white sugar, and then flowered it over the corners and edges with pink, and finished up by lettering it boldly in sugar as "A Present from Edinburgh."

When the cake was finished, he covered it with a strong wrapper of brown paper, and addressed it to "James Burfoot, Fishdealer," adding the name of the town in which they both lived, and the words "*per* rail—carriage paid." He was careful, in writing the address, to disguise as much as possible his handwriting, and, it is needless to add, he did not as usual put a printed label on the parcel bearing his name and address.

Next morning he considerably astonished his son Bob, a boy of twelve, by telling him that he needed him to go an errand.

The command was an awkward one for Bob, who had arranged with two companions to spend the day at a town not far off, at which there were to be races, and no end of shows and sports. Bob accompanied his father to the bakehouse about as nimbly as a murderer going to execution.

Above the cover bearing the name and address, Coglin had tied a wrapper of paper to conceal the address, and inside that had placed a sixpence wrapped in paper to pay the carriage. The parcel thus arranged he sternly placed in Bob's hands.

"You're to take that to Edinburgh, and hand it in at the railway parcel office. They'll find the address and the money inside. You're to say nothing—just put down the parcel and walk out; do you understand?"

"Could I not take it to the railway station here?" sulkily returned his son. "It'll go just as well."

"No! You're to go to Edinburgh, and ask no questions, or I'll half murder you!" cried Coglin. "It's a present, and the—the customer doesn't want the folk to know who sent it, or where it comes from."

"And am I to walk all the way to Edinburgh?" groaned the boy, ruefully.

His father tossed him a sixpence, with the words—

"You can take the train;" and Bob's spirits rose somewhat, but scarcely to their normal level.

At the end of the lane he found his two companions patiently waiting. They were overjoyed to see the sixpence, but the sight of the parcel was a terrible damper. That load was all that lay between them and a day of pure, unalloyed joy. They could have kicked the parcel; and one seriously suggested to Bob that they should quietly drop it into the river or the sea, and go their way undisturbed. Bob reluctantly declined the proposal, but was easily persuaded to go to Portobello first instead of to Edinburgh, and have his fill of fun before taking the parcel to that city.

"It's a present," the boys reasoned, "and they're not to know who sends it or where it comes from, so it doesn't matter whether they get it soon or late, or whether they get it all, for that matter."

Reader, did you ever, when a boy, tramp to Portobello and spend half a day there on a light—a very light—breakfast? I have, and can testify that the edge which that fine seaside resort puts on a boy's appetite would make chuckie stones or hedge leaves seem princely fare. The wonder is—at least my wonder used to be, when we went in droves—that some small boy, juicy and tender, in the gang, did not mysteriously disappear on the return journey. The three travellers enjoyed themselves famously on the sands. The sixpence of train money vanished like magic. They bathed seven times, like the ancient pilgrims of Jordan. They saw the races, and Punch and Judy, and every kind of cheap delights, dragging that parcel about with them, and each taking turns at carrying it through the crowd. At length Bob and another decided to have another bathe, and left their clothes and the parcel in charge of the third on the hot sandy beach. When they returned, the wolfish guardian had the paper covers off the cake, and was volubly explaining how a bit of the sugar coating must have been broken off during their travels. He had eaten the bit, as it was of no further use, and "Edinburgh" had disappeared. The two bathers looked on with wonderful calmness. Their teeth were chattering, and they were longing for a "hungry bite." The remaining words of the inscription were suggestive—"A Present from ———." A mysterious unseen donor was offering them a present.

"The folk wouldn't like to get a broken cake like that," suggested one of the boys to Bob. "If we were to eat it, they'd never miss it."

Hunger quickens the reasoning faculties. Bob at once saw the point, and without waiting to dress he broke up the cake, and they all filled their stomachs. The cake just fitted the three nicely; and then they tore up the covers, annexed the sixpence found within, and had a glorious somersault on the sands to celebrate their victory.

But "pleasures are like poppies spread," and poppies, as everybody knows, contain a deal of poison. These three conquerors were in turn to be conquered—the fate of all. They began to feel queer, as if the wild war-dance had not agreed with them. They got worse, and another bathe was proposed; but their clothes were scarcely off, and their toes in the sea, when they fell down writhing and howling. It was a clear case of cramp. A great crowd gathered about them; rescue-men distinguished themselves in hauling the three boys out of a full inch of water; and they were borne howling to the baths. They roared while they had breath, and then lay limp and insensible. A doctor summoned in haste placed his hand on one of the stomachs—he must have been a family man—a pump was sent for, but before it arrived they had each begun to relieve themselves. Still they were very ill, and it was quite clear to the doctor that they had been poisoned. As they said nothing of the sugared cake they had devoured, but admitted that they had eaten a pennyworth of gingerbread among them, the poor seller of the gingerbread was pounced upon by the police, and lugged off to prison as a wholesale poisoner. The three hapless victims being quite unfit for removal, a telegram was sent to their parents, stating that they had been poisoned, but were expected to recover.

The effect of this message upon the parents of the two companions was alarming, but Coglin it only enraged. At first he stood horrified like the rest, but then, guessing something like the truth, he burst into a fit of passion, and said that it was all Burfoot's doing. His mode of reasoning was this—Burfoot had been the cause of him having to prepare the poisoned cake; through him preparing that cake his own boy had been poisoned; therefore Burfoot, in addition to his past crimes, was guilty of a deliberate attempt to murder the baker's son. What reprisal, what punishment, could be too great for such a wretch?

Coglin resolved to be his own avenger as before, and went to Portobello to see his son. He affected to believe Bob's story of being poisoned by the pennyworth of gingerbread, and reminded him of how often he had warned him against eating anything that was not baked at home. Bob was delighted to get off so easily, and humbly promised to remember the advice, which he did by never again putting a cake baked by his father within his lips. When the boys were brought home, and the unhappy seller of the gingerbread had been liberated, with his raven locks turned grey with terror of the scaffold, Coglin was at liberty to punish the criminal. This time he resolved to make his vengeance sweeping in its character, and to confide the execution of it to no one but himself. To decide on the special punishment required a deal of thinking, but all Coglin's thinking pointed to one qualification—the retaliation must include personal loss to Burfoot. Coglin had already lost considerably by Burfoot's crime; it was but just that Burfoot should suffer in the same manner. While Coglin was at a loss to decide the matter, the newspapers or public press kindly came to his aid. In these he saw described a case of fire-raising by wandering tinkers, who had made up a pellet of chemicals, procurable at any drysalter's, which, on being thrown down among straw or wood, spontaneously ignited, and burned so fiercely that the whole place was speedily in a blaze. Coglin for nights on end devoted himself to amateur chemistry, and with such ardour that he at length produced a pellet, quite good enough to set the whole of Burfoot's donkey-shed and pig-styes in flames. The pellet, when finished, resembled a lump of badly-dried clay; and to ensure its safety, Coglin, when it was finished, placed it in one of his metal confection pans, and locking it in his bakehouse, went to survey his foe's premises and decide upon the best spot for throwing the pellet. He succeeded to perfection. There was easy access to the place, a convenient window to the shed, plenty of straw inside, and the whole of the sheds were of wood as dry as tinder, and promising a grand blaze. It gave Coglin additional satisfaction to know that Burfoot's place was not insured. While the baker was thus settling matters at the other end of the town, a curious incident was taking place on his own premises. His shop and house were in the front street, and the bakehouse in a lane at the back. While Coglin was gone, his wife attended to the shop, and while doing so was asked by a customer for a little barm. To get that she had to take down the key of the bakehouse from its accustomed nail, and go down to the place herself, while the customer waited in the shop. She was not long gone, but woman's curiosity in that short time had induced her to peep into the closed pot. Finding only a dirty piece of clay inside she examined it closely, and then tossed it into a corner among some chopped wood there stacked, and then hurried off to her customer with the barm. They conversed earnestly for a time, and then parted mutually pleased. When the barm-buyer had gone, a boy ran into the shop with the startling message—

"Your bakehoose is bleezing!"

It was blazing, and had been for some time, as the infuriated tailor above could testify. He had barely time to secure his kirkgoing suit and his spectacles when the whole tenement was in a blaze. He swore at the bakehouse and its owner as the ruin of him and his prospects. His furniture and effects were all lost, and he did not hesitate to hint that the whole had been done intentionally.

He was in the midst of these recriminations when Coglin appeared, and stood speechless before the blazing house.

"You did it on purpose, because you kent I wasna insured, and because you thought I went into your bakehouse and spoilt your batch," cried the distracted tailor, pouncing on the astonished baker and trying to throttle him black in the face; "but I'll hae the law to you, or I'll tak' your life wi' my ain hands."

They fought madly for some moments, and were then, considerably damaged, torn asunder by the bystanders. The tailor raved like a madman, and, astonishing to all, the baker listened to his frenzied accusations with the greatest meekness and calmness.

The truth is that the tailor, in his passion, had allowed several words and expressions to escape him which for the first time made Coglin doubt his own acumen in accusing Burfoot of the first outrage, and ask himself at the same time if it was not possible that the real perpetrator was Thomas Elder, tailor. The man had a strong hatred to him, and they had quarrelled quite as bitterly as he and Burfoot.

The words and expressions would admit of no other explanation than Elder's guilt, and now several circumstances recurred to Coglin's memory to confirm the idea. The tailor had bought herrings on that day, and witnessed the quarrel, and might easily have conceived the plan of entering the bakehouse and smearing the window and board with herring scales to convey the idea that the herring hawker was the criminal.

While Coglin was slowly evolving these ideas, a hand was placed on his arm, and, looking round, he found Burfoot at his side with genuine concern and consternation on his face.

"I'm real sorry for this," he said, wringing Coglin's hand, "and if the loan of thirty or forty pounds will help you in your strait, you can depend upon me."

"Good God! no!" cried Coglin, chokingly.

"But I say, yes. I can surely help a friend in distress," persisted Burfoot, warmly.

"A friend?" said Coglin, helplessly. "Yes."

"And I'm almost glad to have the chance, for that tailor has lost everything," added Burfoot, in a whisper. "Nobody can be sorry for him, for, between ourselves, I believe he was the man who entered your bakehouse and spoiled your flour."

"What?"

"Yes; I was told by one who knows, but wanted to keep it quiet, that the tailor was seen coming out of your bakehouse window at about one o'clock in the morning."

"And you never told me!" cried Coglin, reproachfully.

"I can't tell you even yet; I only say I think it," said Burfoot, cautiously.

Coglin was conquered at last, and he and Burfoot left the spot arm-in-arm and fast friends for life. Some of these facts came out long after, when I had the tailor in my hands on another charge, and some were given me by Coglin himself. He is in business still, and prospering in a town on the opposite side of the Forth, and Burfoot often goes through to spend a few days there with his firm friend, golfing on a nice links near the place. As he knows all about the baker's misconceptions and plans for his punishment, and the names are all changed here, I have decided that the giving of the details can do no harm now, and may at the same time teach those seeking revenge that it is possible for punishment intended for another to drop very neatly on to their own shoulders.

ONE LESS TO EAT.

The number of mysterious disappearances in great cities can be calculated upon with almost the same certainty as the death rate. A very few of these are accounted for; a body is found and identified, or a man vanished is found to have been in difficulties, and it is shrewdly or rashly surmised that he has fled to escape the consequences; but the majority of the cases pass into the great unknown, so far as either police or public are concerned.

No. 7 Hill Place, at the South Side, leads to a back court of wretched dwellings occupied by the very poor. At the west side of that court is a block or "land" of houses which are now rather worse than they were at the time of which I write, for a theatre has been built up against the back windows, almost shutting out the light of day from one side of the building. At that time the top windows looked into an auctioneer's yard, and, having a better share of light than the lower flats, were considered rather respectable abodes for working men. In one of these lived George Mossman, a journeyman baker. The house consisted of two rooms, and had been at one time very nicely furnished; but on the Saturday night of which I write the two places were almost empty, for Mossman had been off work for many months with a poisoned hand, which refused to heal, and so kept him and his wife and family "living on the furniture." At first Mossman, who was of a cheery, blithe disposition, had made a joke of his disabled hand, and laughingly declared that he had "an income in his hand, but nane in his pouch;" but as month after month went past, and the hand showed no signs of healing, joking was hushed on his lips. Hunger, starvation, and perhaps death stared them in the face; for Mossman shared the common horror of pauperism, and would have dropped dead before he could have applied at the Poorhouse for a dole.

The terrible pinchings which had been endured by that family were scarcely known outside their own door, for it was believed that Mossman was getting an allowance off some sick fund or trade society. There were two boys and three girls, the youngest of these being an infant at the breast, and the eldest only ten; but these children were so drilled and trained by their parents in their own spirit of independence, that not a whisper of the truth reached the neighbours.

"When things are at their worst they begin to mend." These were the words of the poor, disabled baker to his wife on this Saturday night, but as they did not satisfy hungry bairns, a council was held to accelerate the mending. The house was empty, and the whole family almost naked, so of late they had been seldom outside the house. The general messenger was Johnny, the eldest boy, and he it was who appeared to feel the position most keenly. Johnny was ashamed of his rags, and had a firm opinion that he was a strong, able-bodied man, instead of being the skinny little shadow he was, and that his proper sphere was the sea, to which he had more than once threatened to run away, not returning till he was a captain all covered with gold lace, and with a fair share of the same metal in his pockets for his parents.

"If I was away," he remarked on the present occasion, "there would always be one less to eat."

"We might all say that," said his father, who had grown somewhat sharp and fierce with famine and fretting. "I have thought about it myself often of late. A poor man in trouble and without a friend in the world would be far better out of it."

This sentiment was received with a strong and general protest, the mother especially having got frightened of late at some of the desperate looks and words of the disabled baker.

"You're not without friends, if you like to apply to them," she remarked, after a pause, to let him cool down a little. "There's Borland, for instance, your old companion."

"He's a master now," said Mossman, snappishly.

"So much the better—he may be the readier to help you, for you could work it up to him when you are well. At any rate, something must be done to-night, for the bairns canna want ower Sunday."

"I quarrelled wi' him over a game at draughts," said Mossman, stubbornly, "and I havena spoken to him for ten years, and I winna now. He'd only crow over me."

"You were at the schule thegither, and apprentices in the same shop. I dinna believe he would laugh at ye," persisted the wife, "but if ye like I'll gang mysel'."

"I winna gang, and I winna let you be seen in such rags," said her husband, determinedly.

"I'll gang then, faither," eagerly cried Johnny. "I dinna care though he laughs at me, if he only helps us."

Johnny was kissed by his mother for the brave speech, and the darkness hid the tear that came with it, though Johnny felt the tear all the same. It fired his mind and made him blurt out a thought which otherwise he would have kept in his own head.

"It couldn't be so very bad to steal a loaf," he remarked with a wistful look round on the hungry ones. "I felt near doing it this mornin' when a baker asked me to help his board off his heid. The smell o' the new bread just took my heart, and I was like to bolt wi' ane."

His father's bony fingers gripped him by the ear, and the touch was no gentle one.

"If ever you turn thief while I'm living," he fiercely hissed out, "never come near me or look me in the face again! I wad rather see you deid, ay, and mysel' too," he brokenly added, with a quiver getting into his tones.

The boy was moved and awed, and hurriedly answered—

"I ken that, faither, but I couldna help the thought getting into my heid. I'll run down to Mr Borland's, and ask him to trust you two loaves till your hand gets weel. It'll be nothing to him; I've seen you bring hame as much into your wages."

The father remained silent, but after a little pressing and pleading, said with a weary sigh—

"Do as you please; it'll sune be a' ower noo."

The boy darted out of the house, afraid that his father might change his mind and command him to stay.

Johnny, be it observed, was in rags, and wore boots which a cinder-gatherer would have passed in contempt in a dust-heap. Pinching hunger had given him a haggard and disreputable look, and all that he wanted to pass for one of my "bairns" were a dishonest heart and hand.

Ten minutes' walking brought him to the baker's shop, which he thought was Mr Borland's, but which had been quitted by that master more than a year before, in favour of one in a better locality. However, it was a baker's shop still, and Johnny, noticing no change in the name, and seeing the place closed, began to knock gently at the door in hope that the occupant might be still within. There was no answer, and at length the boy, with a hazy idea that the baker might live behind the shop, went through a narrow entry to have a look at the back.

By the dim light he picked out the window of the back shop. There were bags of flour and shelves of loaves dimly discernible within, but no light and no human face. A moving thing he did see, and a pair of shining eyes gruesome enough to have frightened the wits out of one less hungry, but a steady look for a moment or two showed him that the living creature was only a cat, which had got shut in, and was now mewing most piteously, as if imploring to be let out. The misery of another creature often draws us from our own. Johnny became interested in the cat, and its desperate scratchings and mewings, and, after watching it for some time—quite forgetful of the fact that he might be watched as well—said to himself—

"It would be easy to push up the window and let the puir brute out."

Accordingly, putting his small strength to the frame, he raised the sash high enough to let the cat scramble out into freedom. But, alas! his efforts did not end there.

When the cat was gone his own desperate condition returned to his mind with redoubled strength. There were the loaves in dozens on the shelves within, but there was no sympathising friend present to whom to appeal. How much easier it would be to take a loan of two loaves, and come back on Monday and explain all about them to Mr Borland. If he went home without the loaves, Johnny had an idea they would all be dead before Monday, and then his father need never know anything about it till it was all explained and adjusted.

I am not trying to give his reasoning as sound, but rather to show that when a child is wolfish with hunger he and reason have for the time parted company.

Johnny prised the window sash a few inches higher, and wriggled himself inside. The first loaves that came to hand were grasped at. He meant to take only two, but there happened to be four sticking together, and he concluded that he might as well take the lot. He placed the big square of bread out on the window sill, and then clambered out, and was turning to reclose the window, when something glaring and far more terrible than a cat's eye caught his gaze, and riveted him helpless and speechless to the spot. It was a bull's eye, and the holder was a policeman, who had first been attracted by Johnny's knocking at the front door, and then had slipped in by another entry to watch the whole proceedings from the other end of the green.

The slide of the lantern had been closed till the critical moment when Johnny had accomplished his burglary, when out shone the light, and with a few quick strides the man was upon the trembling boy.

"What! you're young begun," said the policeman, throttling Johnny nearly black in the face, and then shaking him violently lest there should be any breath left in his body by the throttling. "How old are you?"

"Twelve," gasped Johnny at random.

He was barely ten, but with the wild, reproachful thought at his heart that he had disgraced and ruined himself for ever by his rashness had come a queer resolve.

"And what's yer name?" continued the man, who was from the far north, and thought he saw the gallows written in every line of the boy's face.

"Peter McBain."

It was the first name that came to the tongue of the boy, and he blurted it out, with death at his heart.

"And far dee ye live?" continued his captor.

"In the West Port."

Lies, lies! every word of it. Johnny simply named the place farthest from his own home, but then he had an object in view, and the lies wrung more agony out of him than the truth would have done. He was thinking of his father and that fierce warning in the dark—"If ever you turn thief while I'm living, never come near me or look me in the face again."

"How did I ever come to do it? how did I do it?" he bitterly added to himself; but to that there came no answer.

He did not know that famine and excitement had slightly unhinged his faculties; he knew only that in some amazing manner he had become a housebreaker and a thief in the face of his father's commands, and got captured by the police in the very act.

"Then jist you tak' up your bundle and come awa' wi' me to the office," said the policeman; and Johnny lifted the loaves and obeyed, the man closing the window, and taking down the name and address before leaving. While the pair were passing up St Mary's Wynd towards the High Street, I chanced to be coming down, and stopped to learn the nature of the crime. Johnny's face was quite unknown to me, and I could not believe that he or his relatives belonged to the West Port, a suspicion which was strengthened when Johnny became taciturn, and refused to reveal aught of his antecedents. I turned back with them, and went as far as the Central, trying in vain to draw the truth from the poor quivering boy. I should not have taken half the trouble with him but for the fact that he was evidently labouring under great excitement, and that more than once I saw his eyes become brimful of tears. Your true gutter child—the raggamuffin who steals as naturally as he draws his breath—is case-hardened against either tears or trembling. There is no mistaking him; and the first glance at Johnny half convinced me that in spite of his wretched clothing and haggard looks, he was not of that class. As he refused to speak, he was entered as "Peter McBain, West Port, aged twelve," and locked up, charged with breaking into the shop of a baker whom I may name Brown, "and stealing therefrom four loaves of bread, of the value of 2s. 8d. or thereby."

My idea was that he was a runaway from some distant town, who had tramped the boots off his feet, and then been forced by sheer hunger to the robbery. I therefore had him tested with the offer of food. But Johnny was now too excited and overwhelmed with grief and shame at his position, and refused the food with unaffected loathing. Then the last prop was soon driven from my theory by a policeman on the West Port beat declaring, on being shown "Peter McBain," that he believed he knew him well as one who had long been a pest to that district.

While this small and terrible burglar was thus seeing the inside of a cell for the first time, his parents were awaiting his return in anxiety and trembling expectancy. Hour after hour passed, and still the light footfall failed to strike upon their ears, and at last, near midnight, the father could bear the strain no longer, and started out to search for the wanderer. Had the hour been an earlier one, Mossman would have gone in the same direction as the boy had taken, and probably have discovered that the name had been changed. But he logically reasoned that now the shop must be shut, and Borland at his own home, which was a street or two further off.

"He'll have taken pity on the boy and asked him to go home with him," was his parting remark to his wife, and to the home of his old friend he turned his steps—a shabby shadow, walking softly and hurriedly upon stocking soles, for his boots had long since gone to feed the hungry bairns. He was thoroughly ashamed of his appearance, and nothing short of his great anxiety for the boy would have roused him to brave the humiliation of appearing before

Borland. The house was a respectable flat in Lothian Street, and the same which the baker had occupied for years. Mossman made certain by examining the bell-plates by the light of the street lamps, and then rang and was admitted. To his relief the door was opened by Borland himself, who had been busy looking over his books at home after the rest of the household were in bed. The prosperous baker stared at the gaunt and poorly-clad figure rising before him out of the darkness of the stair, and then exclaimed, in lively horror—

"Good God! it's not Geordie Mossman?"

"I've come after my laddie," said the other, hurriedly. "I sent him to your shop hours ago, to—to ask a favour, and he's never come back."

"I'm no an hour hame," said Borland, "and he never came near while I was there. But I'm no in the auld place now, and maybe he's wandered a bit in lookin' for the new shop. Man, Geordie," he added with deep feeling, and wringing the other's hand with a fervour unmistakable, "is it possible ye've been in distress and never let me ken? Come in by and tell me a' about it."

Kindness is more overpowering than cruelty. The poor baker staggered, trembled, and then fairly broke down, and was then hurried into the house, planted down by a rousing fire, and there forced to sit at ease, while the stout baker hastened to pile before him half the eatables in the house. While thus busy diving in and out the room as a means of concealing his own emotion, Borland managed to draw from his broken-down visitor an account of his misfortunes, and the state of things in his home; and then he quietly slipped out of the room, roused his wife out of bed, and sent her off in that direction with a bundle and a basket, which she and the servant girl could scarce carry between them. Then he got a pair of boots and a coat and muffler for Mossman, and the two set out to search for Johnny. Borland advised that they should go to the Police Office first, but that Mossman would not hear of, declaring that that was the last place Johnny would go near. When they had spent an hour in the streets they went to Hill Place in full hope that the boy would be there before them. They found some appearance of comfort in the house, but the poor mother was in tears, and the cause of her grief was explained in a few words—

"Johnny said that if he was away there would be ane less to eat, and he said he would run away and be a sailor. He's away now, and we'll maybe never see him again."

"I never thought of that," gasped Mossman, with a sinking heart. "One less to eat—he's been craiking aboot that for weeks. We'll never see him again;" and then in that relieved household there was more of tears than mirth or rejoicing.

"If I had only gone myself!" the father cried in unsparing self-reproach.

"If I had only known an hour or two earlier," said the kind-hearted master baker.

But the mother was most inconsolable.

"I made him gang—if it hadna been for me he would have been here yet!" she sobbed. "I have done it all."

"Tuts, the laddie is not out o' the world surely," said her husband, with more lightness than he really felt. "I've often heard him speak of trying to find out his uncle, who is a fisherman in Kirkcaldy, and of learning under him. Have patience for a day or two, and we'll hear of him all right."

They waited the day or two, but Johnny was as effectually hidden from them as if he had been buried alive. On the Monday morning he had been placed at the bar of the Police Court, and, when asked if he had taken the loaves in the manner described, said simply that he had, but had never thought of taking them till he opened the window to let out the cat. The magistrate thought for a little, and spoke of sending him to a reformatory, but as there was a difficulty in having no parents to fall back on for the cost of maintenance, he contented himself with a sentence of three days' imprisonment, and a warning to the terrible burglar not to be seen there again or it would be worse for him.

At the trial Johnny's father never appeared, and from that the boy concluded that he was cast off for ever as an unclean thing. Neither was he once inquired for by his mother, which fact cut him keenest of all.

"*She* might have known I didn't mean it," he thought with bitter tears, "but was just led to take them by thinking of them at home."

As "Peter McBain" he served his term of three days, and then was free. Curiously enough, his first thought was of his fisher uncle in Kirkcaldy, whom he had often heard of but never seen. Johnny never thought of going home, but asked the way to Kirkcaldy. He had not a penny in his pocket, and the rags he called clothes could scarcely hold together, and, when he was told that there were two ways to

Kirkcaldy—a short way by the ferry, and a long way by land—he had no choice but to go by land, and turned his face with the utmost coolness in the direction of Stirling.

Very little alters the whole course of a life. As with most boys, Johnny's little head was full of romance, and he had determined either to be a fisherman or a sailor, and actually might have had his desire accomplished had he ever found that uncle in Kirkcaldy. But he had not got many miles on his way when he picked up an acquaintance in shape of a boy a year or two older than himself, who, having been well thrashed by his father for some fault, was "running away" to a grannie in Dundee. He had run away before, and was never tired of describing the glories of life in the mills there, and the kindness of his grannie, who kept lodgers, and was always glad to see him when his own home became too hot for him. So Johnny, who still stuck to the name of "Peter McBain," decided to accept the boy's offer of friendship and guidance, and the two small waifs at length reached that town, where the reception by the grannie was quite as kind and loving to Johnny as if he had been her own grandson. After the boys had rested two days to heal their blistered feet, they went to one of the largest mills, and were readily engaged for some simple part of the jute spinning which could be learnt in an hour or two. At this work Peter McBain showed real smartness, and soon attracted the notice of the foreman. Peter lived with the grannie who had first welcomed him to Dundee, and learned to call her grannie too. The first flush of prosperity was on Dundee at the time; wages were high, and work was plentiful, and anyone showing peculiar smartness was almost certain of speedy promotion.

When Peter had been in the mill for nearly a year, the manager asked him if he would like to learn a trade instead of to be a tenter. Peter was willing, and was taken into the mechanics' shop attached to the mill, there to learn to make and fit up machinery. He grew stout and sturdy, and gave great satisfaction, as he never seemed happier than when tearing in at his work. He never dared to write home, and was mourned as one dead. In six years Peter became a full-fledged journeyman. He was now a tall, strapping fellow, with a good face, and a clear, laughing eye, and was qualified to go anywhere and command a high wage as a first-class engine-fitter. He had been diligent and steady, and had studied drawing and designing to help him in his trade, and altogether was quite a different character from what he had promised as a small and terrible burglar. He had even saved a little money, and it was the thought of that money lying idle, and the heaps more which he was now able to earn, which sent his thoughts homewards and his heart throbbing for dear Auld Reekie. When he had been a few weeks journeyman, and engaged in the same mill at a capital wage, the Fair holidays came on, and Peter's eye caught a bill announcing a "Trip to Edinburgh." Edinburgh! The very sight of the word thrilled him through. He got a ticket and went through next day. He made his way first to Hill Place. His parents had not lived there for years. No one knew them, or had heard of them, and he began to faintly wonder if they could have been all starved to death at that fearful time when he was locked up in prison as a burglar. Then he thought of the bakers' house of call, and went thither and got a great lift to his heart. His father was alive and doing well as foreman to Borland the baker, who had now two shops, and was flourishing also. Peter went to the principal shop, and found Mr Borland behind the counter. As he entered the shop a floury-faced man, in his shirt sleeves, was leaving for the regions below, and the young engine-fitter stared into the face with a palpitating heart.

"That's my faither! that's my faither!" he thought, with a great lump rising in his throat; but he could no more have spoken than he could have flown in the air.

Borland stared at him curiously, and thought from his incoherent words and strange manner that the stranger was drunk. At length he understood that the young man wished to be directed to the home of Mossman, the foreman, and, as he refused to see the foreman, he got the address and departed. Mossman came up from the bakehouse a few minutes later, and was apprised of the circumstance, but thought nothing of it till he was half-way down the stair again. Then something familiar in the face he had seen for a moment in the shop had flashed upon his memory, and he dashed up to the shop, whiter than the flour on his face, and faintly staggered towards his friend and master, Borland, with the words—

"I'll hae to gang hame for a minute. I believe that fellow was my lost laddie—my Johnny come back!"

Meanwhile Peter McBain had gone a street or two farther, and found the house—a much nicer one than the last he had called his home in Edinburgh. A shining brass-plate on the door bore his father's name, and when he knocked, a little urchin, chubby and rosy, whom he had never seen before, opened the door and allowed him to step within. A grey-haired woman sat sewing by the window, and some older children were clustered around, but they all stared at the stranger in blank amazement, and in utter ignorance of his identity. Peter stepped forward and gazed into his mother's face, with the tears creeping into his eyes.

"Dae ye no ken me, mother?" he slowly and chokingly articulated. "I'm Johnny that ran awa'!"

A scream of joy and a wild clasp of the arms was the answer, and then the floury-faced father broke in on them to join in their great rejoicing.

Johnny became a sailor in one sense, for he is now engineer on board one of the American liners, but his heart always turns to Auld Reekie as warmly as when he stood thus before his mother, like one restored from the grave.

THE CAPTAIN'S CHRONOMETER.

The captain had come home with honours—that is, he had saved the ship and a very valuable cargo under his care by sheer bravery and indomitable energy, and been presented with the chronometer by the combined owners in token of their appreciation of his labours. That pleasing memento he carried in his pocket, enclosed in a little chamois leather cover to keep it from dust and wear. It was a ship chronometer, and therefore not meant for use on land or carrying in the pocket; but the captain was proud of his present, and especially of the flattering inscription engraved on the back of the case, and had carried it home to show to his wife and family and any friends he might meet during his short stay.

His ship was at Tynemouth, but his home was in Leith Walk, and about a week of his furlough had gone when he one forenoon met an old friend, and with that gentleman entered a big and respectable public-house in Leith Walk to drink and have a chat over old times. The place was divided into boxes by wooden partitions about six feet high; so customers, though enjoying a certain degree of privacy, could never be certain that their words were not being listened to by others in the adjoining compartments.

Captain Hosking and his friend were too much overjoyed at meeting to think of that, and chatted away in the loudest tones, while a nimble little thief named Tommy Tait, seated at the other side of the partition, swallowed every word. One of the topics was the recent storm and the dangers through which the captain had successfully struggled, and, as a natural result, the chronometer was brought out and displayed to every advantage. The heads of the two friends were close over the valuable present when that of Tommy Tait cautiously rose over the partition.

"It must have cost a good round sum?" said the friend, as he returned the chronometer, and it was carefully encased in the chamois leather cover and returned to the captain's vest pocket.

"Sixty pounds, at least," returned the captain, proudly; "perhaps a good bit more. I know they wouldn't give me a shabby present."

Sixty pounds! Tommy Tait's mouth fairly watered as he prudently withdrew his head, and rubbed his hands in gloating anticipation. Such a prize had not come in his way for many a day. But would the captain be an easy victim to manipulate? There was the rub. Had Tommy Tait's line been one of violence he would have had not the ghost of a chance against the captain, who was six feet two in his stockings, broad in proportion, and strong as a lion. But Tommy's was the delicate art of the pick-pocket, and had the time been night instead of day, and the captain only sufficiently befogged with drink, Tommy would have felt as sure of his prey as if the chronometer already lay in his clutches. Everything was against him. The captain was drinking only lemonade, and had the look of an exceedingly wide-awake customer besides; the sun was shining brightly, and the streets, he knew, were crowded with passengers. Tommy uttered a few strong imprecations under his breath, coupled with a wish that all temperance captains might come to a bad end for creating extra risks and dangers to hard-working fellows like himself. Still the chance was there and must not be missed; and what was a thief worth if his genius could not rise to an occasion like that?

The captain was going towards Edinburgh, as Tommy learned from the conversation, while the friend was going to Leith. So much the better. Tommy would have one pair of eyes less to trouble him. He waited patiently till they had talked their fill, and then followed them out of the shop. They stood for five minutes at the door; but that interval Tommy filled up ingeniously by lighting his pipe at the bar. When the friends fairly parted, Tommy lost all interest in the barman and his dogs, and abruptly closed the conversation and left. As the captain moved on before him with firm and giant-like strides Tommy's heart sank within him. He was a bit of a coward, and he felt certain that if he bungled, and got into the clutches of that powerful man, he would not have to wait long for a sore punishment. Sea captains are accustomed to administer law for themselves, and Tommy's body tingled all over at the very thought of those boots and fists playing about his diminutive person.

The captain wore a pilot coat, the top button of which was fastened. The chronometer, as Tommy knew, was in the right-hand pocket of the vest, with no chain or guard attached. There was both a watch and chain in the opposite pocket, but that was only of silver, and had no attraction for Tommy.

The captain gave no chance till Greenside was reached. There a tobacconist's window had been done out with fountains and grottoes, and real flowing water, as a Christmas decoration, and the crowd around it attracted the captain, and drew a sigh of profound thankfulness from the breast of Tommy Tait. The captain was amused and interested, and pressed closer; Tommy helped him diligently. Looking hard at the window and laughing consumedly, Tommy got his fingers under the pilot coat and touched the chronometer. The absence of a chain was a sore trial to his skill, but at length he got the chamois leather cover between his fingers, and had the whole out and into his own pocket like lightning. But, alas, the thing had been so roughly done, that Tommy was actually ashamed of his own clumsy work. He felt that the captain had started suspiciously and looked him full in the face, and he concluded that it was time to go.

He moved off as unconcernedly as possible for about twenty yards, when the thrilling shout of the captain fell on his ears, and almost stopped the beating of his heart—

"Hi! you! thief!—stop thief!"

Tommy heard no more. Whatever he lacked, he could run with great swiftness, and that wild cry, and the thought of the powerful limbs of the man who emitted the words, made him put on his most desperate pace.

He dived for the Low Calton, in which he managed to burrow successfully, while the crowd, led by the captain and a policeman who had joined, ran on and did not halt till the foot of Leith Wynd was reached. Not a trace of the fugitive was to be found, and the captain, quite breathless with the race, exclaimed resignedly—

"Oh, what a fool I've been! Well, that's the last I'll see of my chronometer."

The policeman, by a question or two, elicited the fact that the captain had got a good look at the thief, and promptly advised him to go up to the Central Office and report the case, assuring him that it was by no means uncommon, when a case was thus quickly reported, for us to recover the stolen property in a few hours. This friendly exaggeration sent the captain up to the Central, when it became necessary for me to tone down his hopes a little. By the description given of the thief, I recognised Tommy Tait unmistakably, for Tommy had certain peculiarities of ugliness about his figure-head which, once seen, were always remembered, and I firmly assured the captain that I could easily lay hands on the nimble pickpocket in an hour's time; but as to recovering the watch, that was altogether a different matter. I could not pledge myself to that.

"Why, it's the chronometer I want," exclaimed the bluff seaman, looking quite aghast. "I'll give twenty pounds this minute to the man who puts it into my hands safe and sound. What do I care for the blessed thief? Though you got him and gave him twenty years on the treadmill, that wouldn't do me a bit of good."

"There's a chance of getting the chronometer, too, if we get the man," I quietly observed. "Just leave your name and address, and all particulars, while I go and see if I can lay hands on Tommy."

I fully expected that I should get Tommy at some of his usual haunts, and return within the hour, but I was giving Tommy credit for far less ability than he possessed. I chanced to know his favourite hiding-place, and went to that direct. He was not there, and had not been near it for days. All his haunts were tried with a like result. Then, a little annoyed, I "tried back," and discovered the entry and common stair in the Low Calton in which he had burrowed while his pursuers rushed by. Two boys had seen him there, and they testified that he had turned back towards Greenside as soon as it was safe to venture forth; and from that point all trace of him disappeared. I hunted for him high and low, for days on end, in vain; and what added to my mystification was the fact that Tommy's relatives and acquaintances were as puzzled and distressed at his disappearance as I could possibly be. At first I thought it possible that he had left the city, but in a day or two had reason to believe that such was not the case. Tommy never went farther than Glasgow or Paisley, and as he had not been heard of or seen in either of these places, a queer thought came into my mind. Could it be possible that Tommy had wandered into bad company and got knocked on the head—in other words, murdered—for the valuable treasure he carried? I note the strange suspicion, not because it turned out to be correct in regard to the loss of Tommy's valuable life, but because the treasure he carried was to bring him trouble quite as unexpected as his disappearance had been sudden. While I had thus been hunting in vain, and Tommy's friends had been almost mourning him as dead, and even ungenerously hinting that I had had a hand in his slaughter, Tommy was enjoying the sweets of a well-earned repose in—of all places in the world the last I should have thought of—the Infirmary! He had got hurt, then—run over with a cab or something—in his flight? Not at all. Seized with a fever, then? Neither. He was as sound in body and limb as myself. It was simply this. Before the chronometer had come in his way, Tommy, who was lazy and hard-up, had gone once or twice to the Infirmary complaining of some imaginary trouble, which the doctors could not understand. His object was to get admitted as a patient, and have a month or two's rest and retirement from the uncertainties of the thieving profession—to be coddled up in bed and tended night and day, and fed up with wine and other delicacies too often denied to the most ingenious malingerer in prison. Tommy was one of those clever malingerers, but he preferred to practise the art in a place where he could at any moment gain his liberty by ending the distressing symptoms of disease.

That was the position. The thought of making the Infirmary his hiding-place came to him as an inspiration. In Greenside he caught a 'bus which took him up to the head of Infirmary Street for a penny. He just managed to get within the gate of the Infirmary when he was seized with such a paroxysm of his trouble that he dropped almost insensible at the feet of the janitor. The house surgeon was summoned, and, as Tommy was then too far gone to be removed with safety to his home, he was borne in an invalid's chair to the nearest ward, and there put to bed. Close to the head of this bed, and below the sash of one of the windows, was a little shelved cupboard, in which was stowed some of the other patients' clothing—tied up in bundles till they should be needed again. Tommy's agony was never so bad but that he could look after the folding up of his clothes, and more especially his trousers, in the pocket of which now reposed a gold chronometer worth at least £60. Such tender solicitude did he evince for the safety of these worn and shabby articles that the attention of more than one person was attracted, and the surgeon sharply demanded whether he had not any tobacco concealed about the pockets, to which Tommy gaspingly replied that he never used tobacco or snuff—a pathetic lie. As soon as the clothes were bundled up and put away in the little cupboard, Tommy had a relapse which occupied the surgeon and nurses for an hour at least, and effectually banished from their minds all remembrance of the little incident of the clothes.

Next forenoon, when the time arrived for the professors and students to make their round, it was found that Tommy's trouble had all settled in his back and neck, for in the one he had such dreadful pains that he could scarcely lie in bed, and in the other a chronic stiffness which a year or two's rheumatism could hardly have equalled. There was much grave consultation around his bed, and Tommy tried hard to learn the result of the deliberations, for he had a wholesome dread of being scarified on the nape of the neck with hot irons, or cupped on the shoulders, as he had been in the prison hospital for a similar attack, but all that passed was spoken in whispers, and sometimes in a language which Tommy did not understand.

Tommy was left ill at ease on two points. He feared some surgical appliance of a painful nature, and he had fidgetty feeling regarding the safety of his hard-earned chronometer. He never took his eyes off the door of the little cupboard except in sleep, and even then the slightest footfall roused him to wakefulness. Then there was a danger of some patient recovering and needing his clothes, and taking out those of Tommy by mistake. Tommy fidgetted himself almost into a fever over that possibility, the more so as he had on one side of him an evil-looking cabman, with a face as bloated as a Christmas pudding, who he was sure was a thorough rascal. In the bed on the other side was an innocent-looking Irishman, named Teddy O'Lacey, who sympathised with him very heartily, and whom Tommy set down as a born idiot and simpleton.

He had no fear of the fool of an Irishman; it was the bloated cabman he watched and dreaded. After considering the whole matter, Tommy decided that the chronometer was not in a safe place, and that night waited till every one in the ward was sound asleep, and the night attendant out of the way. Then he nimbly slipt out of bed, opened the cupboard, took out his clothes, and hid the chronometer under his pillow. He could there feel it with his hand almost constantly, and, if any nurses came to make his bed, could conceal it in his hand till they were gone. At all events he felt more comfortable with it beside him, and acutely reasoned that, even if it were seen, in its chamois leather cover it would excite no suspicion, as several patients had watches hanging by their beds or under their pillows.

Another day passed away, and all Tommy's fears had subsided. The professors ordered nothing but harmless physic, and the chronometer was safe under his pillow, so Tommy settled himself to the full enjoyment of his well-earned repose. He slept soundly that night, and was so refreshed in the morning that he did not immediately think of his chronometer. After breakfast, when he did thrust in his hand, the treasure was gone! Tommy could scarcely believe his own senses. He grabbed wildly under the pillow, over the bed, under the sheet—everywhere; he even forgot in his sweat of mortal agony that he had a stiff neck, and stooped over the edge of the bed to see if haply it had fallen to the floor.

All in vain. The prize had vanished. Worse and worse, he dared not report the loss, for if the chronometer were hunted for and found, no matter who should be the thief, a police case would certainly follow, and Tommy get seven years at least. He looked around. The Irishman was sleeping, as was his wont; the cabman, on the contrary, was eyeing Tommy in a manner that convinced the latter of his guilt.

"You've got it then?" was Tommy's savage thought. "I'll see if I can't take it back from you. I always know'd that cabmen was thieves, but I hardly think they'll match a professional."

The day passed away, and the hour for visitors arrived, bringing Teddy O'Lacey's wife, who spent an hour with her husband, and was introduced to Tommy, and departed, hoping that he would soon be well.

Tommy paid little attention to her kind words, for all his powers were concentrated on the cabman. He watched the man till his very eyes became telescopic, and gloated over the fact that the scrutiny was evidently painful to the suspected one. After the gases were lit his patience was rewarded by seeing the cabman furtively take from under his pillow something in shape of a watch enclosed in a chamois leather cover. The sight was too much for Tommy.

He sprang out of bed, forgetful alike of pains in his back and stiffness of neck, and pounced on the watch with a cry of joy.

"That's my watch, you plunderer!" he shouted; but to his surprise the cabman resisted stoutly, and stuck to the watch, dealing Tommy at the same time several blows, which sent him reeling back on his bed. The man was big-bodied and strong; such an unequal contest could never be maintained by Tommy; so he snatched up a kind of tin flagon, which stood handily near, and hurled it at the cabman's head, closing up one of that patient's eyes and scattering the contents all over his bed. Up sprang the cabman, and the next moment Tommy knew what a real pain in his back meant, for his breast bone had nearly driven the spine out of him through a tremendous blow from his opponent. The din of the battle, the shouts and imprecations, and the cries of the other patients, brought a number of nurses and attendants to the spot; and at length the combatants were torn apart and some explanation offered. Each accused the other of being a dastardly robber in attempting to steal a watch.

The cabman stated his case, and proved beyond question that the watch he held was his own—a silver lever, with his initials engraved on the case. Tommy had then very little to say, except that he had been robbed of a watch, which no one had ever seen, and which was certainly not in his possession when he entered the Infirmary. On the whole, Tommy looked and felt rather foolish, and not even the sympathy of Teddy O'Lacey, who warmly took his part, could quite convince him that he had not done a rash thing. This fear was confirmed when the house surgeon came round and audibly commented on Tommy's astonishing agility and freedom from pain during the encounter, and ended in saying—

"I'm afraid you're an impostor and malingerer, but we'll see tomorrow when the professors come round."

Morning came, and Tommy was sternly asked whether he would rise and put on his clothes and depart, or wait till a policeman was sent for to assist him from the place. With a deep groan Tommy chose to leave the building unaided. It cut him to the heart to make the decision, for had he not been robbed of the chronometer, and was he not thus putting himself farther than ever from the thief? O'Lacey, the simple Irishman, almost wept in sympathy with him, and hoped they would meet again when Tommy was free from all such persecutions and wicked conspiracies. They wrung hands pathetically, while the cabman, with a bread poultice on his eye, audibly wished that he might be present at Tommy's execution.

While this affectionate adieu was taking place, I was entering the gate of the Infirmary with no thought of Tommy in my mind, but intending to see a miserable girl in another part of the building. I wished to see this girl, with the chaplain by my side, and had to get that gentleman before going farther. When this had been arranged, we crossed the quadrangle together, so intent on the subject of conversation that, when Tommy appeared before me, I looked him full in the face without seeing him, and should have passed on had he but been as inattentive as myself. He made sure I had come for him, and dashed away down the steps towards the Surgical Hospital. A high wall surrounded the building, covered with iron spikes, and facing the High School Yard. A ladder left by some workmen stood near, and Tommy pounced on that as a godsend, bore it to the wall, and was up like a monkey before I could reach the spot. The ladder was short, and he had to reach up and grasp the iron spikes to hoist himself up. As he did so, the rotten and rusted iron gave way, and down he flopped at my feet with a sprained ankle, a broken leg, and many more pains and aches than he had simulated for the past few days. He was carried into the building, and his leg set, and then I told him to be ready to accompany me as soon as he was able to leave the establishment. He would say nothing regarding the captain's chronometer; but one of the nurses chanced to speak of the battle, and his strange accusation against the cabman, and I gradually pieced the facts together well enough to clear up all mystifications but one. That was—where was the chronometer?

The cabman had it not; and every other patient and crevice in the ward was searched with a like result. I firmly believed that the chronometer had never been in the place, and that the charge against the cabman was only some eccentric ruse on Tommy's part to draw our attention from the real hiding-place. I visited him occasionally during his stay in the Infirmary, and at length, when he was able to move, took him with me and had him charged with the theft. But here an awkward circumstance arose, apparently to defeat justice. Captain Hosking had gone off to sea again before my capture of Tommy, and was not returned, so that Tommy's identification could not be made. There was nothing for it but to remand him, when he kindly came to our help by confessing all that I have put down. But he declared most positively that he had been robbed of the chronometer during his sleep, and, as one of the nurses had been discharged on suspicion of having pilfered from a dead patient, I lost a deal of good time in ferreting after her. She proved to be innocent, having been out of the building on that particular night, and I was left as far from success as ever. A chance remark of Tommy's about the "simplicity" of Teddy O'Lacey drew my attention to that patient, and one day when I was in the building I walked to the old ward to have a talk with him. He was gone, and his bed occupied by a new patient. I got an outline of his address, and began hunting for him in the West Port. While making this tour through one of the worst rookeries in the place I met a Roman Catholic priest well known to me, and hailed him at once with the question—

"Do you know one Teddy O'Lacey?"

The face of the priest became grave in a moment, and he appeared to me to *think well* before he answered.

"Who are you after now? and what do you want with O'Lacey?" he slowly asked, when he had done thinking.

He was a keen-eyed, intelligent man, beloved as much for his acuteness as for his benevolence, and I saw that his eyes were reading every line and expression of my face—much as I have seen those of an anxious mother do when I have asked for her son.

"Never mind what I want, but tell me where he lives," I laughingly replied. "I want to see him, if you will know."

The priest made no answer for a full minute.

"Mr McGovan," he said at last, with a tremor of deep feeling in his tones, "perhaps I know what you're seeking, and perhaps I don't. But answer me one question—do you believe me? can you depend on my word of honour as a Christian gentleman?"

"From my soul I can!" I warmly responded, grasping his proffered hand.

"Well, then, take my advice, and don't show your face in that land to-day. If you do, *I think* what you seek will be destroyed. Wait another day, and I will try to help you all I can. The man O'Lacey has been very ill, and he believes it is the visitation of God, which I do myself," and he lifted his hat and looked reverently upwards. "Will you have patience for another day, especially when I assure you, on my soul's salvation, that by going there now you will not get, and never see, what you're after?"

"I will," I answered, after revolving the proposition for a moment or two, and so we parted.

Next day a starch box, wrapped in brown paper and addressed to me, was handed into the office. Inside, in many folds of paper, was the captain's chronometer, in its chamois leather cover, bright, beautiful, and perfect as when it left the maker's hands. Pinned to it was a paper, on which were badly written these words—

"A contrite sinner restores what was wickedly stolen, and lifts a mighty load off his mind."

I smiled, and though I made some inquiries after O'Lacey, they never came to anything. Tommy Tait was duly identified by the captain, and sentenced to seven years' retirement, the captain getting back his chronometer, and saying and doing some handsome things on the occasion.

THE TORN TARTAN SHAWL.

A servant in a house at the outskirts of the city had been tempted by the clear air and dry frost to leave a whole "washing" of things out over night. She wanted them to get a nip of the frost, she said, but instead they got a nip of another kind. The girl woke at four o'clock in the morning and happened to look out at the green, when the clothes were there all right. She rose again at six, and, looking out, had to rub her eyes to make sure that she was not still in bed and dreaming. Nearly the whole of the things were gone.

Satisfied that she was awake, she first asked herself if some kind "brownie" had taken the brunt of the morning's work off her hands by taking down and folding up the things; but then, remembering that these useful fairies had all vanished before the steam engine and electric telegraph, she ran out of the house, fearing theft and hopeful of catching some of the thieves. No one was visible. The very best of the clothes were gone; the clothes pegs, all scattered over the ground, the empty ropes, and a few articles of trifling value alone being left to tell of the robbery. At least so the girl thought as she ran into the house and roused all within it with the news. Of course the servant got the blame, and received notice of dismissal at once, although, as she afterwards informed me, it had been by her mistress's express orders that the things had been left out. The lady denied that—it is convenient at times to have a bad memory—and so the disgrace rested on the girl's shoulders. Had the lady, instead of indulging in recrimination and wrangling, sent word promptly to us, the whole case might have assumed a very different aspect, as we could thus have sent word to most of the pawnbrokers by their hour of opening. A good haul had been made, including some gentlemen's shirts of fine linen, the best of the lady's underclothing, and some twenty or thirty pairs of worsted stockings, of all sizes and sorts, as there was a big family. The most of the linen was marked with the letters "A. M. B.," and some of the stockings had the same initials worked into them with pink worsted near the top of the leg.

When the news reached us I went out to see the place and get a list of the stolen articles. Six valuable hours had been lost, and I frankly told the lady that she need scarcely hope to recover all she had lost, and all through that stupid delay. The green had been left exactly as the servant had found it when she rushed out in the morning—the clothes pegs littered the ground; and while I glanced over the approaches to the green, the girl began to pick up these pegs and put them into a cotton bag which hung about half-way up one of the clothes poles. This bag was suspended from a nail at a height convenient for the hand, and at the head of the nail there fluttered a little pennon, which had never been meant for that queer flag-staff. It was a shred of bright coloured tartan, which appeared to have been rent out of some one's shawl, as the owner hurriedly switched past.

"You've been damaging your shawl, Maggie," I remarked to the servant girl, who was busy laying off to me her wrongs and grievances, and the deplorable failings of mistresses in general.

"It's no mine—I dinna wear shawls," said Maggie shortly as she continued her task. Her head was full of her troubles—mine was far away from what she was most anxious to speak of.

I took down the shred of tartan. It began narrow at the nail head which had caught it, and got gradually broader, till it ended, liked a filled-up A, in a fringe of the same colours. I spread the piece out along my palm, and then called to Maggie.

"Look here, now, and tell me if any one about the house, or living near, wears a shawl of that pattern?"

Maggie looked at the scrap of tartan, and declared most emphatically that no one in the household did wear such a shawl, and added with a smile that none of her acquaintances would be seen in such a thing—the colours being about the brightest and "loudest" that could be made for money. The same thought had already struck me, and my thoughts instinctively wandered in the direction of some of my own "bairns." The tartan was of just such a pattern as one may see on scores of shoulders about the Cowgate on a Sunday afternoon. I seemed to see the whole shawl in that shred—a little square thing, folded across, and just big enough to cover the shoulders. By mentally picturing the shawl on a woman's shoulders, and gauging her height by that treacherous nail, I could guess her to be a person rather under than above medium height, and immediately began to ask myself which of my "bairns" given to "snow-dropping" had been lately displaying such a grand shawl. Useless! their name is legion. They nearly all delight in these things, and a dozen at least might wear tartan of the identical colours of the shred in my hand. I began to think that I should make little of my discovery. However, I placed the scrap of tartan carefully between the leaves of my pocket-book, completed my list as far as I could at the house, and left. A bundle of the stolen things was in the Office before me. They had been offered at a pawnbroker's shortly after the opening hour, and pledged for fourteen shillings. The boy who had taken in the things and paid over the money was a *blockhead*. He knew that the pledger was a woman, but could not describe her appearance. He did not think she was very old, and he did not think she was very young. Did she wear a tartan shawl? Yes, he thought so; but then he changed his mind, and thought that she hadn't any shawl. No one could make anything of such a fool, and I strongly recommended the pawnbroker, for his own safety, to get rid of such a stupid assistant, to which the man replied that he would have been happy to do so, had the lad not been his own son. I grinned over my mistake, the pawnbroker helping me liberally, and then left. I then took a long stroll through the likeliest quarters, with a keen eye to every tartan shawl. Twice in the course of that walk did I start joyfully at sight of a shoulder shawl of the identical pattern, but in both cases the owners were decent, hard-working folks, and not a trace of a rent or patch to be found in either of the articles. With my eyes thus grown familiar in the search, I was wearily trudging homewards late in the afternoon with the shawl nearly gone from my thoughts, when on the South Bridge, near the head of Infirmary Street, I came up to a wretchedly-clad woman bearing in her arms a child, round which was wrapped a gaudy and apparently new shawl of the exact pattern I sought. Now, at the first glimpse of this shawl I decided that it was not the one I sought, which I imagined would scarcely be so bright and fresh-looking; but it was the incongruity of that bright shawl, allied to such rags and poverty, which made me slacken my pace, and almost instinctively follow the owner of the child.

The woman was not a professional thief—a glance at her somewhat pinched features told me that—yet her poverty was so apparent that I felt by no means certain that she would not have committed a robbery under such pressure. Poverty and a hungry bairn—where is the mother who could resist the pleadings of these? Then the shawl was the only fresh thing about the queer pair. The mother's clothes were meagre and shabby in the extreme; her boots were mere apologies for foot coverings, and her bonnet only fit for a scarecrow, and the clothing of the child equally poor. They had also a worn and travel-stained look, and stood out prominently among the ordinary passengers as dusty tramps always do when they enter a city. They were strangers, they were poor, and the child wore a tartan shawl of the exact pattern I sought—it could do no harm to follow them, which I did with a sigh for the dinner I had hoped so soon to be consuming.

My interesting pair turned down Infirmary Street, and stopped at the gate of that institution—became, indeed, part of a crowd already gathering there—visitors waiting the hour of admittance to see friends. Five o'clock was the hour, and it lacked nearly ten minutes of the time. Most of these visitors were of the poorest, and they varied the monotony of the waiting by exchanging experiences and expressions of sympathy. My tramp joined in the conversation, and I soon learned from her tongue that she came from the West. The Glasgow brogue was strong in her tongue, but not strong enough, and I soon heard her say that she had come from Airdrie, which accounted for the slight difference in the accent. She was the wife of a pit labourer—an occupation considered far beneath that of a collier, who ranks as a skilled workman; and her husband in working among the hutches had got hurt in some way, and been laid up at home till their little house was almost stripped of furniture. Then the disabled man had gone to Glasgow for advice; and afterwards hearing of the great skill of the Edinburgh professors, he had scraped together enough to bring him through to this Infirmary, into which he was admitted as an indoor patient. He did not write very hopefully of recovery; and at length the wife, reduced to her last penny, had resolved to come through and see him with her own eyes.

"I'm feared that he's waur than he says, and maybe winna get better," she said, shedding tears freely as she spoke. "I've walkit every fit o' the road, thinking I saw a coffin at the end o' the way."

Cheering words and homely sympathy were showered upon her without stint, most of those present seeming to find their own troubles light beside what that slight woman had endured.

"Is that your only bairn?" one asked, to which the mother replied—

"Yes, and I thocht we wad baith a' been frozen to death on the road. It was awfu' caul' last nicht; I never thocht we'd see morning."

"What? did ye sleep in the open air?" cried an old woman, holding up her hands.

"I hadna a penny to pay a lodging; and I was tired and dune, and didna like to gang to a poorhouse," was the choking answer.

The old Irishwoman wiped her own eyes, and then I saw her slowly fumble in her own pocket and produce twopence, which she tried to slip into the hand of the baby.

"Oh, no, no! No, thank ye," cried the mother, in strong protest, and flushing painfully at the proffered help so thinly disguised. "I'm no needing that now; I've got money since then. There's some kind folk in the world yet, and I've as muckle as take me to my mither's after I see how my man is."

I did not hear the rest of her speech, for in putting back the proffered coppers she had thrown up the corner of the tartan shawl—turned it back with a whisk right under my eyes, and there I saw a wedge-shaped rent, as if a piece had been neatly torn out of the pattern near the edge. I was in a manner fascinated and horrified by the discovery, and stood staring at the torn shawl in a manner that must have looked idiotic in the extreme.

"That's a bonnie shawl you've got on your bairn," I at length managed to say, by way of opening up a conversation.

"The bairn's bonnier than the shawl," one woman hastened to add, "but that's aye a man's way o' looking at things. The brightest colours catch his e'e first."

"Have you had it long?" I continued to the mother.

"He'll be eleven months next week," she answered, with a look of pride.

"I don't mean the bairn—the shawl," I said in correction.

"Oh, no, not long," she answered frankly; and then she appeared to catch herself up, and said no more.

"You've torn it a little there," I continued. "The bit seems to be taken clean out."

"Yes, I noticed that," she quietly answered. She did not seem to like me or my remarks—just when she was becoming so interesting to me, too!

"Would you mind turning back the corner of the shawl again for a moment—just to oblige me?" I continued, in no ways abashed by her coldness.

She gave me a look as if wondering at my impudence, and then threw back the corner of the shawl over the baby's shoulder as I had desired. Her look of contempt was beginning to be reflected in the faces around her, but I heeded the looks no more than if they had been the glassy stares of so many wax figures. I took out my pocket-book, turned open the leaves, and produced the shred of tartan. Then I spread the torn part of the shawl flat on the baby's shoulder, placed the wedged-shaped piece I had taken from my pocket-book in the opening, and found that in shape, colour, and size they fitted and corresponded exactly.

The woman followed my movements with no great interest. Her indifference might have been assumed or caused by the door being about to be opened.

"Where were you this morning between four and six o'clock?" I demanded, when I had satisfied myself that I had at last got the right shawl.

"That's nothing to you," she indignantly answered, with a slight flash of annoyance.

"It is everything; and if you won't answer it here, you must go with me up to the Police Office and refresh your memory there."

The woman turned right round and looked me full in the face, more in astonishment than alarm. Then some one whispered to her—

"It's McGovan, the detective," with a significant nudge on the arm, and in a moment she became terribly agitated.

"Do you think I stole it?" she chokingly exclaimed.

"No, not exactly."

"Then what for do you want me to gang to the Office?"

"That is not for me to explain, but go you must."

"I winna! I've trampit a' this way to see my puir man, and I maun see him."

I brought out my handcuffs, whereupon the assembled crowd began to groan and hoot and abuse me to their hearts' content. Would I drag a poor creature like that away to jail at such a moment, before she could even see her invalid husband? I replied that I would not drag her if she was inclined to walk. Then names were showered upon me enough to have stocked a slang dictionary. I pointed out to the crowd that the door was now open, and that through it was their way, while ours was in quite a different direction; and at length, with the aid of a policeman who chanced to pass the head of the street, I convinced them that I was right. The woman was now crying bitterly, and the child was screaming in concert.

"What am I ta'en awa' for? Am I charged as a thief?" she at length sobbed as I led her off.

"Not yet. Just keep your mind easy for a little. It's only your baby's shawl as yet that is in trouble. Why are you afraid to say where you got it, and when?"

She could not see that anyone had a right to ask that. She had not stolen it, nor had she bought it, but she declined to say more, till she saw how serious things looked at the Office.

She was carefully searched, with the result that in her pocket was found a half sovereign and some coppers, but none of the stolen articles. Her baby was then inspected, and on it were found a pair of worsted stockings a world too big for its little legs, with the fatal initials "A. M. B." worked in pink worsted near the top of the leg.

The case now seemed very clear, if a little sad. The woman had been in great want; had been tramping past the place, and under a sudden temptation had taken the clothes and pawned some of them. I fully expected her to admit the robbery, and plead the circumstances in piteous tones in extenuation, but nothing of the kind. She roused out of her torpor of grief, and in the most indignant tones made a statement which seemed to us to have not even the merit of ingenuity. She had been sleeping in the open air on the outskirts of the city, with her child closely clasped in her arms, "to keep it frae the cauld'," as it was but thinly clad, when she was roused by a hand shaking her violently. The disturber of her half-frozen torpor was a woman dressed like a servant girl in a common print wrapper, and carrying a big bundle. The strange woman shook her till certain that she was awake, and then rebuked her strongly for exposing herself and her child when shelter was within her reach.

"I tellt her I was a stranger, and didna ken where the Night Asylum was, and that I hadna a penny in the world," continued our prisoner. "Then she took my bairn in her arms, and kissed it and cuddled it to make it warm, and then she took the shawl off her shouthers—that shawl that you're makin' sic a wark aboot—and wrapped it roon' my wean, an' brocht a pair o' stockin's oot o' her bundle for it, an' tellt me to keep them. Then she gie'd me a shillin', an' tellt me to gang to a lodging in the Grassmarket, and then said she was in a hurry or she wad have ta'en me there hersel', and gaed awa'."

And the half-sovereign found in her possession? How did she account for that? How did it happen that when the mysterious woman with the bundle spoke to her she had not a penny, and now she had a half-sovereign?

"Oh, a gentleman gied me that," she answered, quite promptly. "I was sittin' restin' on a step, when I got in the toon a bit—for I didna think it worth while to gang to the lodging as it was after six o'clock—when a gentleman cam' up to me and asked me hoo far I had come, and aboot my man and my wean, and then he put his hand in his pooch, and brought oot a half-sovereign and put it in my hands. I thought it was a sixpence, for it was dark at the time, and maybe he thought that too. He looked a wee touched wi' drink—drunk, ye ken—and I was gled when he gaed awa'."

Clumsy, clumsy! a clumsy story in the extreme. We tried to convince her of that, and by cross-examining her to trip her up, but she stuck to her statements with amazing firmness, and even volunteered fresh details in confirmation. Finding her obdurate, we gave her up in despair, and she was taken away and locked up in a state of frenzy which looked wonderfully real, and therefore piteous enough.

The only wonder to us now was where the rest of the stolen clothes had been hidden. Allowing for the woman spending some money in the forenoon, she might be reasonably expected to have about ten shillings left of the fourteen given by the pawnbroker, but that disposal accounted for only a part of the stolen things. Could she have had any assistant who would share the plunder? I was anxious to settle that question. I brought in the pawnbroker's son to see her, and he identified her in a haphazard fashion as the woman who pawned the things, but then, as I have recorded, he was a *blockhead*, and his evidence had no great value. I then thought of visiting the Infirmary to see if she had a husband there, and learn if the name she had given—Ellen Hunter—was real or assumed. A little to my surprise I found the husband there, Archibald Hunter by name, as the card at the head of his bed testified; and the moment that a hint of the truth was given him he was so terribly excited and agitated that he would almost have been out of the place there and then had he been allowed.

"Hoo can you blame a starving woman with a wean at her breast?" was his wild inquiry. "Can ye no show mercy where it's no a real thief, but ane forced to it?"

"I daresay she would be shown mercy if she would admit the truth, and declare that she was driven to the act," I replied, "but that she refuses to do. She persists in trying to screen herself and put all the crime upon some imaginary persons who gave her the things. There's nothing new in that story; every thief has it at his tongue's end."

Though we thus disbelieved Ellen Hunter's story, we made every search for the rest of the plunder, and actually did come upon traces of it. Several articles were recovered, which had been either sold or pawned, in which the linen mark had been removed bodily with a pair of scissors. This was particularly noticeable on the gentlemen's shirts, which had been marked on a little tab at the bottom of the breast. In the case of one recovered, this tab had been cut off and the remaining end neatly stitched down. The consequence was that, though morally certain as to the identity of the shirt, the owner could not swear to it, and it was given back to the buyer, who declared that it had been bought from a man, whose appearance he described, and whom he declared himself able to identify.

Meantime the trial of Ellen Hunter came on at the Sheriff Court, to which she had been remitted. No reasoning or persuasion could induce her to plead guilty, or advance extenuating circumstances by way of lightening her sentence.

"They may do what they like to me, but I winna say I'm guilty when I'm innocent," was her firm declaration. "If my wean could only speak, it wad tell ye that I've spoken naething but the truth."

The case accordingly went to proof, and was speedily settled to the satisfaction of the jury, who, without leaving the box, found the charge proven. But then there arose in the Court, close to the bar, a pale shadow of a man, who in broken tones stated that he was the husband of the accused, and pleaded for permission to say a few words in mitigation of his wife's offence. The permission was granted, and, in a husky and broken tone, Hunter proceeded to narrate the circumstances which had brought him to the Infirmary—his wife's devotion, integrity, and sterling honesty; and the dread fear which had brought her on that long journey on foot, and in the dead of winter, with a child at her breast. The speech was given in the homeliest of language, and without any attempt at grammatical correctness; but there was a power and native eloquence about it which went to every heart. The wife was sobbing loudly at the bar with her infant in her arms, and the judge, visibly affected along with the whole Court, was about to pass a light sentence, when there came an interruption, the very last that any would have looked for in that place.

"I will do it, and I don't care for you!" was shouted out in a woman's voice in the audience, and as all looked round a girl known to me as "Sally the Snowdropper," struggled up from one of the seats in spite of the efforts of a man at her side to detain her. Then there was a brief struggle and altercation, and the man rising with her dealt the poor girl a terrific blow in the eyes. The whole Court was aghast, and the brute was speedily collared and brought forward in custody. Then the prisoner at the bar started up with a joyful scream, and pointing to Sally, cried out—

"That's the woman! that's the kind lassie that gied me the shilling and wrappit her shawl roon' my wean. Ask her and she'll tell ye."

Sally came forward, staunching the blood flowing from her nose, and looking pale with excitement, but firm and self-reliant withal.

"The woman is innocent as the child in her arms," said Sally, as soon as she could speak. "A month or two in quod is nothing to me, but it's hard to send an honest man's wife there for nothing. I can't stand that. I never thought it would come to this, or I would have spoken out sooner. I *stole the things*—every one of them—and I met her and gave her the shawl I had on, as her child was nearly dead with cold. I never knew the shawl was torn, or likely to be traced, or I'd never have given it. I gave her the stockings too—the first pair that came to hand in the bundle, and put them on her bairn with my own hands. The mother was half-frozen in her sleep, and at first I thought they were both dead. Just let her go, and shove me in her place, and the thing will be squared."

"She's mad!—she's drunk, and doesn't know what she's saying," shouted the man who had assaulted her; but he was promptly removed and locked up, the immediate result of which was that he was discovered to be wearing a gentleman's white shirt resembling one of those stolen, and having the tab cut away from the breast, and stitched down exactly like the one already described.

Sally very speedily proved that she was neither mad nor drunk by revealing where all the stolen things had been disposed of, and stating that the tabs of the white shirts had been doctored by her own hands. Her companion was next day identified as the man who had sold one of the shirts, and the case was complete.

Ellen Hunter, half frenzied with delight, was set at liberty and taken into her husband's arms; and when our case was complete, Sally, instead of appearing as prisoner, was taken as a witness, and so moved every one that the Sheriff, before allowing her to be dismissed, thought fit to address to her a few words of strong commendation for her generous spirit and truly noble nature, at the same time advising her, in a kind and feeling manner, to try to get out of the debasing life for which she was so ill-suited. In vain! he might have saved his breath. Sally was too far gone to mend her ways; and, while her companion went to prison, she went drifting on to the death and destruction which speedily became her lot. But she left one green spot on her memory. How many such can each of us boast?

A LIFT ON THE ROAD.

A curious difficulty sometimes faces the administrators of the law in dealing with some of that numerous class known as swindlers. A man calls at various houses and represents that he is a clergyman in want or distress, and thus gets money. Some one sharper than the rest runs him down, and he is caught and charged; when, lo! it turns out that the so-called rogue—and rogue he generally is—has actually been a clergyman, and of course is, in common with all broken men, actually in want. The result is clear—there has been no fraud. He has deceived no one; he has told the truth; and though he might be convicted of begging, he cannot be charged with swindling or obtaining money under false pretences.

It is a man of this stamp I have now to introduce. His real name was Alfred Johnston. He was a college-bred man of great smartness, and would have soon made a mark as a clergyman had he not been caught and ruined by a bad woman. Rendered dissolute in his habits and disowned by his friends, he changed his life and became as great a rascal as before he had been promising as a man.

Even with talents such as Johnston possessed this life is not all smooth sailing. There come times of want and danger, when their dearest companions would betray them without reward, or see them drop dying of hunger at their feet without putting out a hand to save. These are the reverses which are never heard of, but which are more common in a life of crime than any other on the face of the globe.

Johnston had tramped on foot the greater part of the road from Glasgow to Edinburgh, and had just crossed the boundary of the shire, which means that he was ten or twelve miles from the capital. His appearance was very much against him, or his route would have been easier. His boots were mere shreds of leather, through which his feet showed conspicuously, and he had no stockings. He had no shirt, and the utmost ingenuity in buttoning up his ragged coat could scarcely conceal the fact. The only trace of respectability remaining about his attire was a shabby and much battered dress hat. Johnston was a very good-looking fellow, with fine flowing black hair, and a big beard and moustache, and was still young—about thirty—but Apollo himself would have had an evil look in such a garb, so this prodigal's lines had been hard ones for some time. In this plight—wearied in body, tired of life, disgusted with himself and all the world—Johnston lay down on a green bank by the road-side, wondering whether it were best to lie there and die, or struggle on over the remaining miles, which seemed to lengthen as they grew fewer in number.

A lovely sunset was shedding glory on the scene, and all was peaceful but the mind of that lost man. In looking listlessly around, his eye fell on a comfortable and well-sheltered residence, the very air of which proclaimed it, to Johnston's experienced eye, a minister's manse. There was a large garden attached, well stocked with fruit trees and bushes, and every other appurtenance that could render a country house snug and attractive. I don't know whether the thought struck him that he might have been the comfortable occupant of such a house—possibly it did, for he was conscious that he had more talent than dozens of the drones occupying manses of the kind—but his immediate action was to rouse himself to consider whether he could not lay the occupant under contribution. A passing field hand, belonging to the village close by, supplied him with the occupant's name and opinions, and, thus armed, he ventured up to the house, gently rang the bell, and with some difficulty induced the servant to take up his name—"The Rev. Alfred Johnston"—to her master.

Johnston stood demurely in the lobby, to which he had been admitted with marked suspicion by the servant, till the Rev. Robert Goodall appeared, in spectacles and slippers, direct from his study. If he had been startled to learn that a brother clergyman wished to see him, he was much more so at seeing the brother clergyman. But Johnston was fluent of tongue, and he had experience in dealing with such surprise.

"I am really a clergyman, as I can prove to you, but have been reduced to this state by my own folly," he hastened to humbly say. "And I have not come to beg or ask you for money, as I daresay there are so many legitimate calls upon your goodness that you can ill afford to succour strangers. But I have walked all the way from Glasgow, and am now nearly fainting with hunger. If you could tell your servant to give me, out on the door-step or at the road-side, enough broken victuals, no matter how plain or coarse, to support me till morning, your kindness will never be forgotten."

The clergyman heard him in silence, and probably scepticism; but on questioning him closely as to his college career, was surprised to find every statement agreeing with his own knowledge. Johnston described the classes; mimicked the Professors; quoted Greek and Hebrew writings with the utmost ease and correctness, and even showed that he had made the acquaintance of personal friends of Mr Goodall who had attended during the same sessions. In this narration Johnston had only to keep to the truth to make it saddening to listen to, and this he did, adding a few pathetic touches about a wife and child left in great want in Glasgow, while he made a struggle to reach Edinburgh on foot, in hope of securing a tutor's place, for which he was well qualified.

"Do you mean to try to reach Edinburgh to-night?" inquired the clergyman, with some pity in his tones.

"No, that is impossible, for I am quite exhausted," said the wanderer, with apparent frankness. "I cannot go much further. I shall rest under some hedge or hay-stack till morning, and then make my way thither by daylight."

"I am sorry for you, a man of education and talent, who might be in so much better a position," said the clergyman, in gentle rebuke. "However, you shall have the food you require, but not out on the door-step. Come this way."

Mr Goodall led the way to a comfortable parlour, where he lighted a lamp, drew the blinds, and then ordered in the remains of his own dinner—cold, of course, but much better fare than Johnston had tasted for many a day. When he had eaten his fill, and finished with a glass of wine brought to him by the kind clergyman, he was in no hurry to leave, and his entertainer was as willing that he should linger. Johnston's tongue was fluent, and he could tell many strange stories of his ups and downs, and in the present case so suited them to a clerical ear that the good-hearted man at length felt strong qualms as to sending such a man out into the darkness. The best plan would have been to give the needy being a shilling wherewith to pay for a lodging at some travellers "howff," but that never occurred to the minister. He was entertained, flattered, and amused by the queer waif cast up at his door, and fancied that the best way to show his gratitude was to invite Johnston to stay there over the night. The wanderer affected to receive the invitation with unbounded astonishment, but was at length prevailed upon to accept the offer, and after patiently listening to some of Mr Goodall's printed sermons, and passing very flattering criticisms upon their logic and learning, he followed the good man upstairs to a spare bedroom, where an old suit of the minister's, with a pair of boots and a shirt, made a considerable improvement in his appearance.

After supper they parted for the night with mutual good wishes, and the minister lay down to a sound night's sleep, conscious of having that day emulated his great Master in doing one good action to the neediest near his hands. Johnston ought to have slept soundly too, for he had travelled far and fasted, and then eaten well, but cupidity was in him stronger than drowsiness. In producing his pet sermons to read them over for his guest's edification, the clergyman had used his keys to a drawer in the writing-table and exposed something very like a cash-box. When the sermons had been restored to their place of security, the drawer had been again locked, but the keys were left in the lock. Johnston, during a momentary absence of his entertainer, unlocked the drawer and placed the keys ostentatiously on the top of the writing-table, from which they were lifted by the owner a few minutes later, all unconscious but that he had himself left them there.

No opportunity occurred during the evening for testing the contents of the unlocked drawer; but in anticipation of there being something in it worth carrying away, he arranged with his kind host that he should be allowed to leave the house very early in the morning.

The thought of that money-box kept him awake for three hours, by which time he guessed rightly that both the clergyman and his housekeeper would be fast asleep. He then slipped down to the parlour on his stocking-soles—the first use to which he put the gift of Mr Goodall—and took from the box about £50 in notes and coin. A gold pencil-case, a silver fruit knife, and a pair of spectacles, which were lying close by, he was mean enough also to appropriate. He then slipped upstairs, and lay down and slept the sleep of the unjust till about seven in the morning.

I don't know what the man's feelings had been when he found that Mr Goodall was up, and had caused the servant to prepare breakfast for him, and when that was hastily swallowed, insisted on accompanying the wanderer back part of the way to the nearest railway station, at which he paid his fare to Edinburgh, and pressed a few shillings into his hand, merely saying at parting—

"Go in peace, and sin no more."

Surely his heart must have got a sore twinge at that moment.

Johnston soon reached Edinburgh, and the telegram announcing the robbery followed an hour or two later. This message contained a brief description of the man, who, however, was known to me by reputation, though I had never seen him. My only wonder was that he had given his real name and antecedents, which, I suppose, may be accounted for by the robbery being an after-thought. With such a sum of money in his possession Johnston was practically at the ends of the earth, and it might be thought foolish to look for him in Edinburgh; but I reasoned otherwise. Your very needy rascal, who has not fingered money for a long time, grudges to throw away much of it on railway fares, or anything, indeed, which does not minister immediately to his own gratification. Besides, Johnston had spoken of going to "friends" in Edinburgh, and I had no doubt but he had in his mind at the moment certain of my "bairns" hailing from Glasgow, and already known to him, who would be glad to profit by his superior education and planning power. By telegraphing to Johnny Farrel I had a list of these "friends" an hour after the receipt of the news, and immediately went out to seek some of them, sending McSweeny in another direction on the same errand. The brief description from the robbed clergyman was supplemented by a fuller one from Glasgow, and thus we were pretty certain of identifying our man, even if we had met him on the street. Now, behold how, when you are most certain, you may be most easily deceived. McSweeny went to a certain house in Potterrow, which he entered without ceremony, and then proceeded to question the inmates. This house had generally a stranger or two in it at every inspection, and the present occasion proved no exception. There were two strangers—one a hawker, and the other an evil-looking character with the hair of his head cropped close to the skull, and his face as smooth and hairless as the palm of his hand. Neither of these answering the description, McSweeny began to make inquiries for Johnston, and was even obliging enough to describe his character and general appearance to those present in that kitchen.

"I believe I saw him not an hour ago," said the cropped-headed man sullenly, after a dead silence on the part of all present.

"Where?" eagerly demanded McSweeny.

"Where I could get him again in five minutes, I think, if it was worth my while," suggestively returned the man.

"Will you take me to him now, then?" cried McSweeny.

"No. But I'll send him up here if you like to wait. Is it worth half-a-crown?"

McSweeny considered for a moment, and then said that it was. The man slowly rose from his place by the fire and held out his hand for the money; but the clever and cunning McSweeny only winked hard, and made a few remarks about great detectives, famous all over the world, not being easily cheated.

"No, no, my jewel," he added; "ye'll get the money when ye've earned it—not a minute sooner."

The man scowled horribly, and slowly slunk out of the room and the house. Was ever an escape more neatly effected? That clean-shaven, cropped-haired man was Johnston! The moment he had entered the city he had gone to a barber and got shaved and cropped—I afterwards spoke to the man who did it—and the alteration which such an operation effects on the appearance can be understood only by those who have seen it performed. Had Johnston been placed at that moment under the eyes of Mr Goodall he most certainly would not have been able to identify his late guest; nay, I am not sure but he might have sworn most positively that that was not the man.

McSweeny waited patiently for nearly half an hour, and then it began to dawn upon him that he had been done. The grins of the occupants of that kitchen as he went out did not tend to soothe his feelings. Not a word was said on either side; it was all understood. What had first roused my chum's suspicion of the truth was the recollection that the man had passed out of the room without a head-covering, and that the remainder of his body was covered with a very loose-fitting old suit of blacks. Now the clergyman had made Johnston a present of just such a suit, and being himself a stout man, had not been able to give him a very good fit. Along with the suit went a broad-brimmed clerical-looking dress hat; but that Johnston had only assumed when out of McSweeny's sight. What made the thing more aggravating was that McSweeny had seen the hat hanging on a window-shutter in one of the rooms in searching the house, yet had never thought of connecting it with the evil-looking wretch by the fire. Not long after McSweeny's discomfiture, one of the county police appeared with a full description of this suit of clothes and broad-brimmed hat—just too late, of course.

When McSweeny had spent a deal of time in hunting for the man who had so neatly escaped him, and appeared to report to me, I was in a very bad temper, for I was conceited enough to think that, if it had been I who had clapped eyes on Johnston, he would not have got off—an opinion which I changed when I knew the rascal better.

Like Jim Macluskey, [See *Brought to Bay*, page 5] he had the rare faculty of being able to change the whole expression of his face by ingeniously contorting his features, and could speak in any kind of language or tone to suit. McSweeny's mistake was really not so surprising or stupid as it appeared to me at the moment, or as it now appears in print.

I had no time to say much, for I felt that Johnston must have realised that the city was too hot for him, and would get out of it at his swiftest. If I was to get him it must be at once.

What route or means was he most likely to take? That was the all-important question with me. First I decided that he would not go near any of the railway stations, else I should have hopefully turned in the direction of the Forth and the North—quite a favourite route for escaping criminals. Then it struck me that, having gone the length of sacrificing his fine beard and hair, and been so successful in thus altering his appearance, he might boldly try the most dangerous route of all, as that on which he was least likely to be looked for— the road for Glasgow. He was not to know that, when it was too late, we had penetrated his disguise, and at that moment was probably exulting over his cleverness. I did not expect him to walk all the way to Glasgow, but thought he might go out a good distance, and then take train at some obscure railway station for whatever town he meant to favour with his presence. My idea was that Glasgow itself was to be thus favoured, but that point did not concern me for the present.

Now, there were the three roads all crossed by the railway to choose from, and I was a little puzzled which to try. He had come by that leading through East Calder, and I scarcely thought he would take that. That left the Bathgate and Linlithgow routes to choose from. I got a gig with a strong stepping horse, and drove out the Linlithgow road till I came upon one of the county police, who satisfied me that no such man had passed along that road within the last three hours. My reason for trying that route was that there was a possibility of him, when once on the railway skirting that road, branching away to the north by way of Stirling, and so escaping. However, there was nothing for it but to drive back in all haste and get on to the Bathgate road, which is the favourite one for tramps. When I was a few miles from the city, I could scarcely believe my own eyes when I saw a man approaching me from the opposite direction, clad in a suit identical with that I was looking for. There it was—loose-fitting, shabby, old, and black, with the broad-brimmed hat to crown all. The man's face had no beard either, but it was roasted brown with the sun, and had on the chin a stubbly growth of hair some days old. Nevertheless, I pulled up and stopped him.

"Here, you!" I said, displaying my staff as I jumped down.

"Alfred Johnston, I've been looking for you. I've a warrant for all Scotland, so step up quietly;" and before he had recovered from his astonishment, or uttered a word, I had the handcuffs on his dirty wrists.

"My name isn't Johnston—that I'll swear," he said, simply, when he got his breath; then a light appeared to break on him, and with a great oath he added, "Now I think I know why the kind gentleman got me to change clothes with him, though mine were sorry rags and them is first-class. Whew! who'd have thought it? He's done something, and the police is after him for it?"

This seemed not bad at all, and quite worthy of the man who had so neatly befooled McSweeny, but I only grinned unfeelingly in his simple face, and said dryly that "I believed so," and bundled him without ceremony into the gig.

"But—but—ye don't mean to tell me ye're going to take me instead of him?" he at length articulated, with a look of half-comical alarm.

"I am—just."

"Then the real man'll get off, and I'll be hanged in his stead!" he cried, fairly breaking down with terror; "for he's footing it out fast enough, I tell ye."

"The real man?" I said, thinking to humour him, as I resumed the reins and turned the horse's head; "and what was he like, pray?"

"A clean-shaved, smooth-spoken gentleman—for all the world like a priest or a minister, only that his head's cropped as close as if he was just new out of jail," was the prompt answer; "though, by my troth, he looked more like a shockerawn in my old duds when I left him."

I started, and began to think. Then I pulled off my prisoner's hat, and found his hair not at all close cropped. I drove rapidly back to one of those wayside stations of the county police, and there left my prisoner safely locked up, every question he answered confirming my impression that he had been speaking the truth. The only difficulty I had with him was in getting him to describe the clothes which he had exchanged for the old blacks he wore. These he either could not or would not name—in colour, shape, or material—a difficulty which I only understood when the rags were before me— and then it would have puzzled *me* to do what I wondered at him not doing. Even a detective can be unreasonable at times.

Leaving the Irish-speaking man thus, I turned the horse's head and made him spin along the road at a fine rate, being not only anxious to overtake the wearer of the "duds," if he existed, but also to escape a storm of rain which had been threatening for half the day and was then beginning to descend. When I had gone on thus for a few miles, and passed a good many on the road—not one of whom answered the description of my man—I allowed the horse to "breathe" in ascending one of the braes by laying the reins on his neck and letting him take his own pace. In thus moving slowly along, I turned a corner allotted to stone breaking, and there caught sight of a dark object huddled in to shelter from the rain. I was all but past, and had just noticed that the figure was that of a ragged tramp, when the man rose and trotted hurriedly after the gig, saying respectfully—

"If you please, sir, would it be asking too much, sir, for you to give me a lift?"

I pulled up the horse and scanned him closely, while I appeared to busy myself pulling up my collar to keep out the driving rain.

"Well," I said, in a tone by no means gracious or obliging, "how far are you going?"

"I'm not particular, sir," he answered with alacrity, "as far as you're going yourself, sir."

"Come up, then."

I had decided that he might not be my man, but I would be as well to have him beside me till I saw if there were any others further on. Besides, it was already growing dark, and I had little time to lose.

The bundle of rags got up, and I had a better view of his face as he made his ragged legs comfortable under the knee cloth. It was clean shaven and by no means so loutish as his speech. His hair, I saw, was cropped to the bone. I drove on till it was dark without overtaking any other, drawing my companion out on the weather and other every-day topics.

"What are you when you are at home?" I at length half jocularly asked.

I had kept him at arm's length, so to speak, all the way, never allowing him to become familiar in the least.

He paused over his answer, looking up at my face through the darkness.

"I'd astonish you if I told you," he at last replied, in a somewhat altered tone.

"Indeed!" I answered, apparently with great indifference, but really trembling with eager curiosity.

"Yes, I am really a clergyman, but reduced to this state by my own folly."

At last I had him! There he was sitting close by me in the dark, betrayed by his own pet phrase, so truthful, and yet so often used to deceive. I could have shouted with exultation, but I was too anxious to see him safe under lock and key. Plenty of time for crowing when I had him in the cells.

I gave a dissatisfied grunt and a dry "Imphum," and remained silent for some time. During that interval a bright thought flashed upon me, and at the first cross road I purposely turned the horse off the main road, and went on till we were stopped by a farm.

I had gig lamps, and these I got lighted, and then I mounted and turned back till we reached the main road, which I boldly turned into—in the direction leading back to Edinburgh.

"Are you sure you're not going the wrong way?" said my companion, after a little.

"I am going my way—this is my road," I replied, with some gruffness; "I can't say anything about yours. I think you said you weren't particular?"

"All right—neither I am," he said, evidently not relishing the thought of being turned out on the dark road in such a rain. "Just drive on, please, and never mind me."

I did drive on at my fastest. I soon reached the little station-house; but before that I had decided that it might not be very safe to trust Johnston in such a place for the night, and I passed it without stopping. At last the lights of the city appeared in front of us, and my companion roused himself to watch them with growing interest.

"What town is this?" he at length asked.

"Edinburgh," I shortly answered.

"What! Edinburgh?" he cried, almost jumping up from his seat. "How can that be? I thought we were driving towards Bathgate?"

"We were at first, but I changed my mind and turned back. Want to get down, or will you go further?"

He considered the matter, though I was really laughing at him in my sleeve while making the suggestion; for, as may be guessed, I had no intention of allowing him to get down—alone. Then he said ruefully—

"Which way are you going?"

"Round by the back of the Castle towards the High Street," was my prompt answer; and he directed me to drive on, signifying that he was going that way too—which was perfectly true. At the Puseyite Chapel he touched me on the arm and said—"I'll get down here, sir, if you please."

I was driving along at a great speed and appeared not to hear him, and in a moment more we were tearing into the brightly-lighted Lawnmarket and High Street.

"I wanted to get down," he said reproachfully, and a little angrily, as we went careering madly down the street.

"It's all right," I said; "I'm getting down in a minute myself;" and sure enough, in less than that time, I pulled up in front of the Central, where I gave the reins to a man, who delightedly exclaimed—

"Oh, McGovan's got him!"

My prisoner gave me a look—long and steady—which spoke more than a thousand words, and then I helped him down with the words—

"Come away, Johnston; we've had a very successful drive, haven't we, though it has been disagreeably wet?"

He replied in the affirmative, but the language in which it was couched was not clerical. That lift on the road cost him just five years' penal servitude. I shall allude to him again.

THE ORGAN-GRINDER'S MONEY-BAG.

When the organ-grinder appeared in a distracted state at the Office, his face was quite familiar to me through seeing him on the streets and at race-courses and other gatherings with his organ. He was a big-bodied, swarthy man, with a full black beard, and, of course, till that moment I had taken him for an Italian. To hear the Irish brogue come pouring in a torrent out of his mouth, therefore, was a little startling. His very grief, and earnestness, and evident unconsciousness of anything ludicrous added comicality to the discovery, and it was with the greatest difficulty that I restrained a smile while he incoherently made known his loss.

"The savings of tin years tuck from me in a lump," he groaned, with a shower of lamentations; "and however the thafe did it, or found out where my money was, or that I had any to stale, I can't for the life of me tell; for even my friend Tom Joson here thought I hadn't a penny, and didn't know where it was kept."

The friend thus alluded to bobbed to me, and I recognised him also as a street musician. He was a lame man, and used a crutch and stick to move about, and his instrument was a tin whistle. Sometimes, I think, he used two of these whistles tied together, and he affected to be much more lame and helpless than he really was. His favourite "pitch" was to squat cross-legged at the edge of the pavement on the Mound with his crutch and stick ostentatiously displayed before him, and a tin mug placed on the kerb ready for contributions, and there he droned out his tunes, generally of a plaintive character, for hours together, with wonderful taste and skill. He got drunk at times, and became troublesome, and had to go to jail to cool down.

That was the man who now bobbed to me, and shook his head dolefully over his friend's misfortune.

"I came here to show him the way, and introduce him to the great detective," Joson volunteered, with a sympathetic snifter and cringe.

"Yes, having been here so often yourself, you were quite qualified for that task," I dryly returned, whereat the lame man cringed and bobbed again, and affected to take the observation as a very good joke, though his mental remarks, I feel sure, were quite unfit for publication.

"You say you have lost a bag of money," I continued to the organ-grinder, after taking down his name as Peter McCarthy. "How did it happen, and how much money did the bag contain?"

"'Twasn't lost—'twas stole from me," cried the organ-grinder, with a fresh burst of expletives on the head of the robber; "and there was two hundred and seven golden sovereigns in the bag—two hundred and seven, sur. 'Twas a heap of money, and it was so pleasant to feel the gold running through your fingers. But I'm afeared I'll never touch it again. And I worked hard for it, sur; if I'd coined every sovereign of it out of me own blood it couldn't have been got slower. Tin years! och, if I lose it, I may creep into me grave."

"You were foolish to carry such a large sum about with you," I could not help observing.

"I didn't carry it about with me—it had got too heavy for that," quickly returned the organ-grinder. "Faith, I only wish I'd never given up carrying it, and I'd have had it now. No; I had it stowed away in a hole of the chimney of my house, where no living being could get at it."

"And yet it was taken—how do you explain that?"

"I can't explain it. I only know that it's gone," he answered with a mysterious look, much as if he thought some greedy ghosts had been at work removing his hidden pile. "My house is a garret in the Grassmarket. I'll take you to it, and show you the place whenever you like. The landlord is a hawker called Jimmy Poulson. He has the other two rooms; but he can't get into my place at any time, as I've a lock on the dure, which I had put on myself, which no one can pick."

At the mention of Jimmy Poulson's name, Tom Joson, the lame man, jerked his head to me significantly.

"I've always till now thought Jimmy an honest man," continued the organ-grinder, "and even if he had got into my house while I was out, how could he have known I had money, or got it out without leaving marks?"

"Ay, how?" groaned the lame man in sympathy.

"You see, sur," pursued the other, "I never had a fire on in my room, for the agreement was I was to get the use of Jimmy's kitchen and fire for a shilling a week extra, so I had a board made to fit the fireplace, and I had that always fixed in while I was out. I'll tell ye how I fixed it so as nobody could move it without me knowing. I always pasted a paper over the edges, and the paper had generally a picture on it. If any one had tuck it down when I was out the paper picture must have shown the cracks and tears. Last night when I got home there wasn't a scratch or tear in the paper—this morning the same; but when I took out the board with my own hands I found that the hole in the chimney was empty, and my bag of gold stole away."

"Stole away!" echoed the lame man, like an obedient chorus, with a doleful shake of the head.

"Then I wondered how it was I hadn't seen Jimmy for three days, for I'd never known him to be away so long before," continued the organ-grinder. "You see, we have both keys to fit the outer door, and when Jimmy's away I just look after things for him. He's a bachelor, and so am I, and likely to keep so if I don't get back my money. Oh, what will my poor darlin', Honora, say when she hears of me being robbed!" he moaned, flying off at a tangent again. "She's waited for me for ten years, and the money was to fulfil a vow I made as a penance to me sowl, for I wance struck my mother, and knocked her senseless, and I vowed before God that if He'd restore her I'd save, and slave, and scrape, and stint myself, and never marry my own devoted girl till I'd bought the little bit of land and the house for the owld paiple to end their days in peace; and another year would have done it. Surely the blessed Lord above us, that heard my vow and helped me to keep it, won't let me be sent broken-hearted to the grave with this cruel loss?"

"You ought to have put the money in the bank," I said severely. "The interest alone during these years would have amounted to something handsome, and allowed you to fulfil your purpose by this time."

"I couldn't trust a bank," he said, with the national prejudice in every word and tone. "When the bank broke I'd have blamed myself for my simplicity and foolishness, but now I blame nobody but the black-hearted thafe. If it's Jimmy Poulson that's done it, he'll never prosper in this world; for it's not me alone he's wronged, but the owld paiple, that are less able to bear it, and my sweet colleen, that would lay down her life for me."

"Oh, but Mr McGovan will soon run him down," observed the lame man, hopefully.

I was not so sure of that, for, supposing the thief to be Poulson, that worthy had already got three days' start. As yet, however, I was by no means certain that there had been any thief in the case. When I had got from the organ-grinder a description of the land of houses in which he lived, I found that it was one well known to me as one of the ricketiest buildings in the quarter, and I quickly formed a theory, from his description of the place and circumstances, that seemed to offer the only feasible explanation. He had thrust the bag of money into a hole inside the chimney; that hole might have been deeper than he thought; might have led into another chimney; and so, in thrusting in the treasure, it was possible he might have sent it tumbling down, like a gift from heaven, into some wretched abode beneath. I said little of this idea at the moment, but anxiety to test the matter induced me to go with the queer pair to the organ-grinder's garret. It was a poor place, and very small. There was a bed at one side, and a window jutting out on the slates. This window was fastened with two thick screw nails on the inside, and had not been opened for years. I tried with all my strength to open it, but it did not yield in the slightest. The place was very tidy and clean, considering that no woman ever got within the door. I turned to the fire-place, beside which stood a square board very much papered over on one side, but showing clean white wood and two cross spars on the other. This fitted the fire-place exactly. Directed by the organ-grinder I reached up inside the fire-place and soon touched a recess in the wall of the chimney. It was a mistake to call it a hole; it was a mere ledge in the wall on which a bag of money might have rested easily, but in which it could scarcely be said to be hidden. There was no soot in the chimney, and my fingers were not even soiled by the inspection. My theory, of course, was completely knocked on the head, but I immediately formed another.

Looking up the chimney I could see daylight at quite a short distance above. The vent was nearly straight till near the fire-place, where it widened considerably. The organ-grinder was positive that the strange door of his safe and its fastenings had been quite untampered with before he himself opened it. He declared that if it had been he should have detected the fact at a glance. The money therefore had not come out at that door; neither had it gone through the wall or down any other chimney; there remained therefore but one way for its abstraction, that was—up the chimney. The lame man Joson, who assisted me officiously during the examination, was anxious when I had concluded to learn what theory I had formed in regard to the robbery, but I did not enlighten him; and though the second theory, like the first, proved to be not quite correct, it was perhaps as well that I said nothing of it at the time. No such caution is necessary here, however, and I may state the theory. I had often seen ragamuffins fishing down the street gratings or inaccessible areas for odds and ends dropped by passers by, their fishing-tackle generally consisting of a long bit of twine and a piece of wood or stone, the under side of which was coated with tar or some such sticky substance. Sometimes, instead of a tarred stone, there was a well-sharpened table fork, which was simply lowered and let "dab" into the article to be hoisted.

If the article happened to lie in any corner "off the plumb," some difficulty was generally experienced in the fishing, though even then captures were sometimes made by setting the fork or sticky stone in motion, pendulum wise, and at the proper moment letting it fall on the article. Now, applying this knowledge to the organ-grinder's money-bag, it seemed to me quite likely that it had been fished out in the same fashion, though I was doubtful if a fork or even a sticky stone could have laid hold of a money-bag of green flannel, especially when that bag was weighted with 207 sovereigns. But even supposing the "fishing" theory correct, boys do not generally wander along roofs fishing down chimneys for possible hoards.

To fish down that chimney implied a knowledge that the gold was there, and that knowledge, the organ-grinder insisted, had been till that day confined strictly to his own breast. Even his own relations in the west of Ireland, he declared, knew nothing of his hiding-place or the amount of his savings. In saying so he possibly spoke what he believed to be the truth. It is possible to betray many a secret without ever using the tongue or opening the lips, and certainly without ever knowing or dreaming that we have revealed what we are striving to conceal. I therefore made no comment on these strong statements, but sought by a series of indirect questions to discover whom he consorted with most, and, above all, who was favoured so far as to be admitted into this house of his, as he chose to dignify the garret.

Only two persons, so far as I could learn, were thus favoured, and these were the landlord, Jimmy Poulson, and the lame man, Tom Joson. The organ-grinder did not make a confidant of either of these men, but if one of them had a higher place in his esteem than the other, that one was Joson. I suspect the organ-grinder was inclined to be miserly, and liked Joson, because the lame man treated him to drink without ever asking him to return the compliment.

The street whistle-player, unlike his dear friend, was a married man, and never got into difficulties with the police except by getting drunk and quarrelling with his wife. He had therefore got into a habit of shunning public-houses when he wanted a comfortable spree—as he knew only too well that there he would be unerringly hunted out by his wife—and going instead to the organ-grinder's garret, where, after the labours of the day, they could enjoy in peace what was denied to Joson elsewhere. Much of this I drew out of the organ-grinder after getting rid of Joson, by sending him out for some writing-paper and ink. When I had drawn from him all I wished, I began to speculate as to whether it was not possible that both Poulson and Joson had participated in the robbery. If I had had any choice in the matter, I should rather have blamed the lame man than the hawker. Poulson was a hard-working man, and had never been through our hands, while the lame man was a bit of an imposition, had often been in jail, though not for stealing, and was exceedingly cunning besides. But there was the condemning fact—Poulson had run off and disappeared, while the lame man not only remained, but had been the adviser and guide of the organ-grinder in seeking the aid of the police. Still I could not see what interest the lame man could have had in so constantly seeking the society of the organ-grinder. What object could he have in view? Had he suspected that the man kept a hoard somewhere about the room, and determined to find out where that hide was?

These were some of the thoughts which troubled me, but I put them past for after consideration, while I made arrangements with the organ-grinder to try a curious experiment, first binding him to absolute secrecy, even from his "friend, Tom Joson." The lost money-bag had been made out of a piece of the green cloth which had covered McCarthy's organ when he was overtaken by rain. He had made the bag himself, and said he would know it again among a thousand. I asked him if he could make one a little like it in size, to which he promptly answered that he could, and out of the same stuff. I then left him, and returned late at night, and long after it was dark. We weighted the new money-bag with a quantity of coppers which the organ-grinder had taken in the streets, and then placed it on the ledge in the chimney. I then mounted to the roof and easily found the right chimney top, as I had made McCarthy light a candle and place it within the fire-place. I then lowered the "fishing tackle" I had prepared for my experiment. This was a leaden sinker at the end of a string, to which was attached an arrangement of hooks, which could not have failed to catch the money-bag if I could only have brought them near it. But there was the difficulty. I fished and fought away for half an hour, but I could never get swing enough on that sinker to bring the hooks near the bag, though I knew exactly where the bag lay, which was more than the thief could have known. As the fire-place widened considerably from the chimney proper, I could not see the bag for which I was fishing, and in the end I gave up the attempt, almost convinced that the robbery had not been effected by any such means. I had gone there after dark to make my queer experiment with a view to keeping the thing as quiet as possible, and also because I thought it likely that the real attempt had been made under like conditions. While doing so I was, without knowing it, within a few feet of what would have given me the real clue to the mystery—I might almost have touched it with my hand—and yet I saw nothing, and left the roof rather more puzzled than when I ascended. Had I gone in daylight all that might have been different.

I had now done with experiments, and set myself to something practical by hunting for the absconding hawker. The finding of his whereabouts was no difficult matter. He was well known, and though out of the city, he had to pursue his calling to get a living, and so a few messages across the adjoining counties soon revealed the fact that Poulson, after an eccentric tour, was returning to Edinburgh for a fresh stock. I was surprised at the news. I had fully expected that a man with 207 stolen sovereigns in his possession would not only cease working for a while, but give the scene of his exploit a wide berth for some time to come. At length I heard that he was in the city, and went to his house to look for him. As I had expected, he was not there, and had not been near the place. There was another place known to him, as I had discovered through Tom Joson, the lame man, in which any one who had means could hide for any length of time. I had been in that den before, and went there direct.

It was a quiet place, down near the bottom of the North Back Canongate. The house was entered by an outside stair in a dark court, where there were excellent corners for concealment.

I took up my position there as soon as it was dark, and had not been long there before I saw a man enter the court, take in all the bearings of the place much as I had done myself, and then select a corner quite as good as my own. In this he ensconced himself so coolly that in sheer wonder I crossed the court and grabbed him by the shoulder. Then in the dim light I recognised a sheriff-officer well known to me.

"Hullo! are you watching for some one too?" I exclaimed.

"Yes, and a bonnie chase I've had," he growled in a whisper. "It's a hawker called Poulson——"

"Ah, indeed! and what do you want him for?"

"Oh, just an affiliation case—decree for ten pounds and expenses, and the usual aliment. I've been all over Fife after him, and he knows it. Fourpence a mile will never pay me for all the trouble I've had. I know he's in here, but I'll wait till he comes out. I wouldn't go into that den for a hundred pounds. They'd jump on me and stave in my ribs, or break my leg as soon as look at me."

"Then, if you're sure he's in here, let's go in together," I answered; "I'll warrant they won't jump on me, or break my leg either. I want Poulson, too; what are we to do with him when we get him, eh?—halve him?"

"Oh, you can keep him if we get him," he returned, with a gruesome shrug of the shoulders. "He'll be as safe with you as any one."

We ascended the stair and knocked, and after some delay were admitted. Poulson, they said, was not there, and of course we did not see him. After locking the outer door on the inside and pocketing the key, I went over the three rooms. In the windows of two apartments adjoining each other there were fixed boxes, with lids, which appeared to be used as seats.

I lifted the lid of one. There was nothing inside, and the space revealed was only about three feet long by a foot and a half deep. I got into the next room after a little, and saw the exact counterpart of this box seat in the window of that. It also was empty, but in length was rather shorter than the other. Something about one of the ends attracted my attention, and I put my hand to it. The whole end moved a little. I touched a small nail in the centre and pulled it. The end slid easily towards me, and, looking through, I saw that the two window seats were one compartment with a movable division. In the long end—that is the end I had searched first—Poulson was lying on his side, and he looked considerably astonished when I hauled him out by the leg.

But when we got him out of the house, and he learned that he was wanted by me more than the sheriff-officer, his surprise increased. He could not understand it at all. When we got him to the Central, and the charge was made known, he broke out into the most indignant protestations of innocence. He had never heard of the robbery of the organ-grinder's money-bag, and had not dreamt of the man possessing such a sum.

"If I had thought it," he added, "I would have asked him to lend me enough to get over this difficulty."

He was locked up, and every search made for the stolen sovereigns, but without success; and after a few days' detention he was handed over to the sheriff-officer. As he pledged himself to pay all his debts, he was released under certain conditions.

This fact having been made known to me, I had him strictly watched, as I had the idea that the money would be drawn from that pile of sovereigns taken from the organ-grinder. No such call, however, was made upon that store. Poulson proceeded to "realise" upon his furniture and effects, and with that and the little money he had for buying a new stock, he managed to clear himself of the disagreeable surveillance of the sheriff-officer. He was still being watched closely by McSweeny, and as he soon became conscious of the fact, he became very unhappy. His recent misfortunes had somewhat broken his spirit, and he began to drink and loaf about instead of bestirring himself to retrieve his position. There was not the slightest indication that he had the organ-grinder's sovereigns hidden anywhere; and in his straits he was dependent chiefly upon the organ-grinder and the lame man, Tom Joson. One day when he had reached his last coin and was groaning over the fact that he was the object of such attention from the police, it was proposed to him by the lame man that he should get rid of the espionage by a sudden flight.

"I'll lend you enough to pay your passage to London," said the generous Joson confidentially; "and to tell you a secret, I'm thinking of going there myself if I can manage to give the wife the slip."

The offer was jumped at by the hawker, the more so as Joson told him he would give him a trifle to start with when he should reach the metropolis. One afternoon, accordingly, they met at an appointed place, and walked towards Granton together. As a touching proof of his confidence, the lame man entrusted Poulson with a bundle of his to carry. The bundle was not very large, but it was heavy. When they reached Trinity, the lame man said he could walk no further, and took a penny ride by rail for the rest of the way, the agreement being that they were to meet on board the steamer. McSweeny, who had got word of the movement from the organ-grinder, was already at the ticket office at Granton Pier. The lame man went on board unchecked. Half an hour later Poulson appeared, carrying the bundle given him by the lame man, and was promptly stopped by McSweeny. The weight of the bundle gave my chum great hope, and for once he was not disappointed. When the bundle was opened at the station-house, there was found within a bag of coarse green cloth, containing 203 sovereigns. Then the hawker confessed that he had got the bundle from the lame man to carry, but was well laughed at for his pains. By that time the London steamer had sailed, and it appeared probable that the lame man had gone with it, for he was nowhere to be found. McSweeny was very proud of his capture, but while he was thus engaged I had been busy in another quarter.

A slater had gone up on to the roof of the house upon which I had made my fishing experiment, and found there a long iron rod, bent at the end and fitted with a sharp hook. The moment I got word of this discovery I made the circuit of the district to find the nearest blacksmith, and from him I learned that the rod had been made to order by him for "a lame man who played the whistle on the streets." Back to the organ-grinder I went, and tried the patent rod down his chimney with perfect success. I hooked up the dummy bag at the very first attempt. At the same time I drew from the organ-grinder a confession that "in drink" he was very loquacious and communicative. I had now no doubt but he had in some such unguarded moment allowed the lame man to draw from him part of his secret, the man's native cunning and ingenuity filling up the blanks.

I now wished very much to see Joson, and with that end in view took the night mail for London. I was in the city long before the steamer arrived, and waiting for it at the wharf when it slowly crept up the river. No tender relative could have looked out for a dear friend with more anxious solicitude than I did for the face of the cripple whistle-player, and, as luck had it, his was almost the first face I saw.

He was looking over the taffrail, and evidently viewing the lively scene with great interest, for he saw no one—not even me—till my hand was laid upon his arm with the words—

"Well, Joson, I'm glad to see you. I hope you've had a good passage?"

The kind inquiry was never answered. Joson appeared to collapse at the very sight of my face, and submitted to be led away without a murmur. Poulson would have had some difficulty in proving his innocence, had not the lame man made a clean breast of it, and pleaded guilty with a view to shortening his own sentence.

For a long time there was one whistler less in the streets, and the organ-grinder's motto ever after was, "Save me from my friends!"

THE BERWICK BURR.

The first time my attention was directed to Will Smeaton, was by a telegram from a Border town which described his appearance, and stated—a little late, however—that he had escaped in the direction of Edinburgh. The message called for Smeaton's arrest on suspicion of a very deliberate attempt at murder, the victim being a sweetheart, named Jessie Aimers. The full particulars followed the telegram, and they seemed to leave little doubt of Smeaton's guilt. Jessie Aimers was a girl of superior education, a teacher in the town, and greatly beloved by all. She and Smeaton had been brought up at the same school, but with very different results—for he became a kind of coarse dare-devil, a brass-finisher by trade, with a strong inclination for salmon poaching; while Jessie grew up refined, modest, and gentle. What possible bond of love could exist between two such natures? is the question which naturally rises to one's lips; yet, with that tantalising contrariety which humanity seems to revel in, the answer was only, that such love did exist, and in no common degree of strength. The question was asked and echoed by all the townsfolk, and debated and wondered over, but the only decision was that Jessie Aimers was foolish to lavish her love on such a worthless object, and very much to be pitied on that account. Simple, short-sighted townsfolk! Jessie's love was her life, her breath, the very pulse of her heart. To give up that would have been simply to lie down in the grave.

The circumstances under which the attempt at murder was said to have been made were these:—Jessie Aimers had left her home about dusk on a fine October evening to meet her lover, who was positively forbidden her father's house. They had met at some appointed spot, and were seen about an hour later wandering slowly up by the river side. Smeaton appeared to be in a bad temper, for he was talking loudly and hotly. Jessie was answering gently and pleadingly. It was then quite dark, but they were readily recognised by their voices. Further up the river, and but a short time after, a great scream was heard, and very soon Smeaton was seen returning along the path alone, in great haste, and so intent on his own thoughts that he passed an intimate acquaintance close enough to brush his sleeve, silent as a ghost. Smeaton had gone straight home, but stayed there only long enough to get some money and his watch, and then made his way to the railway station and took a ticket for Edinburgh.

It was the manner in which this ticket was procured which first excited suspicion. Smeaton did not go to the ticket window himself, but skulked at the other end of the station, while he sent a boy whom he had hailed for the purpose to get the ticket. The boy was known, and the ticket clerk—astonished at him taking such a long journey—refused to give the ticket till he admitted that he was acting not for himself but for Will Smeaton. The boy probably made no mention of the circumstance to Smeaton, for when the ticket clerk went over the train helping to examine the tickets, and came upon Smeaton in an obscure corner, he said to him laughingly—"Were ye feared to come for the ticket yoursel'?" whereat the passenger looked horribly scared and taken aback, so much so that he was unable to reply before the ticket clerk was gone.

While this had been taking place, some young fellows were making a queer catch on the river. They were salmon poachers, and were hurriedly making a cast of a net at a shady part of the stream after seeing the watchers safely out of sight, when suddenly one of them cried out—

"Pull in! pull in! we've gotten as bonnie a beast as ever was ta'en oot the water. I saw the white glisk o' her as she tried to skirt roond ootside the net, but we've gotten her! The sly witch is hidin' at the bottom, but ye'll see her in a meenit!"

Very much more quickly and eagerly than paid salmon labourers, the others rushed the ends of the close-meshed net ashore, agreeing the while that if it was but a single fish, it was a sixty or seventy pounder at least, and in a moment or two had landed the bonnie white fish—sweet Jessie Aimers, with her light dress clinging close to her slight figure, her eyes closed as in death, and her white face gleaming up at them like a shining moon out of the gloom.

"Gude save us, it's a wuman! drooned! deid!" the scared poachers cried in a breath, and by a common impulse they were near dropping her and the net, and taking at once to their heels.

But one more sharp-sighted than the rest, bending down, noticed first that there was a wound on the white brow, which was bleeding, and next, that the features were familiar to him.

"Dog on it, lads, if it's no bonnie Jessie Aimers!"

Exclamations of incredulity and horror ran round the group, and it was only on one striking a match and holding the light close to the cold face that they were convinced of the truth.

They stood there, silent and sorrowful, and with watchers and their own dangers far from their thoughts, and then one threw out a wonder as to how Jessie had got into the water.

"Fell in, maybe?" suggested one.

"Or jumped in, mair likely," said another. "The puir thing has been fretting her life away for Wull Smeaton. I aye thought it wad come to this. She was far owre gude for him."

"Maybe he helped her in," darkly suggested a third. "I've seen them often walking here thegither, and he's a perfect brute when he's in a passion. He wad ding her in as sune as look at her."

This last suggestion found most acceptance. These men knew Smeaton thoroughly—his fiery temper, brutal strength, and impulsive ferocity—and had little doubt but his hand had sent the poor girl to her watery grave. Their only difficulty was how to act in the dilemma.

One thought that it would be safest, in order to avoid awkward questioning by those in authority, to quietly slip the body into the water again, stow away their net in its usual hiding-place, and drop work for the night; but this proposal was not well received, for Jessie was a general favourite, and was admired from a distance by the roughest in the place. While they stood thus in doubt, one of them suddenly exclaimed—

"Deid folk dinna bleed! She's maybe living yet—let's gie the puir thing a chance—row her on the grass—lift up her airms—dae onything that's like to bring her roond."

The result of this electrifying speech was that the whole gang lent a hand in the rough and ready means of restoration, and, with such good effect, that very shortly the supposed drowned girl gave signs of life, though not of consciousness. Thus encouraged, the men made a litter of their coats, and ran with her to the nearest cottage, where she was put to bed, and tended and nursed as carefully as if she had been in her own home.

Jessie's parents were sent for and informed as gently as possible of the accident, and their first exclamation on reaching their daughter's side was—"Oh, the villain! this is Smeaton's wark!"

Jessie was able to recognise her father, and smile faintly when he took her hand in his own, but she was too weak to give any account of the accident or crime till next morning. By that time the flight of Smeaton had been discovered, and telegrams despatched ordering his arrest and detention; and when Jessie woke she found not only the lieutenant of police, but a magistrate at her bedside, ready to hear her statement and act upon her charge. Then they all were surprised to find that Jessie had no charge to make. She would not, by as much as a look, admit that Smeaton had thrown her into the water, or even struck her so as to cause her to fall in or receive the wound on her temple. How had the accident happened then?

"I must have fallen in," said Jessie, after a long pause, and with tears in her eyes.

"Yes, you must have fallen in," impatiently interposed her father, who positively hated her lover, "or you could never have been picked out, but was the falling in purely accidental? Surely, Jessie, I have trained you well enough in truthfulness to be able to rely on your answer in a matter of life and death?"

"Yes, father, dear," meekly answered Jessie, with fresh tears. "I will always be truthful. But I cannot answer every question. I would rather die and be at rest."

"If this wretch attempted to drown you—to take your life—do you think you are doing right to screen him from the just punishment of his crime?" sternly observed her father.

"Will would never attempt such a thing," warmly answered the girl. "He has faults—though not so many as people imagine—but that he would never do. It is not in his nature."

"The police are after him now, and likely to get him, and when he is tried you will be forced to speak the truth," said her father; "you will be the principal witness, and if you do not speak the whole truth, you will be sent to prison yourself."

"I will never say anything against him though they cut me in pieces," said Jessie, with a deep sigh. "Why did they take me out of the river? It would have been better to let me lie than torture me with questions."

As Jessie's condition was still precarious, it was decided to let the matter rest for a little, and meanwhile make every effort to capture Smeaton, trusting to Jessie becoming less reticent, or other evidence turning up sufficient to secure his conviction. On the same forenoon that Jessie was thus questioned, I was going along a street near Nicolson Street, with my thoughts about as far from this case as the moon is from the sun. As yet I had only the brief telegram to guide me, and that contained but a meagre description of the man. He was said to be a native of Berwick, of medium height, and to have curly hair of a sandy hue, and a florid complexion, and to be rather muscular and firmly built. These points might suit a dozen out of every hundred one might meet in passing along the street, and the description interested me so little that the actual features had, at the moment, all but left my memory. What invisible finger is it that guides many of our sudden impulses? When I entered that street I had no intention whatever of visiting a pawnbroker's, but when I came to one of their prominent signs I turned into the stair and ascended it, as gravely as if I had gone south for no other purpose than to visit that particular establishment. I had been there the day before looking for some trinkets which were reported stolen, and as I entered, the thought struck me that I might ask for them again as an excuse for my reappearance. I was in no hurry, however, and as I could hear that there were some customers in before me, I simply took my stand inside one of the little boxes, and nodded to the proprietor to intimate that I should wait my turn. For the benefit of those lucky mortals who have never been forced to enter such a place, I may explain that these boxes run along in front of the counter, and are chiefly useful for screening one customer from another. Once shut in, you are safe from every eye but that sharp million-power magnifier owned by the proprietor or his assistant.

As soon as I was shut in I noticed that the box next to me was occupied by a male customer, who was busy extolling the value and powers of a silver lever which he was trying to pledge. The pawnbroker was quite willing to take the watch, but, as is usual in such cases, the point on which they disagreed was the sum to be advanced on the pledge. The argument was not particularly interesting to me, and I gradually left it behind in my thoughts while I revelled in the queer brogue of the stranger. It was a rich and musical twang to my ears; and when the man came to any word with the letter R in it—such as "tr-r-r-ain"—he rolled that R out into about a thousand, with a rich swell which made one imagine he enjoyed it. I was puzzled for a moment or two to decide on the exact locality of the dialect—though I have often boasted that I can tell the dialects of Scotland and a good part of England to within thirty miles of the exact spot on hearing them spoken.

"The man is from Newcastle," I rather hastily decided; then came a slight mental demur at the decision. There were slight points of difference and many strong points of resemblance. I listened for a little longer, and then smiled out at my own slowness and stupidity.

"I might have known that tongue at the first sentence," was my mental exclamation. "It's the Berwick burr."

While this analysis was going on in my mind, the haggling over the watch was concluded by the stranger accepting a loan of thirty shillings on the pledge, and a ticket was rapidly filled up to that effect, till it came to the important question—

"What name?"

There was a pause before the answer came, and when it was spoken there was much in the careless tone which implied that too much reliance was not to be placed on the truthfulness of the reply.

"Oh, say John Smith."

"I can't take it at all unless you give me your real name," said the pawnbroker, sharply. I have no doubt my presence put a little *edge* on him. "How am I to know," he virtuously added, "that the watch is not stolen?"

"Stolen?" echoed the stranger, warmly. "Man, there's the name of the man I bought it frae;" and he turned out a watch-paper inserted under the back. I could not see the name, but I did make out the words "Berwick-on-Tweed." "I'm no a thief—I'm a brassfounder to trade," continued the man, with energy, "and I expect to lift it again in a week or two."

"A brassfounder?" I thought, with a start. "I wonder if his name is Smeaton?"

While I was wondering the bargain was concluded, and the money paid over, and then the man left. I left my box at the same moment, and we moved out together.

"It's a nice morning," he said, and I returned the greeting.

When we reached the street he turned northwards, and I decided that that was my way too.

"I heard you say you are a brassfounder," I remarked. "You'll be looking for a job?"

No, he didn't think he was—he meant to lie quiet for a little.

"Oh, indeed?—got into trouble, I suppose," I returned, with interest. "Well, man," I added, in a confidential whisper, "I know a place where your dearest friends couldn't get at you. You'd be safer there than anywhere. Care to go?"

He wasn't sure. He didn't mind going, but he did not promise to stay there. He was glad of company, however, and offered to treat me to some drink. I was in a hurry, and begged to be excused.

"You belong to Berwick?" I said, decidedly.

He looked startled and troubled.

"Who said that? How do you know?" he stammered.

"I know the Berwick burr, and you've got it strong," I quietly answered.

"I haven't been in Berwick for mony a year," he said firmly.

"I thought that—that's what puzzled me for a while—you've got a touch of Coldstream or Kelso on your tongue," I coolly remarked.

He stared at me in evident consternation, and getting a trifle pale, but made no reply. I had been studying his appearance, and from that moment felt almost certain of my man.

I conducted him by North College Street, down College Wynd, chatting familiarly all the way, but never extracting from him his real name. I took him that way to convey to him the idea that he was going to some low "howf," in which a man in trouble might burrow safely, and was pleased to note that, as the route became more disreputable, his spirits rose. He evidently did not know the city, and that circumstance aided me. I turned up the Fishmarket Close, and into the side entrance to the Central.

"What kind o' a place is this?" he asked, staggered at the width and spaciousness of the stair.

"It's the place I told you of," I carelessly answered, taking care to make him move up the stairs in front of me. I saw his step become more faltering and unsteady, and when we reached the door of the "reception room," I knew by his ghastly pallor that the truth had flashed upon him.

"Straight in there, Smeaton," I said, as his eye fell on me. "This is an unexpected pleasure to both of us."

He looked at me like a trapped tiger, and I fully expected him to make a dash and dive for liberty.

"What's your name?" he almost groaned.

"McGovan."

"The devil!" he ungratefully exclaimed; and then I led him in, and accommodated him with a seat. He became fearfully agitated, and at length blurted out—

"If anything has happened to the girl, I'm not to blame for it."

He did not once seem to think of denying his identity, and yet till that moment I was anything but certain that I had the right man. He seemed a desperate, callous, and daring fellow, and but for the canny way in which he had been led to the place, would, I feel sure, have given us a world of trouble to capture. But once fairly limed, he became but a quaking coward. I did not understand his terror till I learned that he did not know that Jessie Aimers had been rescued, and her life saved. There was a visionary gallows before the villain at the moment seen only by himself. We were smiling all round, but there wasn't a ghost of a smile left in him. After he had emitted a very brief declaration, he was locked up; and next day a man came through and took him back to the town he had left so suddenly. Jessie Aimers still persisted in her silence, and the only charge which could justify Smeaton's detention was one of salmon poaching. The evidence took some time to collect, and when the trial came on, Jessie Aimers was just able to drag herself out of bed and be present. Smeaton was found guilty, and fined heavily, with an alternative of imprisonment, which every one said would be his reward. But to the astonishment of all, and the disgust of Jessie's father, the fine was paid. No one but Smeaton then knew that the money had been furnished by Jessie Aimers; and yet when the brute was set at liberty, and she waited at the Court entrance to see him and speak with him as he passed out, he was seen by many to push the loving girl violently from him with some imprecation, and walk off with a servant girl of evil reputation named Dinah King. Jessie pressed back the rising tears, and was able to draw on a faint smile before she was joined by her father. Her father had almost to carry her home, and every one looking on that pale face and drooping form declared that Jessie was not long for this world.

Some months after the trial, the house in which Dinah King served was broken into and robbed. Although the plunder was mostly of a kind not easily hidden or carried away, no trace of it was got, and the thieves were never heard of. After a decent interval Dinah discovered that the work of that house was too heavy for her, and gave notice to leave. When she did go she left the town, and Smeaton disappeared with her. Had she gone alone, perhaps no suspicion would have been roused, but his reputation was already tainted, and the result was another intimation to us to look after the pair, as it was rumoured that they had gone to Edinburgh. The very day on which this message arrived a young lady appeared at the Office asking for me, and giving her name as Miss Aimers. As she appeared weak and faint, she was allowed to wait my arrival. When I saw her face my first thought was—"How young and how sweet to have death written on her face!" Yes, death was written there—in the pale, sunken cheeks and waxy lips; in the deep lustrous eyes, and in the gasping and panting for breath which necessitated every sentence she uttered being broken in two. A word or two introduced her, and then I distinctly recalled the former case with Smeaton, and a thrill of pity ran through me as I looked on that wistful face and eager pair of eyes, and listened to her story.

"Every one is prejudiced against him but me," she said with strange calmness. "Look at me. I am dying. I know it, and yet I am calm and fearless. I could even be happy were it not for him, and the thought of him being lost to me through all eternity. I could not exist in heaven sundered from him. It would not be heaven to me. Oh, sir! you have seen much misery and much wickedness, but you know that a woman is not always blind even when she loves with all her soul. He is not so bad; but he is easily influenced and led away. If he is taken and put in prison, through that fearful woman, will you remember that? And if I should not be allowed to see him, or if I am taken away before then, will you give him a message from me?"

I bowed, for I could not speak.

"Tell him I have never lost faith in the goodness of his heart, that I shall love him for ever, and that heaven will never be heaven to me without him beside me. Will you tell him to think of that—sometimes—when he is alone; and of the sweet, happy hours we spent together when we were but boy and girl, full of innocent glee and love, before he was contaminated and led away. Oh, if God would only grant me a little time longer on earth—a little time—just enough to see poor Will led back to the right road and safe for heaven, I could lay my head and say—'Take me, Lord Jesus, take me home!'"

"You may be quite sure that time will be granted you for all that God needs you to do on earth," I softly returned. "He will not take you till your work is done."

I spoke with her for some time, going over many points in her history already partly known to me, but I found that she would not breathe one word against the man. She would not admit that in a fit of passion he had thrown her into the river, or that she owed to that immersion her present feeble condition. She would not listen with patience to one slighting expression or word of demur; her whole soul was wrapped up in him; and no tender, pure-souled mother could have yearned over her child more eagerly than she did over the man whose very name I could scarcely utter with patience. When she was gone I drew a long breath, and mentally wished that I might get my clutches on Smeaton firmly enough to treat him to a good long sentence of penal servitude. I felt as if that would relieve my mind a bit.

A day or two later I came on Dinah and her companion, and took them without trouble, but they had not an article about them which could connect them with the robbery at Dinah's last place. After a short detention they were released, and I hoped that they would take fright and leave the city. During my short acquaintance with Dinah, it struck me that she was a great deal worse than her companion. "She is of the stuff that jail birds are made of, and a bad one at that," was my reflection, and I remember thinking that it would certainly not be long before I heard of her again, supposing they favoured the city much longer with their presence. I saw them occasionally after that, and noted the general decay in their appearance, and guessed at their means of living, but never managed to get near them. One evening I was surprised by a visit from Dinah at the Central. She looked savage and sullen—a perfect fiend.

"You want to take Will Smeaton?" she abruptly began. "I know you do, for you've been after him often enough."

"I would rather take you," was my cold reply, and I spoke the truth.

She affected to take the remark as a joke, and laughed savagely—having the merriment all to herself. Then she revealed her message. Smeaton and another were to break into a shop in the New Town by getting through a hatch, creeping along the roof, and thence descending through an unoccupied flat, and so reaching the workrooms and shop.

"You've quarrelled with him, and this is your revenge, I suppose?" was my remark when she had finished, but Dinah's reply cannot be written down.

My only regret at the moment was that I could not warn Smeaton of his danger. Dinah went back and had dinner and supper with the man she had betrayed—actually broke bread with him and smiled in his face, and appeared more loving than she had showed herself for weeks. A woman, when good, can be holier, purer, and more strong in her devotion and love than a man; but when she is bad, the depths of iniquity which she can reach have never been touched by mortal man.

I sent over a posse of men one by one to the marked establishment, and when Smeaton and his companion appeared and ascended the stair I followed, and so closed up the retreat. They were not long gone. We heard the alarm, and some shouting and struggling, and soon saw Smeaton come scrambling out at the window on the roof by which he had entered, and come flying along the slates towards the hatch. As he got close my head popped out in front of him, and he started—staggered back with an oath—lost his footing, and vanished over the edge of the roof. He was picked up on the pavement below, very much injured and quite senseless, and borne on a shutter to the Infirmary, while his captured companion was marched over to the Office and locked up. Dinah, in ferocious joy over Smeaton's accident, got drunk and disorderly, and was taken to the cells next day. Smeaton remained for the most part unconscious during two days and nights. Towards the close of the second day, a cab drove up to the Infirmary gate, and out of it stepped a young girl, so pale and feeble that every one thought it was a patient instead of a visitor who had arrived. It was Jessie Aimers, who had risen from bed and taken that long journey the moment she heard of the accident. She was helped in to the ward, and sat there with Smeaton's hand in her own till evening, when he opened his eyes for a moment and hazily recognised her.

"Oh, Jessie, I'll never rise off this bed," he feebly exclaimed; and then, as her warm tears rained down on his cheeks, and her lips were pressed to his own, he said—"Dinna! dinna dae that! I dinna deserve it. Pray for me, Jessie, lass; it's a' I can ask o' ye now."

A screen had been put up round the bed, shutting them off from the gaze of the other patients, and inside that the nurses glanced occasionally. They remained there, whispering and communing till Smeaton relapsed again. Towards morning there was a cry, loud and piercing, behind the screen, but the night nurse was out of the ward at the moment. When she appeared, one of the patients spoke of the cry, and the nurse looked in on the pair. Jessie lay across the bed with her arms clasped tight about the patient, and her face hid in his bosom. Smeaton's face was marble-like, his eyes half open and fixed. The nurse knew that look at a glance, and called to her companion that Smeaton was dead, and that she feared the young girl had fainted. Gently they tried to disengage the clasping fingers, that they might raise her and restore her to consciousness, but the deathly coldness of the thin hand caused them both to start back and exchange a look of inquiry and alarm. They bent over her, they listened; all was still—still as the grave, still as eternity. Jessie was dead.

THE WRONG UMBRELLA.

A gentleman drove up to a Princes Street jeweller's in a carriage or a cab—the jeweller was not sure which, but inclined to think that it was a private carriage—in broad daylight, and at the most fashionable hour. He was rather a pretty-faced young man, of the languid Lord Dundreary type, with long, soft whiskers, which he stroked fondly during the interview with the tradesman, and wore fine clothes of the newest cut with the air of one who was utterly exhausted with the trouble of displaying his own wealth and beauty. He wore patent boots fitting him like a glove, and appeared particularly vain of his neat foot and the valuable rings on his white fingers.

When this distinguished customer had been accommodated with a seat by the jeweller—whom I may name Mr Ward—he managed to produce a card-case, and then dropped a card bearing the name of Samuel Whitmore. The address at the corner at once gave the jeweller a clear idea of the identity of his customer. The Whitmores were a wealthy family, having an estate of considerable size in the West, and had, in addition to the fine house on that estate, a town residence in Edinburgh and another in England. There was a large family of them, but only one son; and that gentleman the jeweller now understood he had the pleasure of seeing before him. He was said to be a fast young man, with no great intellect, but traits of that kind are not so uncommon among the rich as to excite comment among tradesmen. The follies of some are the food of others, and the jeweller was no sooner aware of the identity of his visitor than he mentally decided that he was about to get a good order. He was not disappointed—at least in that particular.

"I want your advice and assistance, Mr Ward, as to the best sort of thing to give—ah—to a young lady—you know—as a present," languidly began the pretty young gentleman. "It must be a real tip-top thing—artistic, pretty, and all that; and you must be willing to take it back if she shouldn't like it—that is, in exchange for something as good or better."

"Hadn't we better send a variety of articles to the young lady, and let her choose for herself?" suggested Mr Ward.

"Oh, hang it, no!—that would never do," said Mr Whitmore, with considerable energy. "She'd stick to the lot, you know; women are never satisfied;" and he gave a peculiar wink to convey the idea he wished to express. "You just be good enough to show me the things, and I'll choose what I think best, and you can send them to the house addressed to me. I'll take them to her myself to-morrow, and if they don't suit, I'll send them back by my valet, or bring them myself."

All this was fair and quite business-like, and Mr Ward hastened to display his most tempting treasures to his customer, who, however, speedily rejected the best of them on account of their high price. At length he chose a lady's small gold lever, ornamented with jewels on the back, and a set of gold ear-rings, with brooch and necklet to match. The price of the whole came to a trifle under £60, and the buyer expressed much satisfaction at the reasonable charges and the beauty of the articles.

"You will put them up carefully and send them home, and, if I keep them, you can send in your bill at the usual time," said the agreeable customer; and so the pleasant transaction concluded, the jeweller showed him out, the cab was entered, and Mr Whitmore not only disappeared from the jeweller's sight, but also, as it seemed, from every one else's. As he left the shop, the languid gentleman had looked at his watch, and the jeweller had just time to notice that it was an expensive gold one, with a very peculiar dial of gold figures on a black ground. Some reference had also been made to diamonds during the selection of the presents, and Mr Whitmore had been obliging enough to remove one of the rings from his white fingers and place it in the hands of the jeweller, when that gentleman read inside the initials "S. W."

These two circumstances were afterwards to add to the intricacy of the case when it came into our hands. From the moment when the pretty-faced gentleman was shown out by Mr Ward, he could not have vanished more effectually if he had driven out of the world. Half an hour after, a young apprentice lad in Mr Ward's employ took the small parcel given him by his master out to the stately residence of the Whitmores at the West End, and, according to his statement afterwards, duly delivered the same. There was no name-plate upon the door, but there was a big brass number which corresponded with that on the card left by the pleasant customer. The messenger, who was no stupid boy, but a lad of seventeen, declared most positively that he looked for the number in that fine crescent, rang the bell, and was answered by a dignified footman. He then asked if the house was that of the Whitmores, was answered with a stately affirmative, and then departed. None of the articles thus sent home were returned, and they were therefore entered in the books as sold. A month or two later the account was made up and sent to the buyer. There was no response for many weeks, but at length the answer did come, and in a manner altogether unexpected. A gentleman, young, but by no means good-looking, drove up to the shop door one forenoon and entered the shop. Mr Ward had never seen him before, but the card which he placed before the jeweller was familiar enough to cause him to start strangely. It bore the name, "Samuel Whitmore," with the address at the lower corner—it was, indeed, the *facsimile* of that which had been produced by Mr Ward's languid but agreeable customer months before.

"I wish to see Mr Ward," said the new comer, evidently as ignorant of the jeweller's appearance as that gentleman was of his.

"I am Mr Ward, sir," was the reply; and then the stranger brought out some papers, from which he selected Mr Ward's account for the articles of jewellery, which he placed before the astonished tradesman, with the words—

"I am Mr Whitmore, and this account has been sent to me by mistake. It would have been checked sooner, but it happened that I was away in Paris when it was sent, and as I was expected home they did not trouble to forward the paper."

The jeweller stared at his visitor. He was a young man, and wore Dundreary whiskers, and had on his fingers just such rings as Mr Ward remembered seeing on the hand of his customer, but there was not the slightest resemblance of features.

"You Mr Samuel Whitmore?" he vacantly echoed, picking up the card of the gentleman, and mentally asking himself whether he was dreaming or awake.

"Mr Samuel Whitmore," calmly answered the gentleman.

"Son of Mr Whitmore of Castleton Lee?"

"The same, sir."

"Then you have a brother, I suppose?" stammered the jeweller. "There has been a mistake of some kind."

"I have no brother, and never had," quietly answered his visitor; "and I never bought an article in this shop that I know of, and certainly did not purchase the things which you have here charged against me."

"A gentleman came here—drove up in a cab, just as you have done—and presented a card like this," said the jeweller, beginning to feel slightly alarmed. "Surely I have not been imposed upon? and yet that is impossible, for the things were safely sent home and delivered at your house."

The gentleman smiled, and shook his head.

"I thought it possible that my father might have ordered and received these things," he politely observed, "but on making inquiry I learned that not only was that not the case, but no such articles ever came near the house."

This was too much for the jeweller. He touched a bell and had the apprentice lad, Edward Price, sent for, and drew from him such a minute account of the delivery of the parcel, that it became the gentleman's turn to be staggered and to doubt his own convictions. The lad described the house, the hall, and the clean-shaven footman so clearly and accurately that his narrative bore an unmistakable impress of truthfulness. The gentleman could, therefore, only suggest the possibility of Price having mistaken the *number* of the house, and the things being accepted as a present by the persons who had thus received them by mistake. But even this supposition—which was afterwards proved to be fallacious—did not account for the most mysterious feature in the case—how the things had been ordered and by whom. It was clear to Mr Ward that the gentleman before him and the buyer of the presents were two distinct persons, having no facial resemblance; but the new Mr Whitmore having, in his impatience to be gone, drawn from his pocket a gold watch, with the peculiar black dial already described, a fresh shade of mystery was cast over the case.

"I have seen that watch before," he ventured to say. "The gentleman who ordered the things wore just such a watch as that. I saw it when he was leaving. And he had on his finger a diamond ring very like that which you wear. I had it in my hand for a few moments, and it bore his initials inside."

The gentleman, looking doubly surprised, drew from his finger the ring in question and placed it in the jeweller's hand. The initials "S.W." were there inside, exactly as he had seen them on the ring of the mysterious representative.

"Did you ever lend this ring to any one?" he asked in amazement.

"Never; and, what is more, it is never off my finger but when I am asleep," was the decided reply; and then he listened patiently while Mr Ward related the whole of the circumstances attending the selection of the articles. No light was thrown on the matter by the narrative; but the gentleman, who before had been somewhat angry and impatient, now sobered down, and showed sufficient interest to advise Mr Ward to put the case in our hands, promising him every assistance in his power to get at the culprit. This advice was acted upon, and the next day I was collecting the facts I have recorded. I had no idea of the lad Price being involved in the affair, but I nevertheless thought proper to make sure of every step by taking him out to the Crescent and getting him to show me the house at which he delivered the parcel. He conducted me without a moment's hesitation to the right house. I rang the bell, and when the door was opened by a clean-shaven footman, Price rapidly identified the various features of the hall. He failed, however, to identify the footman as the person who had taken the parcel from him. I was not disappointed, but rather pleased at that circumstance. I had begun to believe that the footman, like the purchaser, was a "double." Being now on the spot, I asked to see Mr Samuel Whitmore, and, being shown up, I began to question that gentleman as to his whereabouts on the day of the purchase. That was not easily settled. Mr Whitmore's time was his own, and one day was so very like another with him that he frankly told me that to answer that question was quite beyond his power.

By referring to Mr Ward's account, however, we got the exact day and month of the purchase, and the naming of the month quickened the gentleman's memory. That day had been one of many days spent in the same manner, for he had been two weeks confined to bed by illness. He could not give me the exact date, but I guessed rightly that his medical man would have a better idea, and, getting that gentleman's address, I soon found beyond doubt that Mr Samuel Whitmore had on the day of the purchase been confined to his own room, and so ill that his life was in actual danger.

"Some of his friends may have personated him for a lark," was my next thought, but a few inquiries soon dispelled that idea. None of Mr Whitmore's friends had looked near him during his illness, and to complete the impersonation, it was necessary that they should have had his ring and watch, which he declared had never been out of his possession.

The discovery of these facts narrowed down the inquiry considerably. They all seemed to focus towards that invisible and mysterious footman who had taken in the parcel.

There is a great deal in a name. The lad Price had used the word "footman" in describing the servant, probably because he had a vague idea that any one was a footman who wore livery and opened a door. It had never struck him to ask if there was any other man-servant in the house, and it might not have struck me either if I had not seen another—a valet—busy brushing his young master's clothes in a bedroom close to the apartment in which we conversed.

"Who is that brushing the clothes?" I asked of Mr Whitmore. "The coachman?"

"Oh, no; the coachman does not live in the house while we are in town; that's my valet."

"And what does he do?"

"Attends me—gets my clothes, helps me to dress—looks after everything, and serves me generally."

"Does he ever answer the door bell?"

"Really, I could not say," was the answer, somewhat wearily given, "but you may ask him."

The gentleman, I could see, had a sovereign contempt for both me and my calling, and was impatient to see me gone; but that, of course, did not disturb me in the least.

I had the valet called in, and in reply to my question he gave me to understand very clearly that answering the door bell "was not his work," but lay entirely between the footman and tablemaid.

"Supposing they were both out of the way, and you were near the door when the bell rang, would you not answer it by opening the door?"

"No, certainly not."

He appeared to think me very simple to ask such a question.

"Then who would open the door?"

"I don't know; somebody else—it wouldn't be me; but they wouldn't be both out of the way at once without leaving some one to attend the door."

"Just so; and that one might be you. Now don't interrupt, and try to carry your mind back five months, and to the 21st day of that month, while your master here lay ill, and tell me if you did not answer the door bell and take in a small parcel addressed to your master?"

"I wasn't here five months ago, sir," was the quick response; "I was serving in the north then."

"Indeed!" and I turned to his master in some surprise; "have you discharged your valet within that time?"

"Oh, yes," he lazily drawled; "I had Atkinson before him."

"At the time you were ill?"

"Possibly so. I really don't remember."

"You did not tell me of this before."

"No? Well, it doesn't matter much, I suppose?"

I found it difficult to keep my temper. I had the lad Price brought up from the hall, and he said most decidedly that the valet before us was not the man who had taken in the parcel.

"Why did Atkinson leave you?" I resumed, to the master.

"He did not leave exactly. I was tired of him. He put on so many airs that some thought that he was the master and I the man—fact, I assure you. He was too fast, and conceited, and vain; and I thought—though I'd be the last to say it—he wasn't quite what you call honest, you know."

"Good looking fellow?"

"Oh, passable as to that," was the somewhat grudging reply. Mr Whitmore himself was very ugly.

"Did he ever put on your clothes—that is, wear them when you were not using them yourself?"

"Oh, yes; the beggar had impudence enough for anything."

"And your jewellery, and watch, too, I suppose?"

"Well, I don't know as to that—perhaps he did. I could believe him capable of anything that was impudent—coolest rascal I ever met. I tell you, Mr—Mr—Mr McFadden—I beg your pardon, McGadden—ah, I'm not good at remembering names—I tell you, I've an idea; just struck me, and you're as welcome to it as if it were your own. P'r'aps that rascal Atkinson has ordered those things, and got them when they were sent home. Rather smart of me to think of that, eh?"

"Very smart," I answered, with great emphasis, while his valet grinned behind a coat. "The affinity of great minds is shown in the fact that the same idea struck me. Can you help me to Atkinson's present address?"

He could. Although he had been wearied and disgusted with the fellow himself, he had not only given Atkinson a written character of a high order, but personally recommended him to one of his acquaintances with whom, he presumed, the man was still serving. I took down the address and left for Moray Place, taking the lad Price with me. When we came to the house a most distinguished-looking individual opened the door—much haughtier and more dignified than a Lord of State—and while he was answering my inquiries, the lad Price gave me a suggestive nudge. When I quickly turned in reply and bent my ear, he whispered—

"That's like the man that took the parcel from me at Whitmore's."

"Like him? Can you swear it is him?"

The lad took another steady look at the haughty flunkey, and finally shook his head and said, "No, I cannot swear to him, but it is like him."

The haughty individual was John Atkinson, formerly valet to Mr Whitmore. A few questions, a second look at the lad Price, and one naming of Mr Ward the jeweller, disturbed his highness greatly, but failed to draw from him anything but the most indignant protestations of innocence.

I decided to risk the matter and take him with me. He insisted upon me first searching his room and turning over all his possessions, to show that none of the articles were in his keeping. I felt certain of his guilt. There was in his manner an absence of that flurry and excitement with which the innocent always greet an accusation of the kind; but his cool request as to searching made me a little doubtful of bringing the charge home to him. It convinced me, at least, that the articles themselves were far beyond our reach. From this I reasoned that they had not been procured for the ordinary purposes of robbery—that is, to be sold or turned into money. The buyer had said that they were intended as a present for a lady: could it be possible that he had told the truth?

I began to have a deep interest in Atkinson's love affairs and a strong desire to learn who was the favoured lady. On our way to the Office I called in at Mr Ward's, but the jeweller failed to identify Atkinson as the buyer of the articles. He was like him, he said, but the other had Dundreary whiskers, and this man was clean shaven. Afterwards, when I had clapped a pair of artificial whiskers upon Atkinson, the jeweller was inclined to alter his opinion and say positively that it was the man, but, on the whole, the case was so weak that it never went to trial.

Atkinson was released, and returned to his place "without a stain upon his character," and so justice appeared to be defeated. The first act of the drama had ended with villainy triumphant.

Let me now bring on "the wrong umbrella." A great party was given, some months after, in a house in the New Town, and, as usual at such gatherings, there was some confusion and accidental misappropriation at the close. All that happened was easily explained and adjusted, but the case of the umbrella. Most of the guests had come in cabs, but one or two living near had come on foot, bringing umbrellas with them. The number of these could have been counted on the fingers of one hand, yet, when the party was over, the lady of the house discovered that a fine gold-mounted ivory-handled umbrella of hers had been taken, and a wretched alpaca left in its place. The missing umbrella was a present, and therefore highly prized; it was also almost fresh from the maker. It was rather suggestive, too, that the wretched thing left in its place was a gentleman's umbrella—a big, clumsy thing, which could not have been mistaken for the other by a blind man. It seemed therefore more like a theft than a mistake, and after fruitless inquiries all round, the lady sent word to us, and a full description of the stolen umbrella was entered in the books.

The theory formed by the owner was that the umbrella had been stolen by some thief who had gained admittance during the confusion, and that the umbrella left in its place had simply been forgotten by some of the guests, and had no connection with the removal of her own. Reasoning upon this ground, I first tried the pawnbrokers, without success, and then, remembering that the missing article had been heavily mounted with gold, I thought of trying some of the jewellers to see if they had bought the mounting as old gold. I had no success on that trial either, but, to my astonishment and delight, McSweeny, whom I had sent out to hunt on the same lines in the afternoon, brought in the umbrella, safe and sound, as it had been taken from the owner's house. The surprising thing was that the umbrella had been got in a jeweller's shop, at which it had been left by a gentleman to get the initials E. H. engraved on the gold top. It was a mere chance remark which led to its discovery, for when McSweeny called the umbrella was away at an engraver's, and had to be sent for.

I went over to the New Town very quickly and showed the umbrella to the lady, who identified it—with the exception of the initials—and showed marks and points about the ivory handle which proved it hers beyond doubt. I kept the umbrella, and went to the jeweller who had undertaken the engraving of the initials. He described the gentleman who had left the umbrella, and, turning up his books, gave me the name and address, which I soon found to be fictitious. He stated, however, that the umbrella was to be called for on the following day, and I arranged to be there at least an hour before the stated time to receive him. When I had been there a couple of hours or so—seated in the back shop reading the papers—a single stroke at a bell near me, connected with the front shop, told me that my man had come. I advanced and looked through a little pane of glass, carefully concealed from the front, and took a good look at him. What was my astonishment to find that the "gentleman" was no other than my old acquaintance, John Atkinson, the valet!

According to the arrangement I had made with the jeweller—in anticipation of finding the thief to be a man in a good position in society—the umbrella was handed over to the caller, the engraving paid for, and the man allowed to leave the shop.

I never followed any one with greater alacrity or a stronger determination not to let him slip. I fully expected him to go to his place in Moray Place, and intended to just let him get comfortably settled there, and then go in and arrest him before his master, who had been very wrathful at the last "insult to his trusted servant."

But John did not turn his face in that direction at all. He moved away out to a quiet street at the South Side, where he stopped before a main door flat bearing the name "Miss Huntley" on a brass plate. A smart servant girl opened the door, and John was admitted by her with much deference. When he had been in the house a short time, I rang the bell and asked for him.

"He is with Miss Huntley," said the girl, with some embarrassment, evidently wishing me to take the hint and leave.

"Indeed! and she is his sweetheart, I suppose?"

The girl laughed merrily, and said she supposed so.

I only understood that laugh when I saw Miss Huntley—a toothless old woman, old enough to be my mother, or John's grandmother. From the girl I learned that her mistress was possessed of considerable property, and that John and she were soon to be made one.

I doubted that, but did not say so. I had no qualms whatever, and sharply demanded to be shown in. John became ghastly pale the moment he sighted my face. Miss Huntley had the stolen umbrella in her hands, and was admiringly examining her initials on the gold top.

"Is that your umbrella, ma'am?" I asked, in a tone which made her blink at me over her spectacles.

"Yes, I've just got it in a present from Mr Atkinson," she answered.

"Oh, indeed! And did he give you any other presents?" I sternly pursued, as John sank feebly into a chair.

She refused to answer until I should say who I was and what was my business there; but when I did explain matters, the poor old skeleton was quite beyond answering me. She was horrified at the discovery that John was a thief, but more so, I am convinced, to find that he was not a gentleman at all, but only a flunkey. In the confusion of her fainting and hysterics, I had the opportunity of examining the gold watch, which was taken from her pocket by the servant, and found inside the back of the case a watch-paper bearing Mr Ward's name and address, and also the written date of the sale, which corresponded exactly with that already in my possession. The brooch and other articles were readily given up by Miss Huntley, as soon as she was restored to her senses. Had she been fit for removal, we should have taken her too, but the shock had been too much for her, and her medical man positively forbade the arrest.

John made a clean breast of the swindle and impersonation, and went to prison for a year, while the poor old woman he had made love to went to a grave which could scarcely be called early. I met John some years after in a seedy and broken-down condition, and looking the very opposite of the haughty aristocrat he had seemed when first we met. I scarcely recognised him, but when I did, I said significantly—

"Ah, it's you? I'm afraid, John, you took the *wrong* umbrella that time!"

"I did," he impressively returned, with a rueful shake of the head; and I saw him no more.

A WHITE SAVAGE.

The woman had a queer and almost crazed look; was miserably clad, with no bonnet on her head, and her hair covered with the "fluff" which flies about factories and covers the workers. I am not sure if she had any covering on her feet; if she had, it must have been some soft material which gave out no more noise than her bare soles would have done.

Added to this, she smelled strongly of whisky, though she was not in any way intoxicated. She had come into the Office at the breakfast hour, and patiently waited till I appeared, without enlightening any one as to her business. "No one but Mr McGovan was of any use to her," she said; and when I appeared and heard her begin her strange story I soon thought that I should be of no use to her either. Her statements were so wild and improbable, and her delivery so incoherent, that I speedily decided that if I was not conversing with a mad woman I was at least beside one suffering from *delirium tremens*. Her age seemed to be about twenty-five, and she was by no means bad looking, had she not been such a miserable wreck.

"I want you to help me to hunt for my man," she said, with perfect self-possession. "My name is Janet Hanford, and I'm married—maybe you'll mind the name."

I thought for a little—or appeared to do so—and then told her that she had the advantage of me, for I did not remember the name.

"Your husband has run away from you, then?" I remarked, secretly not at all surprised at his action.

"No, not that," she answered, and it was then that I began to doubt her sanity. "It was not running away. They told me he was dead and buried, and I believed them; but I saw him to-day riding along in a carriage with a grand lady—a new wife, as I suppose—and I want you to hunt him out. I'm not so good as I should be, but I'm still his wife, surely?"

"Surely," I echoed, thinking it best to humour the maniac.

"You must know that though I've been in jail I'm not a bad woman," she continued. "If I had been, he'd have divorced me, or at least put me away, for he was too poor to afford lawyer's fees. He's only a factory worker like myself."

"How can that be, when you told me just now that you saw him riding in a carriage with a grand lady?" I asked, thinking to catch her up.

"That's the mystery which I can't understand," she answered. "You are to find out all about that. I did not see the lady's face right, as the carriage went by so fast, and I was horrified at seeing him, and could scarcely take my eyes off him; but I know it was Dick Hanford, my husband."

"Some one resembling him in features," I thought. "What were you put in jail for, pray?" I added aloud.

"I was put in once or twice for drink," she said, hanging her head a little. "He wouldn't pay the fines, and so I had to suffer. It's my only failing. I was brought up as a girl behind the bar, and I got to take drink secretly till I couldn't keep from it. Then I was put away, and went into the factory. It's down in Leith Walk. I used to be called 'the Beauty of the Mill,' and all the men were daft about me."

"Good heavens!" was my mental exclamation; "daft about a creature like this!"

"I could have had my choice of a dozen men, but I took Hanford, though his wage was the poorest in the place," she calmly continued. "I suppose it was because I was daft about him. I'm that yet. I never loved anybody else, and never can."

"You said 'once or twice for drink'—were you ever in jail for anything else?" I asked, pretty sure that she had kept something back.

"Yes, I was in for two years. It's only about nine months since I got out. It was then they told me he was dead, and I believed them."

"What were you put in for?"

She trembled and grew paler, and tears came into her eyes.

"I don't remember much about it," she hurriedly answered; "perhaps you will. It was after one of my drinking fits. I was always excitable after them; and they say I sharpened a knife and lay in wait for him for a whole day and night, saying I meant to kill him. I couldn't have meant that, for I love him dearer than my own life. But when he came he was stabbed, and taken to the Infirmary. They said that I did it, and I suppose it's true. I don't remember doing it. He was very badly hurt, and they thought he would die. That's why I was so long in prison before they tried me. If he had died I should have wished to be hanged, so as to be done with everything. You look frightened. Does it seem horrible for me to say these things, when they are true?"

"They do not sound nice from a woman's lips," I gravely replied. "I remember your case now. You hid in the loft of the factory for two days after stabbing him, and it was I who had the hunting for you. I thought it a very bad case at the time, and I remember your husband in Court giving a picture of your domestic life which would have melted a heart of stone. I suppose my plain speaking horrifies you quite as much as yours does me?"

"No; everybody speaks that way, so I suppose I must bear it, though I don't feel so bad as people think me," she answered, with a despairing ring in her tones. "If I hadn't been brought up in a public house, and so learned to drink, I might have been in a very different position. Everybody is against me, and sometimes I feel as if I was against myself."

"There was a child, too, I think," I continued. "Didn't you injure it in some way, or ill-treat it? I forget the particulars now."

"Its leg was broken," she answered, with a quiver in her voice, and tears again filling her lustrous eyes. "I think the doctor said he would never walk right if he lived, because it was the thigh that was broken. It was hurt about the head too. Perhaps it fell down the stairs and hurt itself. Some of them believed that I flung it down. I don't think I could have done that, though I was at the top of the stair when they picked him up. I don't remember anything about it."

"And what has become of the child?" I asked in a low tone, not sure whether to feel overwhelmed with horror or pity.

"They told me he was dead too when I came out, but perhaps they've told a lie about that too. Perhaps he's living, and only hidden from me as Hanford has been. That's more work for you. I have no money, and I must have justice. If he is alive, he is bound to support me; and if he has married that grand lady, he must go to prison for bigamy."

Broken and lost though she was, she seemed to know the law pretty well, but I thought there was little chance of it coming to an appeal of that kind.

"Who told you that your husband was dead?" I asked.

"His mother. That was when I came out of prison. I went home, of course, but I found the house let to strangers, and was told it had been so for two years. Then I went to his mother's, and she would scarcely let me in, or speak to me. She has an awful hatred to me. At last she let me in, and told me he was dead."

"And you believed it without further inquiry?"

"No, I didn't believe it at all at first; but then she got out a certificate from the registrar and showed it to me. I read his name on it with my own eyes—Richard Hanford. If he isn't dead, that name must have been forged. You'll maybe have to take her for that. I shouldn't be sorry at that, for she has caused me many an unhappy hour."

Here was a case altogether uncommon. It is usual for injured persons, not the injurers, to seek our aid.

"You would like your husband to be put in prison too, if he is alive, and yet you fancy you love him?" I remarked. "It's a queer kind of love which seeks a revengeful retaliation like that. I've seen women sunk in degradation of the deepest kind who would make the blush rise to your cheek."

The crimson rose to her face there and then under the taunt.

"I don't wish him any ill, but I am his wife, and he has deserted me and thrown me off, and I want you to find him. I want to try to do better, and live a different life. I want to deserve that he should love me; and I will not allow him to have the love of another while I am his wife."

"I am afraid you have made some strange mistake," I hastened to observe. "Your husband is probably dead, and beyond the reach of your love or your neglect. The gentleman you saw in a carriage possibly resembled him strongly—such cases often come under our notice. Mistaken identity? why, it's as common as day. We had a woman here the other day who insisted upon us arresting a man whom she alleged was her husband, and she would not be convinced till he brought his father and mother and a whole host of relatives to prove that he was another man altogether, and had never been married in his life. And even supposing your husband were alive, how could you prevent him loving another? To retain a man's love is even more difficult than to win it, and can never be done by running a knife into him, or throwing dishes at his head."

"I did not do that; it was the drink did it," she tearfully pleaded. "He said I would never be better till the grave closed over me. You heard him say so at the trial. But I think there's a chance for me yet. It's a dreadful struggle to keep away from drink, but I win the battle sometimes. No one knows what I have fought against; and I'm so poor, and despised, and wretched now that nobody cares to ask. If I were a black savage in a far off country, they'd send missionaries to me and give me every comfort and help; but I'm only a white savage living in Scotland; and I tell you I'm *not* mistaken about seeing my man. I could not be mistaken. I saw him alive and well in that carriage as sure as there's a God in heaven."

"How could a poor factory worker like him rise to such a position?" I incredulously remarked.

"I don't know, but there he was sitting by the lady's side and looking as happy as he used to look when he was courting me; and he saw me too, and turned as white as death at the sight. Perhaps he thought I should die in prison for want of drink, and so married again without waiting to see. I thought of going to his mother's and asking if he was really dead; but then I changed my mind, and came here. It would be better for you to go; you know better how to get at the truth."

"You charge him with deserting you and marrying another woman?" I said, scarcely able to restrain myself.

To this she replied with a wavering affirmative, and then she produced the certificates of her marriage and of the birth of her child, and gave me the address of her mother-in law. She then described minutely the place and circumstances of the meeting with her husband's counterpart, and left the Office. She left her own address also, but I had no expectation of ever needing that. It seemed to me that the supposed fraud, forgery, and bigamy were entirely the offspring of her own drink-sodden brain, and that to ascertain that her husband was dead and buried would be so simple a matter that there was not the slightest occasion for her putting the task upon us. Still I remember thinking—"If the man is really alive, I hope he will really be nimble enough to escape me. It would be an actual blessing to such a man if the jade fell downstairs and broke her neck."

In the afternoon I went to the address of the mother. The house was a small one in Greenside, but the woman appeared a respectable widow, and I found her quietly preparing the supper of her sons, two of whom supported her. She seemed a superior person to be in such a situation; and noting that fact I guessed that her son, though a poor worker, must have had some natural refinement. I told her I had called to make some inquiries about her son, and she probably thought I meant one of the younger members of her family, for she smiled brightly, and invited me to enter. While I accepted the offer

I studied her quiet and somewhat shadowed features, and quickly decided that I had before me a woman who, if she had occasion, could throw as many obstacles in my way as any one who ever hampered a detective.

"It is your son Richard, I mean," I quietly continued, as I sat down at the clean little fireplace.

The mother gave a great start, and I saw the hands busy at the supper grow suddenly tremulous. She looked at me, too, but it was not so much a look of surprise as of searching inquiry or suspicion.

"What about him?" she cautiously returned, when she had recovered somewhat.

"I want to know where he lives, what he does, and all about him," I quickly answered. I fully expected her to blurt out, possibly with tears, that her son was dead, but no such words rose to her lips. She stared at me keenly for a moment or two, as if trying to discover from my appearance what was the nature of my occupation, and then she said—

"What are you? a sheriff-officer or something of that kind?"

"Something of that kind," I lightly returned. "Now, about your son Richard. Is it true that he is dead?"

"I suppose that fiend that he married has sent ye here?" she said with great energy; "but if she has, ye'll get naething oot o' me."

"Well, but you told her he was dead," I persisted; "either he is dead or he is not."

"Ay."

"And you showed her a certificate of death bearing his name?"

"Did I?"

"If you altered that name you committed a felony, and are liable to arrest and imprisonment."

"Am I? I'm no feared," she answered, with a sneer and a toss of the head.

"Will you let me see that certificate?"

"Humph! will I, indeed! Ye'll see nae papers here, I can tell ye."

"We can force it."

"Force awa' then—naebody's hinderin' ye."

"Come, come now—it is quite evident to me that you have something to conceal," I said, fairly baffled.

"Everybody has," she grimly returned.

"Perhaps your son has paid you to be silent?"

A flashing look was the answer; it said scornfully—"As if that would be necessary!"

"Did you forge the certificate?"

"Humph!" The grunt was utterly derisive of me and my powers. After trying her for nearly half an hour I gave the old woman up in despair and left, determined to overhaul the books of the registrar for the district. I did so for a period extending over the two years, but could find no record of such a death. I had not expected to find it. The strange reticence of the mother had convinced me that I had misjudged the broken wife, and that the man was really alive. My visit to the registrar was productive of one discovery, however, which pointed to a solution to one mystery. I found recorded the death of one Richard Hanford, aged 58 years, spouse of the old woman who had proved so intractable under my questioning. By referring to the broken wife I discovered that she had never thought of looking at the *age* of the deceased as recorded in the certificate; and I had a strong suspicion that it had been the certificate of the father's death which had been shown her, with a view to severing the connection for ever.

Back I went to the old woman's home, only to find her flown, and the house shut up and empty. She had taken alarm, then, and deemed flight the most easy way out of her difficulties.

I had now no clue whatever to the discovery of Hanford, and, truth to tell, was not sorry. I heartily hoped that he, too, had taken alarm and left the city, and that I should thus hear no more of the case. But the broken wife, from the hour of the first meeting, had never rested. She was continually on the prowl, never going to her work, seldom eating or sleeping, and almost forgetting to drink. The result was that one night, in watching a quiet hotel or boarding-house at the West End, she saw a man come out and hurry towards a waiting cab, and flew across and pinned him in her arms with his foot on the steps.

"Dick! Dick Hanford! look at me and say why you have tried to make me believe you were dead?" she cried in frenzied tones.

The man was alone, and did not seem greatly surprised, though he was labouring under great excitement and emotion.

"Call me John Ferguson," he said, tremulously, without trying to push her off or escape. "Dick Hanford is dead—dead to everyone."

"Not to me, for I am still your wife," she excitedly returned. "Oh, Dick! I am bad and weak, and foolish—maybe mad at times—but I love you; and I want to be better, and get back my bairn that they say I nearly killed. I think it would keep me from falling. Oh, give me one more chance! I thought you were both in the grave, and that I had put you there, but when I found you alive a new life seemed to spring up in me."

"Call me John Ferguson—Dick Hanford is dead," he still answered, in low husky tones.

He dismissed the cab, and motioned to the broken wife to follow him out to the dark road beyond the city, where they could converse unseen and unheard. He would not say he was married to another woman, nor would he admit that he was Hanford, or this broken woman's husband; though his grave, earnest manner, his gentleness, and every thrill of his voice, convinced her of his identity, if such convincing had been needed.

"I am nothing to you, or you to me," he said; and with a pang she noticed that he never even touched her or offered her his arm. "We are strangers; our ways are different—far apart; just as much sundered as if we were both dead, and buried at different sides of the globe. But I have money now, and I am willing to give you that, if it will do you any good, just to relieve my own mind, if you will let me go in peace. Why should we fight over a dead past? Say how much you want, and it shall be yours, though it should be every penny I own."

"I don't want money, but the bairn I nearly killed," cried the weeping wife. "Money would curse me, but the bairn might lift me up. I'm not the first lost woman who has been pulled up to heaven by a bairn's wee hand."

"That can never be," said the husband, decidedly. "More likely you would drag him down with you. Be content with the ill you've done. Freddy is dead."

"I don't believe it," screamed the broken wife. "He is hidden from me, not dead. I will make a bargain with you. If your love for me is dead, go your way in peace, but leave me the bairn. I'll sell my rights for him. Is it a bargain? or must I put you in prison?"

"You can do neither," was the agitated reply. "You cannot put me in prison, and you cannot touch the boy. You will never see him again. He is far beyond your reach."

They quarrelled over that point, and had to separate without an arrangement. Janet Hanford came to me the same night, demanding that I should arrest the "bigamist," as she declared him to be, and also hunt out her boy, wherever he was hidden, as the care of the child would legally fall to her, who had committed no offence against the moral law. A light task, certainly!

In the first place, I found that the accused persisted that he was not Richard Hanford, but John Ferguson. He had been at the Cape for nearly two years, so he had no one to whom he could refer in confirmation of his statement. He was very hazy as to his antecedents. He had prospered at the Cape, he admitted, but would not say that the money he now possessed had come to him by marriage; he would not admit that he was married at all to the lady who accompanied him, though it was proved that at the private hotel at which they resided they were known as Mr and Mrs Ferguson. The lady herself, being referred to, declined to say whether she was married or not; and when *she* took up that position, I need not say that our chance of bringing home to him a charge of bigamy became poor indeed. Then there remained the charge of desertion, but that could scarcely be brought forward, seeing that the wife had been in prison, serving a term of two years, while he had been away at the Cape and had but recently returned, and so might be supposed not to know that she was alive.

But the weaker Janet Hanford's case grew, the more determined and desperate she seemed to become. John Ferguson's wife had a maid-servant to attend her, and Janet Hanford appears to have taken to watching the girl. One forenoon, when the case was at its most critical point—that is, when there were evidences that John Ferguson and his wife would soon be out of the country—the broken wife saw this girl leave the hotel with two letters in her hand. The girl walked rapidly along Princes Street, with the intention of posting them at the General Post Office; but before she had gone two divisions, Janet Hanford became a highway robber, by snatching the letters from her hand and vanishing like magic. One of the letters was addressed to "Master Frederick Hanford," at a boarding-school some miles from the city; and almost before the amazed girl got back to her master, Janet Hanford was in a railway carriage and speeding towards that school.

The letter she had stolen proved beyond a doubt that John Ferguson was Richard Hanford, and father of the boy, and also revealed the fact that it had been Hanford's intention to remove the boy in a day or two, as he was "leaving the country." Janet Hanford stopped all that by taking a policeman with her, and demanding that the boy—who readily recognised her as his mother—should be delivered up to her. The grief and consternation of the father were terrible to behold, and we had now the singular case of two persons charging each other with a crime, and each demanding the other's arrest.

Hanford made the most strenuous attempts to get back the custody of his boy—who was lame and rather weakly—but failed completely, though he had money and lawyers to help him. An inquiry had been by that time despatched to the Cape, to ascertain whether the so-called John Ferguson had been legally married to Rosa Gladwin, the girl who in Scotland had passed as his wife. In anticipation of the answer to that question being against him, Hanford redoubled his exertions to quicken the slow processes of law which were to give him charge of his boy; but with almost the same result as if he had single-handed tried to push on some great Juggernaut. The ponderous thing moved none the faster, but all the heat and turmoil and excitement fell to Hanford. He was continually running between his temporary home and his lawyers, and in one of these races he caught a chill which he "had not time to attend to."

When the pain became unbearable, he was forced to lie down and send for a doctor. By that time he was almost delirious and in a high fever. The doctor pronounced the trouble inflammation of the lungs, and the case critical.

The moment Janet Hanford heard of the illness she came to see her husband, bringing with her the boy, whom she had hitherto kept studiously out of sight. She was loud in her self-recriminations. She blamed herself for the calamity; in grovelling grief cried aloud to heaven to witness her vow, that if Hanford's life were only spared she would restore his boy, suffer him to leave the country with his father, and nevermore seek to molest either, or wish for anything but their welfare and happiness. The cry was vain; the resolve came too late. Hanford scarcely knew her, and appeared to be living the misfortunes of his life over again; for when his eye did light on her face, he implored those present to take her from him, or at least to save the boy from her remorseless hands. In a day or two he died, to the very last turning from her with aversion, and speaking of his other attendant as his true and only wife, and denouncing Janet Hanford as a curse to herself and all mankind. Of course these delirious utterances could not be taken for his real feelings; indeed, his second wife afterwards assured Janet that the love he bore her was greater than that which he had conceived for herself—it was merely the outside shell of wretchedness and debauchery which he loathed and detested. There was no more concealment of the truth then. It was freely admitted that Hanford had married again out at the Cape, getting a rich settler's daughter and a little fortune by the union, as well as the unselfish devotion of a woman who knew the whole of his past life, and yet did not hesitate to sacrifice her all for his sake. A strange result sprang from that death-bed scene. The second wife imbibed a strong affection for the lame boy, and could not think of parting with him; at the same time a feeling of pity grew up in her breast for the broken wife, who was so prostrated by her great loss that for weeks her life was despaired of. Rosa Gladwin nursed her through it all, and, I suppose, must have discovered in her some good qualities which were hidden from ordinary onlookers, for when Mrs Hanford fairly recovered they did not separate. At first Rosa offered to provide for her by settling on her an annuity quite sufficient for her wants, but the proposal was never carried out. They went out to the Cape together, and no sisters could have been more firmly bound together in affection. Neither of them ever married again, but their lives have been spent in watching the development of Hanford's son, who is no longer a lame boy, but a strong man, bidding fair to leave a big mark in the world's history. The most singular thing in the case, however, is the fact that Janet Hanford left her drunkenness and debasement in the grave which swallowed her husband. Truly there is hope for all, even for the White Savage.

THE BROKEN MISSIONARY.

The place was called a church, but it was really little more than a mission-house thrown out and partly supported by a religious body in Edinburgh wishing to extend its connection. The town is a few miles from Edinburgh, and the building used for the church had at one time been used as a school, then as a slaughter-house for pigs, and at last, with a little painting and fitting up, as a church or meeting-house.

It is not necessary to name the particular sect of which this small church was a part. All churches are formed of men and women, and with these there is always to be found some twist of character, which we, who are twisted in another direction, call an imperfection. Such men as the deacon in the following case may be found in almost any church—men of strong convictions and great pugnacity, who are such heroes for virtue that they never think it possible to fall on the other side.

The little church had no vestry, and but one door, so the minister and congregation all entered from the front. Just within the door there was a small partition, and a folding door to keep the draught off the congregation during the assembling, and conspicuously in front of that, and facing the outer door, stood a three-legged stool bearing a big pewter plate for contributions. The contents of this plate were in general so scanty that they might easily have been counted by the eye, but occasionally, during the summer, visitors from the city would drop into the little place and leave in the plate a practical proof of their interest in the struggling church. After the services, it was the duty of the deacon or deacons to count the collection and place the sum to the credit of the general fund of the church. The minister or missionary, Arthur Morrison by name, was a young man with a wife and two children, who was struggling vainly to exist upon £55 a year. He had striven hard, but had so far failed that he was considerably in debt to different tradesmen about the town. He could scarcely be blamed for that, for his wife was a delicate woman, and most of the expenses had been forced upon him on her account. There was little prospect of his position in that town improving, as only a part of his salary was made up by the church, the rest being a grant from the main body; and as he was a quiet mild fellow, with no great energy or ability, there was little chance of him being sought after by a richer congregation. The poor fellow, however, seemed very earnest and sincere, and to love the work, and had never uttered a word of complaint to one of his people during the three years he had been among them.

That was the position when an incident occurred, so curious and so strange in its results, that it is necessary to put it down minutely, and exactly as it was afterwards narrated by the chief witness in the case, the deacon himself.

It was immediately before the morning service, and the congregation had nearly all assembled. The Rev. Arthur Morrison had not arrived, but an agreeable incident had kept the deacon who stood at the plate from noting the fact. A lady, evidently a summer visitor of wealth, had put a bank note into the plate, and asked to be shown to a seat as graciously as if she had been in the finest cathedral in the world.

The deacon was a man named Thomas Aikman, a baker by trade, a sharp business man, who considered himself the main pillar of that church. He fluttered into the building and showed the distinguished visitor to his own pew—if pew it could be called—placed books before her, and returned to the plate. There was an interval during which no other worshippers entered, and Mr Aikman spent the time in admiring that bank note as it lay in the plate, contrasting so deliciously with the thin strata of coppers below. It was a crisp note of the Bank of Scotland, and so new that it would not remain folded. Of course it had a number, and that number Mr Aikman declared he could not help noting, as the paper lay open before him. He did not mark down the number—did not think of doing so—but he had a good memory, and he could trust to that, and swear by his convictions.

As he gazed the deacon rapidly ran up in his mind all that this bank note would do. There was a trifling debt on the building fund, and this would all but clear it off. There would be no difficulty in getting the other managers of the church to agree to that; they were afraid of the stout and pugnacious baker, and always hurriedly agreed to whatever he thought fit to propose.

While he was settling this matter another stranger appeared, and placed a silver coin in the plate, at the same time asking to be shown to a seat. The half-crown which this gentleman dropped into the plate rested on the bank note already there, and thus the two contributions were left while the deacon went inside and showed the gentleman to his own form. Not a minute was occupied in the task, and during the interval only one person entered the church. That person was the Rev. Arthur Morrison, who appeared heated and flushed as he pressed past the deacon and made his way to the little desk from which he preached. Mr Aikman went straight back to his post at the plate, and the bank note being still prominent in his thoughts, he glanced at once in that direction. Then he started and rubbed his eyes. He himself had been the last to leave the spot—for the gentleman had preceded him into the church—and then the bank note lay in the plate all right, with the half-crown safely weighting it; now, when he got back, the note was gone. The half-crown was there—shining like a white disc among the coppers, but not a vestige of paper money was near it. The deacon looked around. There was no wind, but the note might have got over the edge of the plate, and fallen to the ground. No; it was not in the vestibule. Aikman darted outside; there was not a human being in sight. He staggered back again and stared at the plate till his goggling eyes might have speared a hole in it. There could be no doubt about it—the church had been robbed, and was the poorer by £5 of the deacon's momentary absence. He had no one to advise or assist him, the other deacon on the list having failed to appear, and felt doubly angry and excited over the strange loss from having already mentally decided how the money should be utilised. He was in a fever of bewilderment, perspiring in every pore, and even madly thrusting his hands into his own pockets to make sure that the note had not fluttered in there. Then, after another dart outside to make sure that no prowling thief could have been near, the deacon did a little mental reasoning. No one, so far as he was aware, had entered the church during his absence from the plate but the minister. Could it be possible? No, never! Well, yes it might be. The man was poor and needy, and he might consider the drawings at the door as in a manner his own, or intended for him. Mr Aikman had an old grudge at his minister, who had once dared not only to correct him on some theological points, but had satirized him in a quiet way as well. The man who could utter a joke at the expense of a great man like Aikman was fit for anything, and the bank note could not have gone without hands. The deacon began to understand the whole mystery, and put up the collection and closed the door to go inside and listen to the sermon in no frame of mind to profit by the discourse. At every telling point in the oration Aikman turned up his nose, and mentally exclaimed—

"How can he, with that stolen £5 note in his pocket!"

On the whole, the deacon felt more of pity than of anger at the cool appropriation, but he determined that the minister should know that the robbery had been discovered. How best to make the revelation exercised Aikman's small brain pretty closely during the service. He had not quite settled the matter when the benediction was pronounced. As the lady who had made the handsome gift handed him back the books she had used, and made some remarks about the church, a happy idea struck the deacon. He boldly thanked her for her liberality, and then concluded by asking her—much to her surprise—if she knew the number of the note she had put in the plate. She did not; and as she was too polite to ask the reason for inquiry, no more passed between them, and the lady departed and was seen no more. Had Mr Aikman been of a less active disposition the matter might have ended there. No one had seen the bank note but himself, and it was now gone through no fault of his. But then there was the minister, and the suspicion, and his own old grudge. He could not remain passive.

When all the congregation were gone Aikman steadily fixed the young clergyman with his ferocious eye, and said—

"There was one lady very good to us to-day—she put a £5 note in the plate."

A slight flush overspread the pale face of the young preacher, and he said a little hurriedly—

"Ah, indeed? I am pleased to hear that. Excuse me just now; I must hurry home."

He moved away abruptly, and the deacon stood staring after him, now thoroughly convinced of the soundness of his suspicions.

"A minister of the Gospel to descend to a mean theft like that!" he said to himself. "I must call a meeting of the managers and report the whole case."

It happened to be the month of July, and there was a difficulty in getting a quorum of the managers together, but at length Aikman was promised a full meeting, which took place on the Wednesday following in his own house. There, after shutting themselves in, and making sure that no one could overhear, the four men considered the case of the stolen bank note. Of course they were shocked at the implied guilt of one whom they revered and trusted so much, but Aikman piled up his facts in such a minute and positive manner, that even without additional evidence there would have been little diversity of opinion among them. At this stage, and when Aikman had scarcely concluded, another of the managers quickly exclaimed—

"Why, Mr Morrison changed a £5 note with me yesterday."

"Yesterday?" echoed another, to whom the minister owed a small sum. "And he told me on Saturday that he had no money, and would not have till next quarter day."

"There! What did I say?" cried Aikman with triumphant energy. "Could anything be clearer than that? I know for a fact that he has no money—it is all eaten up long before it is paid to him by me; yet there you have proof that near the end of the quarter he pays away money, and that a £5 note. Have you the note yet?" he added to the man who had received the payment.

He had, and would run and get it. A wiser plan would have been to first make Mr Aikman describe the note put in the plate, and write down its number, and then send for that received from the minister, and compare the record with the note, but that was never thought of. The other deacon had only half a street to traverse, and was back in a few minutes with a crisp bank note. It was of the Bank of Scotland, and nearly new. Mr Aikman snatched it from the bearer—opened it, glanced at the device and the number, and then exclaimed—

"It's a clear case! look at the number for yourselves, '7607'—the very figures of the one I saw lying in the plate. I couldn't help reading them, for the note lay open, and I never forget anything."

A painful silence followed. At length some one asked the question which was uppermost in all their minds—What was to be done? They could not pass over the robbery in silence, and yet it would be a delicate and possibly a dangerous thing to charge a clergyman with such a theft.

"Nothing dangerous about it," said Aikman, brusquely. "I can swear to the note being put in the plate, and the number, and the name of the bank; also, that the minister was the only one near the plate while I was absent for half a minute; and you can swear that he paid away the note to you and got change. What's to be done? Shall we ask him to resign, demand the money back, or give him up to the police to be dealt with as they think best?"

It was quite clear to all present which of these courses Mr Aikman wished followed, and they unanimously decided that the most rigorous course was necessary in dealing with such a criminal. Mr Aikman was therefore deputed to lay the matter before the chief constable of the town, who, however, happened to have a personal acquaintance with the young clergyman, and a great liking for him as well, and not only scouted the idea of him stealing the bank note, but strongly urged Aikman to say nothing of the matter to his minister, whatever other means he might employ for the recovery of the note.

Finding it impossible to move the deacon, the constable at length compromised the matter by agreeing to go with Aikman to the minister's house—it was not a manse, but a little flat, up an outside stair—and see if Mr Morrison had any explanation to offer. They found the young clergyman at home by the bedside of his wife, who was almost a confirmed invalid, and had been rather weaker than usual for some days. The constable was moved at the sight of the young preacher's pale and concerned expression as he hung over the invalid, but the deacon had no such qualms—he looked upon these as indications of guilt, and would have blurted out the charge in hearing of the sick wife but for a huge pinch on his arm by the constable, who at the same time quietly nodded to Morrison, and invited him to speak with them for a moment in the next room.

"There is some difficulty about that £5 note which you paid away on Tuesday to Blackie, the grocer," observed the constable, kindly; while the deacon, as a duty he owed to society, steadily speared the young preacher with his goggling eyes. "Would you mind saying where you got the note?"

The righteous deacon had his reward, for the moment these words were uttered, a startled look came to the worn features of the minister, and his face flushed a deep crimson.

"I scarcely know myself," he at length responded, with considerable hesitation; "is it necessary that I should make that known? What has happened? Is there anything wrong with it? Is it a forged note?"

"Oh, no; the note is good enough," cried the deacon, sternly, still using his spears liberally; "as good as any ever put out by the Bank of Scotland. The lady who put it into the plate on Sunday was not likely to have a forged note in her pocket."

The young preacher started as if the deacon had run a knife into him. He seemed petrified, breathless, and dumb with astonishment.

"I do not know what you mean, or what you are hinting at," he at length replied; "but I know that the note you speak of could not possibly have been in any lady's pocket on Sunday, seeing that it was then lying in my desk here, in this house."

"You'll have to prove that," derisively returned Aikman. "Where did you get it, and when?"

"I got it on Saturday afternoon," answered the suspected man, with calm dignity. "It came to me in an envelope, by post, and without a line to indicate the sender. There were a few words written inside the flap of the envelope, which I had not noticed when I put the envelope in the fire. I snatched it out again and read them. They were—'For the little ones, from a well-wisher.' I was quite overpowered," continued the young preacher, with a quiver in his tones; "I had seen nothing but darkness and trouble before me, as one of my creditors was pressing me sorely for money, knowing perfectly that I had none. I went to God with my trouble in prayer, and that was His answer."

The deacon was horrified. That the minister should steal the note he could readily understand, but that he should account for its possession in such a manner showed a depth of depravity and a hypocrisy which he had not conceived possible to dwell in man.

"You have the envelope, of course?" he sneeringly observed, after a significant silence.

"No; unfortunately I have not. I put it into the fire in case my wife should see it, and—and be pained by the thought of me having to accept such help from an unknown friend."

The deacon looked at the constable with a significant jerk of the head. It was quite evident they could make nothing of a man so lost in wickedness, and so ready with plausible excuses. The constable, however, appeared to be foolishly overcome by the cunning reply of the culprit, and made no remark. It therefore devolved upon Aikman to make a noble stand for honesty and religion.

"Mr Morrison," he impressively began, "that bank note which you paid to Blackie the grocer was put in the plate on Sunday by a lady. I saw it, and read the number of it as it lay. After you had passed the plate, it had vanished. Either admit your crime, or take the consequences."

"Now—at last—I understand you," answered the minister, with more dignity and calmness than his accuser. "You accuse me of stealing the bank note?"

"We do, upon the clearest evidence," snorted the deacon.

"Then I deny it emphatically," said the accused, almost smiling. "I cannot believe you to be in earnest. Steal it! why should I do that? It was put there for the general benefit of the church, I suppose, and that includes me, doesn't it?"

"So you thought when you took it, I've no doubt," angrily returned Aikman, "but you will find yourself grievously mistaken. Constable, I charge that man, in the name of the managers, with the theft of £5. Do your duty."

Matters had now become serious, but the gentleness of the constable smoothed away much that might have been painful.

They walked together to the house of the Fiscal, and, after an account of the circumstances had been gone over, the young minister was allowed to go back to his home on his own recognisance.

The next day I had a visit from the young minister, in at the Central, in Edinburgh. I have but a faint recollection of the interview, but I remember that he appeared greatly excited and agitated, and ended his somewhat incoherent statement of the facts by imploring me to take up the case with a view to—what think you?—with a view to convicting Mr Aikman of perjury or conspiracy! The reasoning of the young clergyman was this:—No one but the deacon had seen a £5 note in the plate, and he alone had reported the note stolen—therefore the note might never have been there at all! From this followed the deduction—the deacon from his old grudge had got up the whole as a revenge on the young preacher to injure his reputation and force him out of his post. In consequence of this appeal I went out to the place and made some inquiries, but was met almost at the outset with clear proof that a £5 note had been put into the plate. The lady who had been the donor was gone, but at the hotel in which she had been staying the landlord had heard her mention the gift to her husband.

The case was tried shortly after at the Burgh Court, the accused conducting his own case. From the evidence led few could doubt the guilt of the poor preacher the deacon was so cool, and clear, and positive in all his statements. On one point alone did he show confusion, and that was regarding his noting the number of the note while it lay in the plate. Here the deacon, from his very evident desire to make all clear and firm, contradicted himself slightly, and then floundered worse under a very simple question from the Sheriff, and was put down in confusion. The result was that the case was dismissed—quite an unsatisfactory result to both parties. The deacon was enraged—having recovered from his momentary confusion, and being now ready with a clear and minute explanation—and the poor minister was quite broken down under the disgrace. When he returned to the town which had brought him so much suffering, he met with so many cold looks from those whom he had believed to be his warmest friends, that he was almost forced to resign his charge. The resignation was accepted with a promptitude even more crushing to his spirit; and then, while he was making preparations to leave the place, his creditors swooped down on his few possessions, and left him and his family with little but the clothes in which they stood.

Morrison appeared to bear it all with calm dignity, but his wife, who was a quick-tempered, high-spirited woman, though delicate, felt the disgrace keenly. They moved in to Edinburgh, and Morrison tried hard to get another appointment, but in vain. The ban was upon his reputation—his name had appeared in connection with an accusation of mean thieving, and he was looked upon with suspicion even by strangers. At length he got employment for a few hours daily in keeping a tradesman's books, for which he got nine shillings a week, and with that and a little copying and tuition he managed for a time to keep himself and his family alive.

But poor diet and a mean habitation among the very roughest characters soon broke the spirit and constitution of his wife, and she passed out of his arms into her long rest before a year was gone. One of the children followed in three months, and he was left alone with the baby. He struggled on quietly and without complaint, shunning all, but ever ready when sought for to go and pray and converse with any of the sick or dying among the very poor who might express a wish for his presence. He became gaunt and thin, and the tradesman who employed him told him he needed a change of air.

I met him more than once in some of the lowest slums, but I failed to recognise the bloodless face and stooping figure. I knew him as "the broken missionary," and it was dimly understood that he had either been in prison or found guilty of some offence against the law, though the poor wretches with whom he conversed and prayed declared their firm belief in his purity and innocence.

One day, at that time, I found a stout, red-faced man waiting for me at the Office, who nodded to me, and appeared greatly pleased at seeing me. I had to tell him that he had the advantage of me, and then he introduced himself as Mr Aikman, the deacon who had figured as such a prominent witness in the case against the minister.

"I have been a cruel wretch, and I deserve ten years in prison for the misery I have brought on an innocent man," he said, shedding tears freely—great hot tears, genuine as genuine could be. "A lady in delicate health belonging to our congregation was ordered to live abroad, and came back only yesterday. The moment she heard of Mr Morrison's disgrace, she came to me and said that it was she who had sent the £5 note to the minister. She sent it from Edinburgh just as she was setting out. I am a sinful and wicked man! God help me! If I could only find out where he is—if you could help me to that—there is no atonement or reparation I should think too great to make to him and his poor wife and bairns. Every penny I have shall be spent in the effort."

I remembered the case then, and immediately set about tracing Morrison, a task which would have been easy indeed if I had thought for a moment of him being identical with "the broken missionary." At length I came upon a solicitor who occasionally employed Morrison to copy deeds, and by him was referred to the tradesman who employed the broken man to keep his books. It was only when we were near the hovel which Morrison called his home that the idea flashed upon me that the broken missionary was the man I was after. I knew where he lived, and went straight to the house, which tallied perfectly with the description given by the tradesman.

When we knocked at the door a low voice told us to "Come in," and on entering we saw only a child of eighteen months creeping about the floor in great glee, with a doll of rags in its hands. But a glance round showed us where the voice had come from. There was a bed behind the door, and in that there was a pale, bloodless face, and a pair of shiny eyes, bearing a shadowy resemblance to the man we sought. The broken missionary feebly attempted to raise himself upon his arm, while the deacon rushed forward, dropped on his knees before the bed, and hid his face and tears in the thin wasted hands he had clasped.

"My poor wronged minister!" he exclaimed; "say you forgive me. We have found out the lady who sent you the £5 note; and I know I have been cruel and wicked——"

A strange convulsion passed over the ghastly face and sunken features of the missionary, while his great eyes appeared to shine out with a perfect radiance.

"Bless the Lord, O my soul, and all that is within me bless his holy name!" he fervently exclaimed, as the great eyes became soft and beautiful with tears.

The child on the floor crowed with delight, and hammered vigorously on the floor with the head of its doll of rags. The deacon gathered the thin form of the sick man in his arms, and hurriedly breathed out all his plans for reparation. He would carry him back with him to his own home; he would care for him, and send him away to the country, to fresh green fields and cool shady woods, where he would have nothing to do but take his fill of the balmy air, and draw health from the glorious sunshine. But the grey head was shaken on his breast in quiet demur, with a pitiful look in the great eyes as they rested on the laughing face of the neglected child on the floor.

"I am going to fair fields and a glorious country," he feebly gasped, "but not there—not there. God has sent his sunshine into my soul, and I can depart in peace."

He fainted away as he spoke, and it was long before he could be restored. The deacon had a nurse and a doctor there in an hour, but they came too late. In the dead of night, with the deacon clasping his hand and wetting it with his repentant tears, the missionary went quietly to his rest.

The child was taken to the deacon's house, and trained and educated, and finally sent to college, and now promises to occupy a distinguished position in the profession which proved so disastrous to his father.

The stolen bank note was never traced, but it was believed to have been taken by a woman who had acted as chapel-keeper, and who was afterwards sent to prison for a theft quite as mean, though less disastrous in its results.

A MURDERER'S MISTAKE.

A toll-keeper on the main road some miles south of Edinburgh was standing at his open door watching the gambols of his two children, when a weary traveller approached and arrested his gaze. There was something uncommon about the dusty tramp when his appearance could rouse interest in an old toll-keeper, accustomed to look with indifference on every kind of wanderer that God's earth can produce. This one was an old man, tall and gaunt and white-haired. So far there was a bond of interest between them, but with age the comparison ceased, for the toll-keeper was stout and well-clad, and had a comfortable expression beaming from every part of his face; while the stranger was haggard, worn, and drooping, like one who had got all that earth was likely to give, and did not care how soon the giving ceased. Above the toll-keeper's happy face was a ticket intimating that he was licensed to sell tobacco; while in one window a few bottles of confections and biscuits, and the words "Refreshments and Lemonade" on a show card, summed up his efforts at trading. The dusty tramp halted in front of the toll-keeper, giving the stout man a full view of his poor clothing and fragile boots, from which his toes were peeping, and his sharp eyes eagerly devoured the intimation above the doorway.

"Good evening, sir," he said quietly, as he fumbled among his clothes for a pocket, and at length produced a penny.

The toll-keeper in general was gruff enough with tramps, even when they seemed disposed to buy his wares, but there was a ring in the tones of this one which struck a chord of pity in his breast, and he returned the greeting kindly. In front of the window showing the biscuits and sweets was a wooden bench. The haggard one limped towards this bench, saying in the same quiet tones—

"Might I rest for a bit on this bench?"

There was nothing arrogant or bold in this request, but rather a ring of indifference or despair. It was as if he had said—"It doesn't matter whether you say yes or no, or whether I sit down or move on, or drop dead by the way. The end is not far off either way."

"Oh, ay, sit as lang as ye like; ye're welcome," said the toll-keeper, heartily. "You look like you had come a far way?"

"I have, sir—a matter of four hundred miles," said the white-haired tramp, knitting his brows; then recovering himself, he said in his former quiet tones, "I suppose you couldn't let me have a penn'orth of tobacco? I've on'y a penny left."

"Hout, ay;" and the toll-keeper brought a liberal length of roll tobacco, which the weary traveller grasped eagerly and paid for promptly with his penny. He bit off a piece and chewed it fiercely, his eye resting steadily the while on the face of one of the toll-keeper's children, a rosy-cheeked girl of seven or eight, who was gazing on the gaunt face and figure in a species of awe.

"It's good for killing hunger," he observed, with his eye still meditatively fixed upon the child; "not that I've felt much of it," he hastily added, as if in fear that the toll-keeper would think that he meant to beg; "I haven't had time to think of that. That's a pretty child," he abruptly added, alluding to the girl.

"Yes, but she's not looking so well as she did," answered the toll-keeper, with a father's pleased look at the compliment. "We nearly lost her with fever a while ago."

"Imphm!" grimly returned the white-haired tramp. "Mebbe some day you'll wish she had been taken. She'll grow up to a fine lass, and then some one will envy you of your bonny flower and crush it up in his fingers, never thinking or caring to think that your heart's inside of it. You'll go mad, then, and think how happy you could have been smoothing the turf on her grave when she was a little child."

"God forbid!" fervently exclaimed the toll-keeper, catching the child up in his arms, as if to shield her there.

"God? What's God got to do with it, I'd like to know?" cried the white-haired tramp, with his hard tones rising to a despairing snarl. "Is there any God? I never see him, though there's plenty of devil about—that everybody can see with their eyes shut. Look you, sir!" he added, clenching one bony hand and smiting the palm of the other in fearful excitement, "I've done with God for ever! When my girl was like that little one I used to go to church o' Sundays, and feel pious and good, and have my heart full of softness and gratitude. I've felt as if I could have took the whole world into my arms to bless it. But that's all gone now, and the devil's the one I speak to. He's been with me all the way, cheering and helping me over the weary miles, and I won't turn agen him now when I'm near the end of it."

The toll-keeper shrank back before the terrible words and sudden hurricane of passion which convulsed the speaker; then he gathered the two children in his arms, and said softly to them—

"Run round into the garden, bairns, and pull some bonnie flowers, and make a fairy's feast in a corner, with rose leaves for plates. I'll come round and see it when it's done. Haste ye now!" and, with a kiss and a smile, he dismissed them.

"Excuse me, sir; I forgot about the little uns," said the tramp, falling back into his former subdued tones, and evidently perfectly understanding the toll-keeper's haste to get the children out of hearing. "I've seen the day when I'd 'a' been horrified at such words myself. It's the way the world goes. We've good occasion to look mercifully on them as is far down, 'cause we may get into their state afore we die. I knew a man once—a Methody he was—who preached a sermon on that man that was hanged for killing his sweetheart up in London. It would have done you good to hear it— how he pitched into that poor chap in the condemned cell. Well, that same Methody quarrelled with a man about some furniture, and went home and got a log of wood, and came back and struck the other over the head till he died, and he was had up for murder, and convicted and hanged for it, as sure as you stand there. I wondered, when I saw him brought out, if he had been pitching into himself when he was in the condemned cell;" and the white-haired tramp laughed a hard, sardonic, unmusical laugh, without a vestige of merriment in the sound.

The toll-keeper fidgeted uneasily, and began to wish this man of such changing moods gone.

"Are you going far?" he asked, wishing to change the subject.

"I'm going on—on—to be hanged," said the stranger, absently; then, recovering himself on noting the toll-keeper's look of horror, he said, abruptly, "What do you call this 'ere town?"

The toll-keeper named the place.

"That's it!" cried the tramp, rousing up and speaking with a kind of triumphant ferocity. "That's the place—I'm not going far past that. I've come to find a man out and pay a debt."

To pay a debt!—a man who had just parted with his last penny! The toll-keeper's suspicions were confirmed—the old man's brain was affected; his wrongs, if he had any, had deprived him of reason. At this stage there came an interruption to their conversation from a field on the opposite side of the road. There was no gate or stile at that part of the field, but over the wall there came clambering a gamekeeper and a gentleman, who had evidently been hard at work with the gun among the woods and coverts further back. The gamekeeper, after a word or two from his companion, walked on with the heavy bag of game, while the gentleman strolled forward familiarly to the toll-keeper's door, wiping the sweat from his brow, and looking almost as tired as the tramp there seated. As he did so, the tramp noted what a fine face the gentleman owned—not so very pretty or finely proportioned, but full of sympathy and gentle courtesy, and altogether likeable and attractive even to a man old, soured, and broken in spirit.

"A warm day, John," the new-comer said, with just one swift passing glance at the tramp on the bench. "A glass of lemonade, as quick as you can, for I'm dying of thirst."

"Will you no come in an' sit doon, sir?" returned the toll-keeper, obsequiously.

"No, thank you—this will do nicely. Now, hurry!" and the gentleman seated himself easily beside the tramp on the bench, where they formed a queer contrast—the tramp old and done, the gentleman in the full flush of youth and strength, and evidently with everything at his command that could make man happy.

"A warm day this," he added pleasantly to the white-haired tramp. "You look tired and thirsty too. Will you have a drink with me? John, another glass of lemonade and some biscuits," he imperatively called out, as the tramp refused the proffered gift, with an instinctive touch at his fore-lock. The lemonade was brought and decanted, the first glass being handed to the gentleman, who politely handed it to the white-haired tramp, who, with another protest, not quite so firm as the first, and the words, "Long life to you, sir!" placed the grateful beverage to his lips and drank it off, the gentleman then following his example. The biscuits had been brought out on a tray, and the frank sportsman lifted one of these, and then crammed the remainder bodily into the hands of the tramp.

"Eat away; I only want a bite. I shall be having dinner when I get home," he said, in a careless, yet kindly manner, which disarmed the gift of anything calculated to offend the most sensitive. "You're English, I think?"

"Yes, sir," answered the white-haired man, in so soft a tone that the toll-keeper felt inclined to rub his eyes to see if it was really the same man.

"London way, eh?" continued the gentleman, toying with the biscuit.

"Yes, sir—Rotherhithe," said the tramp, eating as if he had not eaten for some time.

"Ah, I've been often there myself—a fine place," said the gentleman, with kindling eyes; and then they talked pleasantly of London and its attractions, the gentleman never once showing by word or look that he considered the tramp his inferior. At length he rose to go, took up his gun and paid the toll-keeper, and then, with a pleasant nod to both toll-keeper and tramp, he walked off towards the town.

The tramp looked after him in silence, munching the while at one of the biscuits.

"Who is that?" he said at length, with less gloom on his face and bitterness in his tones.

"Oh, that's young Gowlieden."

"Gowlieden? Good heavens! what a name to go to bed with!" said the tramp. "Well, anyway, he's a good fellow; God bless him, and send more of his kind into this hard world!"

"Gowlieden isn't his real name," said the toll-keeper with a smile. "It's the name of one of his father's estates, and it's our fashion here in Scotland to give the big folks the name of their land. That's the heir, you know, and we call him young Gowlieden. His real name is Stephen Barbour. They live at a place called Frearton Hall, on the other side of the town."

"What!"

The tramp had started to his feet, and given out the word with a shout which almost drove the breath out of the toll-keeper's body.

"Yes, Frearton Hall—what's wrong with that?" stammered the toll-keeper.

"And Stephen Barbour, you say, is his name?" cried the tramp, with every feature of his face gradually overspreading with horror and loathing.

"Yes, that is his name."

"My God!" moaned the white-haired tramp, snatching the bite from his own mouth and dashing it down on the road, and then trampling on it with insensate fury; "my God! and I broke bread with him, and took the drink from his hands, and thought him so kind and noble-looking! And I said 'God bless him,' not knowing any better. Why did the words not blister on my tongue?"

"You know him, then? You have met the young laird before?" said the astonished toll-keeper.

"Never, never! But I know him, the scoundrel! I know him too well."

"He's no scoundrel," cried the toll-keeper, warmly. "He's as good and true a man as any that breathes. Everybody likes him far or near, and never yet did I hear any but yourself say a word against him."

The tramp did not seem to hear the words. He sent the last of the biscuits skimming as far as he could throw them, and, wringing his hands, he dropped on his knees on the dusty road.

"Forgive me, Meg, forgive me!" he muttered in a frantic fashion, with his thoughts evidently far away. "How could I know any better?"

Tears were flowing down his cheeks, and these stopped the harsh words which were rising to the lips of the toll-keeper. The tramp tugged out a ragged handkerchief to wipe away the tears, and in doing so dragged out something hard and shiny, which dropped with a metallic clank on the road. The toll-keeper looked round just in time to see that the dropped article was a pistol, which the tramp was hurriedly putting out of sight again. All his sympathy vanished at the sight of the weapon.

"You had better be going," he said coldly, "for if the police saw you carrying that, they'd soon give you a place to sleep in."

"I'm going," said the tramp calmly, rising and moving off. "I haven't far to go now. Oh, if I had only known!"

Thus he limped away, still wiping his eyes with the ragged handkerchief; and if the county constable had chanced to pass the spot that night, the toll-keeper would certainly have warned him to look after the mad old man, as he thought him. As it was, he got leave to go on to the town, and further. On the north side of the place, and but half a mile from the toll, Frearton Hall stood within its own grounds. There was a lodge at the entrance, kept by the gamekeeper already alluded to, but if the tramp entered there, he had opened the gate and walked in unseen. The dinner at the hall was just over when one of the servants brought a message, which she whispered into the ear of the young laird.

"Wants to see me? Who is he? Did he give no name?" he was heard hurriedly to say.

"No, sir; and he's such an awful-like man—just like a tramp or a beggar," answered the girl.

"A tramp? Oh, I see! Is he old and white-haired?" said the gentleman, remembering the scene at the toll-keeper's house, and the queer character he had assisted there. "Excuse me; I'll be back in a minute," he said to the others in the room; and he ran out, expecting to find the man in the hall.

"He wouldn't come in; he said he'd wait outside," said the girl, noticing her young master's look of disappointment. "P'r'aps he's away by this time."

The young laird stepped briskly through the hall and looked out into the dusk. The sun had just set, and there was still light enough to see any one near the spot. At the head of the walk leading to the house there was a clump of laurels and a drooping ash, and Stephen Barbour fancied he saw a white-haired head look out from behind that, and quickly cleared the space to find his suspicions correct. The queer tramp stood before him, with his right hand hidden down among the rags by his side.

"Oh, it's you again?" said the gentleman frankly, at the same time extending his hand to be shaken.

"You're Stephen Barbour, eldest son of Russel Barbour, aren't you?" said the tramp, taking no notice of the proffered hand, and glaring on the young man with a ferocity which startled the other.

"I am, sir—what then?"

"Then I've come to pay you back for what you did to Meg," said the old man, with suppressed fury. "Take that!" and instantly he raised his right hand, and a pistol-shot rang out on the soft evening air.

Quickly as the hand was raised the victim had time to throw out his own in a futile grasp at the old man's arm; then, when the bullet reached him, though desperately wounded, Barbour, with a loud cry, threw himself upon his assailant, grasping him tightly in his arms as if he would have squeezed the breath out of the man's body. The tramp had made no attempt to escape, and probably meant to make none; but the grasp annoyed him, and he struggled violently for a moment, and at length, as the senses of the wounded man were leaving him, succeeded in throwing Barbour backwards. At the same moment a coachman, turning a corner of the house with a pitchfork in his hands, ran forward to learn the cause of the disturbance, and seeing his young master in the act of being thrown down by a ragged tramp, he ran at the old man full tilt with the prongs of the fork, one of which passed clean through the tramp's arm.

This assault seemed to rouse the old man to a pitch of insane fury, which gave him an unnatural strength. He rushed at the coachman, wrenched the pitchfork from his hands, smashed him furiously over the head with the long pole, and then, throwing down the new weapon, turned and vanished.

The spectacle which met the eyes of the alarmed household when they rushed out was that of two men lying prostrate on the ground, with the pitchfork and pistol near them, and the first impression naturally was that the coachman in an insane moment had turned and attacked his young master. In a minute or two the true state of affairs was made known; the wounded man was borne into the house, and messengers despatched in every direction in search of the murderous assailant. From the first the medical man summoned gave very little hope of Barbour's recovery, and positively forbade him being questioned in any way. But when the news of the crime had been sent to Edinburgh, and I went out to get the facts of the case, the toll-keeper had spoken to the county constable of all that took place at the door, and, after a visit to that worthy, I thought I had the true solution of the mystery, which was far from being the case. During some of his visits to London the young heir had met the old tramp's daughter; the usual heart-rending result had followed, and the visit of the father had been undertaken solely for revenge. That was my view of the case, and in spite of the deadly determination with which that vengeance had been wreaked, my sympathy lay more with the poor father than his victim. To my surprise, however, both the toll-keeper and the county police strongly dissented from my opinion. Stephen Barbour, they strenuously declared, was quite incapable of such villainy. His character was singularly pure, and his whole life had been known to these men to be honourable and upright. From the lowest to the highest, every one had a good word for Stephen Barbour, and at the time of the shooting he was about to be married to a gifted young lady, who for years had been sole mistress of his affections. Without troubling to argue the point I set out to trace the murderer. Edinburgh was not a great distance from the scene of the attack, and the nearest large city, and my experience is that a genuine red-handed murderer always seeks safety among the masses of the biggest town within reach, unless he can at once leave the country. This one was poor—his last penny had been expended—therefore he could not go far quickly. I returned to Edinburgh, and the same afternoon met a man at the Night Asylum who had given the old tramp twopence, and a bit of white cotton to bind round his wounded arm. He had come upon him at the roadside near the city trying to remove the ragged coloured handkerchief with which he had bound up the arm, and which he was afraid might poison the wound.

On getting this news I started for the South Side, and had got as far as Minto Street, when, looking up one of the quiet streets leading towards St Leonards, I saw a tramp seated on a gate step, and moved up to have a look at him. So minutely had the man been described to me, that I recognised him at a glance. He was seated on the step holding his wounded arm, and staring straight before him in despair and apathy, his face white as his hair, and his whole expression that of a man longing for death to end his troubles.

I stopped before him, and when his dull eyes at length rose to meet my own, I said to him sharply—

"You were out at Frearton Hall last night?"

A slight flush came into his bloodless face at the words, and he faintly tried to rise.

"Yes, sir," he answered. "You're a pleeceman, though you don't wear the clothes?"

"Take care what you say—it'll all be used against you," I said, as I gave him my hand to help him to his feet.

"Oh, I don't mind that a bit," he said in a woeful and weary way that went straight to my heart. "Is he dead?—the man I fired at—is he dead?"

"He was not when I left him, but they're expecting that," I curtly answered. "Can you walk with me to the Central—it's more than a mile—or would you need a cab?"

"I'm willin' to walk as far as my strength will carry me," he said, with child-like obedience, as he took my arm for support. "Only to think that I've been an honest working man, striving to do what's right all my life, and yet to come to be hanged for murder after all! And I'm not sorry, either. I'm glad I've killed him, for I expect my Meg to die through him."

I looked at him curiously, thinking that his mind was affected, but the quick eyes took in the look at once, and he added—

"I'm not touched here;" and he put a finger-point to his forehead; "don't think that. I'm as right in the head as you are—only worn out and done. I was strong enough till it was all over, and then I seemed to have not the strength of a sparrow."

I thought he was right, and at the end of the street hailed a cab from the stance, and we drove to the Central, he looking out on the crowded streets with great interest, and making another of his queer remarks.

"I s'pose it's the last time I'll see so many people till I'm brought out to be hanged," he said, stolidly. "Well, it won't be any worse than what I've felt already here—here;" and he put his hand on his breast and quickly added, "Be you a family man, now?"

I nodded gravely.

"And you don't look a bad 'un—you didn't kick me or pull me about as I've seen some do, never thinkin' they'll be old themselves one day. You've a gal, mebbe?—one you've sort o' set your heart on!" he added, hooking his bony fingers on one of my arms and fixing me with those searching eyes of his. "How'd you feel if any one stole her out of your bosom, and ruined her, and cast her at your feet—a poor, bleeding, crushed thing, ready to lie down and die? Wouldn't you feel like killing that man? I see it in your face. Well, that's just how I felt; we're both alike, only that I've done it, and you haven't come to that yet."

At the Office he quietly and calmly gave his name as Philip Huddlestone, and when asked if he had any statement to make, he said—

"I've nothing to say but that I shot the man, and that I'm not sorry I did it. I'm only a poor man, a journeyman painter by trade, but I've my feelings the same as the richest. I've a daughter I set my heart on, and though she was only a barmaid, you mustn't think she wasn't good and pure. That man—him that I shot, and ain't sorry for—met her at the bar, and got talking to her about love and nonsense, and kept telling her of his estate that he'd come into when his father died, and of the money he had coming to him. Well, the poor gal didn't know no better, and made up to run away with him to Paris. He was to marry her there, and I believe did go through some affair of the kind to blind her eyes when he saw she was set on coming back if he didn't. But then the law ain't strong enough there to make it binding in England, and he knowd she was no more his wife in this country than I am. Well, he kept her till he was tired of her, and then bolted and left her. She got helped across the water, and then came back to her poor old dad. I didn't know my own gal—my own flesh and blood. I think she's dying, and I left her in safe hands while I came up to Scotland to see her righted. She sent me to do that, but she didn't know I meant to do it with a pistol. I walked most of the way, 'cause we're very poor, and I'm not so able to work as I used to be."

That was the substance of the prisoner's declaration, and, after emitting the same, he was taken away and locked up, his wounded arm being first properly dressed. But before a week had elapsed there came a surprise for us all. The wounded man had so far recovered as to be able to receive an account of the prisoner's declaration, when he expressed the most unbounded astonishment, and emphatically denied all knowledge of the circumstances. That he spoke the truth few could doubt, for it was ascertained beyond question that Stephen Barbour had not been in Paris for more than a year. The complication seemed so mysterious, and the statements of both men remained so emphatic, that a messenger was despatched to the prisoner's home, and that man found the daughter as emphatic in her statements as her father, and in the end brought her to Scotland to see the wounded man whom she claimed as her lawful husband. This step proved a wise one, for on the poor girl being introduced to the invalid, she at once cried out—

"That is not Stephen Barbour—he is like him, but older and fairer."

This answer gave the old laird the first clue to the mystery. His second son, a fast youth whom it was impossible to keep at home, spent most of his time in London, and often got into good society by passing himself off as the eldest son and heir. Thus he had been introduced to the pretty barmaid, and by the name of Stephen he had been married to her in Paris.

This, his latest piece of villainy, plunged the whole family into grief, involving as it did not only the family honour, but almost costing his innocent and beloved brother and another man their lives.

So enraged were his relatives that the case was given into the hands of the police, and Adam Barbour, to his profound disgust and surprise, was arrested in London, and tried and convicted of false impersonation, for which he was sent for three months to prison.

Stephen Barbour made a good recovery, and was able at the trial of Huddlestone to speak so feelingly and kindly of the prisoner, that all—even the accused—were moved, and the sentence was the light one of nine months' imprisonment. The daughter Meg was cared for by the Barbours, and ultimately, I believe, on the death of the man she had married, received the second son's portion, supplemented by a handsome addition from Stephen Barbour. Her father rejoined her in London at the expiry of his sentence; but either the excitement of his journey to Scotland, or the prison life which followed it, had been too much for his slender frame, and he scarcely saw the end of the year.

A HOUSE-BREAKER'S WIFE.

Going down the Canongate one day I was accosted by a little treacherous rascal known as Dirty Dick. I suppose he had followed me down the street for the purpose of so addressing me, but at the moment I did not think much of the circumstance. Dick was not particularly dirty in his appearance or person, so it is possible he had got the name rather for some dirty trick or act of treachery. He had the distinction of being heartily despised by every one who knew him, myself included.

After a little preliminary patter, to throw me off my guard, Dick said—

"Bob Brettle has finished his time and got back here."

That, then, was Dick's business with me. Had he quarrelled with the convict and ticket-of-leave man he named? I knew perfectly well that the reckless Bob Brettle had returned, for he had duly reported himself to us, as bound by his ticket-of-leave, but I thought proper to say innocently in reply—

"Has he, really?"

"Yes," continued Dick, with animation; "I've seen him often, and know where he hangs out—Brierly's, in the Grassmarket. Is a straight tip of any use to you?"

I looked at the rascal, and if the imp had only had the sense of an owl he would have seen how contemptuous was the glance. But it is given to some natures to be perfectly unconscious of the loathing they inspire, and Dick's was one of these.

"I'll tell you when I get it," was my reply. I did not expect Dick to give me any news or promp me to anything that was not likely to benefit himself.

"Well, you'll soon have Bob Brettle in your hands again," said Dick, button-holing me with an affectionate caress, which made my flesh creep. "He's planning something now. I don't know what the job is, but it's something dashing and daring. If he was took at the same old game, wouldn't it be ten years this time?"

"What was his last term?" I asked, affecting ignorance.

"Seven."

"Well, you don't need to ask, knowing that," I said, making Dick uncomfortable with a steady stare.

"If you was to watch him well, and get me to help you, I believe you'd be sure of nabbing him," said the traitor temptingly.

"Oh, you've quarrelled with him, then?" I sharply returned.

"Not me!" he exclaimed with great fervour.

I set the answer down as a lie, but pursued—

"Well, you think to get money for the dirty work of betraying him?"

"Not a penny," he vociferated, with a tremendous oath, "and there'll be no betraying about it. Only I thought you'd be always glad to hear the news or get a tip. You helped me so much in that last fix that I haven't forgot it;" and the villain tried to put on a sentimental and grateful look by way of drawing a red herring across my path.

I was not deceived, but Dick's next words were lost to me. I was thinking hard, and trying to account for Dick's sudden zeal in the cause of law and order. He did not want money—I was bound to believe that at least;—could he have an old grudge at Brettle, or was this freak of treachery only the result of a quarrel?

I could not see how it could be either, for Brettle was not the man to associate much with a cur like Dick, but I resolved to make some inquiries with a view to laying bare the informer's motive.

Brettle was a man who, in spite of the fact that we were professionally enemies, called out from within me a deal of admiration and sympathy. He was a powerfully-built fellow, still under thirty, and had once been handsome. He had not been born into a life of crime, but had been a hard-working silversmith, led off his feet and ruined by a pretty woman. The woman was really a beauty, but with the figure and face of an angel she had the heart of a devil.

She was known as Pretty Polly, and Brettle conceived such a passion for her that he actually married her. Brettle's dash and daring carried him on for a long time unscathed, but at length he was caught and had a smart sentence. Pretty Polly supported herself as a barmaid during the interval, but being detected in helping herself from the till, she went into prison just as Bob came out. When her three months were finished they got together again. Brettle had another spell of good luck, till in a moment altogether unexpected by him he was neatly trapped, and laid past for seven years. I had the taking of him, but I was quite ignorant of the source of the information upon which I had acted. There had been a traitor, but I did not trouble to seek out the person, when the act brought grist to my mill.

Now, in surveying Dirty Dick's shifty countenance, the thought came to me for the first time—Could he, that insignificant looking wretch, have been the betrayer of Brettle before his last conviction? I could scarcely credit it, but if it was he, then the fact would point to a long-standing grudge and a revengeful feeling not yet satiated. Now, I had never given Dick credit for brain enough to conceive and nourish a good hatred, and one does not care to discover a flaw in his own estimate of another's character.

After a little further conversation, from which I learned that it was not yet settled how Brettle was to distinguish himself, I parted with Dick, he kindly volunteering to "see me again" as soon as he had important information to tender.

For a day or two after I could not be called idle. The foremost question in my mind was—Why does Dirty Dick wish Brettle laid up for ten years? and all my work was in the direction of a feasible explanation or answer. I searched, and questioned, and ferreted in every conceivable direction, but was only left more puzzled than before. Dick, I found, had had no quarrel with Brettle, nor could I discover that he had any grudge against the ticket-of-leave man. I discovered also that it was absolutely impossible that Dick could have been the cause of Brettle's last capture, as at the time Dick had himself been fulfilling a three months' sentence for theft.

I happened one afternoon to meet Brettle himself, and, though he generally showed great hostility to me, and never exchanged words with me if he could avoid it, I thought I would have a word with him in passing.

"How are you getting on Bob?" I pleasantly asked, before he could hurry past.

"Not getting on at all," he gloomily answered. "I've been trying to get work, but can't."

I opened my eyes to their widest, and for a moment could scarcely speak.

"What kind of work?" I cautiously inquired, thinking he might mean his adopted trade of housebreaking.

"Any kind—anything to keep life in me," he cried, with some bitterness. "I'm sick of prison, and don't mean to go inside of one again if I can live on the square."

I could scarcely trust my own senses. I had never expected such words out of his mouth; and then, after the hint I had received from

Dirty Dick, I was doubly suspicious, and must have looked the feeling. Could it be possible that he was trying to deceive me for some purpose? I could not believe it. It was quite out of his line. He was not of the stuff out of which a good hypocrite could be made.

"I'm glad to hear that you've come to your senses," I dryly remarked. "What has given you the notion?"

"I don't know, but the spunk's all gone out of me," he dejectedly answered. "I haven't my wife now."

"Oh, indeed! what has become of her?" I asked with fresh interest.

"Gone," he said, with a sorrowful shake of the head and a quiver of the lip.

"Gone where?"

"Gone dead, I'm afraid," he huskily answered. "If she'd been alive she would have met me whenever I got out. She worshipped the very ground I trod on. I hear she went on the stage as a ballet-girl after I was laid up, and that and the loss of me killed her, I suppose. We had a bit of a tiff before I was took. I was so hanged jealous of her—but that was nothing. The like of her doesn't walk the earth. True as steel, and she loved me so!"

I said nothing; for if I had spoken I should have had to say that if the loss of Pretty Polly made him adopt an honest life, her absence would be a blessing.

I chatted away for a little, and then said abruptly—

"What was your object in telling me you were going on the square?" I thought perhaps that he might want assistance.

"What was your object in speaking to me?" he roughly and snappishly returned. "I had no object at all. I know that the more thieves there are the better it is for you."

"You're mistaken there, Bob, and I'll prove it some day," I answered pleasantly, and then I left him.

My curiosity was roused regarding Brettle, and I took the trouble to have him watched, when I discovered that he really was trying to get work, and even undertaking the meanest drudgery to earn a living. Everything was against him, of course, and he went back steadily till his clothes would scarcely allow him to appear on the street.

In making these investigations I was continually contrasting Brettle's condition and evident inclinations with Dirty Dick's prophecy, that

I should soon have the ticket-of-leave man in my hands again, and with no success so far as a solution is concerned. The promised "tip" had never come, and even Dick was a mystery to me. I was at a loss to know whence came the money which Dick spent so freely upon himself. He did not work; he was too cowardly to engage in any act of plundering likely to produce much gain; and yet he had abundance, while Brettle was in great want. Dick had the reputation of being able to arrange a robbery very nicely, but would never risk his own liberty in the affair, however tempting the gain; but even knowing that to be a source of income to him, I was at a loss to account for his seeming wealth. Thus it chanced that my attention came to be more earnestly fixed upon Dick than upon the man he had promised to betray into my hands. When I saw Dick moving in a stealthy and cat-like way before me, one day when I was passing along Princes Street, and knew that he was quite unconscious of my presence, I was quickly roused to an interest in his movements. I had not watched him long, when I thought the solution of the whole mystery was in my hands. It seemed to me that Dick's new line was pocket-picking, and that he was following a likely plant—an elderly gentleman and a lady—with the intention of exercising his new art. After a time it dawned upon me that Dick's cowardice was against him. Several chances occurred which he did not attempt to make use of. At length the gentleman went into one of the shops alone, and then, to my surprise, the lady, who had remained standing at the window, turned slightly, noticed Dick standing near, moved a little closer to him, and addressed some words to him in a hurried and constrained manner, which Dick as swiftly answered. The lady then took out her purse, and, placing a coin in his hand, turned once more to look in at the window, while Dick passed on with the crowd as if nothing had happened. Now, had Dick been the first to speak, and had the lady's manner been different, I should have considered it an ordinary case of begging, and had no scruple in following and taking Dick. But as it was I could only wonder what connection such a haughty and evidently wealthy person could have with a miserable coward like him. Instead of following Dick I followed the lady as soon as she had been rejoined by the white-haired gentleman, whom I took to be her husband. From the side glimpse which I had of her face she seemed to be quite young and very good-looking, though there was a nameless something in the expression of her face which told me that she had not always been in such a position. In order to get a better look at her, I got past the couple on the opposite side of the street, crossed over while they stood inspecting a window, and then, as soon as they moved, sauntered slowly forward and met them full in the face. Purposely I got directly in front of the lady, in seeming forgetfulness, and, as she stopped in haughty surprise, I had a good look into her eyes. Then I started and looked again, upon which her glance fell before mine as surely as those of one of "my bairns" ever did. In a moment more she was past, and I was left wondering. I was puzzled and bewildered. The face seemed strangely familiar to me; I could have sworn that I had known the owner of it long before, and yet I could not tell her name or recall a single circumstance in her history. I stood there cudgelling my brains till I had almost lost sight of the couple who had so interested me; then, unable to make a better of it, I roused myself and followed them for a full hour, till they entered one of the biggest hotels in the city and remained there. A waiter running out a moment or two after, on being stopped by me, said that the couple were "Mr and Mrs Harper, from Glasgow," and that he understood that the gentleman was very wealthy. They were in Edinburgh on a pleasure trip, and, so far as he knew, had no children.

That was all I could get from the waiter, but the news did not banish that beautiful face—so full of sweetness and innocence, if a certain flash could have been taken from her fine eyes. That flash was the only thing to turn the scales, and it did that most effectually. It gave just such an expression to the whole face as I could imagine Lucrezia Borgia to have owned.

Later in the day, when thinking of Brettle and his affairs, by some queer turn of memory I recalled the name of Pretty Polly, and then her sweet-looking features rose before me as vividly as if I had seen them only the day before. But that was not all; for lo! as I looked, the fine features became somewhat stouter and coarser, and rapidly changed into those of Mrs Harper, whom I had that day followed along Princes Street.

"How like they are to each other!" was my mental exclamation. "It must have been that resemblance which puzzled me. But could they be the same person? Never! Brettle says Pretty Polly is dead."

This reasoning did not convince me, for there still remained the curious fact that the haughty Mrs Harper had allowed her glance to fall before my own in that fashion so suggestive to me of "auld acquaintance." Could Pretty Polly have had a sister who resembled her? I thought not; for had not Brettle himself said, "The like of her doesn't walk the earth?" Besides, if she had a sister, and she in such a good position, I could scarcely believe that the lady would be so heartless as to allow her brother-in-law to almost perish of want while she revelled in luxury.

I was waited for by Dick at a street corner on the afternoon of the following day. When I saw him I was a little pleased, as I thought it possible that I might get out of him all I wanted in regard to the strange woman. But as Dick was full to the eyes with his own affairs, I let him chatter about them first.

"I can give you the straight tip about Brettle at last," he eagerly began.

"Do you expect me to pay you for it?" I quietly interposed.

"No, no, not a penny."

"You work for nothing, then—for the mere love of the thing?" I said, with a palpable sneer.

"Just that," he said, swallowing the insult smilingly. "Brettle is to break into a shop in Leith Street to-night—Calderston's, No.—. The place above enters from the Terrace, and the key of that is sent home every night by a drunken porter. Brettle will treat him on the way, get the key from him, and work inside all night. Perhaps he will stay there over the Sunday. He is to work the job single-handed, and take the plunder out by the Terrace stair in different lots."

"And who arranged all this for him?" I asked, nailing Dick's shifty glance with a steady stare.

"Oh, I don't know—himself, I suppose," he confusedly answered.

That was enough for me. I saw that Dick had arranged it all as a nice trap for Brettle. What could be his object?

"Dick," I said suddenly, after noting down all he had revealed, "have you any idea what has become of Brettle's wife, Pretty Polly?"

The start the man gave! and his face! I never thought that there was such a blush in him.

"Dead, I think," he guiltily stammered, after a horrible pause.

I thought not, and said so.

"She couldn't be married again, to a richer man?" I suggestively observed. "I understand she and Brettle were lawfully man and wife."

Dick's face was the picture of guilt and confusion. If the ground could have swallowed him at that moment I imagine he would have been thankful. I was reading all the answers to the questions which had puzzled me for days in his tell-tale features.

"You have seen her lately, then?"

"No," he faltered, while his face said "Yes," and cursed me into the bargain.

"And have you no idea where she could be found?"

"Not the least," he said, with the lie almost choking him.

"Imphm! Well, that's all I want with you just now," I coldly remarked, and with a dive he was gone.

I saw the whole plot now, and felt sure that that beautiful devil of a woman was at the bottom of it all. But was I to allow that miserable man—that well-meaning convict who had actually made an effort towards a life of honesty—to walk into the shambles? No doubt it would look like a feather in my cap to take him in the act and walk him off for his certain ten years' penal; every one would think it neat and clever, and speak of the vigilance and sharpness of the police, &c., but there would still be a voice within me crying out against the whole as a crime—an offence against a law that never was written. After giving the matter some thought, I went out to the Grange to a gentleman with a big heart and unbounded faith in myself.

"I want you to give me some money," I said, as his hand grasped my own, "without asking any questions. It is to help a convict and ticket-of-leave man till he shall be able to help himself."

"All right, Mr McGovan; you shall have it," was the frank response. "Just say how much it is to be."

I named the sum, and it was placed in my hands. Little more was said, and I left that wide-souled and big-hearted man to have a hunt for Bob Brettle. I expected to find him quite easily, but I did not; and what gave me more concern was to learn in the course of my search that Bob had broken out—that is, had been drinking hard, and was, when last seen, in a state of savage ferocity and excitement, which, I feared, would not help me greatly in my mission. Still it was no time to delay. I must see him then, or be forced to take him as a house-breaker a few hours later. I persevered till I found him in a public-house—savage and fierce as could be. He would scarcely answer me, and only consented to speak with me alone when I told him he *must*.

"You've had a struggle lately, and I promised to prove that I had no interest in you remaining in the old line," I quietly began. "I've brought you some money which a gentleman has given, on my assurance that it would not be thrown away, to help you till you get work."

"Take it back to him then—I don't need it now," he angrily returned. "I've got work, or at least expect to get it."

"Yes, I can guess what kind of work you mean," I pointedly answered. "Do you know what your next sentence will be, Bob, if you're taken at the old game?"

"I'm not taken yet," he confidently answered, with an oath and a thundering blow of his fist on the little table of the box in which we were secluded. "He'll be a clever man that will take me; ay, and he'll need to be a strong man too!"

"Bob Brettle!" I cried, starting up and leaning across the table towards him, "you're a fool!"

"What!" and his big fist was clenched as if to let drive at my face.

"A fool—a perfect baby—a blind idiot, who would walk into a trap chuckling all the while over his own cleverness and daring. Man alive! what is all your bravery or daring against the wiles of a wicked woman?"

"A woman! what woman?" he faltered, apparently pulled up by my very abuse.

"Why, the woman you call your wife—Pretty Polly—who is now in this city with a wealthy man to whom she is married. Her name is Mrs Harper now, and I suppose she feared that your claims on her might be awkward, and so employed Dirty Dick to prepare a job for you—that Leith Street affair which you mean to go to as soon as you leave this place, and at which I am to take you in the act, so that you may be booked for ten years at least. Now, smash out at me now, and say I've an interest in keeping you on the cross!"

"My wife—Pretty Polly—living and married to another man!" he breathed, with a look positively frightful settling on his heavy features. "I—don't—believe—a—word—of—it!"

I folded my arms and said nothing. The idea was a new one to him; I would let it work. I had not long to wait. I could see the workings of the demon Jealousy in his face, in his twitching lips and flushed cheeks, in his clouded brow and clenched hands.

"You've got a name for telling the truth," he at last hoarsely observed, with a look of piteous agony on his haggard face, "but I must see the woman before I believe it. Tell me where she lives, or take me to her. The she-devil! Oh, if it's only true!"

"Rest content with my word. I shall not give you her address—at least not now. It wouldn't be safe. When you are sober and calm you shall have it."

"I am sober," he quickly returned; and he seemed to speak the truth, for every trace of drink had vanished like a flash, "and I am calm—as death. Give me her address!"

I refused most positively, and at length he rose, deliberately put on his cap, and quietly walked out of the shop with the simple remark that he would see me again. I knew enough of Brettle's character to warn me that the sooner Pretty Polly was got out of his reach the better it would be for her.

I therefore hurried over to the hotel, and learned that she and her husband had gone out about six o'clock, and not yet returned. I sat down to wait for them, little guessing that I was to remain there till nearly eleven o'clock, they being at the theatre, as I afterwards learned. While I was thus waiting at the hotel, Bob Brettle had taken action in a style characteristic of him and his passionate nature. He hunted through all the dens till he came upon Dirty Dick singing songs in a half-gleeful and half-fuddled condition. Dick remained gleeful not one moment after he saw Brettle's face. The housebreaker invited him out to the darkness of the stair-head, and there brought out a long-bladed clasp-knife, at the same moment throttling Dick with his left hand, and forcing him down on his knees. There, with the point of the knife at Dick's heart, he dragged out of the quaking wretch a full and abject confession of the plot, and also of the name of the hotel at which Pretty Polly and her wealthy husband had put up. When Dick had finished, Bob simply swung round his powerful left hand, and in a moment Dick lay groaning on the landing below with a broken leg and fractured rib. Paying no attention to the injured wretch or his cries, Brettle ran down the stair and made for the hotel.

A waiter at the portico told him that the Harpers were not in, but were expected shortly. Brettle stood sentry there at the door or near it for a full half hour, and at length was rewarded by seeing a cab drive up, and a gentleman get out and hand forth a sweet-faced and elegantly dressed lady—the veritable Pretty Polly.

With a bound like that of a tiger Brettle was upon her, and had her taper wrist clenched in his hand, and her face swung round to the light of the street lamps with a force that almost crushed the delicate bones.

"You jewelled serpent!" he hissed, "you would sell me to the shambles! Look at me, you beautiful devil, and say, if you can, that it is not true!"

A shriek—appalling enough to reach my ears above, and bring me rushing down—was Pretty Polly's only answer.

Her husband, however, laid a hand on Brettle's shoulder—

"How dare you, sir? Who are you?"

"Her husband!" shouted the infuriated house-breaker; and at the same moment there was the flash of a knife and an agonising cry from the wounded woman, and a rush upon the assailant from all sides. I was among the number, and Brettle recognised me with a quiet nod.

"I'm not going to struggle or bolt," he quietly observed, as Pretty Polly was lifted from the pavement and borne insensible into the hotel, with the blood gushing from a deep wound in her breast. "I'm satisfied now. I have paid her off. I've taken it out of her, and she was the only woman I ever loved!"

Bob's grief, however, seemed quiet and tame compared with that of Polly's second husband, upon whom the revelation came with a shock which nearly proved fatal. Mr Harper quietly slipped away out of Edinburgh without once asking to look on the face of the woman who had deceived him. Brettle went to prison, of course, and Pretty Polly, as soon as she could be moved, was sent to the Infirmary. She lingered long, but did not die. In about six months she was pronounced able to leave the hospital. She appeared as witness against Brettle, and helped to fix a year's imprisonment on him, and then she drifted out to a life of hardship and degradation which ended her before Brettle's sentence had expired. Brettle heard the news unmoved when he was liberated, and then disappeared. I have never heard of him since.

McSWEENY AND THE CHIMNEY-SWEEP.

The things were missed from one of the rooms in a house in George Square not many hours after the sweeps had been there, and of course suspicion at once fell upon these men. Who ever trusted a chimney-sweep the length of his own nose? The blackness of their faces is supposed to be nothing to that of their souls, and what was the old and popular portrait of the devil but a chimney-sweep with a tail tacked on? There were three articles taken—a gold bracelet, a very valuable necklet and pendant, and one gold ear-ring.

The leaving behind of one of the ear-rings gave the robbery an odd look, for the whole of the things had been taken from the drawer or a dressing-table, and the ear-ring left was the first article which caught the eye of the owner when she opened the drawer.

Either the thief had wanted only one ear-ring, or had been scared in grasping at the plunder, and so left the odd trinket. The drawer had been locked, but the key had been left in the lock, and must have been made use of by the thief both to open and refasten that receptacle. Mrs Nolten, the lady of the house, was the first to make the discovery, and, not knowing that the sweeps had been in the house, fancied that one of the servants might have taken the use of the jewels.

A furious ring at the bell brought the two girls up in great consternation, and then the truth was known. Neither of them had been near the drawer of the dressing-table, and one of them, while admitting that the sweeps had been there, declared that she had "kept her eye on them" all the time, and so could scarcely conceive it possible for them to be the thieves.

Mrs Nolten paid no heed to the remark, but wisely sent word to us in all haste. When the report arrived it was about eleven o'clock in the forenoon, and I was on the point of starting off to look after a much more important case. However, as I had to go southwards, I decided to take George Square on the way, and then let McSweeny do the rest. We soon got to the house, and were shown into the dressing-room from which the articles had vanished.

The two servants were brought up, and from one of them I learned that the sweeps had been simply a man and a boy. They had both been in the room for a little, and after the man had helped to lift out the grate and fasten up a blanket in the fire-place, he had gone up on the roof to complete the work, leaving the boy in the room alone. They believed that the boy was the sweep's own son. I examined the carpet in front of the dressing-table. It showed no marks of sooty feet. I then looked at the drawer in which the articles had been secured, and finally took the key from the lock and smelt it. There was a distinct smell of soot about it, but then the whole room had a flavour of the kind just then, and the smell on the key might mean nothing. After taking down a minute description of the articles missing, and getting the sweep's address, we left the house, and I directed McSweeny to go to the chimney-sweep and see what he could make of the case. We then parted, with the understanding that I also was to call at the sweep's on my return. The man's name was Sandy Brimely, and his place only a couple of streets from the spot.

It was a dark dingy hole below the level of the street, and consisted of three rooms or cellars, lighted through gratings on the pavement. One place was used as a kitchen and sleeping-place, another smaller place was also used as a bedroom, and the third hole was used as a store-room for soot. This third place was in reality part of the first, but had been divided off by the wooden partition which kept the soot from sliding all over their living room.

Sandy was standing at the head of the stair leading down to this sooty abode when McSweeny arrived. His work was generally over by that time, except when a godsend came in shape of a chimney afire, and Sandy leant against the wall enjoying his pipe as peacefully as if there had been no such beings as detectives in the world. He was a sly, oily tongued fellow, but so far as I know had never been convicted of any worse crime than beating his wife, or occasionally taking more whisky than he could carry unassisted.

After a little preliminary blarney on both sides, during which it appeared that Sandy knew both McSweeny's face and his profession, my chum considerably startled him by saying abruptly—

"You were at Mrs Nolten's, in George Square, this morning?"

The sweep took the pipe from his mouth, with his pleased look effectually banished. If he had not been so sooty he might have been said to turn pale, so constrained and almost scared did he become.

"Let me see. Yes—yes, I was there," he awkwardly answered. "I was there doing two vents."

"Did you take anything away wid ye?" said McSweeny, pointedly.

He expected the man, if guilty, to show signs of concern or confusion; but, if anything, the sweep looked brighter after the question.

"Away with me?" he echoed, to gain time for the answer. "Of course I did. I took the soot."

"Nothing else?" suspiciously pursued McSweeny.

"Nothing else, sir, as I'm a living man," energetically returned Sandy. "I hope you don't think I would touch an article belonging to any one else?"

The question was a delicate one, and McSweeny did not attempt an answer, further than to state that some things had been missed, and that he was there in his official capacity to investigate the case, and try to find the articles missing.

Sandy allowed him to talk on, drinking it all in and becoming brighter and more beaming at every word.

"I hope you'll search every hole and corner in my place, sir," he fervently exclaimed, when McSweeny had done. "I want my character cleared, and my honesty established. What," he added grandly, "what is dearer to a poor man than his good name? and what would become of my business if folks took me for a thief? I insist on you searching my place—never mind about a warrant, or anything else—my honour is at stake, and I must have it done at once."

He led the way downstairs to his abode, in which McSweeny found quite a crowd of small sooty children scrambling about the earthen floor in noisy glee. These were all sent outside, and then Sandy explained to his wife with much warmth the absurd suspicion which had been raised against his character.

"I see it all now! I see it all now!" he suddenly exclaimed, smiting his sooty brow with tragic force. "Could anybody believe they would be so cunning?"

McSweeny hinted that an explanation would be acceptable.

"Why, don't you see, sir—the servants—the servants; they're at the bottom of this. They've taken the chance while we were there to steal the things, knowing the blame would fall on me. You've no idea," he continued, waxing pathetic, "what sweeps have to put up with. There's scarcely a house we go into that we're not watched like glaziers on tramp. You can see it in their eyes. It's hard to be looked at like a thief when you're doing your best to earn an honest living."

"Are you quite sure now that the boy you had with you mightn't help himself if he got a dacent chance?" suggested McSweeny, by way of appearing to sympathise with the sweep.

"Him? Why, he's my own son!" exclaimed the sweep, as if that quite settled the matter. "But he's just out in the square there playing at the bools. I'll send for him, and you can question him yourself."

This was done, and the sooty apprentice appeared, and denied all knowledge of the missing articles.

McSweeny, on the invitation of the father, somewhat gingerly searched the sooty clothes of the boy, but found nothing. He then performed the same office upon the father, with a like result. The wife also turned out her pockets for inspection, and then McSweeny settled himself to the not very agreeable task of searching the house. The furniture was poor and scanty, and the floor an earthen one, so there was no great difficulty in the task. But there was soot everywhere. It was on the floor, on the shelves, in the very beds, and so pervaded the whole atmosphere of the house that McSweeny had soon drawn such a quantity into his nostrils that he would willingly have paid half-a-crown down for the pleasure of sneezing his own head off. He went gaping, and blinking, and sputtering over the place till he had searched every part but the soot cellar. Before that he paused ruefully. I firmly believe he would have shirked searching that altogether, and that the resolve was showing itself in his face, when the cunning sweep affected to make a suspicious movement or two with his hands near the partition, as if in the act of dropping something into the soot.

"What's that you're after now?" cried McSweeny, starting round sharply and dragging forth the sweep's hand.

"Nothing—oh, nothing, sir," was the glib reply; "I was only feeling how high the soot is."

McSweeny suspiciously lifted a candle, held it over the partition and peered down into the soot-bin at the spot, but could see nothing to indicate that any article had been dropped. This partition was about two feet and a half high and immediately behind it the soot was fully a foot deep, sloping up thence to the back wall to a height of about three feet. Against that wall several sacks of soot were piled, and resting on one of these sacks was the end of a spar of wood which reached across the soot to the wooden partition, upon which the other end rested. This plank was evidently used as a standing-place from which they could conveniently empty their soot-bag after a morning's work. McSweeny thought it possible that there might be a hide of some kind behind these soot bags, and, candle in hand, clambered up on the partition and thence on to the spar bridging the soot. As he stepped across the frail bridge he had to turn his back for a moment to the innocent-looking sweep, and knew no more until he had dived down nose foremost into the sea of soot.

He always declared that the sweep had shoved the end of the plank from the partition; but when he scrambled to his feet among the soot, sputtering, gasping, and sneezing enough to rend himself, there was Sandy standing gravely by him with a look of earnest and sorrowing condolence on his grimy face. The wife went into fits of laughter over McSweeny's appearance as he stood in the soot, with his face and beard thickly coated with the soft black, and only his well-rubbed eyelids beginning to show white through the sable covering, but she was solemnly rebuked and sworn at by her demure-faced husband.

"Eh, sir, to think that the plank should have slippit just when it wasna wanted to slip," cried Sandy, handing McSweeny a sooty rag with which to clean his face and clothes; "but it'll dae ye nae herm, sir, nae herm. Soot's a healthy thing, sir—healthier than clean water."

"You—you—ah—ah——choof!—you did that!" cried McSweeny, as soon as he could speak, ferociously fixing Sandy with his eye. "You'll suffer for—ah—ah——choo—oof! Begorra, I've a good moind to stick your head in it, and make you swallow a bag of it before I let you out."

"Me, sir!" cried Sandy, in pious horror. "May I never soop another lum if I ever thought o' sic a thing. See, I'll gie ye a brush doon, sir. It's a kind o' a pity ye had thae licht-coloured troosers on, but they'll clean at the dyer's, and never look a whit the waur."

"Don't thrubble yourself to brush me, for I'm not done wid the hole yet," savagely responded McSweeny; "but for this I'd have let you off aisy, but now, sweet bad luck to you! I'm as black as I can be, and I'll see to the bottom of this before I stir."

McSweeny at the same moment seized a big shovel which he found in one corner of the soot-bin, and deliberately began to spade out the soot into the middle of the kitchen floor, carefully examining every shovelful before he pitched it over the partition. While he was thus engaged bending over a spadeful of the soot, Sandy managed to make a sign to his wife, who stooped to the floor, picked something up, and threw it over into the heap of soot rising in the middle of her kitchen.

McSweeny was just conscious of some swift movement having taken place, but saw neither the movement nor the direction of the pitch.

"What divil's game are you two up to now?" he suspiciously growled, looking from one to the other. "I'll have to take yez both. You throw'd something just now—what was it?"

The sweep and his wife raised their hands as if horrified at the accusation, and solemnly declared that McSweeny's imagination had deceived him; that they had nothing to throw, and they would as soon attempt to fly in the air as to try to deceive such a world-renowned and keen-sighted detective as he. McSweeny, still suspicious, came out of the soot-bin and searched about for a little, but found nothing; and then, after a deal of snorting and swearing, went back to his work, and soon had all the loose soot out in the kitchen. There remained then only the sacks at the back to be removed, and McSweeny was diligently setting his brawny arms and shoulders to them when I descended the stair and stood before them. I stood transfixed with astonishment at the strange scene, till a familiar grin from the demon of darkness at work in the soot-bin made me look at him more closely, and then I faintly recognised my chum.

"Good heavens! what does all this mean?" I exclaimed, after a hearty laugh at McSweeny's solemn face and the eloquent burst of abuse which he heaped upon the sweep and his wife.

"It means," he responded, making a virtue of a necessity, "that I'm not afraid to do my duty properly, even though I do get a little black by it, and spoil a good suit of clothes into the bargain. Jamie, avick, I've found nothing, but we may take them both on suspicion, for a pair of bigger blackguards never walked the streets unhung."

It seemed to me that had the sweep been an innocent and honest man, he would have resented this language hotly. He did not. He was all smoothness and politeness still, and officiously offered to help me in any way. What I liked worse was to observe that he was also all cheerfulness. There was even a twinkle of gloating and delight in the corners of his demurely drawn eyes over McSweeny's grinning and discomfiture, or possibly over the consciousness that he was perfectly safe. Now, I had never believed that we should find the missing articles in that sooty den, and had hinted as much to

McSweeny. Supposing the sweep to have nerve and effrontery enough to commit such a robbery, he would have been an arrant fool to have kept the stolen trinkets about his house. After a look round the place myself, and a short conversation in an undertone with McSweeny, I decided that we might go, and trust to tracing the missing articles elsewhere. But there was the sweep's kitchen in a dreadful state of confusion, with a great pile of soot filling the centre of the floor; it would never do to leave the poor man's house in that state, and I promptly said so.

"Oh, that's naething, sir—I'll put back the soot mysel'," smoothly and graciously answered the sweep. "Dinna disturb yoursel', sir; I'll see ye up that stair, for it's very dark and narrow. This way, sir; this way."

He quickly made for the stair, but I paused before following, and exchanged a look of inquiry with McSweeny. The wife, squatted by the fire with a pipe in her mouth, watched us furtively out of the corner of her eye. That sly, cautious glance decided me. The sweep had shown a trifle too much alacrity in wishing to bid us good-bye and see us out. I stood still and conversed in a low tone with McSweeny. The sweep looked back from the doorway somewhat anxiously.

"We're not quite ready yet," I quietly said; "we must put things as we got them." Then I added with apparent coolness to McSweeny, "Shovel it back *carefully*."

The face of the sweep, sooty though it was, showed a visible and concerned change as I spoke, and I felt that I had scored a point.

"I'll help you, sir; I've another shovel here," he cried with alacrity after the first stagger, pouncing on a shovel and approaching the soot heap.

"Thank you—no," I coldly and sternly returned, pointing to a seat by the fire; "sit there till I tell you to rise."

He sat down, or rather flopped down, with an attempt at a gracious grin, and, taking the pipe from his wife, began puffing fiercely, watching us anxiously all the while. McSweeny slowly and deliberately shovelled up the soot in small quantities, according to my directions, narrowly inspecting it as it was returned to the bin, and before the half of the soot had been so lifted he paused to inspect a soot-covered object which had got into one of these small shovelfuls. I was at his side in a moment; and as the glitter of metal caught my eye I glanced towards the sweep and saw that he was painfully anxious to look indifferent. The object, when cleared of soot, proved to be a small handle of gilt brass, fastened to a flat piece of ivory, on which was some neat carving. The four eyes at the fireside were goggling, like distended telescopes, at us as we stood clearing the strange object of soot.

"What's this?" I sharply demanded of the sweep.

"That, sir?" and he took a stride or two forward to look at the fragment. "I'm sure I dinna ken; it's a thing ane o' the bairns found oot on the street and brought in to play wi'."

Sandy's face said "lie" all over in spite of the soot as he made the hurried answer, and I said nothing. Every thief has "found" these things, or had them given him, or innocently brought into his house by some third person not conveniently at hand. After a close inspection of the fragment I was inclined to think that it had formed part of the lid of an ivory box or casket. No such article was in our list so far as I could remember; but the expression of the sweep's face and his general manner induced me to say that I would take the fragment with me.

"Certainly, sir, certainly; it's of nae value to me," cried Sandy with forced alacrity. "Will I wrap it in a bit paper for ye?"

I declined the officious offer, put the fragment in my pocket, and shortly after took leave with McSweeny, who made a dive at once for the baths in Nicolson Square. A wash in water and a brush at the fragment seemed to confirm my suspicion. The ivory appeared to be fine, and was prettily carved, and it seemed to have been rudely smashed. I took the piece to a dealer in such articles, and he not only confirmed me in my suspicion, but showed me a complete casket of the same style of workmanship. It was a small thing, about six inches long by four broad, and might be used, the dealer said, for holding either jewels or money. They were very expensive, and but few were sold. This last bit of information I found to be correct, for after going over all the dealers in such articles in Edinburgh I could not find one who had sold a casket answering the description of the fragment I had found. I wished to find the owner for a particular reason. In examining the ivory one day it struck me that it had a smoked appearance—a kind of dingy hue which could never have been imparted by simply lying among soot. How could it have got that tinge? Not by being thrown into the fire, for there was not a burn on the whole fragment. Could Sandy have hung it up his own chimney like a red herring or a ham to give it that colour, or had it been so tinged when it came into his possession? The chimney in

Sandy's house had been the place which we searched most rigorously, so I was tolerably certain that he had no other interesting herrings there in pickle. I thought the owner of the bit of ivory and brass might help me to an answer, and at length decided to advertise for him. "An Ivory Casket, Carved," was notified in the newspapers as having been found, and the owner was requested to call without delay upon me. The day that this advertisement appeared, Sandy called at Mrs Nolten's house in George Square, and asked permission to go up on the roof to get a rope which he believed he had left there on his last visit. The request was put before the lady of the house, and promptly refused. Sandy then went to the next house and made the same request, and received as prompt a refusal. After the second appearance of the advertisement, a gentleman named Dundas called, and requested to see the "Ivory Casket." There was a strange reserve about him, which I only understood when in confidence he imparted to me the suspicion that his own son had been the robber, at the same time emphatically stating that he was firmly resolved not to give in any charge against the runaway. On being shown the fragment, he identified it as part of the lid of an ivory casket stolen from his house, and containing at that time nearly £10 in gold and silver. The casket had not been missed till after the flight of his son, who had left a good situation and gone to London with the craze strong upon him to be an actor. I found, however, that Mr Dundas had a distinct recollection of employing Sandy to sweep his chimneys about that time, and as six months had since elapsed, Sandy had been there on the same errand but a month or two ago. On calling the gentleman's attention to the smoky appearance of the ivory, he declared that it had not been so tinged when in his possession, and spontaneously remarked—

"It must have been hanging in some chimney."

In a chimney certainly, but what chimney? whose chimney? I revolved the matter in my mind, and at length concluded that Sandy would never have been foolhardy enough to conceal anything in his own chimney. And yet there was pretty palpable evidence that the stolen article had been in *a* chimney.

After half a day's cogitation, an idea struck me which gave such a feasible explanation of the thing that my only wonder is that it did not occur to me earlier. Sandy, if he wanted a chimney as a hide, was not limited in his choice to one or twenty. He visited some at regular intervals, and was in these cases the only man employed. What was to hinder him from using them boldly as establishments of his own? depots for goods which he could not conveniently store at home? I began to wonder how I could get hold of a list of these houses that I might inspect the chimneys. In sweeping a chimney it was often necessary for Sandy to lift out the grate, when it was what is known as a "Register," and it seemed to me that in doing so he could easily make use of the space behind as a hide when the grate was put back; but in making this guess it will be found that I gave Sandy credit for less ingenuity than he possessed. While Mr Dundas was diligently hunting for the address of his runaway son, that he might fairly ask him if he had been the thief of the casket and its contents, I was ferreting out the most prominent of Sandy's customers. In making the round of these it is singular, but true, that I never thought of calling at Mrs Nolten's, and when I did find myself there, it was more by accident than from choice. Being on the spot one day, I thought I would go in and have the register grate lifted out; but when this had been done in presence of the lady and myself, and nothing found, Mrs Nolten recalled the recent visit of Sandy, and detailed to me the circumstances. I immediately conceived a strong desire to go up on the roof and have a look for that "rope which he thought he had left." I did not look about the slates or rhone pipes, but went straight to the chimneys, though I confess I was at a loss to understand how anything could be safely concealed in them. After going over all the chimney-cans, I came to one inside which, just at the bottom where the can was embedded in mortar to secure it to the stones, I saw sticking a common three-inch nail.

It was all but hidden with soot, but enough was left bare to show that it had attached to it a bit of twine, which hung down inside the chimney proper. I grasped at the nail, easily pulled it out, and drew up with it the bit of twine. Something dangled at the end of the twine, which proved to be a paper parcel not very neatly tied up. I felt the contents of the parcel through the paper, and smiled out broadly.

"What a dunce I was not to think of this sooner!" was my comment upon myself.

I distinctly felt the shape of a bracelet through the paper, and did not trouble to open the parcel till I should get down into the house. I went down, and Mrs Nolten, seeing me smile and the parcel in my hand attached to the sooty string, instantly grasped at the truth.

"You've found them in my own chimney?"

A woman's instincts seldom mislead her. The lady was right. I opened the paper parcel, and there, snugly reposing within, and not a whit the worse of the smoking, were the bracelet, the necklet, and the odd gold ear-ring. I left the house at once, taking the interesting parcel with me, and in a minute or two stood before Sandy in his own home.

"It's a fine day, sir," he graciously began.

"It is—a very fine day," I returned, with emphasis. "Do you remember that bit of ivory, Sandy, with the brass handle attached, which we found here?"

Sandy found his memory conveniently defective.

"I had quite forgot aboot it, sir," he said awkwardly, when I had refreshed his powers a little.

"Well, I've discovered the gentleman who owns it, and strangely enough he declares that *you* were in his house sweeping some chimneys the day before it went amissing."

Sandy's sooty face was a curious study, but he wisely made no audible reply.

"Don't say anything unless you like, but did you ever see this parcel before?" I gently pursued, as I brought out the parcel and showed him its contents. "Nothing to say?—very good. Just put on your coat and cap and we'll go, then. I'm only sorry," I added, as I put a handcuff on his wrist, and retained the other end in my hand, "that I haven't a pair of these with a longer chain between the bracelets, for I never come close to you, Sandy, without sneezing for half a day after."

Sandy grinned a feeble and ghastly assent, and then went with me without a word. We could easily have proved both robberies against him, but he decided to make the best of his position by pleading guilty, and so got off with three months imprisonment.

THE FAMILY BIBLE.

To men of business or wealth, accustomed to handle large sums of money, bank-notes for large sums—such as £50 or £100—suggest nothing but convenience of handling and counting. With those who never owned £50 in their lives it is very different. The sum represented seems fabulously great—a fortune in itself. And then the thing is so small—a little oblong square of paper—so compressible—so thin—that the second stage—that of temptation—easily follows. Fifty or a hundred pounds in gold would be a good weight to carry, and a sum difficult to conceal; but a slip of paper! how many cunning and impenetrable places of hiding could be devised in a few minutes for that?

I have to give here the adventures of three £50 bank-notes. These notes had been paid to Mr George Lockyer, a builder, who dabbled a little in money lending, by a friend in quittance of a bond on some property. The payer of the money was but a working man, else the transaction would probably have been settled with a cheque; and the fact that this man was in working clothes had an important bearing upon the whole case, apart from the absence of a cheque altogether. The money had been drawn from the bank, but neither the teller who paid over the notes nor the receiver of them thought of noting the numbers.

Mr Lockyer, however, though anything but a careful or methodical man in regard to money, chanced to notice the number of the top note, from the fact that it was formed of two twenties, thus—"2020."

The notes were scarcely opened out—they were quickly counted—the necessary papers handed over to the payee, and the whole transaction, and some friendly conversation as well, was all over in about fifteen minutes.

When the payee was gone, Mr Lockyer lifted the lid of his desk, and carelessly placed the notes, folded in three, on the top of some papers, intending to take them out in a short time, and bank them on his way home to dinner. He did not take them out or bank them—he forgot all about them. About half an hour later he left the little office, locking the door after him, and taking the key with him.

This little office was part of a small erection attached to the building yard. That part which Mr Lockyer used as an office was not above ten feet square. It was fitted up with two desks, as at times the builder employed a clerk, but at that time was entered by no one but himself, or any callers he might have to receive while there.

The remainder of the erection was used as a kind of tool-house, and was fitted all round with shelves. This apartment entered from the building yard, and at one time the door between the two places had been open, but now it was not only closed and locked, but crossed on the tool-house side by the shelves aforesaid. This door had not been open for years, and the builder had not even a key for the lock. The other door, and that now in use, entered from the street, close to the gate of the yard.

Mr Lockyer remained away from his office during the whole afternoon, the reason being that he found some friends waiting him, and had no particular press of business to call him away. Late in the evening, however, he remembered suddenly of the three £50 notes left so carelessly in his desk at the office, and started up and whispered to his wife that he would have to go out on business for half an hour.

"I have left some money in the place which should have been in the bank or here," was his explanation, "and I must go and get it, for the place is a mere shed;" and as the word "money" rouses the strongest instincts of some wives, he was suffered to depart in peace.

He reached his office in ten minutes, and found it to all appearance exactly as he left it. It was then quite dark, but he was so sure of the spot on which he had placed the three notes that he did not trouble to strike a light, but merely raised the lid of the desk and groped for the notes. His fingers did not touch the soft, greasy papers, but the harder and smoother pile of accounts which had been beneath them. He groped and groped; he struck a light—first only a match, then the gas—but in vain. The three bank-notes were gone.

"Did I leave them here? Did I not put them in my pocket?" was his first wild thought, followed by a hurried groping and searching for his pocket-book.

The notes were not there. Then he distinctly remembered placing them in the desk, and the fact that he had never removed them. He searched the whole desk, turned out every scrap of paper and article that it contained, carefully examined the room from floor to ceiling, turned over everything in the other desk, and finally sat down with his hands in his pockets, thoroughly baffled and puzzled. He had locked the notes in that small apartment; the key had never been out of his pocket, yet, on returning a few hours later, he found that they had vanished.

The builder glared about him in a state of great excitement, imprecating under his breath, and heartily abusing himself for his carelessness, though he had done the same often before with impunity. While he sat thus vainly seeking a solution his eye fell upon the disused door. There was no key to it that he knew of, and the outer door of the tool-house, entering from the yard, he felt sure was locked. Still there was a possibility of entrance in that direction, and that fact set the builder a-thinking. But one man had the entry of that tool-house—a disabled mason, named John Morley, whom out of charity he kept employed about the yard. Morley had injured himself permanently by lifting a heavy weight, and could do little but look after the things in the yard, and give them out as they were wanted by the men. Mr Lockyer had known him nearly all his life, and had never found him to do a dishonest action. Yet still the fact remained that there was a man, very poorly paid—his wage was 12s. a week—having a wife and two bairns to keep, and with a possible means of access to the missing money. Might the money not have been taken in a moment of strong temptation even by a man like John Morley, reputed sterling and honest?

"If he has taken it, I can hardly blame him," was the generous reflection of the builder. "They have a sair struggle to make ends meet, I've no doubt; and I was a fool to leave the money lying about. But I never knew him to have a key for that door, and how could he possibly knew that the money was there, even if he had a key? I had better act cautiously, as much for my own sake as for his and his family's. I must say nothing to the police or any one till I see John himself."

Mr Lockyer had been kind to his yard-keeper; he had all but supported the man and his family during Morley's illness; then he had devised how he could employ him at some nominal task by way of making the man feel less dependent; and lastly, he had promised to assist him and his family to join a brother abroad who was in a more flourishing condition and had promised him work suited to his bodily strength. The builder, therefore, could scarcely believe that the man he had so helped and shielded could return the kindness by robbing him of £150; and he locked up his office and turned in the direction of the yard-keeper's home, resolved to be as guarded in his words as possible, so as not to hurt the man's feelings. Mr Lockyer was a man who had risen—a bluff, hearty, generous-hearted fellow—and had always a lenient hand for a working man in difficulties.

Morley's home was a cellar in Buccleuch Street—a dingy, damp hovel, lighted by a grating under a shop window. The place was not far from the yard, and therefore was speedily reached by the builder. Morley was at home, smoking by the fire, and the bairns were playing in a corner. The wife was out washing, as she often was, in order to eke out their income.

Morley looked a good deal surprised at the visit, and scarcely asked his employer to enter. Mr Lockyer, however, walked in and seated himself, and, after a few preliminary words, said abruptly—

"John, was there anybody about the yard this afternoon?"

How Morley looked it is impossible to say, for the light was only that of the fire, and his back was towards it.

"No, sir," he answered very readily.

"Nor in the tool-house?" continued his employer.

"No; it's been lockit a' day," said Morley, decidedly.

"You're sure?"

"Quite sure, sir."

There was an awkward pause, and then Morley, with a slight tremor in his tones, said—

"Is there onything wrang?"

"Yes; I left three notes—bank-notes for £50—in my desk when I went away to dinner, and they were gone when I got back half an hour ago."

"Impossible!" The man looked shocked and astonished, but there was nevertheless a something constrained or unusual in his manner which the builder did not like. "Naebody could get into the office by the tool-house," Morley hastened to add; "that door hasna been open for years, and the key's lost. Besides, there's the shelves in the road."

"How could they get in, then?" cried Mr Lockyer. "The front door was locked, and the key in my pocket; and it's not likely that they would pick the lock in broad daylight in the front street."

"Oh, thieves are clever now-a-days," observed Morley; "they're fit for onything."

"They may be, but that's a little beyond the ordinary," drily returned his master. "How were they to know I had left the money in my desk, or how long I would be away?"

"Ah, that's it!" said Morley.

"Do *you* know anything about it?" said Mr Lockyer at last, with an effort.

"Me! Do you think I'm a thief?" said Morley, flushing up. "If you do, you're welcome to search the house now."

"Oh, I daresay!" sneeringly returned his master, liking his yard-keeper's manner less than ever. "It would be easy finding three notes, wouldn't it, if you liked to hide them well? I might as well look for a needle in a haystack. No, no, Morley; I don't say you took them, or that you didn't, but they're to be found, and I'll leave that to the men that are bred to the trade—the police or the detectives."

"Yes, they're the best hands at that," said Morley feebly.

No strong and indignant protestations of innocence; no hot words, or tears, or reproaches; nothing but that meaningless answer, and that look of guilt and fear.

"The man's a thief if looks are to be trusted," thought the builder. "If it turns out so, I'll never be kind to mortal being again."

Mr Lockyer had done a foolish thing; he had let the man know he was suspected; but in the action he had been prompted by the best of intentions. He had failed in these, and he now did the next best thing to redeem the mistake—he came to us with news of the robbery. He described the circumstances of the robbery and the position of the place much as I have put them down, and concluded by stating it to be his firm belief that Morley was either himself the thief, or knew how the clever robbery had been accomplished. I agreed with him, but blamed him strongly for going near the suspected man.

"It is the money you are most anxious to recover, and yet you go and put the man on his guard. You may make up your mind now that you will never see the notes again. They will either go into the fire, or be put away in some hiding-place far beyond our reach."

"That's nice comfort to a fellow," observed the builder ruefully. "Is there anything you can do?"

"Oh, yes; we can do our best to make up for your blunder, by hunting for both the thief and the notes; but I have told you what is most likely to be the result."

I had no expectation of making anything by a search in Morley's house, but I thought it advisable that the form should be gone through, if only that I might study the man's face the while. I could have gone and done it there and then, but deemed it best to wait till morning.

There was a possibility, as Mr Lockyer suggested, of Morley repenting of his act and returning the plunder in the night time, and, besides, by delaying till morning, we might take him unexpectedly. Of course I afterwards regretted the delay; we always do when we find ourselves disappointed in results.

Morley appeared as usual at the yard before six o'clock, and made no allusion to the interview of the night before beyond asking his master, when he appeared about eight o'clock, "if he had got any word of the missing money."

He got a very curt and ungracious answer, and spoke no more. At the breakfast hour, when Morley locked up the yard and went home, I was waiting near the spot with two assistants skilled in searching. We just allowed John to enter his house and get comfortably seated at his porridge, when we knocked and were admitted. He did not seem greatly disturbed when I gave my name and showed the search warrant.

"You didna need a warrant to search my house," he said boldly. "I tellt the maister that he was welcome to search it whenever he liked."

He sat down and finished his porridge with evident zest and appetite, while we turned over every article in the little den of a house. The place had not been disturbed so much for many a day. Morley's wife seemed much more distressed at the charge than he, and assisted us with the greatest eagerness and anxious concern. We found no trace of the notes, and Morley's manner convinced me that they were not in the house. He was too cool and careless. Had they been hidden there—however securely or effectively—he could not have concealed some perturbation when we came near the spot or grew "hot" in our little game of "hide and seek." Just once did I notice anything like a change in his expression of face. When we had turned over everything in the house, I chanced to say to Mrs Morley—

"These are all the things you have, I suppose?"

"Oh, yes, sir," she earnestly answered. "Since John rackit himsel' we've had to make shift with less and less."

While she thus spoke, I saw her eye run round the room as if in search of something; then she began poking about with the aid of one of our lanterns, and finally she turned to her husband and said in a kind of whisper—

"Where's the famil——"

She did not get the sentence finished, nor even enough of it to be intelligible to me. Morley was standing close to her, and whether he kicked her on the leg, or trod on her toe, or merely gave her a look, I cannot tell, but he checked her speech most suddenly and effectually. I just saw enough and heard enough to make me suspicious, for the den was dark, and I was not expecting the words so unguardedly uttered by the wife. The last word sounded to me like "fummel," and I racked my brains for many an hour after to discover what on earth a "fummel" was. I had no doubt at all *now* of Morley's guilt, and, of course, I could have arrested him; but what good would that have done? There was no evidence whatever to support the charge, and likely to be none with Morley locked up in prison. Besides, I now felt tolerably certain that the notes were not destroyed, but concealed in the "fummel"—whatever that meant. I wanted badly to find that "fummel," and reasoned that I was more likely to do so with Morley moving about in freedom than with him cooped up in prison. The secret of the hiding-place was known to Morley alone; that was quite evident to me from the eagerness of the wife to assist me, and help to prove her husband's innocence, and also by the simplicity with which she had let out the remark about the "fummel." I determined to draw off my men, with so many apologies that Morley should think himself quite safe from further trouble or suspicion. To confirm this impression, I directed his master to take no further notice of the matter, and to keep him in his employment as usual, which was done.

I now had Morley carefully watched during the hours he was free from his work. I changed the men occasionally, and never watched him myself, that he might not take alarm, but nothing came of the watching. Morley never once attempted to change a fifty pound note, never appeared a penny richer than before the robbery, and never went near any place likely to be used for the concealment of the notes. The only thing that concerned me was the fact that he was preparing to leave the country, nor could I make that a ground for suspicion, as he had begun those arrangements long before the date of the robbery. At length I grew impatient, and took to relieving the men watching him after dark, as then there was little chance of him recognising me. Morley generally took a solitary stroll after partaking of his frugal supper, and on one of these occasions he stopped before a broker's in the Potterrow, a place suspected to be a kind of "wee pawn"—that is, an unlicensed pawnbroker's. Morley looked in at the window first, then all round him, and then walked into the shop, and was soon engaged in a violent altercation with the boy in charge. He stormed, and he threatened, and he swore, and I could see his arms moving about more energetically than those of a preacher "dingin' the poopit cushion a' to bits," but I was afraid to venture near enough to hear the words and understand their meaning. At length he left the shop in a furious and excited state, volubly threatening to "send the police" to them. I was strongly tempted to offer my services, but, being curious to learn the cause of the dispute, I allowed the blustering man to depart, and then entered the shop. The boy was a smart young shaver named Tim Cordiner, and knew me perfectly.

"What did Morley kick up such a row about?" I asked.

Tim put on an air of simplicity and said—

"Who's Morley?"

"That man who was here just now."

"His name isn't Morley—it's Peter Mackintosh," said Tim, with an air of superior knowledge.

"Oh, is it? I beg your pardon," I returned, with a fine-drawn sneer, which Tim perfectly appreciated. "Well, what was he in such a state about?"

Tim fenced cunningly, but finding me in dead earnest, was forced at last to say—"He's in a state about something which he sold to my father, and wants now to buy back again. He says the agreement was that it was to be kept for a month, to give him a chance to buy it back. Did you ever hear the like? We're not allowed to do that," the monkey solemnly added, "it would be as bad as keeping a 'wee pawn.'"

"Oh, come now, Tim, don't try that with me; play 'the daft laddie' with somebody else," I laughingly returned. "What was the article he sold or left with you?"

"A Bible—a Family Bible——"

"Good gracious!"

"Ay, you may say that. Bibles is a drug in the market; and to expect us to keep one when we had a chance to sell it! Family Bibles is out of fashion now—can't get the price of the binding for them—and the last we had lay for a year in the windy."

"And so you sold this one?" I said quietly, having got time to think during Tim's speech. "Who was the buyer?"

"Blest if I can tell—seemed a sort of 'revival,'" by which Tim meant a "revivalist," a name given to a sect of religious enthusiasts then newly started in Edinburgh. "Was it you who sold the Bible to him?"

"Yes, that's why that man kicked up the row. He says my father knew it wasn't to be sold. I wasn't to know that, and I was glad to get rid of it. The 'revival' was near not taking it because the Family Register was cut out—tried to beat me down two shillings for that. Religious folks are always the biggest screws."

"You must be terribly religious then," I calmly remarked to Tim, for I knew that that youthful precocity could drive a bargain which would have drawn a blush to the cheeks of the biggest rogue of a broker who ever bartered and sold.

Tim grinned delightedly at the tribute to his genius.

"Would you know the 'revival' again?" I asked, beginning to think I was fairly done at last.

"Oh, fine. I've seen him before, giving away tracts on the streets. He left me one, after buying the Bible and trying to beat me down two shillings."

"Have you got it now?"

"No; I used it to light the gas—it saved a match, you know."

I thought if any one was likely to save money and die rich that one was Tim, but I was to change my opinion soon by discovering that the smart young broker was as great a spendthrift as he was a screw. After some further conversation I warned him to say nothing to Morley of my visit, should that worthy return, as I had no doubt he would, to see Tim's father. I am doubtful if Tim kept his promise. Certainly if any one offered him a shilling to break it, the promise would instantly kick the beam.

After the visit to Tim the suspected yard-keeper seemed a good deal depressed. He went back once, and had a hot quarrel with Tim's father, threatening the police again, but failing to fulfil that threat. He said the Bible must be got, and the broker promised to do his best—which meant nothing.

In the meantime I had been much occupied in thought about Tim himself. His answers to me had appeared frank and truthful enough, but a dire suspicion that it was possible for the monkey to cheat and deceive even me crept into my mind. I discovered that Tim was squandering money right and left, quite unknown to his father. He sometimes went to Portobello, or Leith, or Musselburgh with his companions, and spent a day there, Tim always paying the entire expense, like a lord of the land.

Could it be possible that Tim was himself the purchaser of that Family Bible, and the "revival" merely a creation of his vivid imagination?

So strong a hold did this idea take of my mind that I gave up watching Morley, and turned my undivided attention to Tim. I could not find that he had changed a £50 bank-note, but I did discover that he had been seen with two twenties. I, therefore, only waited till he should be out with his friends for a day's squandering, and then I pounced on him in the midst of his jolity. Tim appeared mightily crestfallen, but grandly demanded to know what was the charge against him. I replied by asking where he got all the money he had been spending. His reply staggered me a little.

"What! is it my father who has set you on to this?"

Now, why should Tim blurt out that? To me it implied that Tim had taken the money from his father. I threw out a hint about a Family Bible being a good bank to draw from. Tim looked puzzled, and really did not seem to grasp the idea. I did not enlighten him with an explanation, but I myself was enlightened next day by his father, who had discovered that his smart son had broken in on a hoard of his own, and lessened it by nearly £60. He nevertheless did not wish to charge Tim with the robbery, but merely requested that that clever monkey might be handed over to him for punishment.

I could not oblige him, though he promised that the chastisement should bring Tim as near the grave as he would ever be without entering it. I had now to put the matter before Tim in a plain, straightforward question—"Had he or had he not lied about the sale of that Family Bible?"

He loudly protested his truthfulness, and offered to help me to find the buyer.

"How can you do that when you say he left neither name nor address?" I impatiently returned.

"Oh, we could easily find him at some of the revival meetings," was Tim's quickwitted reply. "He'll be at the door giving out tracts when the meeting breaks up. I know his face fine."

I stared at Tim, and then spoke out the thought that flashed across my mind. "Tim, if you don't turn out a thief, you'll maybe be a detective some day."

"A detective!" he echoed, with a merry twinkle in his eyes. "Oh, no, Mr McGovan, I haven't enough wickedness in me for that."

Tim and I went to a revival meeting that night together. By going together I mean to imply that we were closely attached to each other—by a pair of handcuffs. Tim could not have gone forward to the penitent form though he had been ever so strongly inclined. We did not need to wait till the close, nor look out for a tract distributor, for one of those who rose to address the meeting was instantly identified by Tim as the buyer of the Family Bible. The lad was quite young, and had on his face as he spoke a look of etherial happiness and rapt delight which could never have been assumed. I think I see that fair face before me now. It looked noble, exalted, thrilling—just such a face as we could imagine smiling at the stake, and breathing forth forgiveness and peace amidst the roaring of the flames.

When the address was over, the young man had occasion to move through the hall and past the place where we sat. I touched him on the arm, and drew him out to the door. He promptly admitted that he had bought a Family Bible, second-hand, from the boy before him. He had it at home, but though he had used it twice every day in his home, he declared most earnestly that he had found nothing in it. At my suggestion we walked with him to his home. He was evidently unmarried, for the home was presided over by his mother, a quiet, respectable-looking widow.

The Family Bible I sought occupied a place of honour in the little home, and the owner had only to point to it and tell me to take it down with my own hands. I opened the book, and he quietly informed me that the only alteration I should find would be at the beginning, where he had inserted a new leaf as a Family Register.

I turned to the leaf and read there his own name, and quite a recent date, in the column of "Births," with the words below—"Saved from wrath by the mercy of Jesus Christ." Without a remark I sat down and turned over every single leaf in that book, but found nothing.

When I had finished, and was in despair, I happened to notice that the paper pasted against the inside of the back board did not correspond in colour and texture with that on the front board. A little examination revealed the cause. The lining of the back board was simply one of the fly-leaves pasted down at the edges. I passed my fingers over the pasted leaf. There was a feeling of something below. I took out my pen-knife and ran the point into the sheet and round the pasted edge—the whole family, and Tim in particular, looking on with goggling eyes. When I turned back the leaf, I found it glazed and yellow on the under side, like that inside the front board, but I found also other three slips of paper neatly ranged above one another, flat against the board of the Bible—three £50 banknotes. The owner of the Bible looked simply and truly surprised. Tim looked terribly disappointed and chagrined.

"If I had known they were there, I'd never have sold it so cheap," he blurted out.

"Maybe not at all?" I suggested; and Tim did not deny the soft impeachment.

The notes were readily identified by the builder by the number "2020" which one of them bore; but when we came to look for Morley, he had vanished. From another country he afterwards sent a detailed confession of the circumstances which led to the crime. The payer of the money was dressed as a working man, and asked at the gate for Mr Lockyer. Morley at once conceived a suspicion that the man had come after the post of yard-keeper, and applied his eyes and ears to the inner door in the tool-house to ascertain the truth. He saw the notes placed in the desk, and the temptation followed, for he had found a key shortly before in the tool-house which fitted the lock perfectly. After taking the notes he dropped the key into a street "siver," or we might have stumbled on it during our search. Tim was set free, but he has not yet developed into a detective.

CONSCIENCE MONEY.

An old man, a jobbing gardener, named Alexander Abercorn, stopped one of the day policemen at the West End one morning in July, and said in great concern and agitation—

"Man, I'm afraid this house has been robbed in the night time. And the worst of it is I have the keys, and they'll be sure to say it's been done by me."

The house in question was a big one known as the Freelands, and occupied by a Mr Arthurlie and his family. The family were gone to country quarters, and the house was empty even of servants. Abercorn hurriedly explained, what indeed was already known to the policeman, that he had a contract for doing the gardening about the place, and, being a tried and trusted man, had been left with the keys of the place, with orders to enter it every day to see if all was safe. Other families had left him a similar charge, and he had some half-dozen bunches of keys, which he showed to the policeman in confirmation. Hitherto his task had been easy, and the result satisfactory enough, but now for the first time a calamity had come, and he begged the officer to step in and see. They entered the house, and the old gardener walked straight to the pantry, in which was built an iron safe for containing the plate and valuables of the family. This safe was inserted bodily into a large cupboard, which had an ordinary wooden door fastened with a common sixpenny lock, and so looked innocent enough outside. The wooden door stood wide open, and so also did that of the iron safe within, though both had hitherto been locked.

There were no breakages, or marks of prising with crowbars or chisels—the door appeared to have been opened in the ordinary way, by inserting a key and turning back the bolts of the locks. The detectors on the lock of the safe showed that no skeleton keys had been applied or used, and yet the old gardener declared that the key of the safe had never been intrusted to him. He did not know who had it, or where it was kept. He had the keys of all the rooms, and also the key of the press in which the safe was built, but not the actual key of the safe. The entire contents of the safe had been turned out on the pantry floor, and the thieves had then shown great discrimination in the selection of their plunder. None of the plated articles had been removed; only genuine silver, and, as some of these exactly resembled each other, the thieves had shown a skill almost magical.

The old gardener, of course, knew nothing of what had been in the safe; and, seeing the plated articles littering the floor, he only said he *thought* the place had been robbed. It was only after word had been sent to the Central Office, and we had telegraphed to the Arthurlies, that we learned that the value of the silver plate alone was upwards of £500, and that there had been in the safe other articles of value which brought the total loss nearly up to £800.

Within an hour of the report being sent in, I was out at the house, and was shown over the various rooms by the old gardener. To say that the old man looked excited and strange would be but faintly to describe his appearance. He was deathly pale; he trembled at the slightest question or look; his teeth chattered when he spoke; and he gave the most stupid and confused answers to some of the simplest queries. I had not been long in the premises when I found that there were several peculiarities about the robbery which marked it off from the ordinary burglary. There were three doors to the house. Two of these—the area door and the back door—had never been touched. They were bolted and locked just as they had been left. No window had been forced; every one was closed, and fastened, and shuttered exactly as it had been left. This narrowed the means of ingress to one door—the main door, which was secured by two patent locks. It was the keys of these locks which the old gardener carried and used in entering the house. I examined these locks closely, and when done, decided that they had not been opened with skeleton keys or tampered with in any way; either the door had been left unlocked, or the keys, or duplicates of these keys, had been used in effecting an entrance. The second peculiarity was that no room in the whole house of three storeys had been entered but the pantry. There had been no rummaging through bedrooms for valuables, no turning out of rare china and curiosities in the drawing-room, though there were articles of that kind there far exceeding in value the plate stolen. The thieves appeared to have had but one object in view— the contents of the safe—and for that they had made without a single divergence right or left. Now, that is not at all like the ordinary housebreaker, who is never satisfied with a moderately good haul, but must go tearing, and searching, and smashing, and destroying all over a house before he is convinced that there is no more to carry off. Then, what professional housebreaker could have resisted at least tasting a bottle of those rare wines which were within arm's length of him in the pantry! I have caught them drunk on the spot just through that weakness, but I never knew them to be so rigidly abstemious as to pass good drink untouched.

When I had concluded my examination, the old gardener was very anxious to know my opinion. Had any one else plied me with the question, I might have answered, but with him I was forced for the present to be silent. The truth is, I suspected him, and nobody but him, as the thief. He was a poor man to begin with; the clothes he stood in were not worth ten shillings; and I was led to believe that being somewhat old and frail, and having a daughter entirely dependent upon him, these formed almost his sole possessions. I could not conceive, indeed, how so many had thought fit to trust him with the keys of their houses, but then I did not know that he had the reputation of being a sterling and honest man, respected alike for his deep religious feeling and humble worth. He had a poverty-stricken look to my eyes, and then his confusion and agitation, and the other discoveries, were against him. The same afternoon Mr Arthurlie and his wife came to town by express; and then I got from them the surprising intelligence that the keys of the safe were always kept secreted in a little niche in a wooden cupboard exactly opposite the press containing the safe. This precaution had been taken through the keys once having been lost by being carried about, thus necessitating the fitting on of a new lock on the safe. Until I saw the hiding-place I thought this arrangement one of the most foolhardy imaginable; but when I went out to the house I found that the nail on which the keys were usually hung was in a place the last that an ordinary thief would have looked to. It was in behind the hinge of the door of a wooden press or wine rack. You had to open first the door of the press, then grope in behind the left-hand door and get the keys. No one knew of this place but the tablemaid and the housekeeper. The Arthurlies kept no man-servant. They were positive that the old gardener, Abercorn, did not know of the keys being thus hid in the place, though they admitted that he might have discovered them if he had exerted himself to search. I had found the keys of the safe lying on the floor of the pantry under some of the discarded plated articles, so it was certain that the thief had not only searched for the keys but found them and used them. I began to question the Arthurlies regarding old Abercorn, the gardener, and they, divining at once the drift of my suspicions, assured me that I was quite mistaken, and gave me such a description of the man that I felt half ashamed of my own convictions. I had thought of at least a search in the gardener's humble home, but implicit trust and strong protestations of the Arthurlies forced me to shelve that idea for the present. So long as the man was not a prisoner or formally accused I could question him to my heart's content, and I resolved to take full advantage of the circumstance, by making him account for his actions from the time he had been in the house on the morning before the robbery until the discovery of the robbery as already described. He had asserted most positively that upon his last visit there had been not an article out of place or the slightest trace of a robbery, and if that were true the whole must have been executed within the twenty-four hours. Again, it was not likely that a thief would choose the day time for such a feat, so this further limited the time by twelve hours at least. What had Abercorn been about during that night? If he could not account for that time I should have a fair excuse for arresting him.

I therefore said no more to the Arthurlies, but got the address of the old gardener—a little cottage down by the Dean—and next day went down to have a talk with him. The place was easily found, for he had in front of the cottage a strip of ground full of all kinds of flowers, and "Alex. Abercorn, Jobbing Gardener," conspicuously painted on the little gate. An old woman opened the door, and I asked for the gardener.

"He's no in; he's working," was her reply, and the news was rather pleasing to me than otherwise.

"Oh, well, I daresay you will do quite as well," I said pleasantly. "You're Mrs Abercorn, I suppose?"

"Na, na, I'm only his hoosekeeper," she promptly answered. "Mrs Abercorn's deid three years syne. I never was married, and maybe never will be."

As she was old enough to have been my mother, I thought her marriage by no means a likely occurrence, but took care to throw out no hint to that effect. We chatted together very nicely for a minute or two, during which I got from her nearly her whole life story, and then she invited me to enter and see the gardener's daughter. But for the fact that this daughter, Jeanie, as she named her, was an invalid, the old woman declared that she would not have been needed in the place, as they were "very poor." I followed her into the front room, in which was a bed facing the window. In the bed was a young woman of perhaps twenty-five years. She had a sweet face, and a delicate complexion, gradually tinging out into rosy cheeks, and a pair of big, lustrous eyes, which were turned on me, wide open with wonder, as I entered. But the beauty of the face, and its fine hues, and even the brightness of the great eyes, was not of the kind to draw out one's admiration so much as to stir in the bosom a thrill of pity, for the stamp of death was over it all. Consumption was written on that face, with a sure and early death, as plainly as if the green turf had already been spread above her. I scarcely liked to look into the face—it was so eager, and bright, and beautiful.

It was a little difficult to explain my business, but before I had made much of an attempt in that direction I was surprised to find that neither the invalid nor the old housekeeper had heard aught of the robbery. I was staggered. Why had the old gardener concealed that from his little household? I had to put aside the query and go on with those more important. Could they remember what time the old gardener had come home the night before last?

Oh, perfectly. He had been home about seven o'clock, for he was rather busy, and might have stayed at his work later, but for the fact that Jeanie had taken a bad turn that day, and he was anxious to be beside her.

Did he stay long at home?

The question appeared to puzzle them both, and then, when I explained, they said, as a matter of course, that he had never gone out again the whole evening. Why should he, indeed? His daughter was all in all to him; he was never happy but when he was beside her; and if walking round the world barefooted would have made her well, he would cheerfully have undertaken the task.

"I never will be well, though, till I go abroad," added the girl with a smile, which made her look still more lovely. "The doctor said so long ago, but father is so poor and has to work so hard for every penny, that till lately he could not think of it. But now it's settled that I'm to go before the winter comes on. Father has got the money from some one. He wouldn't say who it was, but it's a kind friend anyhow who would lend such a sum—and I'm to get strong and go back to service next spring."

Her very heart seemed to overflow with exultation and proud hope as she uttered the words. It almost drew tears to my eyes to witness her joy.

"Then your father was with you in this house all night? You're quite sure of that?" I said, reverting to the old theme.

"Oh, quite, for he was never away from my bedside. He did not go to bed at all, seeing me so ill, but just dovered the best way he could in that big chair. I watched him all the time, and when he did fall asleep I couldn't help crying a little to think what a hard lot he has, all on account of me being so weak and ill. What I would give for strength to work and slave for him as he deserves—oh, what I would give!"

"And the bunches of keys he has—the keys of the houses that are empty just now—where were they all the time?"

"Oh, in the box there," said the housekeeper, taking up the question at once, and without the slightest trepidation. "I put them in there myself. They lie there every nicht."

"And would it not be possible for any one to get at them there?" I pursued. "I mean any one who wished to make use of them to effect a robbery at one of the houses?"

"Oh, no! They both assured me that such a thing was impossible. Not a soul ever came near the house, and certainly no one had been within the door on that particular night." The daughter concluded by saying proudly that she was quite sure that no one would ever get near the houses, or into them, so long as her father had charge of the places. He was so careful and reliable, that he was better than twenty policemen.

"He has not told you, then, that one of the houses has been entered?" I said, in an unguarded moment of surprise.

"No; was it really?" they both exclaimed in a breath.

The expression of the two faces was a study. The withered face of the old woman was scarcely stirred—it showed interest indeed, but merely that of a passing curiosity. The face of the invalid girl, on the contrary, was full of changes and fluttering emotions, as her own mind was evidently full of tumult. She questioned me rapidly, and I answered her as guardedly as possible, but her features as I proceeded became slowly blanched with a kind of rigid horror. That strange look—so full of far-reaching thought and deep anguish—I could not at the moment understand. To say that suspicion was hovering over her father did not account for all that was pictured in her face—there was something behind all that, and I am afraid my words became somewhat incoherent in trying to fathom what that secret was. I never saw a face which told so much, if I had but had the key to those flitting expressions.

Her horror, and anguish, and deadly despair, and the tears which would force themselves into her eyes to make them more pitifully beautiful, arose from something I had said, which had evidently more meaning to her than to me, and I cudgelled my brains in vain to recall anything which should so affect her.

I did not remain long after this queer change had come over the invalid, for with that change had come reticence, thoughtfulness, and silence. Her brightness and loquacity were gone, and the gossipy old woman had all the talking to herself. My impression of the whole case, when I had left the cottage, was that there was guilt behind all I had seen, and that the best plan would be to arrest the old gardener, and have his house thoroughly searched.

That was the substance of my report; but against this was brought the strenuous request of the Arthurlies, and the arrest was delayed that I might have the suspected man watched, and, if possible, accumulate stronger evidence of his guilt. I was not sorry for the delay in the light of the curious incident which followed. Two days after my visit to the cottage a parcel was handed in at the Central Office, which on being opened was found to contain bank-notes to the amount of £70, and the following brief note:—

"One of those concerned in the robbery at Mr Arthurlie's returns his share of the proceeds, which his conscience will not allow him to keep."

It needed but one reading of these lines to convince one that no professional thief ever composed or penned them. The diction was too correct, to say nothing of the spelling; and whoever heard of a professional housebreaker having a conscience, or returning entire his share of a robbery on that account? Then in looking over the note it was evident that there was a painful effort to disguise the handwriting—to make it heavy and lumpy, and strong like that of an unlettered man, while the verdict of all who looked upon it was that the writing was that of a woman. Who could that woman be, and how could she have accomplished the robbery? If she had got only a fair share of the proceeds, there must have been at least seven or eight more in the robbery. The parcel had been handed to one of our men outside the Office by a boy, who had walked off the moment he got rid of it. He had spoken enough, however, to reveal that he was of that class of country folks living outside the city proper—the accent of these being strong and broad, and easily distinguishable from that of the city.

The moment these facts were made known to me I had a cab brought, and drove rapidly over to the Dean, taking the man with me. When we got to the place we dismissed the cab and took up our station near the cottage of the gardener. I was in hope that if the boy had been sent from that place he would return to report, but I was mistaken. We waited about for fully an hour, and then gave up the task in despair, and wandered through the little village to have a look at the faces. In doing so my companion spotted a boy at play, and collared him sharply with the words—

"It was you who gave me the parcel at the Police Office, wasn't it?"

The boy denied it stoutly, but in a tone which left no doubt on our minds that he was lying. When threatened with the cells he admitted that he had got sixpence to deliver it, from old Marjory, the gardener's housekeeper! Taking the boy with us, we went to the gardener's cottage. Old Marjory was outside cutting vegetables in the garden, and the moment her eye fell upon us I felt convinced that we would have no easy task in getting information from her.

"You sent this boy with a parcel to the office, Marjory?" I began. "Where did you get it?"

"Somebody gied me it, and it wasna Maister Abercorn, either," she dourly answered.

"Do you know what was in it?"

"No, me—I never asked."

"Did you not write the letter that was inside?"

"No, I canna write, or read either—a'body kens that."

"You could rob, though, at a pinch, I suppose?" I dryly returned.

She flashed a pair of angry eyes on me, and then said—"I never robbed onybody in my life, and it's no likely I'll begin now."

"Well, you'll have to tell all you know about that parcel, or go to jail, that's all," I shortly answered.

"I canna leave the lassie," she said, dourly, "she's rael ill, and there's naebody can attend till her like me."

"I thought she was going away abroad?"

"She's no gaun now," said the queer old woman with a slight softening in her tones. "She'll never get to a foreign country till she reaches the better land. The puir thing's sinking fast. I wad ask ye to come and see her, but I'm feared the sicht o' you wad upset her as it did before. She's never been weel since ye was here."

This news startled me. Why should my presence agitate the invalid? Could it be possible that she was the thief? How could she, when she had not been able to leave the house for months?

The old woman determinedly refused to speak, and while we were arguing the point, Abercorn himself appeared. He appeared quite overwhelmed with confusion when the position of affairs was explained to him. I told him that his housekeeper, Marjory, was arrested, and that he must go with her. He made no complaint or demonstration of any kind, except when I regretted that his daughter was so ill that I could not take her too, when he gave me a glance so full of anguish that I half regretted having spoken the words. He quietly asked leave to go in and see his lassie, and to satisfy myself that the girl was really unable to go with us I accompanied him. The girl, by a kind of instinct, seemed to read the dreadful truth in our faces, and I thought she would have died before we got her and her father parted. Only one exclamation I thought strange—that was when she was clinging to him and raining her tears in his face, and cried bitterly—

"Oh, father, I've brought all this on you—I've brought it all on you, and I meant to save you!"

When the old man and his housekeeper were examined they had no declaration to emit—nothing to say. They had made it up between them, I suppose, to take refuge in stern silence, and perhaps on the whole the course was as wise a one for themselves as any they could have been directed to follow. Not an hour after they had been locked up, I got an urgent message from the invalid daughter to come and see her. How urgent it was may be judged from one expression in the message, which was, "Come to-night—to-morrow may be too late, for then I may be dead."

I found her in a state of great prostration; but she roused up at the sight of my face, and was able to dismiss her attendant, in order that none might hear what passed between us.

"You can never know what I have suffered since you were first here," she said with an earnestness fearful to behold. "I have sent for you to see if it is not possible to save my father. It is the real robber you wish to put in prison, is it not? My father is innocent, except that he was tempted, and that his love for me made him weak. Would it not be in his favour—would it not save him—if you were put in the way of taking the real criminal?"

"I cannot pledge my word that it would save him, but it would certainly go far to lighten his punishment," I soothingly returned. "If he is really innocent it can do him nothing but good to reveal all you know. Nothing is more certain than that, as the case now stands, he will be convicted and probably severely punished."

"I will trust all to you—I may not live to see it, but I will leave you to do what is best for my poor old father," she said, weeping freely. "I only suspected something of the truth when you came here first and said there had been a robbery. I had noticed something strange about my father for a day or two, and when he told me that at last he was to get the money that was to take me abroad and make me strong, it was said in such a queer way, that I didn't know whether to cry or be glad. I fretted over the horrid thought for a whole night, and then I spoke to him about it. I saw by his face that he had done it—that he had become a criminal for me. I was horrified, but could I be angry? It was his love for me—it was to save my life he had risked his whole life, and reputation, and immortality. Who could be angry at being so loved? Then he told me all he had done. The Arthurlies used to keep a man-servant, but he was put away for drunkenness and dishonesty. I have seen him once or twice. His name is David Denham. This man met father one day and asked for me, and was sorry to hear that father could not get the money to send me abroad. Then he said that *he* could get the money, and would get it if father would just lend him the keys of the Freelands for one night. Father would not hear of it at first, but the other kept tempting him, and saying how cruel it was of him to let his only daughter die, and at last he gave in. The keys were only out of his keeping for one night, and Denham knew where the keys of the safe were kept, and so got at the silver plate and carried it all off. It was sent to Glasgow to some one who had agreed to buy it, and Denham brought the money to father after dark. I could not bear to look at it or touch it. I seemed to see in it the thing that was to part me and my father for ever, instead of letting us spend eternity in heaven, with neither poverty nor suffering. I bundled it up and wrote the note which you would get with it. I felt so happy when it was gone, and I made Marjory send it in a way that would not give you a chance to find out the sender. But you did find it out, and I have done more harm than good. It would have been better for my poor father if I had had no conscience troubling me."

I soothed and cheered her as well as I could, and then went after Denham. I found he had gone to Glasgow, and, by sending off a telegram, had him neatly nipped up at the station by Johnny Farrel. Denham was thoroughly taken by surprise, and in his amazement did a rash thing. He had had some disagreement with the fence about the plunder, and had gone through to settle that, but only to find himself nipped up at the station. What could be clearer? He had been betrayed by the swindling fence. Would it not be a fair retaliation to betray the fence in turn? He thought it would, and did so; which greatly rejoiced our hearts, for it enabled us to recover a deal of the plunder before it went into the melting-pot.

Jeanie Abercorn declined rapidly after her statement to me, and in a week had passed to her long rest. Her last message was to her father in prison, telling him that she was only going out of his sight for a time; that God would forgive him, whether men did or no, knowing that it was his great love for her that tempted him to the crime. The old gardener received the message in a stupefied state. He had never appeared the same man since the arrest. He was told that he would be accepted as a witness against Denham, and agreed in a dull, listless manner to tell all he knew, which he did, with the result that Denham was convicted and sentenced to five years' penal servitude. When the trial was over, the old gardener was told that he might go.

"What have I to gang to?" was his reply, as he wrung his hands and tottered out. "What have I to gang to?"

In a month or two the poor old man had drifted away to join Jeanie in the Great Unknown, beyond earth and sky.

A WOLF IN SHEEP'S CLOTHING.

"Once a criminal, always a criminal," is a pretty safe maxim. When a man—and more especially one of education—is degraded into a thief and a liar, who would believe him if he expressed a wish for a better life? Nay, if he actually did change, and became a very anchorite or saint, would not the whole world howl out "Hypocrite?"

In the present case there was neither the profession of repentance nor the desire for a different life. The "Rev. Alfred Johnston," already alluded to in "A Lift on the Road," [See page 218, *ante*] on being released from prison, was in bad health, bodily as well as mentally. Some of the wages of sin had been paid out to him during the last year in prison, and he went out into the world a mere wreck, the shadow of his former self. He cursed me as a cause, and the whole world besides—and he even at times, I suspect, cursed himself—but he had no power to retaliate or avenge his fancied wrongs.

The glory of man is strength, and when that is gone, the best bed and blanket are the grave and a green turf. There was still the genteel begging left to him, but somehow the returns were now poor compared with his former gains, and Johnston was impatient for a chance which should allow him to leave this country for the Cape with a good pocketful of money at his command. During his seclusion his consort had drifted out to that colony as a barmaid—his real wife had been laid in the grave years before by his brutality and dissipation—and the moment he learned the truth he conceived the plan of following and joining her there. The climate was just such a one as he needed to restore his health, and a bold rogue, he thought, might in that place realise a fortune in a very short time. He had been landed in Edinburgh, as being the scene of his capture and conviction, and so it was around on the Edinburgh citizens that he now cast his eyes with a view to his own welfare. What is really one's welfare none can decide for himself, and Fate often steps in and with inexorable hand fixes that for him. I daresay Johnston had often, in his better days, preached that truth, but he had either ceased to believe it, or allowed it to become buried in his mind, for at the strange turn events were to take none could have been more surprised than himself.

By studying carefully the subscription lists of the various local charities, and making diligent inquiries, Johnston decided upon a Mr

Samuel Cooper, a retired merchant, living at Bonnington, as the likeliest man to make an easy victim. Mr Cooper was old, and benevolent as well as wealthy, and what was more important, he did not read the newspapers much, and so was not likely to know of Johnston's past misdeeds. He was indeed a quiet, modest, feeling-hearted man, and the greatest tribute to his goodness was this very selection of him as a victim by the shrewd and unscrupulous Johnston. For a wide radius around his home, and more especially among the poor of Leith, this good man had raised up to his name a hedge of blessings and prayers; and who knows but these were now to be his protection in the hour of need?

The appearance of Johnston at this time was interesting. He had been a good-looking man, and the strict prison life and diet had removed the bloated look from his features, while his cough, and weak chest, and gasping for breath, only served to make him a pitiable object for charity and help. His clothing was the same wretched garb in which I had taken him more than four years before, but that too helped to excite commiseration.

This was the spectacle which greeted Mr Cooper one afternoon at his own home, when he had been told that a visitor, in the person of the Rev. Alfred Johnston, wished to speak with him, and awaited him in the adjoining room. Instead of a gentleman in blacks, he saw before him a ragged outcast, coughing painfully and looking ready to drop into the grave, and he started and looked round the room in wonderment.

"I am the Rev. Alfred Johnston," said the outcast, reading aright the expression of Mr Cooper's face. "I am really a clergyman, reduced to this state by my own folly and the wicked persecution of others. I have heard of your goodness—of your great heart, and your truly Christ-like compassion, and therefore I have crawled here to implore your help. Christ did not turn away the greatest sinner, and if I have sinned you can see I have also suffered. Ah, sir! if my life were but given me to begin again, how different would be my condition!"

"But how do you come to be thus reduced?" cried the benevolent old man, exceedingly sceptical of the truth of the statement. "Surely you have friends to whom you could appeal before a stranger like me?"

"Friends!" echoed Johnston, in a choking voice, and with a bitterness which was not exactly assumed; "when did a friend cling to one in adversity? No, sir! Give me the cold, callous world—the most unfeeling stranger—before the dearest friend. But I do not ask you to trust to my statements being true. Write to some of the deacons of my former church—with all their prejudice and ill-will they will at least bear testimony to the truthfulness of my statements;" and at random he named a small town in the west, the furthest away he could think of on the spur of the moment.

"Give me their names," gravely returned Mr Cooper. "I may write, and I may not, but it can do no harm to leave the address. One is so liable to be imposed upon," he soothingly added, afraid that he might have hurt the feelings of an unfortunate and injured man.

Thus cornered, Johnston gave two names, assuring Mr Cooper that the town was small, and that no other address was necessary to find these prominent deacons. He then launched out into a history of himself, partly real and partly imaginative. He had been unfortunate—exceedingly—in his congregation, and had roused opposition and animosity by his very bluntness and truthfulness. At length he had been forced to resign, and supported himself by tuition and other means till reduced to the verge of starvation. Then a wicked woman got up a plot against him, and, because he refused to marry her, lodged information with the police and had him arrested on a false charge. This charge she supported with gross perjury, and Johnston had been sent to prison a martyr to his own resolute goodness. The confession regarding the prison experience was thrown out merely in case the good man to whom he appealed might know something of it already. It would be quite impossible to convey in writing any idea of the plausible manner in which his story was concocted and narrated. As a preacher Johnston had been eloquent and persuasive; and now, when so much depended upon the exercise of these gifts, he carried all before him. It was not all false, and the hardships he had endured were not all imaginative. Several times Mr Cooper was moved to tears; and when Johnston concluded by saying he did not want money, but merely some decent clothing and his passage paid to the Cape, the good old man was on the point of giving him what he wished without a word of inquiry. Prudence prevailed, and in the end Johnston was delighted to hear him say—

"If all you have told me is true, I shall see that you are helped as you desire. I shall interest several members of our own church, and perhaps the pastor as well, in your unhappy circumstances, and possibly they may be disposed to give you help as well."

"Excuse me, sir," interposed Johnston, getting alarmed at the proposal; "spare a sensitive if a fallen man the degradation of having his sins and sufferings paraded before others. I had rather want their help than have to appear before these gentlemen and answer their questions. Let me creep out of the country unseen and unknown, to begin in a far-off land a nobler life, fearless alike of recognition and of censure."

This seemed such a natural request that Mr Cooper hastily agreed, and promised strict secrecy to all in the city. He then dismissed him with a trifling sum for his immediate needs, and the request that he should come back in a day or two—as soon, indeed, as it was possible to receive answers from the deacons, whose addresses he had just taken down.

Those who do not know the boundless resources of the rogue of education will imagine that Johnston had got to the end of his tether, and would never again dare to look near the benevolent Mr Cooper, knowing that certain exposure would follow the written inquiries. Nothing of the kind. The circumstances were just such as roused Johnston to his keenest activity. From Mr Cooper's house he went to a stationer's and bought some notepaper and envelopes of different kinds, and, being accommodated with a pen and ink, he wrote out two polite notes, addressed to the postmaster of the town in the west he had named, in two different hands, and signed with the names he had given to Mr Cooper, requesting that any letters which might arrive for him should be re-addressed to two different addresses in Edinburgh. No one but an expert looking at these notes could have guessed that they were penned by the same man—the handwriting, the phraseology, the notepaper, and the style were entirely different. They were posted at once, and thus arrived one mail in advance of Mr Cooper's two notes, which were at once re-addressed as directed, and duly delivered into Johnston's hands. To write replies for the two imaginary deacons was then an easy matter; to get them duly authenticated with the post-mark of the town in question was more difficult. But during the interval, Johnston had called upon Mr Cooper, and made such rapid progress in his favour that he had not only been provided with a complete suit of clothes, but had been allowed to dine with Mr Cooper and his wife. So much familiarity implied also the gift of some money, and part of this money Johnston now hastened to use in a trip to the west. He left Edinburgh by an early train, posted the letters in the town, and took the first train back to Edinburgh, which he reached in time to take tea with the good man he had imposed upon. The same evening Mr Cooper chanced to mention that in a day or two he would have in his possession a large sum of money, out of which he intended to pay a steerage passage for Johnston to the Cape. The place where he kept his money was already known to Johnston, from the fact that a pound note had been taken from the drawer as a present to the broken-down minister. This place was a small parlour on the ground floor, easily accessible from a green behind the house. The window was fastened with an ordinary spring check, but that was no impediment to a man of Johnston's experience; and the shutters were seldom closed, and certainly not fastened at night. A great scheme flashed upon Johnston's brain. At first his only desire and concern had been to get clothing and a passage to the Cape; now, however, the bloodthirsty excitement of the old convict and jail-bird crept over his faculties, and goaded him on to a greater haul. He would empty the drawer the first night the money was there to take. There would be but one night in which the crime could be committed, for Mr Cooper had shown no reserve or concealment of his plans, and Johnston knew that on the following day most of the money would be paid away in quarterly accounts, &c. With part of the money given him by the benevolent man, he bought some housebreaking implements—a thin putty knife to force open the spring fastening of the window, a bracebit to cut an arm-hole in the shutters if they should happen to be closed and fastened; and lastly, a leaden-headed neddy or life-preserver with which to smash the skull of anyone who might oppose or attempt to capture him. Fate might order it that that victim should be the white-haired and warm-hearted man who had helped him in his sore plight—well, so be it; he had not the ordering of fate, and was content to risk even that. As to escaping after the crime, he trusted to his own experience and skill in disguising himself; and even if a swift flight were impossible, he knew several who would be only too glad to hide him, with such a sum in his possession, till the hue and cry were over.

Thus provided for every emergency, Johnston went down to the house at Bonnington one evening after dark, ostensibly to hear the result of Mr Cooper's letters to the imaginary deacons, but really to ascertain if the money was in the house, and to see how the room lay for his midnight attempt. He was shown into the very parlour he was most anxious to reconnoitre, and left there so long alone that he began to get alarmed, although the interval had given him the opportunity to draw back the spring fastening of the windows and reclose the shutters as he found them, adjusting the slender hook which fastened them so lightly that a mere touch from the outside would drive them open. At length Mr Cooper appeared, looking grave and concerned, but Johnston's alarm was speedily dispelled by hearing his benefactor say—

"You will excuse me for keeping you waiting so long, but the truth is my grandchild—the little girl you saw at the table the other night—is not very well, and we have thought it advisable to send for a doctor. I thought she had only caught a little cold, but now she has lost her voice and can only speak in a whisper, and seems, besides, to be in a state of high fever as well. Oh, if anything should happen to her, I could never get over it. She is only ten, and the last one left to us."

Johnston offered a few commonplace words of a soothing nature, and then adroitly turned the conversation to the subject of the letters from the "deacons."

"Oh, I have got answers from both, and they are satisfactory in every respect," said Mr Cooper, rousing himself a little, and producing the two letters concocted and posted in the West by Johnston himself, and frankly placing them in the hands of that arch-rogue. "You may read them for yourself, and consider it settled that I shall give you the assistance you require—a passage to the Cape. Willingly would I give twice that sum to see that poor child well and strong as usual——"

A ring at the door-bell interrupted the speech, and Mr Cooper started up and again left Johnston alone, with the words, "Ah! at last, there is the doctor."

The intending criminal sat there and heard the doctor admitted and led to the bedroom of the sick child. Then there was a long stillness, and at last the footsteps sounded in the lobby; the doctor whispered for a time with Mr Cooper, and finally the front door closed and the carriage drove off. Some slow and feeble footsteps then came in the direction of the parlour door, and in a moment or two Mr Cooper stood before Johnston, ghastly pale, and tottering, and with the tears gathering thick in his eyes.

"Oh, my friend, the worst of news!" he at length found voice to say, as he sank feebly into a seat and covered his face with his hands. "The doctor says it is not a simple ulceration of the throat, as we imagined—the trouble is diphtheria! and—and it is so far gone that he does not believe she will recover!"

Before that awful grief and those flowing tears Johnston was stricken dumb, and he uneasily began to wish himself a mile from the spot. In broken accents the stricken old man proceeded to describe the nature of the disease—how a kind of fungus had begun to grow across the windpipe, which would shortly choke the breath out of the young body as surely as if a strangulating cord had been tightened about the neck, and how the child, though still chatting cheerily and brightly in its hoarse whispers, was actually within a few hours of death and heaven. Johnston felt more uncomfortable than ever. He started round not to see the grief-stricken face, and something heavy hit him sharply on the leg. It was the leaden-headed neddy in his coat pocket, with which he had been prepared to deal out death to any one opposing him in robbing the man before him. The blow on the leg, however, was nothing to the knocking which was at that moment going on in his heart.

"Oh, my friend! you—you are sent to me as a blessing from heaven in my hour of sore trial!" exclaimed Mr Cooper at last, starting up and clasping Johnston's hand in his own, and welling it over with his warm tears. "Little did I dream of this when I first thought to help you. God has a purpose in everything. You will come with me to my darling child; you will pray with her and speak to her of heaven. How could I pray when my whole heart is rising in rebellion against God taking the dear child from us? Forgive me! forgive my wickedness—but she is the only one left—the only one!"

If Johnston had been asked to go up to a cannon's mouth, that he might be blown into a thousand fragments, he would have gone more cheerfully than to the task required. His pale cheeks crimsoned—the first blush that had visited them for many a day—then he as swiftly became a ghastly white. He tried to speak, but the words choked him, and the hand which grasped that of his benefactor was nerveless and feeble, and cold as ice.

"Excuse me," he at length managed to falter forth, "but I'd rather not. I had a girl of my own once who was taken away much in the same way, and to go through the same experience again would tear my heart open;" and he sank down in a chair and abjectly covered his face with his hands.

"Your are not in earnest—you cannot be!" cried the old man, opening his eyes in wonder. "You surely will not desert me in my hour of need? I cannot believe you are ungrateful, and your very experience in the same affliction should help you to console us. I do not care so much for myself, but my poor wife has set her whole heart upon that child. Come with me and speak to her—tell her of your own child—of all you endured, and how God blessed the calamity to your soul—come, for I fear she will go mad!"

Who could hold out against such an appeal? Johnston rose, and allowed the old man to lead him slowly to the sick chamber. He was in a dream—the present and much of the past had fallen away from him as by magic, and he was looking on a familiar little room, with a sick child and a tending mother, both of whom hung on his words with reverence and love. He saw the whole as vividly as if he had looked upon the real faces there and then, and a great cry struggled for utterance in his heart—

"My God! my God! have mercy upon me, a sinner!"

He felt some one place a book in his hand, and he opened it mechanically, and began to read part of Christ's Sermon on the Mount; but all the words which fell, in such rich tones and eloquent accents from his lips, seemed to him to come from the mouth of his own visionary sick child. The gentle eyes seemed to flash out fire into his very soul as the words were uttered—"Beware of false prophets, which come to you in sheep's clothing, but inwardly they are ravening wolves. Every tree that bringeth not forth good fruit is hewn down and cast into the fire."

Johnston was a splendid reader. To listen to him reading was to be thrilled, but the one most thrilled in that little group was himself. He seemed for the moment to have been wrenched suddenly out of his degraded life into a holier, nobler one, long since buried in the past. They told him afterwards that his conversation with the sick child seemed inspired—that the very gates of heaven seemed to open before their eyes under his eloquence, but the man himself remembered nothing of it.

He saw *those other faces* all the time; and if his tender words seemed such as could only come from the lips of a father, it was simply because he seemed to be addressing his own child. But when his benefactor led him from the sick-room back to the little parlour the spell was broken, the vision vanished, and the stricken wretch fell on his knees and groaned out—

"I am a wretch! I am a scoundrel! Why has not God struck me dead before your eyes?"

Tears, groans, and imprecations against himself followed; and then, to the astonishment of his benefactor, Johnston poured forth an abject confession of the truth—how he had deceived him with the letters, and actually meditated a midnight robbery with violence against the very hand that was now pressing his own in such gratitude and affection.

Mr Cooper, though shocked and horrified, heard the narration as only a Christian man could. He could not believe that Johnston was half as depraved and wicked as he imagined himself, and gently and feelingly reminded the cowering wretch that he had already confessed to many faults and shortcomings. In the end Johnston was shown out, and grasped as warmly by the hand in parting as if what he had just confessed had raised him tenfold in his benefactor's estimation. As they were thus bidding each other good night, in the expectation of meeting again in the morning to arrange for the passage to the Cape, I stepped out of the shade close by the doorway, and laying my hand on Johnston's arm, said sharply to Mr Cooper—

"Do you know that this man is a released convict, and a thief and housebreaker?"

"I know all that, and more, for he has just confessed all to me," was the mild reply.

"Let me warn you that he has this very day bought some housebreaking tools, which he may use at any moment, even upon your own house," I continued, a little astonished that Johnston made no attempt to escape.

"I know that also, for he has already delivered the tools into my hands," said Mr Cooper. "If you choose to come in, you may take them away with you."

Quite nonplussed, I accepted the offer, allowing Johnston to depart, and in a few minutes was told all that had happened. I placed no reliance upon Johnston's contrition, and while taking the implements, again warned Mr Cooper to be strictly on his guard in dealing with such a wretch.

Very early next morning Johnston returned to the house at Bonnington, and spent nearly the whole day with the sick child, tending it, nursing it, and conversing as sweetly and gently as any mother could have done. This continued for some days, till at length the doctor pronounced the child out of danger, when Mr Cooper actually, in the height of his joy and gratitude, went down on his knees before the degraded minister, and blessed God aloud for sending the man to his house. A few days later a passage was taken for the apparently contrite and reformed rogue to one of the colonies, and Mr Cooper made no secret that he intended to give Johnston, when fairly aboard the vessel, £50 to start a new life with on the other side. But on the very morning when the passage-money was paid, Johnston discovered something wrong with his throat, and his pulse high and fevered, and went to the Infirmary to ask advice. The house surgeon looked at his throat, and told him he must remain as an indoor patient, as the trouble was diphtheria, and the case a serious one indeed. Before night Johnston had lost his voice, and next day the disease was in his windpipe. His last words were a written message to Mr Cooper and his grandchild, bidding them farewell, and adding—"I was asleep in sin, but God through you awakened me, and now I am not afraid to die."

Milton Keynes UK
Ingram Content Group UK Ltd.
UKHW021843130624
444169UK00005B/137